THE
BUFFALO
COMMONS

THE
BUFFALO
COMMONS

RICHARD S. WHEELER

A Tom Doherty Associates Book
New York

This is a work of fiction. All of the characters and events portrayed in this novel are either fictitious or are used fictitiously.

THE BUFFALO COMMONS

This book is printed on acid-free paper.

A Forge Book
Published by Tom Doherty Associates, Inc.
175 Fifth Avenue
New York, NY 10010

Forge® is a registered trademark of Tom Doherty Associates, Inc.

Design by Patrice Sheridan

Library of Congress Catalog Cataloging-in-Publication Data

Wheeler, Richard S.
    The buffalo commons / Richard S. Wheeler.—1st ed.
        p.   cm.
    "A Tom Doherty Associates book."
    ISBN 0-312-86262-8 (acid-free paper)
    I. Title.
PS3573.H4345B78   1998
813'.54—dc21   97-29843
                                                        CIP

First Edition: March 1998

Printed in the United States of America

0   9   8   7   6   5   4   3   2   1

The world was all before them,
  where to choose
Their place of rest, and Providence
  their guide.
They hand in hand with wand'ring
  steps and slow
Through Eden took their solitary way.

John Milton
PARADISE LOST

Sweet is the breath of morn,
  her rising sweet,
With charm of earliest birds;
  pleasant the sun
When first on this delightful land
  he spreads
His orient beams on herb, tree,
  fruit, and flower,
Glist'ring with dew.

John Milton
PARADISE LOST

THE
BUFFALO
COMMONS

PROLOGUE

The wolves did not know what to do, so they watched from a grassy ridge. Far below them, in a prairie hollow protected from the bitter wind, the Hereford heifer struggled with her first birthing.

The wolves had never preyed on cattle; that was outside of their experience. There had always been ample game where they came from, and they had learned from their elders how to hunt and kill what they needed. They knew the ways of the elk and deer and mountain sheep and coyotes, but not cattle. They were hungry. The antelope on these vast pastures usually outran them and the mule deer were hard to catch if they were healthy. So these wolves starved even though meat abounded. For this was cattle country and had been for over a century.

Far below them, the bred heifer struggled to produce a calf, writhing on her side, her back against chokecherry brush, panting heavily as she pushed the unyielding calf toward daylight. She paused a moment and then redoubled her efforts, this time feeling movement and some tearing that shot pain through her. She had come here alone, wanting to birth in private as most females of most species do. On her left rear flank she bore a brand, a lazy N quarter circle, one of several owned by Nichols Ranches.

She had eluded the manager of this, the westernmost of the Nichols ranches, by pushing into a thicket of red willow and buffaloberry brush and waiting for her pursuer to pass by. He had intended to put her, along with his other bred heifers, in a pen close to the ranch buildings where they could all be observed, and helped, through their difficult first delivery.

She had never seen a wolf, and lacked the means to defend herself or her calf. She was hornless, and thus all the more vulnerable. But the wolves did not know that. They did not know much about cattle. And she knew less about wolves.

The seven wolves in this group—they could scarcely be called a pack—included a bred female, two adult males, two female yearlings, and two male yearlings. Neither of the adult males was clearly the alpha, or dominant, wolf, and neither had sired the litter being carried by the bred female. She had been bred far away by another male before her world changed.

The pregnant female had been the alpha in her pack. She was a beauty, about eighty-five pounds, lithe and sleek, her muzzle tan, her body brown shading to black—not the usual color of wolves, although wolves came in various shades. She was carrying eight half-formed pups, and was wildly hungry. The rest of the wolves watched and waited and did nothing, but she could wait no more. She had eaten nothing but field mice for two days and madness was in her. She needed ten or twelve pounds of meat a day. Below her was a great unknown creature, but one she could kill. Maybe this one could scratch or bite or kick her to death or gore her, as elk could, or a bull moose, or a bear. But she didn't know, and her spirit was listening only to the pangs of her belly.

She rose, feeling the harsh wind ruffle her silky pelt, sniffed the icy air, and slithered downslope in short rushes. The beast below her didn't seem to notice. The wolves on the ridge hung back, uncertain not only of the prey, but of her dominance. She ignored them, growing more restless as she edged closer to the hollow. The wind quieted there, and she could hear the heavy breathing, the struggle sounds of the creature. She could smell the birthing and understood it. Boldly she approached, sniffed at the half-emerged white-and-brown calf poking wetly into the world. Food.

But still she did nothing, respecting those heavy cloven hoofs that could kill her with one stroke. Instead, she rounded the struggling Hereford until she could see its head. Now at last the heifer spotted the sleek brown-black wolf, and grew agitated, her gaze frantic, her breath exploding in gusts. She tried to rise, wallow to her feet. But it was too late. The wolf clamped powerful jaws over the heifer's windpipe, the canines piercing it even as the jaws crushed it closed, blocking air. The wolf hung on while blood gouted over her muzzle, hung on as deadweight, like a lamprey on a fish, while the heifer thrashed and then died in a widening pool of bright blood. The dying had taken less than a minute.

The wolf released her jaws and let the heifer sag into the barren earth, its muscles spasming. Then she barked sharply, summoning the others to their first full meal in three days. She paraded proudly, deferring her own hunger a moment to let them gather over the feast and bite savagely into hot flesh. One young male ate the newborn. Another wolf gutted the heifer and gorged on the soft entrails. Another tackled a flank, tearing at red muscle, ripping away curly-haired hide. For an hour they gorged, and then retreated to the lonely ridge top to sleep and play and watch in the timid March sun. They were not done with the carcass and intended to protect it from coyotes, magpies, ravens, skunks, wolverines and other creatures.

It had been so easy. The beautiful, strong-limbed female felt content. She was once again an alpha, the dominant wolf in this group, as she had been before, in another place. Living here on these vast plains would be easier than the life she had led in the mountains. There were thousands of these helpless animals, fat and clumsy, without speed, without horns, without lethal teeth, with nothing but hooves and weight and mass to protect themselves. They would feed a thousand wolves and more, her pups and their pups and all the pups to come.

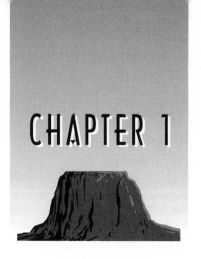

CHAPTER 1

Cameron Nichols watched the telltale plume of yellow dust trace the progress of a car up the long lane that linked his home to the Otter Creek road.

That would be Hector Truehart again, and the car would be the white Lincoln the lawyer drove. Nichols waited patiently, knowing the answer to Truehart's proposition would be the same: no, not now, not ever, not in a hundred years. He liked Truehart, and even liked the lawyer's persistence. Over the years, Nichols had formed some impressions of Texans. They came in two sizes, citified peacocks, or good-old-boy sharks. But Truehart didn't fit either bill.

In a minute the white Continental would pull into the circle drive, and Truehart would emerge, a rumpled, quiet, diffident man in a gray suit and quiet paisley cravat, carrying his venerable black attaché case. Nichols preferred that honest attire to the fraudulent and gaudy Western attire worn by ranch brokers and insurance salesmen.

These meetings were important occasions, and Nichols dressed for them. He was not a man to do business in faded, torn jeans, boots soaked in corral muck, or shirts and jackets gummed over with manure, scours, animal blood, bull semen, calf slobber, or the residue of birthing. So he had adorned his lean, fifty-four-year-old weather-stained body with slacks, slip-on black shoes, a white shirt, and a woolen Palm Beach sport coat. That attire never failed to surprise Truehart.

The man braked the dust-coated Lincoln before the rambling ranch house in a cloud of grit. The early spring had been ominously dry again. From the doorway, Nichols watched the man fold his glasses and poke them into his breast pocket, pluck up his portfolio, and approach in an apologetic gait that could disarm the most militant, shotgun-toting No Trespass rancher.

"The answer's still the same," Nichols said.

"Ah, Cameron—may I call you that?—I just want to talk a little."

"Sure," Nichols said, leading him into the quiet, sunny living room his wife had decorated in French provincial themes he didn't care for. "Scotch, right?"

"Oh, it's a bit early. I always admire this room. That wall of mullioned windows; the view clear down to Otter Creek."

"It started as a cabin. Each generation's added to this house. This room was added by my mother. She liked the view in winter."

"You have roots. It's hard to give up a place that's been in the family for generations. A pioneer place."

"We're not giving it up. Horoney must know that by now."

"No, he's a determined man. He doesn't know it. Cameron, have you and your family really thought about what it'll be like, being all alone? Not a soul around?"

"We've been living with that for ninety years. We're not isolated."

"Not isolated? Here?"

Nichols adjusted a Venetian blind at the rear of the room. "See that?" he asked, pointing to a grassy upland. "My Cessna takes me anywhere fast. See that phone line? We talk to friends, e-mail them, fax them. See that satellite dish? We're as connected as anyone in a city. See my four-by-four pickup? I can be in Miles City in two hours—my grandparents needed two days. Did you see that mailbox on the Tongue River Road? The postal service delivers there. FedEx and UPS right to this door."

"They won't, though. Not when this is launched. Tell me frankly: does Mrs. Nichols want to stay?"

"She says she does." Nichols laughed. The lawyer laughed.

"I thought so," Truehart said. "Family dissension."

Nichols didn't reply. This family was torn by it all. He wished it had never happened; that life could continue as before. But it never would. And the divisions were there long before the National Grassland Trust polarized his own kin.

"What would it take? Laslo Horoney's willing to set you up in a cattle operation as large as this, on better pasture, in a wetter climate. Or he'll pay market value for this."

"Yes, we've been over that. We Nicholses are rooted down, Mr. True-hart. We've been here—well, not from the beginning, not the open range days, but not long after. This is home. Come on, I'll show you something."

He led the Texas lawyer through the dining room, the kitchen, and out the battered back door, and walked swiftly toward a slope shepherded by majestic cottonwoods. The harsh March wind tugged at Truehart's fine suit, and the man was probably getting chilled, but Nichols didn't pause until he came to a half-acre plot of prairie enclosed by a black iron fence. Within were the generations, and the stones that marked them; lives begun, spun out, and ended at this pinprick place on a map of eastern Montana. Nichols opened a gate, and ushered Truehart in.

"I wish you could see this in late spring," he said. "It draws range agronomists from all over the area. They love these last bits of untouched native prairie." He smiled wryly. "You might say this plot was our undoing; the prank our ancestors played on us."

"How is that?"

"These bits of virgin prairie are what started the whole thing," Nichols said. "Patches like this are the yardstick the agronomists used to tell us we've ruined the prairie. Two hundred species of life to a square yard in here, and a root system that captures moisture, holds the earth down when it blows, helps the grasses rebound after a drought or a grazing."

Truehart smiled, expectantly.

Nichols did not disappoint him. "The pasture isn't what it was. Can't argue with that. That wind's going to chill you, but I just wanted you to see these stones. Over thirty now. The oldest is dated 1914." He stopped at a simple marble slab flush with the earth. Graven into it was a name, Mabel Sterling Nichols, and two dates, January 3, 1931, and August 17, 1984.

"My mother," he said. "Young. Lung cancer. She smoked."

Truehart nodded.

"Great-grandparents, some of their brothers and sisters. Three of four grandparents, some of their siblings. Two infants. Two cousins. An uncle who broke his neck falling off a horse at nineteen. Some folks related to us by marriage." Abruptly he turned, led the lawyer back to the ranch house, and shut out the moaning wind. He wished he could shut out other winds of change as easily as closing that door.

"That's where my children will plant me," he said, rubbing his hands to warm them.

Truehart stared out the window that overlooked the Otter Creek Valley. "Sometimes things happen that require people to adjust to new circumstances. This is one of those things. As much as you love this place, it won't ever be the same again," he said. "I think you know that . . . Did the foundation make you a fair offer?"

"You call it an offer?" A flash of anger laced Nichols's voice. "You call all of this an offer? Tearing apart everything that people like you and me spent blood and toil and tears to build?"

Truehart smiled gently. "Have you considered what'll probably happen? How long do you expect to have electrical service? A telephone?

How long will a fuel truck deliver heating oil and gasoline and aviation gas? Especially when the roads break down? You'll be taxed—but will you receive services? A landfill? Roads? Will the nonexistent school bus take your grandchildren to some nonexistent school over nonexistent roads?" He paused, apologetically. "Forgive me, Cameron. I'm only describing what's likely to happen. I know how it hurts."

"Look, Mr. Truehart, my parents and grandparents got along just fine without services. This ranch wasn't even connected to phone or electricity until the late fifties—like most Montana ranches. If dealers won't deliver products like gasoline, we'll go get them. If the phone company rolls up wire, we'll use our cellular. If the electric lines come down, we'll resort to solar panels or a generator." Nichols pushed back the heat building in him. "If you think you can isolate us, consider this: a nice retirement community, right on the edge of your buffalo land—your big zoo—would draw a lot of people, and a lot of friends. If you isolate us, we'll do it. We've a dozen children on our ranches—just right to run our own school. Sorry, Mr. Truehart. You can't roll back history. You can create a sort of zoo or museum for people to glimpse the way things were—but you can't return to another time."

"Mr. Horoney believes the past holds the key to the future. And buffalo are the future—the best future for a nation squandering its future. Our *future*."

Nichols smiled tightly, wrestling back his temper. All Nichols men had it, he more than his father or son. "Maybe we'll be forced to see what the courts say. Horoney's foundation isn't a public body; it has no right to condemn land for public purposes. It's as private as this property."

"Ah, Cameron, is your property so private—BLM land, Forest Service land, state school sections, leased railroad land . . . ?"

"You know that it is, Mister Truehart. Nichols Ranches are one of the largest private holdings in the West."

"And riddled with holes, public land in the middle of yours, and in every hole, buffalo will roam."

"You'll build a lot of fences, then. Strong enough and high enough to contain your buffalo. Cattle fences won't do. Mine won't do. It'll be your responsibility, your animals. I won't let your buffalo trespass. And if they spread brucellosis, and my herd is condemned and destroyed, you'll find yourselves in court."

Truehart nodded. "A mess. Easily avoided with some flexibility." He looked impatient, as if jousting with Nichols wasn't his idea of getting things done. "Let me tell you where we are," he said.

Nichols already knew, but listened impatiently.

"We've got crews out rolling up fence. When we're done, there won't be any barbed wire dividing the land between Interstate 94 in Montana, and Interstate 90 in Wyoming. We've other crews cleaning up ranch sites, salvaging metal, and burning the buildings to prevent squatting. That, ah, is going slower. Lots of metal buildings there. Lots more metal grain silos than we'd counted on. But we're progressing. And the utilities are rolling up phone lines, disconnecting electricity—give or take a few lines that power the oil fields."

All this amused and saddened Nichols. They were tearing out the web of settlement—what they could of it, anyway. "It's an illusion, this wilderness," he said flatly. "The whole area's dotted with telecommunications towers on hilltops; interstates, roads, oil patches, strip mines and power plants. You think it'll all return to wilderness?"

"Of course not. But it'll still be the Big Empty, the place where buffalo roam, the dream of millions of Americans."

"It's a fantasy. Buffalo and grass. You think you can wipe out square miles of sagebrush and prickly pear?"

"Our agronomists say the prairie'll recover swiftly from most of its abuse. Mr. Horoney won't put any buffalo on it the first year; and if it's a dry year, he won't put anything on it the second year. After that, he'll put five thousand bison on it, drawn from South Dakota and Ted Turner's herds. A handful of animals on a grassland the size of West Virginia."

"And the sagebrush?"

"You'll see range fires again when the grass returns. They burn off the sage, and then native bluestem grass crowds it the next year." He paused. "We won't control natural range fires. They're healthy. And they won't stop at your ranch fences. And there won't be fire trucks or neighbors to help you."

Nichols stared out the window at the world he knew and saw it crumbling.

"Cameron, let's get things on the table," Truehart said. "Mr. Horoney's authorized me to tell you that the foundation will withdraw its offer if it isn't accepted by June one. You've a fair offer for the Nichols ranches, all two hundred twenty thousand acres. Twenty-five million, and you keep the proceeds from your cattle and equipment. After June one, it'll be worth—" he shrugged. "Of course the foundation would always be willing to buy out Nichols Ranches, but not at their present market value. When your ranches become isolated patches within the National Grassland Trust, I'm afraid they'd be worth—"

"Nothing," said Nichols, "and everything."

CHAPTER 2

No sooner had Truehart wheeled down the lane than Sandra Nichols emerged from her mysterious lairs in the rear of the old house where she hid whenever the lawyer came. The sight of her always warmed Cameron. The years had been kind to her body, at least, and those same chiseled facial planes, scattering of freckles, and red hair, softened now with white, hadn't changed much over the years.

"What did he say?" she asked.

"He said the foundation's withdrawing the offer on June 1."

"That's awful."

He wondered how she meant that. They played a game. From all appearances, she was rooted here, supported his wish to remain in a homestead and business his family had run for generations. But he knew that somewhere within her soul she desperately wanted to leave. She had never borne the isolation of ranch life well, this Butte utility executive's daughter who was accustomed to a broad, intense, and patrician social life. And now things were much worse. The neighbors had vanished, sold out to the foundation. Her diversions now were the satellite dish and gin, and he ached for her. He had sensed over the long years that she felt she had married beneath her. Still, she had been loyal, outwardly enthusiastic, and added a fine grace and warmth to this isolated household. It was as good a marriage as any man could ask for, really—until the last few years.

"I've been expecting it," he said. "Their dream is to complete the buffalo commons in the millennial year, and so they're not pussyfooting around anymore."

"What will you do?"

He shrugged. "What would you like me to do?"

"You have to do what's right for the family."

Fencing again. He wished she would just say she was lonely; with their share of all those millions they could go to the Sunbelt, see the world, meet entertaining people, start living. Once she had wanted him to learn how to golf. Now he could learn. The thought amused him.

"I'll talk to everyone. Maybe I'll be outvoted." But he knew that wouldn't happen. Nichols Ranches, actually, were three corporations and a trust in which his ninety-one-year-old grandmother was the beneficiary. The trust could not be dissolved, except under the most unusual circumstance—which indeed, this was. But a court would have to approve.

"I wish this were settled," she said. "It's getting on my nerves."

"Well, it'll be up to Dad." His father, Dudley, held the controlling interest in the largest corporation and was the trustee for his mother's share.

"Did Mr. Truehart threaten?"

"Oh, in a way. He pulled the plug, if that's what you mean. Laslo Horoney's quite a man, and I don't believe he's trying to harm us. He just wants the Big Open and wants to offer it to the country in the Year Two Thousand. Hector Truehart's as comfortable as an old shoe—even when he's dishing out an ultimatum."

"We'll have to give up the place. It's such a pity. All these roots and things."

Cameron laughed, and she smiled contritely. All those roots and things. "There's no one left to invite over for dinner," he said. "But whatever Dudley does, we don't have to stay here as much. The ranches run themselves most of the time, and I've a few aces up my sleeve. How'd you like all the friends you could ever want—and right here?"

"Oh," she said softly, her composure wavering for just a moment.

"I'll go tell Dudley," he said.

He shrugged into a thick woolen ranch coat, her games grating on him. He sure as hell didn't plan to quit. He just wanted to live out his life as he always had, running one of the largest livestock operations in the West, but somehow he found himself in the path of other people's visions. No, religion. That was the exact word. The divinity of unsullied nature; the devil of civilization.

He stormed into the March wind, choosing to walk the three hundred yards to his father's house, which was newer and smaller than the rambling main ranch house—and less permeated with memories. But Dudley Nichols had made it a home. He belonged there, bound by invisible webs of habit and sanctuary.

The wind assailed Cameron, drove needles down his neck, raised dust—probably off some nearby wheat ranch—and drove it into him. The dryness worried him, but drought was an ancient enemy the Nichols family knew well. Eventually, after one or two or three years, the rains always returned. He and his ancestors before him had fought this parsimonious land, loved and hated it, exploited and nurtured it, ruined and rehabilitated it, milked it for all it was worth and rued the sagebrush and prickly pear that resulted. But most of all, they loved it and employed a native cunning, passed down across generations, that enabled them to weather crises in a fragile, dusty, High Plains area in the rain shadow of the Rockies. It was the sort of cunning that kept them afloat while others came and went, victims of drought, cattle cycles, indebtedness to banks, plagues of grasshoppers, and the relentless advance of sagebrush, knapweed, leafy spurge and foxtail barley across pastures that once were free of them.

But it wasn't all so dark. Even as he walked, he could see a faint haze of lime green forming on the band of cottonwoods along Otter Creek, far away. And the air around him was as fresh and clean as air could be, and the good earth under him was his and his father's and grandmother's, and some of it belonged to his children now, too. And four generations, going on five now, had prospered there, stronger than city people because they made a hard living. He owed his ancestors something; he owed his children and grandchildren more.

He entered the house with a brief rap and a halloo. But his father had seen him coming from the picture window, and was waiting.

"What did that lawyer want?" he asked in that familiar, sharp, gravelly voice.

"To buy us out. And to tell us we have until June one or they pull the offer."

Dudley Nichols snorted. Cam knew that sound. It erupted from the soul of a stiff patriarch, a slim, erect, wire-haired man not yet showing much gray in his black hair; a man who diligently clung to his self-image as a Westerner and cowman; a man in gleaming Tony Lamas, pin-striped woolen trousers, and the most expensive Western-cut shirt money could buy, this one blue with a darker blue piping.

"They'll have to dynamite us out—in bits and pieces," Dudley said.

That's what Cam figured. The larger the buyout offer, the more it had excited Dudley's pride. Turning down twenty-five million was a lot better than turning down the original twenty million offer.

"Dad, we'll have to operate eight cattle ranches without services. We're going to scrape our own roads, get our own gasoline, install solar panels, and switch to cellular phones. And run our school, too. Melanie Marble, over on the Powder Ranch, is already home-schooling her kids. It won't be hard. But we'll probably have to make some compromises.

Isolation hurts. We're going to need friends, good company. And that means importing them. I'm thinking of starting the Buffalo Estates—twenty-acre parcels right on a fence line."

"What kind of son did I raise? Selling tracts!" Dudley retorted.

"That's not the response I want from you."

"You want to sell land?"

"A few acres. The only thing that's hurting us is the isolation. And we can fix that. Sandra's already sinking—her friends are gone. And I don't want her to suffer any more. She's in trouble."

Dudley looked about to say something he'd regret—probably about spoiled Butte women—but didn't say it, and Cam was grateful. Instead, the old man retreated into legalisms. "I can't break a trust. It's my mother's place—this one is. It supports her. That nursing home; it's a money sink. And each corporation's a different deal. Different directors, shareholders. We can't just sell off land. I don't want some subdivision in here. We're cattle people. We raise beef. That's all we've raised. Hereford people. We're breeders. Our bulls are prized animals. I don't want anything else around here."

"We're going to have to make some changes, Dad. I'll deal with that."

"We don't sell land—especially for a resort. Cam, we're Nicholses."

"We're also Garwoods, Sterlings, Cassadys, Joiners, and a lot more."

His father smiled suddenly, unexpectedly. "I like a fight," he said.

"So do I. But we're in for it. We'll be watching buffalo knock down our four-strand fences as if they were string. Watching our cattle get out and wander a hundred miles. Watching the wolves eat our beef. You can count on it—those nature nuts'll put in wolves, too. Just like Yellowstone. The wolves didn't stay in the park. They reduced the elk herds and took off. They killed so many sheep around Big Timber last year, those sheep men threw in the towel. You can't shoot 'em; they're supposedly an endangered species. Shooting one's worth about a year in prison and half the profits of a ranch. They're like India's sacred cows. But I have a few notions about that, too. There's a way to deal with wolves—and legally."

"I don't understand it," his father said. "Deliberately destroying civilization. Destroying food production. Do you know how much wheat and beef and sugar beets and wool and mutton and canola oil come out of here? Enough to feed a small nation. What are they trying to do? Starve the world? I don't understand it."

"Dad, we'll weather it. In a few years people'll get their fill of wolves and buffalo, and beef'll look good on their tables, along with a hundred things that are made of wheat—and that'll be that.''

They wrestled their dilemma some more, not without a certain respect and a bond of blood and kinship, but Cam got nowhere with the stiff old man and was falling into a black mood, so he slipped out into the quietness of the afternoon. The wind had faded. In a few days—if it wasn't too dry—the pastures would bloom with emerald grass, and pasqueflowers, and life. The meadowlarks would return, along with the mallards, and sandhill cranes, and killdeer.

Dudley had gone brittle after Mabel died. It was an odd thing, Cam thought. His father needed his mother, and when his mother left him, Dudley turned prouder, more rigid, more negative, and less effectual, until at last Cam had quietly taken over running the ranches; heavy responsibilities for a young man.

But Dudley Nichols held the cards; only one small corporation, which held the two most recent ranch acquisitions in its shell, was not Dudley's to command. Cam and Sandra and the children controlled that one.

Cam scarcely knew what to do. There were no good solutions.

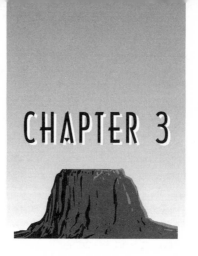

CHAPTER 3

Laslo Horoney received his capable attorney, Truehart, in the parlor of his suite atop the Mirage in Las Vegas. He didn't like to do business across a desk, which he considered a barrier to trust and intimacy. So he conducted it in easy chairs and couches, writing occasional notes on a legal pad perched on his knee.

Truehart had found Horoney here, but might just as easily have tracked him down in La Jolla or Phoenix or Miami or Hilton Head. Laslo and Dolly were at home anywhere, among all sorts of people, and preferred to keep suites here and there across the Sunbelt rather than maintain an ostentatious home. Their base, actually, was a modest home in Arlington, Texas.

"How did Nichols take it?" Horoney asked.

"I don't know. It's really up to his father, you know, but the old man refuses even to talk to us."

"How many people are still hanging on?"

"A lot. We're maybe forty or forty-five percent of the way along. There are probably fifteen hundred people in the area, and probably over a hundred large holdings in Montana, and another thirty in Wyoming. And lots of small fry, of course. They're waiting for the Nichols family to decide. A few are just holding out for the best price. A few have sold to speculators and they're trying to stick us. We're simply ignoring them, of course. It's a racket. The project has attracted half the con artists in the country. But if we can move Nichols off, and add those two hundred twenty thousand acres—it'll all be over."

Horoney sighed, and ran a hand through his unruly white-shot brown hair, which he wore long, giving him the look of an aging hippie. "This is the hardest part," he said softly. "The part that gives me the most anguish. I admire these people. They've wrestled a living from a dry land that was never meant for agriculture. They've done it with cunning and courage and patience, weathering the dry years, fighting back, putting every drop of water to use." He sighed. "So tragically—for the land, and ultimately for themselves. I would do anything I could to make it easy for them to move."

"I've adhered to your guidelines, Laslo. Used persuasion mostly. Every one of those ranchers and wheat farmers has heard the case for restoring the prairie. Every one's been offered an appraised market price."

"Would it help if I went up there and talked with the family?"

Truehart nodded. "You've shared this vision with the nation; become its apostle and advocate. You might try it. But you're talking to people who call that place home. *Home.*"

"I'll go. I know something about homes and what they mean. How's the rest coming? In particular, what's going to happen in the Wyoming legislature?"

"I think this time they'll go ahead and create the new county and enact the tax base we want. I emphasized that the towns around the buffalo preserve will do an estimated fifty million in new tourist and guiding business, and hotel and restaurant business. Gillette is looking at a boom, just as Miles City and Glendive are."

"Good. Keep me posted. This is the millennial year. I want the commons a going operation before this year passes."

Truehart had a few more items on his list, and then hastened out to catch a redeye flight to DFW airport, leaving Horoney alone for a change.

Dolly was back in Arlington. Horoney wished she were at hand. He liked to engage in a socratic dialogue with her, and found her counsel worth more than anyone else's on earth. He loved to watch her wade through a reception, enjoying all the people she met, at home wherever she might be. He loved to watch her play romantic Chopin on her concert Steinway, or recite one of her adventuresome narrative story-poems. He stood at the window, looking at the array of lights blinding the night's eye, enjoying the glitzy world built on exploiting dreams. He had never invested in casino stocks and never would, as a matter of conscience. But that hadn't stopped him from enjoying the town and its effervescence.

He woke up one day to discover he was one of the wealthiest men in America, but he scarcely knew how he had gotten that way; nor did it matter. He had pioneered shopping centers in the Sunbelt way back in the fifties, then pioneered the enclosed air-conditioned mall, and then branched out into commercial real estate—all in the booming South and

Southwest. An odd vocation, he thought, for a man who had done advanced work in botany at Baylor; for a man fascinated by nature in all its mystery and complexity. He had never abandoned his absorption with nature, and over the years had read the scholarly journals and contributed to various research projects.

He spoke with a faint accent even though he had been born in the United States in 1939, a son of Hungarians who had fled war-clouded Europe, choosing freedom from terror over the financial security they enjoyed in Prague. His parents didn't speak English, and it was Laslo's second tongue, but one he mastered very early. Like so many immigrants or their children, he loved this country more than those born to it did. He could be whatever he wanted here in America, and nothing would stop him except his own inadequacies.

Then, with a spin of a wheel of fortune, he was rich; then very rich. His thoughts had turned more and more to giving money away, rather than making it. He would start a foundation, perhaps—but when he looked into them, he discovered that few had adhered to the express instructions of their founders, and some were utterly perverse. He discovered and read Andrew Carnegie's thoughtful essay, "The Gospel of Wealth." The great industrialist had proposed that the rich should return most of what they had garnered, and in their lifetimes instead of at death. Carnegie had proposed, moreover, that the gifts be put to good purpose, not to foster dependency but to help people to help themselves. Thus had Carnegie endowed libraries across the country, fountains of information and wisdom by which ordinary mortals could advance out of ignorance and poverty.

Horoney had liked that, but his sensitivity to nature and the interdependent systems of plant and animal life led him in another direction: The whole nation—including some of his own shopping centers—was ravishing nature, and would ultimately pauperize itself if it continued to abuse its resources. Oddly, the homeless gave him his clue. They had plagued his commercial buildings, gathered in his malls, collected at the back of restaurants on his property. He ached for them, set up a foundation to help them. Could it be that plants and animals were homeless as well, driven out of their natural habitat by the onslaught of civilization?

Odd how his thoughts devolved from the homeless to the homelessness of plants and animals, driven from their habitat by man. Nothing was in its proper home anymore. He wanted to give the world homes. Not just nomadic habitations, Bedouins' tents, but places of kinship and security, places where all creatures belonged and were nurtured by the webs of life and love. Out of all that mental jumble he had arrived at a vision of homes, proper places for mankind, and proper homes for animals and plants. Every species had its home.

This, then, was the gift that would pay his debt of gratitude to a country that had sheltered his parents and himself, given him abundant wealth, a beloved wife, three quiet and serious children, and the chance to count for something before his arrhythmic heart failed him. Somehow, after the long detour into commerce, his interest in the natural world had surfaced anew, along with a sense that what man had deranged was really the homes of all things.

Beaches? Oceans? Mountains? Forests? Endangered species? He chose grass, largely because it had few defenders. The fragile ecology of the High Plains had suffered grievous abuse, and a national treasure was being wasted. He supposed it would seem eccentric for a shopping-center man to make the restoration of the featureless and unloved plains the capstone of his life, but that didn't matter, either. He had found his life's cause. He would restore a home to the world's exiles.

He found allies. Some Rutgers sociologists had discovered that various eastern counties in Montana and Wyoming and other High Plains states had, over many decades, depopulated themselves, and now had one or two people per square mile—roughly the Indian population before settlement. Drought and climate had triumphed over all the engines of civilization. The plains had emptied. And thus had been born the dream of restoring the area to its primitive estate; a sea of grass, buffalo, wolves, deer, coyotes—and the short bunchgrasses that flourished there. Man didn't belong there.

He went to Congress and proposed the National Grassland Trust, but the lawmakers demurred, finding no compelling reason to evict tens of thousands of hardworking Americans from their lands and enterprises. At first Horoney was taken aback—Congress didn't share his vision. But soon he counted the setback a blessing. His defeat had reminded him that this was a free country that protected its citizens in their lawful commerce, and that a person's home was protected from government intrusion by common law and the Constitution itself. He ultimately approved of Congress's reluctance. But he intended to have his buffalo and grassland commons, this time through his own resources.

Employing the entrepreneurial genius that had won him one of the world's great fortunes, Horoney set to work. He talked to state legislators about the grasslands. He lobbied for a change in federal policy, and finally got it: the president directed the Forest Service and Bureau of Land Management to cooperate with Horoney's new foundation, thus integrating federal and state lands into the new National Grassland Trust.

He selected a target area—southeast Montana, below Interstate 94, and northeast Wyoming, above Interstate 90, and a large piece of North and South Dakota west of Highway 85, much of it already National Grassland. Later, in a second phase, he would add the empty grassland north of Interstate 94, embracing much of northeastern Montana, and enlarging the nature preserve to a tract of fifty thousand square miles, about the size of New York State.

He flew over the target area, drove down its dirt roads, counted ranches and wheat farms, observed power lines, noted natural-gas pipelines, oil fields, telecommunications towers, railroads, mines, grain elevators and agribusiness. It wouldn't become wilderness; only romantics supposed it might. But it would do. Range managers told him that under the right conditions, the abused High Plains might rebound in ten or fifteen years; that wheat farms could be returned to buffalo grass; that the varieties of native grasses and other plants would increase—and that the natural sporadic grazing of buffalo herds would hasten, rather than discourage, the restoration of the prairies.

He enlisted foundations, consulted with the Nature Conservancy, hired agronomists, and drew his friend and attorney Hector Truehart into it. Working quietly at first—Horoney shied from publicity of any sort, and in any case he didn't want to drive up land prices—he began buying rangeland from ranchers ready to quit. There were many. No one could ranch that country without fighting it. And all the while the Sierra Club and Wildlife Federation and other Green groups watched, mesmerized, as this unlikely ally began the first phase of his plan, to purchase approximately twenty-four thousand square miles of land to turn into nature's own garden.

Some had laughed—the sheer magnitude and complexity would defeat him, they said. Some hated him—he was demolishing civilization, they said. Someone in the Department of Agriculture—which bitterly opposed him—noted that he would destroy much of the nation's beef supply, and radically reduce its wheat production. Realists jeered. Many environmentalists did, too, complaining that the National Grassland should be in federal hands. They sniped at him, insinuating that he toadied to agribusiness and was too kind to those rich corporate farmers who'd sucked the life out of the plains and turned them into an arid ruin of sagebrush and cactus and inedible weeds.

None of that fazed him. He quietly sold off malls and skyscrapers and funded his foundation, a difficult task because buyers were few, and such properties were largely illiquid. He sent the ever-gracious and diplomatic Truehart and others down lonely dirt roads to talk with ranchers and grain farmers and cut deals if they could. He studied plots—schoolyards and cemeteries and little parks—that had never been grazed and learned still more about massive root systems and biodiversity. He studied fenced sections that had been left untouched for five, ten, fifteen years by far-seeing ranchers. He learned what there was to know about the miraculous, efficient buffalo and how they grazed, and how the prairies had endured periodic drought for eons. Botanists and county extension agents showed him good and bad pasture: some rich with native grasses, some bare earth and trash weeds, demolished by abuse.

What had begun as a simple idea grew portentous to those in the area. Suddenly the plains tribes, Sioux, Cheyenne, Crow, Assiniboine, Gros Ventres, Blackfeet, remembered their ancient way of life, and began to stir with dreams of buffalo upon an unfenced sea of grass. Yes! Tear away every fence, and give it all back to the Indians! On the other hand, ranchers and wheat farmers, shopkeepers, horsemen, bartenders and businessmen located at every crossroads began to rage at the very idea of a buffalo commons, and accused Horoney of tearing apart the woof and weave of civilization. Without intending it, he found himself surrounded by history and faith and belief and the largest of all questions. What was good?

He needed to talk to the Nicholses, whom he had never met but admired boundlessly. They were the sort of Americans who had made the nation great.

That evening he called Dolly and invited her to go on a jaunt. She loved the idea, looked forward to his adventures, and came with him whenever she wasn't embarked on one of her own. Then he called his pilots in Dallas, arranged to have his Gulfstream V fly him to Miles City, and to bring Dolly with them. And he had his executive assistant, Bailey, arrange to have a four-wheel-drive pickup truck ready when he got there.

It was time to talk about his vision to those who wanted least to hear it.

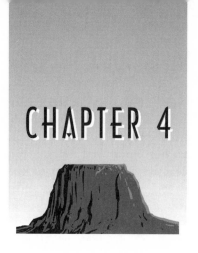

CHAPTER 4

Martin Dudley Nichols dreaded these regular meetings with his faculty advisor, Leonard Kazin, chair of the new Environmental Sciences Department. But Kazin and a select committee would soon be judging Martin's thesis, and the man's criticism had to be considered—and weathered.

He headed through a raw March day to the western edge of the campus at Bozeman and entered a new building there as one would enter a dentist's office for root canal work. A month ago Dr. Kazin had warned Martin that the thesis was taking on a certain tone, a certain reach of opinion that went beyond what had been warranted by Martin's research.

Completing the thesis was all that stood between Martin and his master's degree and dream of a position with one of the environmental organizations, especially one with deep pockets. The thesis, *The Social and Natural Ecology of the High Plains, from the Fur Trade to Modern Agribusiness,* was actually a wedding of rural sociology and grasslands ecology, and a caustic history of exploitation, ignorance, and ruin, largely focused on his own benighted family, although they had yet to learn of that.

Well, he thought, they would soon enough. And they'd be pissed. But by then he'd be employed, and not spending his father's cash, every penny of which came from bleeding the plains white and raising beef full of fat to coat the arteries of everyone who ate it. He himself was a virtual vegetarian. Maybe, if the world followed his example, the rape of the Great Plains would grind to a halt.

He found old Kazin waiting for him in his office, really a crowded warren of books and papers stacked into dangerous columns. Martin didn't dislike the old man, who'd been in the Biology Department forever—from the late fifties, before there even was an Environmental Sciences Department, someone told him. He was just an old fart who'd been around too long. The younger faculty mostly ignored him because his ideas weren't progressive, and Kazin could sometimes make them uncomfortable. Martin would have preferred someone else, but he had no control over that, and he'd wasted too much of his life at Montana State University to pick fights now.

Kazin looked like death warmed over, and that wasn't far from reality. The man had battled prostate cancer, and wore a gray pallor like a shroud.

"Martin," he said. "Have a seat, young man. How are you coming?"

"I hope to finish the writing by the end of summer, and have the typing and proofing and notes done by the end of the year."

"Slow, eh?"

Martin nodded. He was impatient. Kazin knew all this, but he asked the same question at each of their meetings, as if civility required it. Why couldn't the old man get on with it?

"Let's discuss Chapter 3, plains ecology prior to the arrival of white men. I'm a little concerned about romanticizing the plains."

"Sir?"

"Portraying the plains as a shining sea of knee-high grass, Eden before Adam and Eve arrived."

"I don't know what you're talking about, sir."

"Green religion, Martin. It goes like this. In times past, the world was an Eden. Nature was without evil. In this Eden was the High Plains, populated by buffalo and wolves and all the rest, and a few Indians who'd learned to live in perfect harmony with nature, never despoiling it, never taking more than they needed for food and shelter, a people sensitive to all the natural world, a people without sin. But into this Eden came white men, exploiters, rapers of nature . . . greedy, racists, all the rest."

"I don't know anyone who believes that, Dr. Kazin."

Kazin grinned. "Neither do I. Odd, isn't it, how the notion keeps cropping up in the literature."

"I've never seen it in the literature."

"Well, here now—page thirty-eight of your thesis—all this about the first settlers reporting abundant grass, knee-high, waving in the breeze, Eden—all that on that page and the following. It wasn't like that."

"Well, that's what the settlers said. It's fully documented. Primary sources, every one."

"But that doesn't make it the whole picture, does it? Those same settlers starved out when the drought years arrived."

"I discuss that, sir. The plains cycled between wet and dry years. That's all documented."

"Oh, I suppose, in an abstract way. But you give the impression that the plains were solid grass, with no sagebrush to speak of. Is that quite what you mean to say?"

"Yes, I do."

Kazin swiveled slowly to a stack of papers, plucked something from the stack, and handed it to Martin. It was a Government Printing Office document, dated 1867, entitled *Report of the Secretary of War.*

"That's the report of the Raynolds Expedition of the Army Corps of Engineers. Captain Raynolds explored the Yellowstone basin in 1859 and 1860. He had the old mountain man, Jim Bridger, as his guide. By the way, they more or less crossed your family's ranch land. This exploration occurred twenty-odd years before the earliest settlement or the earliest open-range ranching, or the earliest cattle. You'd better read it. It's rare; take care of this and return it to me."

Martin eyed the report sourly. "What do you want me to look for?"

"Well, let's look at page thirty-six. Right there. Just what I've underlined. They're on the Little Powder, in July of 1859."

Martin did, irritably.

THE RIVER IS NOW VERY LOW, and in many places the water is standing only in pools. The bluffs bounding the valley are barren and present a chalk-like appearance and it is only upon their summits that grass could at any time grow, and even thus has been consumed by buffaloes, which have been far more numerously visible to-day than heretofore.

AT A FEW LOW POINTS WE found a coarse grass that the buffalo had rejected but our mules ate with avidity. The supply was not sufficient, however, and the deficiency was met, both last night and to-night, by hewing down cottonwood trees and allowing the animals to feed upon the bark. This they did with apparent relish, and the branches were peeled as thoroughly as it could be done by hand. This is an expedient that is frequently resorted to by the Indians when the grass fails or is covered by snow; Bridger asserts that, in case of necessity, animals can be subsisted upon this bark through an entire winter.

THE SCARCITY OF GRASS IS INDEED becoming serious, and it is only in rare spots that we can find sufficient pasturage to herd our mules. The soil is also poor, and I doubt if a single section of land in sight would produce sufficient to furnish an ordinary family with a respectable meal.

Martin was amused. "So? This makes my point for me. There shouldn't have been any settlement of the High Plains."

"Ah, not quite. It suggests, doesn't it, that the plains were no Eden prior to the arrival of white men? Read the rest of it at your leisure. Especially the stuff about sagebrush. The expedition was trapped in sagebrush so thick they could scarcely cut their way through. Two decades before the earliest settlement. That's not Eden, Martin."

"What do you mean by Eden? I don't claim it was. It's cyclical. A wet year would have given Raynolds a different view."

"Just as describing a dry year might give your readers another view of your Eden. Rigor, Martin, rigor. Everything nailed down and nothing ignored, including evidence that may not support your thesis. A serious work of scholarship requires all that and more—a passion for truth no matter where it takes you."

Lecturing again. Old Kazin was prone to that. Martin smiled sourly and said nothing.

"The very concept of wilderness touted by the Sierra Club and the Greens is essentially racist, Martin. Ever think of that? This vision of an Eden, uninhabited, the processes of nature advancing without human interference—it just happens to ignore something. The Indians. They were present across North America, and were major predators. I've seen good work suggesting they were the most important predators—more important to ungulate populations than wolves, lions, and other predators combined. It hasn't been true wilderness, not for eons, and man was very much a part of the ecology for many thousands of years. Time to get past the Eden idea."

Martin found himself totally rejecting the idea. Indians never mattered much. Old Kazin didn't even know what wilderness was, or what nature could be, unsullied by mortal activity.

"Now let's see, Martin, I have another note here. Ah, yes, prairie dogs, eradication thereof. I see nothing about it, but of course you may still be planning to include something—"

"Prairie dogs?"

"Yes. Destructive little devils, and not just because their holes broke horses' legs. They denuded square miles of High Plains, hundreds, maybe thousands of square miles, left them bare as a billiard table, prone to erosion—until ranchers killed them, shot them, poisoned them off. Then the prairies bloomed."

"The killing off of the prairie dogs was an ecological disaster," Martin argued. "Because of that, the fox and eagle and hawk and coyote populations dwindled. The black-footed ferret, which feeds entirely on the prairie dog, is almost extinct. It disturbed the balance."

"And restored hundreds of square miles of grassland to good condition."

"That's debatable, sir."

"Well, then, debate it. That's what a rigorous paper does, you know. Focuses on issues that divide us. But I have the sense that you'd rather not debate it because it might cut against your hypothesis that settlement demolished an Eden."

"I'll think about it," Martin replied tightly. He didn't want to clutter up his thesis with junk like that. The thesis was inarguable—settlement had wrecked the plains. Why pick nits?

"Ah, Martin, I apologize," Kazin said. "You're doing a fine piece of work. Maybe I should just let you take your chances with the master's committee."

"No, sir, I appreciate your help."

"I grew up in a different world, before academia became a springboard for—social change might be the polite term. We were after something else, you know? The federal government—Park Service, EPA—they're offering research contracts right and left, and guess what? All that research is generating exactly the results the bureaucrats were hoping for. My oh my! The government's bought most of the university environmental sciences departments in the country. One wonders about the future of science."

"I don't follow you, Dr. Kazin."

"Oh, I can't explain it exactly. Let's say that if this thesis of yours remains valid over time—say, over your career—you'll have achieved the thing my generation set out to do. But if, a decade or two from now, it's thoroughly refuted, knocked down by the next young scholars coming along with their own buzzwords and fancies, then you'll know what I'm talking about."

Martin ached to escape, but couldn't.

"I think I've upset you. Perhaps you should consult with Dr. Chambers, Martin. He and I don't agree about much of anything, and he's a sociology man, too. Maybe I'm all wet. Maybe he'll give you the perspective you want. He's a fine man, right on the cutting edge. A gifted scholar. I admire his work."

"I'll do that, sir. I have some things to review with him. That book, *The Territorial Imperative*—I want to talk to him about it."

"Yes, see Bill Chambers."

They spent an hour reviewing details, and Martin didn't escape until dusk, and when he did he was in a sour mood. The Raynolds report felt like a rock in his briefcase. Maybe he could allude to it in a footnote. Yes, that was it. Reduce it to a damned footnote. Either that or use it to buttress his thesis, that the plains were uninhabitable.

It wasn't that people couldn't live there; it was that the life there was rotten, like his own, growing up isolated, friendless, stuck with a family full of outdated ideals, like those of his grandfather. The thought of Dudley Nichols softened his harsh feelings a little. He liked his grandfather, in spite of the old man's antique notions. His grandfather had virtually raised him, spent hour after hour with him during the long summers, spinning tales of the frontier, showing the boy how to saddle and ride a horse, how to rope and brand, how to shoot and hunt, how to look for old Indian campgrounds, with tepee rings, arrowheads, maybe even ancient buffalo bones. And all the while, his grandfather had taught Martin everything he knew about ranching and weather and grass and cattle—especially cattle. Maybe the old man had simply been preparing the next generation of Nicholses to take over someday, but it had been friendship during a lonely childhood.

He shared a small room at the rear of one of those big old Victorian houses on Willson with his Chinese girlfriend, Mary Linn. He was ready for some microbrew, maybe Moose Drool, and a salad of alfalfa sprouts and mushrooms, with maybe some tofu in it, after a lousy afternoon.

Kazin. The old fogey made a bundle giving talks to cattlemen and stock growers and wool growers and the National Farm Bureau and all the rest of the corporate land-killers. Let him get in bed with them. He never would.

He thought of someone he'd like to be in bed with, and hurried to his room, where he was stuck because his rich father was too cheap to give him a decent apartment. There wasn't anything he could do about a drunk of a mother and an exploiter father except fight them.

CHAPTER 5

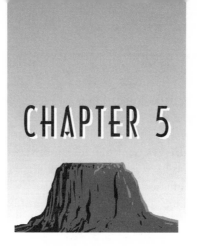

The news from John Trouble, who managed the North Ranch, certainly didn't sound good. Four probable wolf kills, the first in the area. A heifer and newborn calf, a yearling steer, and a cow. All within a mile of one another.

"Look, John," said Cameron into the phone, "I'll call Bill Marshal and tell him we want him *now*. It'll take him an hour and a half. I'll be over as fast as I can. Find out anything else you can."

"Cam, I've been hearing wolves at night, only I didn't believe it and I wasn't sure. For a coupla weeks, maybe. I went out there with the ATV for a look."

"I'm glad you did, John. I'll see you in an hour."

Cameron hung up, anger percolating through him. Wolves. It was going to happen sooner or later, but he wasn't ready for it. Yellowstone Park was a long way west, and he had hoped—naively, it seemed—that the wolves would hang around the country over there.

He called Bill Marshal's office in the Rosebud County Courthouse and discovered the county extension agent was out to lunch. Cameron left a message. He'd follow through later with his cellular phone from the truck.

He was going to blister Marshal's ear for a while. Marshal was an old friend and good troubleshooter, and he knew what Marshal would tell him: keep it legal, get the experts in, and don't shoot wolves because it could cost Cameron a few years in a federal lockup and several tens of thousands of dollars. Wolves were a protected species.

Nichols wasn't sure he would heed the advice. Some of the outfits around the Yellowstone country were dealing with wolves their own way: shoot, shovel, and shut up. Angrily Cam unlocked his gun cabinet, selected his favorite varmint rifle, a Marlin, collected a handful of shells, and locked the cabinet again. He wasn't much for hunting; like most other ranchers, he had seen all the blood and death and dead meat he cared to see. But just then he would have put every bullet in his possession into the wolf that was butchering his stock.

There was one more item to collect, this time from his office. He loaded his Yashica camera and spare film into a bag, scribbled a note to Sandra, and headed out the door, getting hotter all the while. The goddamned environmentalists and their goddamned wolves.

He jammed his white GMC three-quarter-ton pickup into gear and spun down the lane, spitting gravel behind him. North Ranch was an hour's dirt-road drive north and west. It would take Marshal two hours to get down from Forsyth—even assuming the agent left immediately and wasn't on other business. Cameron drove recklessly, ignoring the rattle of the truck as it hit potholes and skidded over gravel ruts. He had pounded trucks into hulks for years, deliberately abusing them when he couldn't abuse anything else.

He wished he hadn't called Marshal. They were right, those old boys in the Yellowstone country. Shoot, shovel, and shut up. Except that they kept getting caught, fined twenty-five grand, and sent up for plenty of long months of remorse.

The roads to the North Ranch took him through country he loved, rough ridges laced with ponderosa, cottonwood-lined gulches and creeks, grassy meadows winding through long serene valleys. The route took him past wind-carved sandstone outcrops that harbored the nests of thousands of birds and had sheltered him in rough weather. Most of his ranches yielded sanctuaries, hidey-holes where he could retreat during a sudden hailstorm, or a brutal drop of temperature, or a deluge. Some were animal dens full of scat; others were overhanging ledges wind-carved in sandstone. Some were nothing but juniper or willow thickets a besieged man or horse could push into, out of murderous weather. This harsh land had frozen and baked him, pummeled him with golf-ball-sized hail, drenched him miles from refuge. Now, in the fullness of his years, he knew where to head when the sky turned black, knew how much time he had.

His corporations owned much of this country but the ranches weren't contiguous and the Custer National Forest poked fingers of public land into it, and vice versa. He'd negotiated with the Forest Service for years, trying to trade sections so both he and the government could consolidate their holdings, but the environmentalists had put a stop to it, called it a giveaway to corporate agribusiness. The Forest Service had backed off even though the government was the net winner of two wooded sections in the exchanges they had worked out.

A faint haze of green covered the fields, the earliest hint of grass in a brown-and-gray world. He liked that green, liked its promise of nurture for domestic and wild animals. But this trip he barely noticed the first faint stirrings of spring. How many wolves? A pack? How many carcasses? How much loss in hard dollars and cents, and in softer calculations, such as time spent at damage control, fending off bureaucrats, and the rest? He stopped those lines of thought abruptly, aware suddenly that he didn't even know for sure that wolves were responsible. It could be lions. The big cats, also a largely protected species, had multiplied and were taking more and more domestic stock now that they had wiped out much of the mule deer population.

He wheeled at last past the rural mailbox and up the twisting rutted road that led to the West Ranch buildings nestled under a protective ridge, and to his old Northern Cheyenne manager there, John Trouble, as good a man as ever handled livestock, except for the week or two a year he drank. No one knew for sure the origin of that name and there were three or four versions of the story. But it was known that John's ancestors were among those who in the autumn of 1878 fled Indian Territory, Oklahoma, where the Northern Cheyenne had sickened in soul and body, determined to return to their homeland or die. Many did die. John's ancestors, with Little Wolf, made it. Soon after, the family had acquired the name Trouble, and whoever was patriarch was known as Big Trouble. John was the patriarch now.

The stocky manager was waiting in the cold wind as Nichols wheeled to a stop. Trouble wore his gray-shot hair short, almost a crew cut, which only made his rawboned face rawer and heavier.

"Marshal called, cellular. He's on his way, due here in twenty minutes," he said.

"Good. Was it wolves for sure?"

"Some paw prints in the dust. Dry this spring, isn't it. Biggest damned wolf I've ever—" he paused. "I've never seen one, except that they come to me in dreams. Maybe I've a bit of wolf brother in me. Those paws looked the size of saucers. Not cats. Wolves for sure, at least at two carcasses. The third's in brush."

"Herefords?"

Trouble nodded. The Nichols ranches bred the Herefords, but they often ran other cattle, whenever they could be purchased at the right price. "Helpless creatures," he said. "Now if they were buffalo, they'd have a good set of horns. Wolves won't mess with a healthy grown-up buffalo unless he's alone."

"How long ago did you find 'em?"

"First one yesterday afternoon. I was out in the ATV, checking on things, scared up some ravens. It got ate two, three days ago and it's mostly hide and bone. The other two are within a mile of there."

"Can we get there with the pickup?"

"Pretty close."

"You said you've been hearing wolves?"

Trouble smiled ruefully. "I did, woke me up sort of, but I didn't believe it. Not wolves. You know how it is. Coyotes maybe. But it was wolves. Big damn wolves howling on the ridges. Makes me wild. Half of me wants to go howl with 'em, the other half wants to shoot 'em and protect the cows. Mavis, she don't like 'em. Neither does Little."

He was alluding to his elder son, Garland, better known as Little Trouble.

"John, how do you feel about the wolves—as a Cheyenne?"

Trouble's brown eyes glowed, and his weathered face crinkled. "They sing songs to me, Cameron. They're music. But they're devils. This is now, not a century and a half ago. But you talk wolves, and the Skins all howl." He was using a term, condensed from redskins, that Indians used to identify themselves but which was forbidden to white men.

"You all right with tracking 'em down? Getting 'em out of here?"

Trouble shrugged, and Cameron could only guess at the man's private thoughts. In spite of all the years ranching together, in spite of Trouble's good salary—higher than most—and in spite of the television and satellite dish that fed an alien world into Trouble's mind, there were sudden swift chasms that opened up now and then between them.

The Rosebud County agent drove in, pulled a briefcase from his truck, and joined them. "Gotta make a report," Marshal said. "You know what wolves are? They're paperwork. Animal Damage Control, United States Park Service, United States Fish and Wildlife gets a copy. Montana Fish, Wildlife and Parks, three Ag agencies, and the Forest Service. All right, let's go."

Cameron waved Big Trouble into the driver's seat of Cam's GMC, and the others crowded in. He headed west, through two wire gates, into a ponderosa-guarded flat, and stopped half an hour later at a dense stand of chokecherry in a draw.

"This here's the bred heifer," Trouble said. "I stayed away so's the experts could look at those prints."

"Don't look at me," said Marshal, a man more at home fighting sagebrush, cactus, drought, and leafy spurge.

There wasn't much left of the newborn except a chewed-on skull. And the heifer's bones were well scattered. The wolves and a dozen lesser predators—coyotes, crows, skunks, weasels, and anything else with a taste for flesh, had reduced the carcass to a scatter of bones and hide.

Trouble pointed at a dog print, then another of a different size. Big prints left in the dust, half–blown away now but still identifiable. Front paws wide, with claw prints usually visible. Rear paws more diamond-shaped, claws visible also. These weren't the round, wide and clawless prints of a big cat.

"Just a minute," said Marshal. "I'm new at this." He dug in his briefcase and pulled out an Ag Department animal-print guide. But it didn't have wolf prints. He did find the images of lion prints.

"I don't make it out to be a lion," he said. "Don't know for sure it's a wolf, but it's no lion."

Cameron pushed back his impatience. All he needed to know was what a dog print looked like.

"Wolves," said Trouble.

"I imagine," Marshal said.

"I'd like to shoot the bastards," Cam said.

Marshal stopped writing. "Don't do that, whatever you do. The feds—fish and game—are now running stings. They put a radio collar on a wolf—fancy collar that tells 'em the instant a wolf's shot—and then release the wolf near the outfit of someone who's suspected of shooting wolves. They're so good that they land on the guy before he's got his rifle put away. Forget the shoot, shovel, and shut up."

"I'd like to shoot the bastards," Cameron repeated.

Marshal grinned uneasily. "Cam, there's something you should know. United States Fish and Wildlife has the legal authority to seize assets of anyone it suspects is killing endangered species. Up until a year or so ago, the wolf was listed as experimental, which meant that Fish and Wildlife could deal with wolves even if ranchers couldn't. But now they've got full endangered species status—ever since, oh, early 1998. Right now, Fish and Wildlife doesn't even need proof and it doesn't have to wait for a guilty verdict. If they even *think* you're killing wolves, they could tie up this place, or your livestock, or your vehicles—whatever they want. Don't get into that kind of trouble."

"How can they do that? This is the United States."

"They can do it. They can seize whatever they feel like and if you're proven innocent down the road, they can take their time giving it back to you."

Cameron digested that angrily, and then took pictures, close-ups of the prints, longer shots of the bones.

"I can't figure out why they came here when there's so many sheep close to Yellowstone Park," Marshal said.

"A wolf travels," Trouble said.

"How many do you figure took this heifer, John?"

"I don't know. What makes me an expert on wolves?"

"I thought you might know," Marshal said apologetically.

Trouble drove them across the pasture to the other two kill sites, which Nichols photographed. He was two thousand in the hole now and this was only the start. Where would it stop?

"How do I get this back, Bill? What about those outfits, like Defenders of Wildlife, that offered to pay any ranchers whose stock was killed by wolves? You remember, back in the early nineties, when people were raising hell about putting wolves in Yellowstone? They raised a hundred thousand dollars and promised to pay."

"Oh, that. They disbursed the entire amount and last I knew they were raising more. There's a chance you could get something from them," Marshal said.

"I hope they keep their promises," Cameron said.

"The wolf reintroduction was, ah, a bit more successful than they figured. All those nice wolves liked the taste of sheep and cows after all. A lot of those greenies want to cut off the payments. Why pay money to all those rich sheepmen and stockmen—agribusiness, giant corporations, with millions of dollars in assets? You'd better apply fast, before they back out. There's not much help from predator control, either. The wolf population expanded too fast. Animal Damage Control fought a losing battle for four or five years. Now they want their budget doubled so they can trap more predators and put radio collars on 'em and monitor 'em with helicopters."

"So I'm probably stuck. Two thousand in beef out the window, just for starters."

"There's no program—"

"Programs," Nichols snapped. "Programs. I'll start my own program."

CHAPTER 6

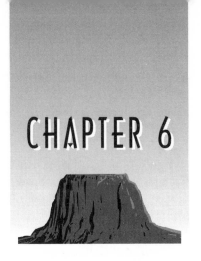

Laslo Horoney called Nichols from the Miles City Airport, while Dolly waited in the rented pickup. He did not receive a welcome.

"I've got a problem on my hands, and we have nothing to talk about anyway," Nichols said curtly.

"A problem?"

"Wolves. A pack of them. My family hasn't dealt with wolves since the teens. Getting the federal government to remove them is another problem. So you see—"

"My wife Dolly and I had simply hoped to drop by—make your acquaintance."

"And twist my arm."

"No, not talk about that."

"We're not budging, Mr. Horoney."

"All right then. But it might be of value to you to know what the foundation has in mind. I think it would remove some of your worries."

"My problem is wolves, sir. Right now they're killing one animal every other day. Two or three thousand dollars of beef a week."

Horoney paused. Nichols had a problem that would only expand when the buffalo commons was functioning. What better argument was there for Nichols to sell the ranches? But he would come to that conclusion himself.

"Mr. Nichols, I'll say something that might surprise you. I'm not a member of any of the environmental or wildlife groups—I don't belong to the Sierra Club, the National Wildlife Federation, Earth First!, or even the Nature Conservancy, and of those groups I admire only one—the Nature Conservancy—because it works with people instead of trying to tear our world apart."

Horoney heard only silence for a moment.

"That does surprise me," Nichols said. "Well, all right, you come on over and give us the pitch. I'll get us all together—my father, my daughter Deirdre—DeeAnn, we call her—and her husband, my wife—and we'll listen."

"Could we make this simply a social occasion? I have my wife, Dolly, with me."

Nichols laughed. "Come on over and have a drink. Hang on a moment while I talk to Sandra. She cooks the best standing rib roast in Montana . . . Ah, you eat red meat, don't you?"

"You bet. Everything in moderation, including a good rib roast."

Nichols returned moments later. "She's up to it. It's a dinner party, Mr. Horoney. You can do your soft sell over some bourbon or Scotch or whatever suits your fancy. But don't expect to change things."

Horoney liked the man.

He had quietly explored this country, but it was new to Dolly. He drove the interstate over to Rosebud, and then cut south through a land of massive slopes, rock outcrops, and ridges alive with ponderosa.

"I thought the High Plains were flat as a pool table," she said.

"Some of it is—awesome in its scope. I've driven in places so huge, with such a towering sky, that they made me feel small as an ant. But not around here. This is some of the prettiest country you've ever seen, and that's one reason people like the Nicholses love it and cling to it. It nurtures something in them."

"I feel sorry for them, Laslo. They didn't ask for this in their lives."

He liked that and smiled at her, endlessly glad of his good fortune to have her for his mate and friend and lover. "It's the hardest part. The most painful to me."

"I never thought of eastern Montana as a place I might enjoy. It's just—here. What do these people do? Aren't they lonely and bored? I would be."

"Well, let's find out. I'm curious, and you are, too."

"You like driving this pickup."

"It beats sitting in the back of a stretch limo trying to sell skyscrapers."

"There's nothing here."

"You mean no people. Just us."

"Sort of lonesome."

"That's it. The plains have been depopulating themselves for decades. Back in the twenties, they were full of people, little railroad towns each with a grain elevator, small ranches and farms. It didn't work. The climate's too dry. The small outfits were all consolidated into giant ones. Now these people live isolated lives. You know what they lack? Neighbors."

She smiled wryly. "Maybe the little push you're giving them will lead them to a better life. People cling to things."

Horoney traversed a good gravel road along Otter Creek, and turned at last into a long, inclined lane that would deposit them at the Nicholses' home ranch nestled under the eastern bluffs. They came to a small complex, several white frame buildings, including a rambling ranch house that had its own odd grace and exuded permanence, joy and perhaps pain.

Cameron Nichols was on the veranda, awaiting them.

Horoney introduced Dolly, and Nichols looked faintly startled as he gazed into her thin face, which was framed by glossy brown hair. A face without makeup. He had obviously expected something else.

"You were expecting a Dolly to look like a busty blond singer," Horoney said, "and found a slim, brown-haired beauty instead."

They laughed. Within the wondrously comfortable and much-lived-in old house, the Horoneys met Cameron's wife Sandra, who displayed a bright smile that didn't show in her eyes, fading carrot hair, a face that suggested intimacy with hard drink, and a dubious sincerity; then Cameron's father Dudley, impeccably groomed in costly Western clothing, knife-edged Western-cut twill trousers, a bib-style plain blue Western shirt, and pointy high boots polished half to death, and a barbering that had pronounced death upon any stray hair. The man was making a statement with his attire, and his statement said *cattleman*.

Horoney shook hands with the reserved and silent man who didn't really want to shake hands, and then met the daughter and her husband.

"This is Deirdre—DeeAnn—my oldest daughter, and her husband Mark Cassady. They do the real ranching around here. Her kids are out in the barn, and you'll meet them."

DeeAnn wore Western attire, too, the cut oddly out of sync with the stuff in Shepler's these days, rather like her grandfather's nineteen-twenties outfit. Horoney sensed the granddaughter and grandfather shared a certain view, and were less flexible than her parents. The only thing Western on Cameron's lean frame was a big belt buckle on a big belt.

Horoney found himself being stared at, which is what most people did when meeting the second-richest man in the United States, a man who was creating a prairie wilderness of about twenty-four thousand square miles for starters, and doing it largely out of his own pocket. Horoney had guarded his privacy zealously, avoided photographers, and had managed to keep Dolly and himself free of harassment. They could travel and not be recognized, and that was the fruit of his long struggle against notoriety. But his fortune made life awkward sometimes, and he had taught himself to ease his companions along toward ordinary intimacy.

"Dolly and I were hoping to get the Cook's tour," he said.

That did it. Cameron showed them the old house, and how it had been added to by several generations; showed them a wall full of ranching trophies, blue and purple stock fair ribbons, breeder's cups—Herefords, it seemed—and some old rodeo trophies, the antlers of a giant elk shot on the ranch in 1917, and a weathered buffalo skull found in a coulee. They showed the Horoneys a map of the ranches that covered a whole wall in Cameron Nichols's office, section by section, spread across a plain from Colstrip to Broadus, twining around the Northern Cheyenne Reservation, and surrounding some of the Custer National Forest. The Horoneys were taken to the cemetery plot that Truehart had told him about, the place with virgin prairie in it.

They talked stiffly at first, put off by Horoney's power and prominence, but he warmed to them, softened their stiff politeness, and won Dolly and himself a small corner of comfort. Then Cameron Nichols opened the bar, Scotch to the Horoneys, bourbon on ice to old Dudley, beers to the Cassadys, gin and tonics to Sandra and himself. Sandra took hers, added more gin, and vanished into the kitchen.

"Quite a spread, Cameron," Horoney said. "When I think of all the troubles people have had settling here, I'm all the more impressed."

Nichols liked that. "We had to learn how to deal with this country," he said. "We carry no mortgages, no debt. Bank debt's what kills ranches. We keep enough hay on hand to feed for two dry years, and that doesn't include what we can grow on some irrigated fields." He glanced sharply at Horoney. "And in spite of what people think about corporate agribusiness raping the land, we rest about ten percent of our land all the time, giving it a two-year break without a cow on it. And I have a man who does nothing but war on cheatgrass, thistle, knapweed, spurge, and other weeds. The pasture's all we have, our only asset, and if we destroy it, we're done for. We live with that every day, but all I see in the press is how agribusiness is wrecking the land. We've planted shelter belts for wildlife, fought off the Russian olive tree, which is our northern version of your mesquite down in Texas—it crowds out other trees and eats range. We learned by trial and error. Dudley, here, passed along to me what he knew. And he had gotten his wisdom from his parents, who had weathered the Great Depression. Grandma Nichols is still alive, in her nineties, doing fine in Miles City. A nursing home there. And—" Cameron smiled apologetically. "I don't mean to go on."

"Impressive," Horoney said. "I never did believe that most ranchers—a few bad apples apart—ruin their range. One agronomist told me that private ranch pasture throughout the west is generally in better shape than BLM or Forest Service land . . ." He sipped the good Glenlivet malt, and smiled. "You must wonder about me. If you'd like to know how a real estate man with a foreign name and his wife, who has a degree in English literature, got into this, I'll tell you."

He told them about being a man trying to give his country a gift, and how he had thought about the homeless, and how civilization had deranged the homes of man and creature alike, and how he had turned to the High Plains, in part because no one else cared about them. He told them that the restored plains was one of the greatest of all gifts to a crowded world; that this proposed wild land would become a home to its own again, and would remind future generations of what it means to live in harmony with nature. He told them about how the idea caught fire, how schoolchildren wrote him, how people in the proposed trust area donated their lands—twenty-one sections given to the foundation so far—and how he had struggled to get the necessary legislation through statehouses.

He talked of his growing fascination with buffalo, an animal that seemed to do less damage to the fragile arid pastures of the plains when allowed to roam freely; that buffalo had lived on the plains since the last ice age, were more adapted to them than cattle, could endure winters better, could feed themselves more efficiently, and—not least—offered mankind a low-cholesterol red meat. He talked of the restoration of ruined range. For two years, since 1998, the foundation had been buying ranches, and not a domestic animal had grazed them since. He talked of restoring the original buffalo grass, bluestem, and how there wasn't seed enough in the world to do it, so he had started up a bluestem seed farm in Colorado. He told them about the foundation's efforts to destroy the worst of the alien grasses, cheatgrass, squirreltail, and foxtail barley, all mostly unpalatable for hooved animals, so that the bluestem, the grass best adapted to the area, could grow again. He talked about thick root systems that endured drought, about random grazing, about nature restored to harmony with itself.

Old Dudley was bristling now and then, but the rest listened intently, and Horoney knew that he was reaching something in these people.

He told about children sending their dollar bills to the foundation, about artists donating paintings, publishers doing books, grassroots organizations springing up in Montana and Wyoming and the Dakotas to pressure their legislatures into enacting the necessary tax and governmental changes. He told them about East Coast Americans exuberant about the return of the buffalo, the magic animal that had been a part of America from the beginning and was once celebrated on its nickels. He talked about the wheat farms, the one-crop monoculture that left the land naked to the wind that swept away the precious topsoil year after year until it was now half-gone.

He acknowledged that the new buffalo commons would not be true wilderness: it would be laced with oil patches, quarries, coal mines, high-voltage transmission lines, radio facilities, beacons, dams, windmills, stock ponds, geometric windbreaks, old roads, and military installations. But all these, he assured them, would be nothing compared to the sweep of empty land, rich with bluestem, needle and thread, western wheatgrass, and prairie June grass, a restored piece of the continent and a home to the creatures that had adapted to it.

There was so much more to talk about—but he paused.

DeeAnn spoke first. "What about the pain? You have no idea how much you're hurting people and even sending them to their graves."

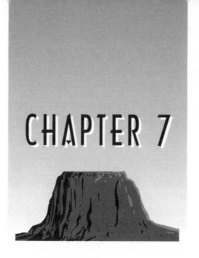

CHAPTER 7

Somewhat to DeeAnn's surprise, Dolly Horoney answered the question.

"Mrs. Cassady, what actually happened surprised us. Most of the people who've sold ranches to the foundation were happy and relieved. They talk about how the foundation was just the prod they needed to sell out; how tired they were of fighting the arid country, falling behind, getting in debt over and over. How it wasn't home anymore. For most of them, selling out was like stopping a toothache. It's been so heartening to us."

That was a good response, DeeAnn thought, but it didn't allay her own pain, or her anger at what was happening around her. Did these incredibly rich people really know how it was? Two years earlier, she still had a circle of friends. They might be forty minutes of dirt-road driving away, but they got together. Now they were gone. Family after family. She and her husband were trapped and isolated, and she felt only the helplessness that people feel when confronted by bottomless power and wealth.

"The dislocation is the saddest part," Horoney said. "I don't know any way around it, except that we have full-time staff trying to make resettlement easier."

DeeAnn watched her grandfather stare at Horoney as if the rich man were a grasshopper. The man's incredible wealth didn't intimidate Dudley, who glared at Horoney's hair, combed straight back and then cut off at shoulder level, with a hatred that was palpable. She knew what her grandfather was thinking. The man was a hippie, and hippies were scum who shouldn't be allowed in the Nichols house.

She saw more in Horoney than he did, and it troubled her. The man had a fine-boned, sensitive face, almost too ascetic, hollow-cheeked and tender. An odd face for a man who had triumphed in the hurly-burly world of commercial real estate and shopping centers. Neither of the Horoneys were what rich people should look like. She confessed to herself that she liked both of them, even though they were the cause of her misery.

"I'll tell you what I want to know," Dudley said, truculently. "How's this country gonna eat once you start feeding wolves? That's all you're doing, feeding wolves, you know. By the time you're done buying up wheat farms and running cattlemen out of business, you'll reduce wheat production by ten percent, and almost that for livestock. And in a time when grain's tight, too."

Horoney grinned. He was ready for that one. "We worried about it. But right next door in the Dakotas, there's prime wheat country. And the state agriculture department tells us there's still land that could be put into wheat there. It's better land than here, too, because there's just about the right rainfall for spring wheat, and the eastern half of those states is wet enough so you don't need to farm dryland style. Now, all this wheat country in Montana—it's blowing away. This type of wheat farming—alternating fields each year to preserve moisture—that just leaves bare ground, naked to the wind. Half the topsoil's gone, and it'll never come back. It's a wasting asset here, a doomed enterprise. So—to answer your question, Mr. Nichols, we're helping wheat farmers resettle in the Dakotas, and we're going to put that naked land back into blue-stem—buffalo grass—just as fast as we can. We're all for keeping the topsoil, aren't we?"

Dudley muttered something, obviously hating to agree with anything Horoney said.

DeeAnn tried a new tack, the one that lay like a ticking bomb beneath this wary meeting. "We've got wolves now. What's your foundation going to do about them? Do you want them, or will you ask the government to move them?"

A sudden tautness infected the old room, as if this were the real issue they were dancing around and avoiding.

Horoney shrugged. "The wolves aren't compatible with livestock."

"I was hoping for more of an answer."

"That's a very good answer, DeeAnn," said her father. "We finally got a federal Fish and Wildlife man in today to look at our wolf kill sites. He said there were several wolves, some pups. He couldn't say how many—it's too dry for good prints. He's the one who told us we'd lose three or four of our beeves a week. Two thousand dollars a week; a hundred thousand a year. And they won't help us. He said this'll be part of the Buffalo Trust Lands, and it was pointless to ship out the wolves." He stared bleakly at Horoney. "I hope your people didn't have anything to do with this."

"Of course not." Horoney was uncomfortable. "We'd just as soon not have to deal with wolves until the buffalo herds are reestablished. After that . . ." He shrugged.

DeeAnn understood the shrug. A few years down the road the foundation would want wolves on the national grassland.

"Looking at those bones is like looking at a grave in which our lives'll be buried," Cameron said. "I can't think of a better way to drive out people like us who want to stay."

"If the foundation people are doing business that way, I'll stop it immediately," Horoney said. "I won't have it."

That was forthright, but DeeAnn felt distrust worming through her. Those wolves came from somewhere, and she wanted to know where. They were a long way from Yellowstone Park.

"But there'll be wolves someday," she said.

"Yes, eventually. In a decade."

"So what you're saying is that you're against pressuring people like us with wolves during this time when you're buying land and building your buffalo herd, but not afterward."

"That's correct, Mrs. Cassady."

"Well, that's on the table, at least."

"Wolves are a necessary predator. They balance nature. My agronomists tell me that wolves sometimes stampede buffalo, and the latest research suggests that it was the stampedes, the churning of the prairie earth, that made the prairie grasses flourish. An odd and delicate interaction. Wolves started buffalo stampeding, which churned the soil—and the result was lush bluestem grass."

"I don't trust those eggheads," said Dudley. "Next week they'll have a new theory. And in ten years they'll discover that buffalo meat gives people liver cancer and everyone should eat beef instead. So you'll slaughter all the buffalo and put Herefords on again."

They laughed.

DeeAnn had more bones to pick. "Why do all your people hate civilization?" she asked. "You're tearing it out. In other times, people celebrated growth and development. Conquering the wilderness and making the world safe for settlement. You're far from our reality, safe in big-city Texas. What would you think if some wolves roamed through Dallas, eating pets and maybe children."

"There's no known case of wild wolves eating people," Horoney said. "That's an ancient European mythology, a lot of it rising from Russia. There's some interesting studies of that phobia I'd like to show to you.

The Indians don't consider wolves to be demonic—wolves are their friends."

"Well, I'm not so sure about that."

"Perhaps my information is incomplete, Mrs. Cassady." He smiled. "I enjoy playing *Peter and the Wolf* to our grandchildren. It's not exactly politically correct, but who cares?"

Why did she enjoy this man she was trying so hard to dislike? No wonder he had become so rich. "Wolves mean the end of civilization," she said.

"You know, I sense that, too. An undercurrent, let's call it, against civilization—or at least Western, European civilization. I sense it among my foundation people, and sometimes I ask them about it but all I get are denials. But it's there and it puzzles me. I've quietly removed two or three staff people, actually fine agronomists or botanists or environmental scientists, because of a certain attitude. I call it the Eden assumption—wilderness is Good and Pure and Noble. Civilization is the Devil, the Tempter. But—here's the odd puzzle—they mean only *our* civilization. Not India's or Africa's or China's or Burma's—no matter how badly other people corrupted and ruined their home on earth."

She smiled at him. Why did he do this to her when she wanted so much to dislike him? For two years, ever since she began witnessing the sale of land around her, neighbors packing up, selling off herds, pulling out, she had thought about this, thought hard until her head ached with her thoughts. What was happening? She had tried to explain it all in terms of money, economics, gain and loss, style of living, material things. But none of it made much sense. Why did some people want wilderness, and rejoice in every retreat of the fragile web of civilization?

There was something more profound at work in all of this hue and cry about the buffalo lands and wilderness. Something that Horoney had realized, too. The man had thought about these things. Could it be religion? Did one side worship Creation as pure goodness and innocence, while the other side worshiped a Creator? Did one side regard man as the demon who corrupts Creation, and thus arrayed itself against civilization? Did the other side believe mankind should subdue the wilds, make them a home and a garden, and nurture life within that home and garden? The thoughts had excited her. What separated the two sides was nothing less than *theology*. She wondered where Horoney fit into all of that. And Dolly, too, for that matter.

It had amazed her that she had come to that perception, and she wasn't very sure about it. She had a bachelor of science degree from

Eastern Montana College in Billings and hadn't ever thought of herself as a scholar or anything like that. But there she was, driven for answers when she needed them, and that answer had formed and solidified within her. And here was Laslo Horoney, the author of all her family's anguish, largely affirming her every private thought.

"Dinner's ready," her mother said from the dining room doorway. They rose, perhaps gratefully.

DeeAnn wasn't done with him, and she wasn't done with this civilization issue, either. It puzzled her, this Green hatred of civilized life. The stock response of the environmentalists was that they really were the saviors of civilization, they were putting it on a sound ecological footing. But she knew in her bones it wasn't so. They wanted to purge paradise of Adam and Eve. Maybe the world's richest man, if that's what he was, would give her a clue.

The succulent rib roast, sizzling in its roasting pan, filled the dining room with heady odors. Her mother could cook beef like no other mother on earth, and took pride in it. She had gone all out this time, pulling out the heirloom Wedgwood, spreading the linen tablecloth that usually appeared only for Thanksgiving and Christmas feasts, setting the table with her monogrammed silver salvers, snowy napkins in rings, and artificial iris as a centerpiece. She had prepared new red potatoes, asparagus in hollandaise, everything an exacting lady who loved company loved to display.

"Sit, dammit," her mother said.

DeeAnn realized her mother was drunk, and what looked like the sheen of a hot kitchen on her face was in fact tears.

CHAPTER 8

J. Carter Delacorte didn't like the way his pulse was soaring as he drove into the Wild Horse Port of Entry from Alberta, Canada, just after dusk. But it would soon be over; he was an old hand at this. Everything was in order.

The Customs inspector looked over the flatbed pickup and the trailer behind it, obviously recognizing it for what it was. Two rows of steel dog kennels were bolted to the bed, each carrier containing one of Delacorte's prized Alaskan huskies. Two supple hardwood racing sleds and other gear were lashed to the trailer behind.

"Have a run at the Iditarod?" the inspector asked.

Delacorte flashed his thousand-watt smile. "I got whipped this time," he said. "But I'm getting better, and I'm learning more about the dogs. It's exhausting."

"It's not a sport for the poor," the inspector said.

"The race alone cost me about thirty thousand," Delacorte replied. "And that's just the starters."

The Customs man grunted and ran his flashlight along the rows of dog containers, and then over the sled and gear in the trailer. "I guess I'll have a look in some of that," he said.

Delacorte nodded, annoyed at him. He opened the door and stepped into a blustery cold night, while the inspector trained his light on the cab interior, briefly, an authoritative sweep that missed nothing even though it seemed casual.

Something was bugging the guy; maybe Delacorte's quartz crystal, dangling on a gold chain from his neck. These bureaucrats all had some sort of bone to pick with someone, and maybe he had it in for people who believed in holistic healing. Delacorte opened trunks of racing gear and let the Customs man poke through gang lines, draglines, harnesses, snow hooks, paw boots, dog coats, spare snaps, blankets, snowshoes, face masks, goggles, dog bowls, a sleeping bag, cooker and alcohol fuel, an ax, wind shirt and pants, mukluks, a fur-lined parka, bags of Charlie Champaine Mix dog food, fish oil, and much more.

"Let's have a look at your suitcase," he said. "And of course the papers."

Delacorte shrugged and pulled it out from behind the seat in the club-cab pickup, and handed it to the man. Three minutes later the inspector snapped it shut, examined the Jackson Hole veterinary papers for the dogs, the receipt for the $1,750 entrance fee to the Iditarod, and a pile of receipts for food purchases in Alaska. He then walked the length of the truck again, shining his light into the containers, on the muzzles of the dogs, and sometimes into the interiors of the kennels. The man seemed uneasy, and Delacorte winced when the beam lingered too long in some places. At least the Customs man didn't pull out a scanner. Ever since 1993, Iditarod dogs carried a tiny microchip, the size of a grain of rice, embedded hypodermically in the scruff of the neck. The coded chip was intended to reunite owners and lost dogs and provide instant veterinary information about lagging dogs cut out of teams at the checkpoints. Only half the animals in Delacorte's truck kennels wore the chip, which made him all the more nervous.

"They've all been vaccinated with Vanguard 5/CV-L. That covers the lot," Delacorte said. "My vet in Jackson says that's the best."

"This veterinary log's for sixteen dogs. You got an empty cage."

"Lost one. She got into a fight and I had to have her put down."

The Customs man grunted. And then suddenly it was over; papers checked, inspection complete.

"All right, sir," the man said, in a tone of voice that suggested it wasn't all right.

Delacorte ran a hand through his cornsilk blond hair, hair that women loved to fondle, shifted into drive, and crawled south. His pulse began to slow. It had been easy. Why had he worried?

He had a hard trip ahead, nonstop driving before the ordeal killed another one. Captive wolves sometimes died for no reason—just because their life seemed over. One had died coming down from northern Alberta, where he had picked them up. Just died. Like that. They were expensive, these wolves, five thousand dollars each to a trapper who kept his mouth shut. They had been caught in exactly the fashion that the Yellowstone wolves had been caught—with a head trap that sprang a tight collar around the neck when the wolf poked its head through to reach the bait. The wolves had been kept in a steel holding pen until

Delacorte could pick them up, then sedated and stuffed into the custom-built kennels. They would not have food or water until they were released because he didn't dare open the doors to feed them.

This haul included three half-grown pups, three pregnant females weighing eighty or ninety pounds, and a giant gray male weighing a hundred and ten pounds, who barely fit into his kennel and glared murderously out of it. The younger wolves looked something like his fifty- or sixty-pound Alaskan huskies, a racing breed evolved from wolflike malamutes and Siberian huskies. The adult wolves were another matter, significantly larger than sled dogs, a terrible force pent up in a tiny steel box. As camouflage, Delacorte did bring back eight of his huskies, amiable dogs to release and show to the Customs men if he had to. But it hadn't been necessary. It had all been a lark. He laughed. It'd be a great tale to tell to his Earth-mates in Jackson someday in the distant future. He owned a fine holistic lodge there and had apologized to the pines that went into building it, as well as a condo overlooking San Francisco Bay.

He drove hard through the moonless night, hoping to reach his destination and release the wolves well before dawn. These predators, like the others, would strike a blow for the National Grassland, and strike a blow against the exploiters and agribusiness corporations whose miserable greed had wrecked the plains. Monkey-wrenching, that's what this was. Edward Abbey had shown the way. Knock 'em for a loop. Foul up their operations. He admired the tactic. He remembered that mysterious Chicago-area activist called The Fox, who struck at polluters in ways so ingenious and diabolical that he had transformed the Movement and harvested reams of publicity back in the seventies.

The marvelous thing about the wolves was that they were *untouchable*; they were a protected species. There wasn't a thing the Nichols family could do about them except shoot them—and land in the federal lockup. He laughed again. This was the second bunch. There'd be a third and fourth. And each pack would eat a fortune in beef each year—and more when they multiplied. God, what a monkey wrench! Old Ed Abbey, wherever he was, would be beaming.

Delacorte intended to heal the Earth his own way, with holistic cures and love and spiritual insight. Right now his sole objective was to get rid of the exploiters. They needed a push, and what better push than one that ate their profits? Horoney was too soft. He wasn't a part of the Movement, not really a Green, and no one trusted him. He was a corporate polluter himself, and didn't really grasp the evil he was contending with. But it didn't matter. Soon the High Plains would heal, and those rotten, cholesterol-laden beef cattle and all the other corruptions of civilization would be out of there forever.

It was a terrible drive: Wild Horse to Havre, Havre to Harlem, then down a long lonely road that would require switching to his second gas tank, and on to Roundup, which might or might not have an open service station. Then he would drive east to Forsyth, and south down Rosebud Creek, and east over endless dirt road to his destination, Pumpkin Creek, and the largest of the Nichols ranches, the Antler. He had driven it all before, knew every turn, but in the deeps of the night he felt insecure and worried. What if he were caught?

But he wouldn't be. He had selected the perfect place for the release, hidden from the lonely dirt road by a stand of willow brush that would conceal his entire rig. He had worked it all out, every contingency but the loneliness. Only madmen could live in eastern Montana. He eyed the black skies nervously—some snow showers had been predicted and he didn't want to leave tracks or hit ice. But the weather held, and he drove grimly onward, across naked plains and hollows where no one lived or ever would live. He plugged a Deepak Chopra New-Age tape into his player and listened transfixed to the message of self-esteem and the gifts that self-confidence bestowed on a wounded world. It buoyed him.

When he was tired he ate a granola bar and drank some herbal tea from a thermos. He was careful about his food, and that care kept him youthful, his face sculptured into sharp planes, his electric blue eyes bright, his sexuality vibrant, which was important to him. He avoided all meat, including dairy and egg products, but compensated with brown rice and pinto beans and megadoses of vitamin B-12. Refreshed, he drove the last lap as the night waned, desperately wanting to be in and out before the cloak of darkness lifted. But when the sky grayed along the lonely horizon, he knew he had lost the cloak.

Releasing the wolves would be an ordeal. Slipping them past Customs was nothing compared to persuading them to leave their cages. He arrived at his chosen place just as his surroundings became vaguely visible. He took no chances, and turned off the road into a rough trail that led to the creekbank, which he followed until the truck and trailer were invisible from the road. No one would come by—no one ever did—but he would be careful anyway. Monkey-wrenching required smarts, and he had plenty of those. His pulse lifted again, and he wished he had taken a beta-blocker. He had trouble with fibrillation.

He unwrapped some cuts of beef, bait actually, although the wolves wouldn't really be hungry. These he laid alongside the creek, on frosty ground. The real bait was the creek itself. Then he clambered to the top of his cages, slid heavy gauntlets over his hands, and began unlatching cage doors—all of them except those of his sled dogs. Then he gingerly swung them open. Nothing happened. The wild animals were innately cautious, and would take their time about leaving. All but one. A sleek pup jammed through the door as swiftly as he opened it, shocking Delacorte. The half-grown wolf, a gray male with black marks, scorned the beef and walked into the creek, sniffed the strange water, lapped tentatively, and then drank, scarcely bothering to observe his surroundings. Delacorte stood atop the cages, trapped there until he could safely return to the cab of his pickup.

The quiet was eerie. The freed wolf stood, sniffed the air, ignored the beef, and waited. None of the others moved. Delacorte did not even feel any stirring from within the opened cages. His pulse skyrocketed, and he knew he must make his cab and take a beta-blocker at once. He'd fibrillated once, and never traveled without them now. The cab would be more comfortable. The sharp cold was already numbing him. Gingerly, half in panic, he eased to the front of the kennels, passed the ones with his Alaskan huskies, and swung into his cab, relief flooding through him. He had the sensation that these prisoners of his would gladly tear him to bits.

Nothing happened. Were they dead? The thought appalled him. All of this for nothing? They had been alive, and tranquilized with a narcotic injection in Alberta. But that had been more than twenty-four hours ago. He felt the truck lurch slightly and found another wolf on the ground, this one a female, an adult tan-and-black beauty who lifted her muzzle, sniffed, scratched the earth violently with powerful claws, as if to dig a nest for her pups, and then drank.

The gray pallor lifted a little but the utter silence depressed him. He needed to take a leak, but didn't dare leave the safety of his cab. Who knew what angry wolves might do to him? He wasn't about to test the issue. The stars began to fade a little. He buoyed himself through the long wait with visions of wolves spreading through the area, wreaking havoc, peeling down the numbers of Herefords, leaving piles of bone and hide in every coulee, driving black ink to red ink, slaughtering the calf crop, turning black ink into red. Ah, what a joy! Wakan Tanka, the Great Spirit, would rejoice!

Then, for some mysterious reason, the other captives fled their cages simultaneously. He felt subtle movements, saw dark forms alight on frosted ground, leaving prints where their warm footpads hit the frost. He counted seven. They drank, stared, sniffed, growled gently. One of the females licked the face of a half-grown pup. They were beautiful creatures that apparently mated for life, fed their young faithfully, and drove back the terrible blackness of civilization that desecrated the altar of the world.

Delacorte started his truck. The wolves bolted straight through the creek and regrouped on its far side while he eased his rig past the brush and onto the dirt road once again. Only when he was a mile away did he stop and shut all the kennel doors. No one had seen him; no one ever came this way this early. He would head for breakfast on the interstate, and then go on down to Jackson and a day or two of well-earned slumber. He had monkey-wrenched the Nichols family for the second time. When they succumbed, the rest of the corporate agribusiness holdouts would sell out, too, and a world devoted to Nature and Love and Harmony would be born.

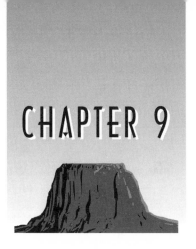

CHAPTER 9

Martin Dudley Nichols watched the field house fill, barely able to contain his anxiety. This would be his coming out. Years ago, that term applied to debutantes being introduced to society. More recently it had taken on other connotations, which amused him. But his own coming out would be different; he would in the next minutes introduce himself to his own family.

This was a major event, and the sponsors—the Environmental Sciences Department and several of the Green groups, had engaged the big, geodetic-domed field house of Montana State University as the only place in Bozeman large enough to contain the anticipated crowd of students, faculty and outsiders. A faint odor of athletics pervaded the place, sweat and tennis shoes and the stink of lost causes.

He, an obscure graduate student, would play only a minor role in the program this evening, and only because his last name was Nichols. The principal speaker would be Dr. Peter Andrew Brooke-Carson, the world-renowned expert on the delicate ecology of the High Plains as well as impassioned essayist, a man Martin devoutly wished were his faculty adviser.

Those who entered the field house this brisk March evening received several pamphlets handed out by the new Zeta Alpha Ecology Sorority, but the only important pamphlet carried the bold legend, STOP HORONEY. The headline was not an anti-Green sentiment, but one deploring the privatized version of the National Grassland as an unspeakable sacrilege and corporate rape of the plains. This would be a gathering to encourage Congress and the president to federalize the project and create a National Buffalo Trust.

A podium and some chairs for the speakers had been set up on one end of the basketball court, and there, under the glare of distant spotlights high above, Martin sat, summoning courage to sever himself from his benighted family. His parents had known, over the years, that he didn't think much of their ranching or their conservation practices and cautious politics. After this night, they would know how far distant he was from them all, and what he thought of their fascist politics, their stupidities, and their ruination of the land. He peered into the shadowed tiers of seats vaulting upward on all sides, realizing that several thousand people had collected here. How could he address them? His heart raced.

At last, ten minutes after the hour, Dr. Brooke-Carson arose. The professor had a mane of salt-and-pepper hair and looked formidable, like a starved lion. In his youth he had been a fiery activist in the upheavals of the sixties and seventies. In a way, he still was.

"Good evening, friends and fellow travelers on the road to the pres- ervation of the world," he began. That was all it took to unleash ap- plause, which rose upward, held, like surf thundering against a seashore, and then subsided.

"You are busy people and we shall dispense with formalities. I am going to begin with a review of what's transpired, and then tell you what we need to do about it. Then there will be other speakers, each with a valuable message."

Martin felt the crowd settle into attentive silence. It would be recep- tive to the gospel preached here this evening.

"Now, a brief review, a bit of recent history," Brooke-Carson began. "Those who envisioned a buffalo commons, the Big Open, a restoration of the High Plains to its original estate of many years ago, scarcely imag- ined that the project should be attempted by private means. We had always believed that the federal government, and only the federal gov- ernment, had the resources and sovereign authority to do the job.

"But along came Laslo Horoney, an incredibly rich capitalist and ex- ploiter of urban populations, who had somehow absorbed the vision and made it his own without really grasping the difficulties. For all his riches, he lacks the resources to do the job properly. Wealth, it turns out, is not the only thing needed to create the Big Empty. Authority—namely, fed- eral authority—is needed.

"Why? Because with federal authority comes the power of eminent domain, the power to condemn, for the public good, private lands and remove private holdings by force if necessary. Horoney's project fails on that ground, and for many other reasons, which are now vividly and painfully apparent.

"The net result of all of Horoney's effort has been the pending ac- quisition of about three-quarters of the lands, but because his foundation is merely a private entity, he isn't able to budge the rest of the corporate agribusiness interests, and has no recourse. So the grassland remains incomplete; a failure. Some agribusiness holdings sit like tumors upon the commons."

Carson paused a moment to let that sink in. "But worse, much worse, were the compromises Horoney's foundation was forced to make to obtain tax preferences from the state legislatures of Montana and Wyoming and South Dakota. In exchange for relief from property and livestock taxes, and other concessions such as redrawing county lines to create the new Buffalo County, the legislators forced compromises on Horoney's foundation that permanently ruin the prospect of a true restoration of High Plains ecology. One of these was the work of the hunting and fishing lobby.

"As you know, in this state, hunting and fishing are cults. Anything on four feet is considered a fair target for a bullet. Anything that flies is considered a fair target for shotgun pellets. Anything in a river is a fair target for a hook. If it's wild and it lives, it shouldn't. The result was a howl against Horoney's project, one that legislators certainly could not ignore. The foundation was forced to agree to permit hunting and fishing on its vast holdings. In this alleged wildlife refuge of Horoney's, there will be regular deer and antelope and elk and game-bird hunting seasons, fishing seasons, and all the rest. All of this is obviously going to be ruinous to the ecology of the plains, and makes a mockery of the whole idea.

"Worse, as far as ecology is concerned, our friends the Native Americans got into the fray, and insisted that since the lands were stolen from them in the first place, they should have the right to harvest buffalo. The net result of a lot of negotiations between the state, the foundation, and the tribes is that the Sioux, Assiniboine, Crow, Cheyenne, Gros Ventres, Blackfeet, and Nez Percé-Bannacks will each be entitled to kill five hundred buffalo a year in the commons after the herds reach a certain size. And since these tribes traditionally prefer cow meat, which is more tender than bull, this selective harvesting of female buffalo will have grave consequences for the life of the herd. Each year, that is, thirty-five hundred buffalo, mostly cows carrying calves, will be slaughtered. Horoney was forced by the lobbies and legislators and then the tribes to accede to it.

"Now, there may be social justice for our Native American brethren in all this, but in ecological terms it is intolerable. Someone has to stand up to these predatory lobbies, and declare this preserve to be inviolate, a national trust land. And I have not even mentioned the problem of poaching. No mere foundation can prevent poaching on twenty-four thousand square miles of wilderness, poaching by persons in airplanes and snowmobiles, persons armed with nightscopes and technology. Horoney's foundation could file civil suits for poaching or trespassing, but lacks the legal means even to prosecute those it catches. Only the federal government can do that."

Carson paused, pregnantly. "Horoney's foundation has eleven directors, but only three of them are environmental scientists. Three Green tokens. The rest are Wall Street financiers, executives of giant corporations, former government officials, and one or two executives of other foundations. Corporate America! That tells you all you need to know about Horoney's intentions.

"We're here to put a stop to private landgrabs. We're here to sign a petition to the president to set aside this land as a national trust, to nationalize this project and turn it over to the Park Service. He can do it with a stroke of the pen. We're here to contribute to groups that will lobby for a proper national trust, and not some rich man's fanciful dream that could end up simply as a giant landgrab, a steal, from the American people . . ."

Sternly, Carson elaborated his Six Nonnegotiable Demands: declaration of a National Buffalo Trust; federal takeover of the project; immediate removal of agribusiness and other despoilers from the area; immediate federal prohibition of hunting and fishing on the commons; immediate establishment of an antipoaching police force; and immediate nullification of Horoney's deals with the tribes.

His auditors listened raptly, obviously ready to contribute anything, sign anything, do whatever was needed to federalize the buffalo commons. Martin found the eminent biologist's ideas almost mesmerizing, so laden on the one hand with scorn for a private buffalo grassland won at such cost to ecological balance, and on the other hand with such hope of a true commonwealth of nature, kept pristinely by the National Park Service and its legions of experts, including Brooke-Carson himself, on a governing board.

Then at last, Brooke-Carson wound up his exhortation and introduced Martin.

"This young man, pursuing a master's degree here, bears the name Nichols and comes from the family that remains the principal roadblock to success," Carson said, into a profound silence. "But this young man has intellectual courage, conviction, and above all, has grown beyond the limitations of his background. He is going to tell you his story, and from it you will discover even more reason why corporate agribusiness must be forcibly removed from the proposed commons."

Martin rose, feeling a certain queasiness, and a certain cold hostility burdening the atmosphere of the field house. He wasn't at all sure this had been a good idea, but it was too late now. Before this evening ended, he would sever the cord to his family.

"I won't take much of your time," he began apologetically, into the microphone, "because this is a dull story. I'm here simply to tell you that people on isolated ranches live stunted lives, unable to enjoy the company of others, miserable in their constant war with a region never meant for ranching because there isn't enough rain, and because only giant ranches can survive.

"I grew up alone, except for my parents and sisters, and mostly on a school bus. Yes, a school bus, not a big one but one of those runty ones because there were so few of us. Hours of sitting dumbly on a bus before school; hours of boredom coming home from school. You can't study on a bus; you grow weary of other students and sink into silence. And once home, you have no neighboring children to play with. That is especially true in the summer, when you scarcely see a child your age. So you go your lonely way, angry with your life. Multiply that by every child in similar circumstances and you have the outline of a social tragedy that nothing—4-H Clubs, Future Farmers of America—nothing helps. It is simply the result of families stubbornly living in realms that nature never intended to be ranched.

"And it is not only children who are afflicted. In our isolated ranch buildings, falsely called homes, we suffer from alcoholism, early death, family feuding, disease, escape of younger generations—I left; one sister lives in Denver; only a remaining sister stays on, unable to escape. Why should anyone be there? Is this an idyllic life of a rancher's son? So what if I could saddle up my favorite horse? Who was there to ride with? Whom do my parents see? Can they invite people for dinner or meet people for lunch? Of course not. Their lives are little more than what comes to them in their satellite dishes.

"My message is, don't feel guilty about pushing people out of the National Grassland. They shouldn't have been there in the first place. The area never should have been settled. The railroads at the turn of the century were largely responsible for that, promising people—including my great-grandparents—a paradise. Rain follows the plow, they said. Plow the earth and you attract water from the skies. Well, they plowed virgin prairie—and the rain didn't come, and the prairie blew away, and half the topsoil there has been forever lost. And then the population vanished. Those little towns died. Ranchers and wheat farms quit and vanished, and their holdings were absorbed by larger and larger companies, such as Nichols Ranches.

"There are only thirty-some people on my family's two hundred twenty thousand acres, and that includes a handful of children as miserable as I was. All they need is a push, and you're here to give them a push. As long as Horoney's private foundation is attempting to create the commons, agribusiness can't be pushed out. This project requires the power of eminent domain, the power to take private property for the public good, and that requires public ownership. And only federal ownership can transcend all the state and local politics that compromised the Horoney venture. I respect the plains, which is why I want to see people removed from them. I respect people, which is why they should not be permitted to live on the plains. I am talking about homes. I was never at home there. But buffalo are. Wolves are. I am one of the homeless. Right now, buffalo and wolves are among the homeless. We need to restore good order."

On he went, not talking about the fragile ecology so much—he'd leave that to men more eminent—but talking about how agribusiness ruined the High Plains; how his blinded family, locked into hollow tradition, was still ruining the range.

He realized, suddenly, he had talked too long and his auditors were restless, so he wound up his litany of pain and loneliness, and sat down to polite and perfunctory applause. He obviously hadn't been the attraction; the charismatic Brooke-Carson had been the one all those people had come to hear.

He felt angry and didn't know why. They didn't even care about him, one of the walking wounded. They didn't even know that he had just broken, utterly and shockingly, with his family and that they had witnessed an act of anguish and raw courage.

Numbly he sat through two other talks, one by a young Blackfoot woman who said it was wrong for her tribe to insist on killing buffalo in the new buffalo commons, and another from a dissident hunter who said that ecology was much more important than Boone and Crockett records. He argued that killing defenseless animals should be left to wolves rather than mortals because wolves were selective, attacking the halt and weak, while bullets were not.

After that they heard an exhortation from Brooke-Carson to sign the petition, contribute fifty dollars each to the fund, and enlist others to the great cause. Horoney had to be booted out—for the sake of the High Plains. And agribusiness like Nichols Ranches had to go, too.

Martin Dudley Nichols listened and wondered what lay ahead in his lousy life. And what his family would think. And whether the checks would still come.

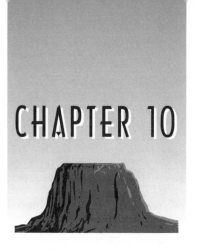

CHAPTER 10

Dudley and Cameron Nichols sat in Dudley's dark den, listening to an audiotape huckstered by Montana State University Students for Wilderness. Dudley listened first to some fancy professor attack Horoney and demand the ejection of the Nichols family from their homes and ranches, and then, astonishingly, to his grandson approving the entire business and whining about his deprived childhood.

Dudley felt old. At seventy-one he no longer understood the world, and felt that he had outlived his times. He heard his grandson's wavering voice fiercely asserting that the plains were not fit for human habitation, all of which was news to Dudley. But much worse was Martin's criticism of his upbringing, and accusations that the Nichols family had desecrated and exploited the lands it held. Dudley knew it was not so. Maybe in his day he had pushed the land too hard, but Cameron had inaugurated a major range-restoration program, which idled about ten percent of Nichols pasture every year, and had raised the caliber of several poor sections to fair, and several fair sections to good, by County Extension Service standards. They had spent over a hundred thousand dollars eradicating sagebrush. It was an ongoing effort; in a decade, the majority of Nichols pasture would be categorized as good, although none of it was in excellent shape. They could not afford that.

But that wasn't what hurt.

After a pitch to send money, the tape ran out. Dudley watched Cameron slump mutely in the leather easy chair and stare at a pine-paneled wall from which hung, in sentimental array, the memorabilia of the old days: branding irons, horse collars, hames, ancient high-spade bits, battered Stetsons, angora chaps, black-and-white photos of favorite ranch horses. The world wasn't like that anymore. Most of the employees, John Trouble for example, drove cattle with all-terrain vehicles rather than horses, wore duck-billed caps in summer, and Scotch caps in winter.

They branded with propane-fired heaters, and processed cattle through squeeze chutes. All of which made Dudley feel older than hell.

"We did our best for him," Cam muttered. "I don't know what to do. Cut him off, maybe."

"What good would that do?"

"He's bit the hand that feeds him."

Dudley adjusted the Venetian blinds to let more light into the gloomy room. The window opened on a sloping pasture that descended to the creek, which was bordered now by a mass of gray limbs that soon would green. It was a stark view; the plains were stark, and their niggardly beauty was one of the things that set sons against fathers and mothers. There had been a day when Cameron himself, angry with his father's ways, had raised hob, had it out with Dudley, and ended up pitching out dozens of costly old ranching traditions, one of which was pasturing three hundred head of stock horses. Dudley had sorrowed, known that his son was right and the horses were cutting into the thin margins, and watched big semitrailer outfits load up the horses and take them to the sale ring in Billings. Now there were about twenty good geldings spread over the ranches, and not a stallion or mare in sight.

"Times change," said Dudley.

"I'm not going to let that brat get away with it," Cam snapped.

"Not much you can do."

Cam stared. "He waited until he was almost done with six years of college. Took the filthy cattle money from his evil agribusiness family right to the end, six goddamn years . . . Do you know how Sandy feels? She's been crying and drinking all day."

"DeeAnn'll run the outfit someday. She has sense," Dudley said.

"One out of three," Cam said. "There were places here for all three. Three young families, taking over from us."

"DeeAnn knows the business and likes country living," Dudley insisted.

"I'd like to punch that punk kid in the nose," Cam said. "Where the hell does he think the money came from? Money for all those years in college so he could get his master's degree? Why didn't he at least wait until he had a job?"

"I think it was important to him to do what he did right now—before the job."

"Giving me the middle finger, that's what you're saying."

"No, showing us he's his own man. You might try being proud of him," Dudley said, wondering where that crazy thought came from. But he knew. Sons needed to get out of the nest. Some of them did it by rejecting everything their parents stood for or did. If anything, young Martin had been slow about it.

"Proud of him! For what? Slicing up my family, his mother and me, trying to get Congress to evict us? Whining because he sat in a school bus—as if we could do anything about that? When they consolidated the schools, was that somehow the fault of Nichols Ranches?"

"Cam, let go of it. The boy's bright. He's got a fine career ahead of him. Maybe he'll give the world something we'll be proud of."

Cameron glared and Dudley swiftly retreated.

"I may as well drop this tape in DeeAnn's lap," Cam said. "See what she thinks of her brother."

Dudley nodded. He had said too much.

Cam left abruptly, leaving the old man in the quietness of an April afternoon. He heard the engine of the pickup turn over, and the sound of tires on gravel. The world outside his window seemed the same as ever, eternal, the shoulders of the land just what they were centuries earlier, just what they would be long after he lay in that plot yonder. But it wasn't really the same.

All his life he had walked this earth and knew it as his own. The United States was home. Montana was home. Powder River County was home. The neighbors made it home. More than that, the things he shared with them made it home. That was the difference: he didn't share much of anything with anyone anymore, and that set him adrift in an alien land, surrounded by people he didn't understand, people who mocked his ideas, the things he had grown up with. People like ecologists, who even condemned civilization and thought of Dudley Nichols as an intruder.

It wasn't his world anymore, and that was natural enough. Young people had their own visions. But this was different. Every generation had built a nation; but now Martin's generation was dismantling one, and suddenly this sturdy house, which turned the weather and sheltered family and friends, was no longer a home. He remembered all the time he had spent with Martin, when the boy was blotting up everything there was to learn about ranching; remembered Martin's love of horses, including the ones Dudley had given him. Remembered how he and Martin had ridden to the farthest corners of the ranch together, grandfather and grandson, enjoying Nichols land, the vast prairie, and their lordship over it. Dudley had always loved the boy, and had nurtured in him a love of the earth, and tradition, and country. Now, it seemed, Martin had pitched all that out. This new, adult Martin was an enigma, and a torment to an old man.

Dudley yearned suddenly for the world that had been his home, and headed for his phono, where he kept tapes he had bought from a nostalgia music company. He had grown up during World War II, on a ranch without electricity or phone, but on the occasional trips to Ashland or Miles City or Forsyth he had heard that music, his music. Later, in 1947, when he was drafted into the peacetime army still occupying Germany and Japan, he heard a lot more of the big-band music and loved it as his own. They had put him in the Quartermaster Corps and stationed him, improbably, at the presidio in San Francisco, and he had loved it there, loved the white city on the sparkling bay, loved the buoyant people, the turmoil of postwar life, and above all, the big bands.

He slipped a cassette into his player, and soon the room was filled with real music, not the tuneless bombast he despised so much. Real music! Melodic, sung by women in slinky evening gowns, men in black tuxedos or dinner jackets. Glenn Miller, Artie Shaw, Harry James, Tommy and Jimmy Dorsey, Les Brown and his Band of Renown, Claude Thornhill, Doris Day, Helen Forrest, Helen O'Connell, Dick Haymes, Kitty Kallen, Frank Sinatra, my God, that was music, and that was a world so vibrant and sweet that his soul responded like a blossom to sunlight whenever he thought of it.

He listened to Fran Warren sing "A Sunday Kind of Love," and remembered Sunday kinds of love when he had courted Mabel Sterling out there in San Francisco. The tape switched to Helen Forrest singing "Skylark" and he remembered how he had wondered whether there was someone for him, waiting in a meadow to be kissed. He heard Doris Day sing "Sentimental Journey" and remembered how it was to take the train back home when he got his first furlough. He remembered how he had proposed to Mabel out in Golden Gate Park one chill evening and how she had kissed him for an answer. And that was as far as they went because in those days you didn't just sleep with a woman, especially one who would become your wife, because it was right to wait, and it also showed respect. They hadn't slept with each other until their wedding, the day after he was discharged, and then it had been awkward and she cried, and it was a long time before they knew much about it. But their very innocence had given their honeymoon a haunting gaiety he would never forget. There had been something else, something that all these young people today didn't have, something he couldn't put words to. He and Mabel had something sacred—yes, that was as close as he could get—something sacred that young people didn't have now, and that sacredness had lasted until her death from cancer. It still lingered in his mind like some sweet fragrance, like that lilac cologne she used on special occasions, such as anniversaries and the few times they had gotten away together and could romance each other.

Back then, at the ranch, he didn't hear much music because they didn't have electricity. Mabel was a brave soldier. She had to accustom herself to pumping water from a well, and heating up bathwater in the reservoir of the kitchen range, and splitting stove wood. But it was fine; there were neighbors everywhere, and life was just grand. They had one party after another. Mabel loved to have people over, and often quietly set a meal before people who had just dropped by and hadn't expected to stay. Beef! They always had lots of that.

The babies came, Nicholas, Eloise, and Cameron. Cam stayed, the others moved to the coast. One or another always stayed with the place. Now DeeAnn was staying, while Julia was making a life in Denver, and Martin Dudley in Bozeman.

Odd how the world began to change in the seventies, maybe the late sixties, too, though it all seemed distant and immaterial. For one thing the government started telling them what to do. They couldn't even burn out a sagebrush patch if the BLM didn't want them to. They couldn't spray stuff. They had to have their wells tested. There were new rules about selling cattle that had been doctored. Grazing fees shot up. Bureaucrats came sniffing around looking for septic tanks two feet from where they should be. That's when they incorporated. They couldn't just own ranches anymore. Taxes were crushing and the government was publishing regulations and insurance companies jacked up rates, state fish and game people started bossing them around, and you couldn't even drill a well anymore or put in a stock pond without getting permission from half a dozen agencies.

He couldn't say just when he grew aware that this old earth wasn't his anymore. But one day a few years earlier he had awakened to it. The damned place wasn't home. The United States wasn't home. These damned young people were treating him as the enemy, the despoiler of grassland, the overpopulator, the killer of buffalo and the sinister fellow who coated the veins of innocent people with cholesterol. And beef became Satan! They all switched to chicken and fish and stuff like that and ate alfalfa sprouts and began saying that cattle had to go, ranchers had to go, the BLM should charge higher grazing fees, and everything that Dudley had built ought to be torn down.

He stood at the window, watching the wind rustle the dead grasses, remembering Mabel, who lay up there in the plot, a place beside her reserved for him, and he knew he wasn't at home anywhere now, and not having a home is the same as death, and he wished he could go up there and lie beside her.

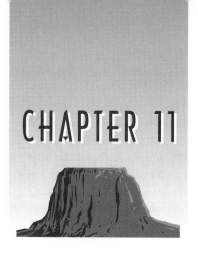

CHAPTER 11

The phone call from Joe Hardy, manager of the Antler Ranch forty miles east, troubled John Trouble.

"You still got wolves?" Hardy asked.

"I'm afraid so. I hear 'em every night, and we're documenting a kill every couple of days."

"Are you sure? Because we got some here, too."

"I don't know how that can be unless the pack split up."

"Well, we got 'em. I've got two dead heifers and wolf prints. And the cattle are acting spooky."

"Have you told Cameron?"

"I'm about to. I just got back. Those carcasses are two hours away. But I thought I'd just check with you, first. Isn't this the damndest thing? Wolves? And we can't even point a rifle at them without going to jail?"

"Cam's been working on it. There's supposed to be a federal predator-control outfit coming here. It's a helicopter. They're going to drop a net on some of the pups in the pack and haul them off somewhere. Take the pressure off the adults. They say that then the wolves'll stick to deer and antelope. Some joke, eh?"

"They're nuts, those people," Hardy said. "Well, I'll call Cameron. He ain't gonna be thrilled. If he gets to losing two, three, four beeves a day, you and me will be looking for another job."

"That's the truth of it, Joe. My regards to the missus."

He hung up, pensively, wondering how in hell a wolf pack could be in two places at the same time. Unless more wolves had drifted in from somewhere. Yellowstone Park had become a sort of wolf nursery, and the elk population was dropping so sharply there that it was inevitable that the wolves would head for the cattle country—and all the meat they would ever want.

"What was that about?" asked Mavis, his wife, who was watching satellite TV.

"Wolves on the Antler."

She smiled. "Maybe that's good."

He stared at her. That gentle observation opened up chasms he didn't want to think about. "Forget that," he said dourly. But he couldn't.

He headed into the night, wanting to think it out again. He was a man split into parts that would never go together.

Outside, he felt Cheyenne. Indoors, he felt almost white. Maybe it was all the conveniences—propane heat, electricity, refrigerator, washer and dryer, food in plastic and stories dropping out of the sky and into their satellite dish. Maybe it was the security. House and utilities and beef free, and eighteen thousand a year to manage the North Ranch. By Northern Cheyenne standards he was rich. He even had a daughter, Estelle, in college in Billings. A Skin with a college-educated daughter— that was something.

But out here in the faint light of a quarter moon, he felt Cheyenne. He could function in cold like this; didn't even need a jacket. He had a Cheyenne body, stocky, big-bellied, dark-skinned, kept in pretty good shape with white men's medicine, blood-pressure pills, cholesterol-reducing pills, stuff like that.

But that didn't keep him from feeling Indian. Like Mavis said, maybe the wolves were a good thing. Clean out the ranches, the white men, bring back the vast, open plains where his people had once freely roamed. Toss out the Baptists and Evangelicals, and listen to Sweet Medicine, and the songs of the wild ones, and hunt the four-foots again. Horoney's buffalo commons had stirred every Plains Indian he knew, including himself. The white men were going away. The fences were going away. The buffalo were coming back. Maybe this was the end of the white man's time.

Hell, all that was nonsense. This was the year 2000, not the year 1850. You couldn't go back. But a lot of young men on the reservation a few miles away wanted to go back. They were fired up with tribal memories of a different era. They were having visions now, seeing the restoration of the old ways. Kick out the damned white men, hunt the buffalo, declare themselves a sovereign nation, wear braids, wear buffalo robes and get rid of polyester forever. Get rid of packaged food that tasted like sawdust. Eat real meat, buffalo hump, full of power, and not the soft gummy beef of the white men.

Trouble snorted. That was nonsense. Buffalo was a good meat, all right, and he had a taste for it, but these buffalo were going to be Horoney's, and five hundred a year wouldn't feed the Cheyenne People. It was a rotten idea anyway. Killing buffalo cows for food was all right when the plains were black with buffalo, but killing cows out of a struggling herd would ruin it. They knew that; all the tribes that had negotiated the deal knew it, and didn't give a damn. That was the white men's problem.

They were crazy back there in Lame Deer and Ashland. He had quietly driven to a few of their meetings, and it sounded like the American Indian Movement all over again. The People were cleaved in six new directions, and the younger they were, the more militant they were. Suppose they did kick out the Nichols ranches and all the rest. Suppose they did return to the past, hunt buffalo, get rid of mobile homes and pickup trucks and TV and plastic food. Suppose they did. Then what? They'd starve, that's what. People like himself, who had gotten a steady paycheck for years, would be dirt-poor again, that's what.

Did they think they could just go out and kill buffalo in Horoney's big park? That his foundation wouldn't resist poaching? And trespassing? And if the whole thing was turned over to the federal government, and all of a sudden Smokey Bear cops were everywhere, what was in it for the People? Did they think they'd be happier wearing skins again? That a buffalo robe would be better than a goose-down parka along about January and forty-below-zero nights? That a buffalo-hide lodge would be better than even their tin-can trailer houses?

He fired up a Camel, gusted smoke into the night breeze, and felt itchy. What was good? The stories of his people? Cheyenne religion? All the traditions that lay half-dead and forgotten, except in white men's books? He sure as hell didn't know.

He heard the wolves howl from a ridge not far away. They had come closer and closer to his home, but this was the closest. He listened to the wolf brothers singing their songs into the frosty night, enjoying them, enjoying their wild, ribald, mocking howls that lifted like laments to the One Above and then faded into gossip. Mocking, that was the word. The wolves were mocking white men. Mother Earth had not heard those sounds here for a long time, and he welcomed them. He knew intuitively that his own spirit helper was the wolf, and now, when he was turning gray, he heard the wolf again upon the lonely land, and something within him stirred.

He had taken some measures after consulting with Nichols. They had decided to push the cow-calf pairs to the southernmost pastures, as far from the wolves as possible. These several sections had been sequestered as part of Nichols's range-restoration program, but now they would be grazed again. Nichols had bought a few hundred common cattle, all of them horned, and these had been turned loose in the wolf-infected areas only the day before. Neither Nichols nor Trouble had any notion of whether horned cattle could keep wolves at bay, but surely they had a better chance than Nichols's closely bred Herefords, whose horns had been removed and whose sole weapon against predators was a good kick. Trouble didn't have much faith in horns, not when a cow or heifer or steer faced a whole pack of wolves, but desperate circumstances required desperate measures. The common cattle would grow slower and have less carcass weight than the registered Herefords, and might in the end cost the ranch money. But what else was there to do?

There weren't many options.

He sucked one last drag from the Camel and flipped it into the breeze, where it arced orange sparks on its way to the ground. He laughed softly. Smoking had been all but outlawed by white men afraid of death. But Indian people had always loved tobacco, and weren't so terrified of dying, and if a good lungful of tobacco made a hard life a little kinder, what business was it of the Food and Drug Administration? It had reached the point where cigarettes were barely accessible—except on Indian reservations, where they were cheap and abundant.

He turned into his ranch-style 1970s house and found Mavis sewing on her latest star quilt. It was gorgeous, with bold primary colors radiating outward in star patterns on a pale green ground. She had walked off with grand prizes at all the Indian fairs and powwows, much to the consternation of the Crow, whose women were famous for their quilts. Trouble enjoyed that. The Northern Cheyenne alluded to the white-hugging Crow on the neighboring reservation as amateur Indians. Amateurs indeed, and mostly mixed bloods, after two centuries of copulating with whites. There were other differences, too. The Crow had always been loose sexually, while the Cheyenne had been strict, almost puritanical, to borrow a white man's term. Cheyenne girls—at least those who hewed to tradition—kept their virginity.

"I heard wolves," Mavis said. "So close."

He nodded.

"They will eat the cattle and we will be going away from here."

"I don't think Cameron's throwing in the towel."

"I can see what is coming," she said. "I hope Estelle can finish college. She calls me and says she went out with a Blackfeet." Mavis laughed cynically. "A Blackfeet. I guess that's better than a Crow."

"We're all 'Native Americans,'" he said. It was a joke. She laughed.

They laughed at the polite white men's term. They liked Indian better.

Native American, what kind of term was that? Everyone was a native American. He knew what they were: Cheyenne Indians. Bound by the Four Sacred Arrows, some of which still existed among the Southern Cheyenne in Oklahoma.

Restlessly he headed for a closet, where he kept something for the People. Years ago, in part because of family tradition, they had made him the keeper of the winter count and given him an ancient buffalo robe with a pictograph of each winter, each year, from the 1880s upon it. But these had stopped. The last winter, the white man's 1936, had been depicted as the Year of the Last Lodge. Then, nothing more. No one had painted the succeeding winters on the ancient robe, no one kept the history of the Northern Cheyenne, nor had he been expected to.

But something drove him, and he dug out the rolled-up buffalo robe. Slowly he unrolled it, wrestling with the stiff, brittle leather which didn't want to unroll after its long slumber, until he was able to spread it over their kitchen table. There it all was, a history of the People. Something welled up in him, and he hunted around for some paints, settling at last for some rust-red latex barn paint. At the site of the last entry, the image of a falling lodge, he began adding dots, one dot for each unrecorded winter, sixty-four dots all in a row in the spiral design around the hairless side of the robe. After he had completed the sixty-fourth dot, and counted them again to make sure, he began his drawing of a wolf's head. This would be known henceforth in Cheyenne tribal history as the Winter of the Wolf. And the year when the Keeper of the Winters kept count again.

CHAPTER 12

For days, Sandra Nichols dreaded Cam's rebuke for the Horoney debacle. But it never came. Dear Cam, her friend and lover, had simply swallowed the whole affair into that mysterious interior of his, and she never heard the condemnation she expected, or a plea to stop drinking. If anything, he had been a little more tender. That night, in the privacy of their bedroom, he had simply hugged her for a long time even though she was barely able to stand up. But she knew he was keenly disappointed in her. She was getting loaded all the time now.

Deirdre had rescued the moment, more or less, springing to her mother's help, laying the great platter with the sizzling standing rib roast before Cam, who did the honors. Deirdre had led her mother back into the kitchen to "get the vegetables," and there had steadied Sandra, given her a towel to wipe away her tears, and then helped her to her seat at the shining table, opposite Cameron.

But none of it had escaped the Horoneys. Sandra had sat stupefied, smiling inappropriately, weaving slightly, avoiding conversation, her words slurred. She had been aware of Dolly's probing gaze, and aware that conversation had been deflected away from her. So the dinner passed, and she could remember very little of it. But she had been drunk in the presence of one of the world's richest and most powerful men, and a woman of such great achievement in her own right that Sandra had been awestruck.

She could not explain why it happened. She starved for parties out in this damned wilderness. She might have enjoyed the ultimate party, hosting two of the world's most sought-after and fascinating people. But she had downed four double martinis as she pulled out her snowy linen, pulled out the silver and swiftly polished some of it, sipping martinis as she salted and spiced the rib roast, started the potatoes, mixed the hollandaise. Loaded beyond help when she pulled the rib roast from the oven, burned herself, peered into the living room with terror, imagined what might happen if the billionaires didn't like her fare or her small talk or the dogs or something else.

It had all been smoothed over, except that Cam had started to ask small questions: Would she like to travel? Would she like to check into Mayo's for a once-over? Were things all right? No rebuke, although twice he had simply taken a glass of booze from her and poured it down the drain. Dear Cam, always tender; that was what she loved about him.

Then came Martin's diatribe against his own family, and she celebrated by getting so bombed that Cam had to carry her to their room and put her between the covers. Martin! Her own son, surly and mean-spirited, without charity toward her or his father, taking their money for an advanced education while loathing his flesh and blood. That was too much. She cried and drank and scarcely bothered to dress, while Cam sank into a rigid black silence.

One April evening she surfed the satellite channels, as she usually did, never landing on one for long, sipping her gin as she usually did until she was drunk enough to sleep. She always got to bed later than Cameron, whose workday exhausted him. She never had anything to do, so she anesthetized herself.

This night, she headed for their suite, with its king-size bed, the only place she was ever happy now. She loved the nights, when Cam was beside her, a comforting bulk and an anchor in a world she no longer cared about. She had always loved him; she'd been dotty about him in school, and that had never changed.

She meandered into the bath, tugged at clothing, rubbed moisturizer into her middle-aged face, examined her fading red hair and decaying flesh as she always did. She stayed trim because the instinct to do so was innate in her. Then she pulled on some navy-blue sweats, which she preferred to nightgowns because they kept her warm through Montana winters.

She headed for bed, but this one time Cam wasn't asleep. He was propped up in the dim light, waiting for her.

"Not tonight," she said.

He didn't respond for a moment, and then gently kissed her while she settled beside him. "I want to talk to you," he said.

That sounded serious. He was taciturn with her by nature, but they communicated well enough. She just settled into her down pillow and waited.

"There's a place in Billings, a foundation, where you could get some help for the drinking," he said. "I've been talking with them. You could get some counseling—therapy if you want—and some routines for dealing with this. They're very good, and you'd be glad you went. They'll take you if you want."

"I don't want to. I like my sauce. It keeps me from going crazy."

Cameron sighed. "They told me you wouldn't get much from it if you didn't want to go. I'd like you to go. It'd be for a couple of months at the most. You'd enjoy it."

She shook her head. "And what would I come back to? More of the same?"

"They have skilled people, Sandy. They can help you . . ."

She laughed shortly. "I don't trust those people. They'll tell me I'm codependent. Twenty years ago they'd have done transactional analysis. Thirty years ago it would have been Freudian analysis. Next year it'll be some new junk."

Cameron would not be put off. "I'd like you to try it. It's not a prison. If you don't like it, come home. It's out of control, Sandy."

"That's where I want it to be."

She had him there. He was expecting her to agree with him about the sauce. But she liked to drink. She didn't know why she drank. One reason was as good as another. She drank because she enjoyed booze and obliteration. Cam thought it was because she was lonely and bored and isolated, but those weren't reasons. There really weren't any reasons. She knew that, even if Cam didn't.

"I'd like you to think about it," he said. He sounded disappointed. "Would you at least drive in to Billings with me and talk to someone? Frances Macamer is her name, and she's a clinical psychologist—specializing in substance abuse."

"If booze is what makes me happy, why do you fight it?"

He didn't respond for a long time, and then he pulled her to him, held her tight, his strong arm holding her so that her breasts crushed against his flannel pajamas. She liked that.

"What would make you happy?" he asked.

"To see you happy. I want that whole grassland trust to go away so you wouldn't worry so."

She felt him tense. He pulled free and stared across to her. "For once, say what you really think, Sandy."

She didn't like that and wished she had poured an extra drink before she came to bed.

"I want to go to sleep now."

"It's hard for you here. We've no neighbors anymore. Horoney's foundation looks like salvation to you because then we'd move, maybe live in a city, be close to people, have a home, and you could be yourself again. I know that, and I've lived with it for years, and I owe you an apology for a life you've barely borne. You've courage and loyalty, Sandy, sticking by me, making yourself a Nichols, living here, twenty miles from Ashland, Montana, in the middle of nowhere."

She did not want to cry, so she refused to let herself. She hated the moment because he had torn apart the comfortable stories by which they had engaged each other. She was tempted to protest that she did like it there, loved it, but instead she pulled free and turned her back to him so he couldn't see her tears. Then she turned off the bedside light and lay rigidly in the dark, homeless in Cameron's home.

"You're the best thing that ever happened to me, Sandy," he said, and slid away from her, resigned to defeat that night. "Please help me keep you."

She lay in the dark, tears leaking from her and sliding down her cheeks into her pillow. She loved Cameron so much, after all these years. She'd been crazy about him in college at Bozeman, her big cowboy. That had never stopped. At first it had been magic. But then it had evolved into something richer and more profound. They were boon companions.

She had come to the ranch as a bride in 1968, determined to love everything that had nurtured Cameron. The Nichols family raised live-stock, and wore Western clothing, and went to stock shows and rodeos, and read journals she had never heard of, like *Montana Stockgrower,* and talked of shipping prices, scours, quarter-horse racing, Justin boots, typey configuration, rain, irrigation, sagebrush and cheatgrass. She was the stranger, the city girl from gaudy Butte, where the Anaconda Company and Montana Power Company were still kings.

Her new life was all so strange, but Cameron was her anchor, and as long as he buffered the no-man's land between herself and her in-laws— and later her own children—everything was all right. They had neighbors and she loved to entertain. What did it matter that some of the neigh-boring men sat down to a meal wearing their straw hats? What did it matter that she ordered her clothing from Peck and Peck, and I. Magnin, and Saks, and loved to go to San Francisco or New York to shop? What did it matter that she looked awful in Western clothing—except for Santa Fe-style squaw skirts and turquoise? She met, entertained and loved the Nicholses' hardy neighbors, Angus men, Hereford men, Charolais men, rodeo queens, quilt-makers, 4-H moms, Future Farmers of America peo-ple, hard-drinking horsewomen who thought nothing of supervising stal-lions covering mares; country people, in their own way much more worldly than her own social class in Butte.

So there she was, looking like a Junior League wife amid another world. She dressed her children in boots and jeans, bought them saddles and bridles and handsome saddle blankets, listened to their country-western songs, drove muddy pickup trucks across endless seas of grass, worried through Martin's rodeo years when he rode broncs and bulls—and, she suspected, a few girls, too. She drank a lot, but who didn't? That was bourbon country, and Butte had been much the same, a hard-drinking place, and some good booze lubricated life and made it sweet.

But even then, people were leaving the country one by one, and by the late sixties, the shrewd Nichols family had bought up the land—and in the process driven away neighbors until the nearest were ten miles from her door. Her dinner parties dwindled because it took so long for people to come and go. Lunches were no longer possible; the remaining women were too busy and too distant, and in any case the few restaurants in the area dwindled, too. Churches folded, clubs and societies fell apart, young people fled instead of staying in the area, no one married anyone, no one even died because those who retired had fled to warmer and more populated precincts to die in the sun, maybe on some Arizona golf course. And suddenly in the late seventies she realized she was living in a hollow place, a forlorn backwater, a vacuum, and everything had somehow fallen apart.

Now she had the satellite dish, the phone, Cameron, Deirdre, and alcohol. She wept silently into her pillow, knowing Cameron was awake, aching to talk with her, and that they both were trapped. She had never complained, and she wouldn't now. She desperately wanted to leave here before she withered away, but she was a Nichols now, and that was her fate.

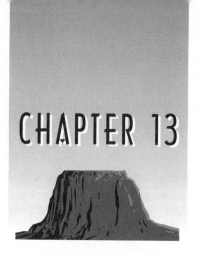

CHAPTER 13

Cameron stood back to the wind, staring sickly at the bones and hide of a registered Hereford cow, number C1448. It was the fourth carcass he'd seen that day of sorrows at his Antler Ranch in Custer County.

Anger and fear churned in him. Beside him stood his manager, Joe Hardy, a short, phlegmatic man who gnawed on a toothpick. Others were present this time: the Custer County agent, Bill Borg, who'd gathered this group together in a hurry, Drew Phillips, an itchy functionary with Animal Damage Control, and a ponytailed gaunt young man in rimless glasses, Sanford Kouric, a biologist with a Ph.D., connected with the U.S. Fish and Wildlife Service in Helena.

Nichols waited irritably while Kouric took notes and photographed the pile of ribs and red-and-white hide that had once been one of his prized, award-winning cows with a breeding history that made other ranchers envious. The Antler was the breeding operation for Nichols Ranches, in part because of its rich grasses, good minerals, wind-sheltered hills, and winter havens. The Antler had no ponderosa pine on it. Cows sometimes ate the needles of the ponderosa, which were an abortifacient, and cost Nichols Ranches some calves until Cameron had cut down the last of them and planted cottonwoods where they were suitable. Here the best cows and prized bulls produced the heavy, chunky calves that matured months faster, ate more efficiently, and carried more carcass weight than common cattle. Through this ongoing upgrade program, Nichols Ranches were continually producing beef more economically.

But it had not been cheap. This dead Hereford cost approximately twice the price of a common cow. The other two dead cows and the calf were also worth plenty. He had seen the butchery of about six thousand dollars of registered, computer-tracked beef this day, and wondered how long even a large livestock outfit could endure it.

The others sensed his rage, and dealt gingerly with him.

"Mr. Nichols, yes, these are all wolf kills, I'm sorry to report," said Kouric. "These are typical. Wolves usually kill cleanly, going for the throat. The pattern's quite distinctive compared to, say, a pack of wild dogs, that tear at a victim. Wolves don't hamstring, contrary to popular belief. Why would a wolf risk a good kick? They race in under the neck and grab the throat with those big trademark canines, bite into the arteries, and hang on until the prey drops."

Nichols wasn't much interested in the details. "Well, what's ADC going to do about it?" he demanded.

"Not much, I'm afraid, sir," said Phillips. "Ever since the executive order requiring us to cooperate with the Horoney Foundation, our policy has been to abandon predator control in the targeted area."

"I've lost maybe six thousand here, and around eleven thousand on North Ranch, and you're not going to do anything?"

"I'm sorry, Mr. Nichols."

"How can that pack be in two places? Did it split up? Where'd it come from?"

Kouric answered. "That's a mystery. Usually, when a pack moves, it leaves a trail. We can follow it. Sometimes radio collars help us. But we don't know where these two packs came from. This one has at least four adult wolves, probably more, and it's an odd bunch, maybe without an alpha female. I can tell that much from prints and scat."

"Are they Yellowstone wolves?"

Kouric shrugged. "Could be, but my instinct says no."

"So I'm stuck. This can bankrupt a ranch outfit in months."

"No, contrary to what you've heard, Defenders of Wildlife is still paying ranchers for predator damage. They did go through the original hundred thousand they raised in nineteen ninety-two as part of their efforts to encourage wolf reintroduction, but they've raised more since then. They shelled out big during the Big Timber sheep crisis last year. The same rules apply. The kills have to be certified by a county agent or someone authorized, like me, as true wolf kills; they'll pay up to two thousand per animal; in doubtful cases they'll pay fifty percent."

That didn't mollify Nichols. "I'll still lose. Those three cows were part of a pedigreed breeding program. This one was a fifteen-hundred pedigreed cow. This leaves holes in my breeding. You don't just go out and buy new breeding stock. You're aiming at a type that works, and you breed to it, weigh the animals, measure everything."

"That's all true," said Kouric gently. The man seemed agreeable, unlike some of the wolf cultists Nichols had seen at public hearings about wolf reintroduction.

"Let's talk about these killings," Kouric continued. "Wolves prefer the prey they understand—moose, elk, deer, hares, buffalo, and so on. For thousands of years they've been conditioned to hunt those animals. Imprinted with a food image, you might say. They hardly even recognize cattle and sheep as food. Given plenty of natural prey, they tend to ignore domestic animals. That's been demonstrated over and over. The cattle kill rates in Minnesota, where there are almost two thousand wolves, are microscopic, a fraction of one percent, even in the wolf zones. Ranchers have more trouble from domestic or wild dogs. That's true in western Montana. We have solid data now, based on years of observation. Cattle ranchers can live with wolves, although sometimes sheep ranchers will have trouble."

"That doesn't help me any."

Kouric nodded. "You're right. And statistics conceal the pain any individual rancher might feel at something like this. Your problem, Mr. Nichols, is that natural prey for wolves is largely absent here, so these wolves are killing your cattle. The mule deer population is thin because there's so little browse; few white tail; no elk to speak of; some antelope that can usually evade wolves—they have a great sentinel system—and not much else. Before settlement, the various populations of predators and prey were in balance here. The prey, buffalo and deer and elk, knew how to survive amidst wolves. Some ran; others employed their horns and hooves. The wolves killed the weak, the injured, and the old, which was actually desirable. But wolves killed young stock as well, which was less desirable.

"Ever since wolves were exterminated early this century, this land's been turned over to cattle and sheep—animals with no natural defenses. If this were now the National Grassland, with buffalo, elk, deer, and even feral horses—mustangs—you'd see a different result. Wolves are hell on foals, by the way. They checked the growth of mustang populations when the Spanish introduced them. That's sort of an exception. Wolves go after game that they've been conditioned by eons of time to bring down. You'd suffer losses, yes, but not the sort of catastrophic losses you're experiencing now, if there were buffalo and elk here."

None of this placated Nichols. "Look, Kouric, wolves are radiating out of Yellowstone Park after a five-year eating orgy, and now you want me to believe that wolves don't migrate from one end of the country to the other, killing cattle. What am I supposed to do?"

Kouric paused, choosing words carefully. "Yes, certain wolves leave the packs. It's biologically ordained. They migrate vast distances. The original Glacier Park wolves traveled clear into Colorado, west into

Washington, north to the country in Alberta and Manitoba and British Columbia they came from, and across Montana. We know that from the radio collars. The telemetry keeps us posted. We tried to collar one wolf in each pack until they became too numerous. I have to confess something. Like most wolf biologists in the early nineties, I thought the Yellowstone wolf population would stabilize at about one-fifty. We were wrong. The wolves had it too good in the park, with about three hundred prey to every predator. The wolf population shot up to two-fifty or more, and then, when the park elk population shrank radically a year or two ago, the wolves migrated. It was wishful thinking. We've had to learn as we go along."

"If they're so numerous, why are they still an endangered species? Why can't I just shoot them? They're in no danger of extinction."

Phillips replied. "It's public policy—"

"Then remove them for me!" Nichols snapped.

"Well, we can't do that—"

"Yes you can. That's what Animal Damage Control has done for generations. Back when it was in the Interior Department they were always ready to help—"

"Well, sir, this is a new era now."

"Look," said Kouric, "we can do something. We can collar these packs, and we can tell you where they're going, if they move. And you can do something. Raise animals less vulnerable to wolves. Ever think of raising buffalo?"

"A lot of help that is."

"I don't know where these came from. Something's odd about this. I'll arrange for some spotting flights, and maybe we can net one or two and take some blood samples. We can do some genetic traces that'll tell us they're either Yellowstone wolves or some other group. You may see a copter around here. That'll be me with a net. We drop the net on one, tranquilize it with a jabstick, take blood, photograph it, check for existing ear tags, put on the collar, and wait for it to revive."

"Cameron, here's the certification you'll need to collect from Defenders of Wildlife," Bill said. "Sanford Kouric and I've both signed."

Nichols pocketed the papers. The April wind sliced cold air around his neck and ankles. Something told him that he was about to bleed the Green group's predator fund out of existence—and then what?

He addressed the county extension agent. "Bill, what should I do? I've got a lot of money locked into this operation. It's not just mine; it's the family's. My grandmother, my father, my children, my new grandchildren . . ."

The agent looked away.

"You're all as quiet as stones, and what you all want me to do is get the hell out of the country, give up, quit, turn my life work, my family's heritage, into your zoo."

"Cameron—"

"Well, it's true. So I collect a few dollars for this bunch. Where does it stop? Next week there'll be a few more carcasses, and I'll call you again, and you'll certify more wolf kills, and . . ." He shrugged. "Maybe I'll start talking to congressmen and reporters and voters. What else is left?"

Kouric braved the wrath. "I understand the Horoney Foundation would pay you well and help you resettle."

"This country is my *home*. This ranch is Joe Hardy's *home*. He has a family here."

"This was once the wolves' natural home, and the buffaloes' home, and the home of elk and even grizzly—until ranchers drove them off so they could raise helpless animals. Mr. Horoney talks a lot about the homeless—people outside of their sphere, animals, even grasses and vegetation being driven out of their homes. Maybe it sounds crazy, but there's something to it. You've made a home here, and I admire your courage. You've fought a dry country that isn't hospitable to the human race. That's something to think about, sir."

Nichols stared at the hippie and seethed, but then controlled himself. Kouric at least had been forthright while the rest weaseled and waffled and stared at the overcast sky.

Phillips studied his watch. "Well, I have to get back to Billings. I have a report to write up. I'm going to have to report the tenor of your conversation and your threat to us, sir."

"Threat?"

"You've been very hostile. Publicity would only hurt your cause. Ninety percent of the public approves of the wolves. Copies of this will go to U.S. Fish and Wildlife, the Park Service, ADC, you know."

Nichols's massive, weather-stained paw grabbed a handful of Phillips's coat, and just as quickly released it.

"I'll report that, too. Assaulting a federal officer is a criminal offense, a felony. You've done it at last, Nichols."

"Cool off, Phillips," Borg said. "He didn't assault you."

"You stay out of it, Borg."

"Let it go," said Kouric, sharply. "Nichols is hurting. I didn't witness any assault."

Phillips glared, then headed for the federal Bronco.

Nichols watched him go, loathing bureaucrats more than ever. Pretty soon bureaucrats would own America, and no one else would own anything, including their own lives and liberty.

Without knowing how or why, Nichols found himself shaking hands with the ponytailed Doctor of Biology who was a part and parcel of the movement that was tearing his ranch business to bits.

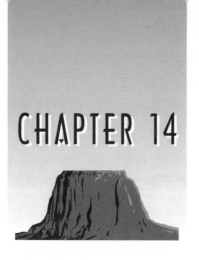

CHAPTER 14

Dolly Horoney sat across from Laslo in his den, listening to a tape of the Bozeman rally. She watched him, wondering how he would respond to all that calumny. He lounged in his plush swivel chair behind his black walnut desk, his feet crossed before him, his mind rapt. He looked so young sometimes, and never younger than when something troubled him.

Dolly had met virtually all of the world's billionaires, and of them all, only Laslo seemed boyish. The rest wore masks of hard calculation and will; he wore no mask, and bared a vulnerable face to an unbelieving world. No one could quite understand how Laslo had done it, but she knew.

It had taken both of them, really. He had a mercurial, intuitive mind and the native impulse to act. He had never been a logical thinker and his dizzying leaps from one precipice of the mind to another left the world puzzled. It sometimes left her bewildered, too. Take the little pep talk he liked to give to groups interested in his National Grassland project. He would begin with the homeless he saw in his shopping centers and end up with homeless animals and even homeless plants and grasses, and the need to restore everything to its natural, ecological home. She didn't quite follow that, nor did she grasp how restoring everything to its proper home, such as buffalo and wolves and bluestem grass to the High Plains, and moving people to areas more suited to human nature, had anything to do with anything, especially the homeless who lived a subterranean life in the great cities of America.

But it all made sense to him, and she never disputed his perceptions. That leap of intuition that short-circuited logic and rational argument had been the essence of her husband's genius and success. But he had other resources, namely her own quiet logic, which she employed when they were alone together. Sometimes his plans made no sense at all, and then she asked the questions, and he listened. She had rescued him from some bad moves, such as buying the Rockefeller Center.

They listened to Brooke-Carson, whose arrogance was palpable even on this unspooling strip of magnetized iron oxide, and heard him denounce as a landgrab Laslo's great passion to restore the High Plains, and call Horoney's vision unworkable, and claim it was corrupted because he had business people and financiers on his board, and insist that only the federal government could rescue the National Grassland.

Laslo frowned, laughed softly, crossed and recrossed his lanky legs, smiled at her, and listened. All of it seemed incredible to her. Without her husband there would be no grassland project. Congress had rejected it. The federal bureaucracy lacked the funds and authority to create it. The foundation had spent, so far, four billion of Laslo Horoney's dollars to create the Grassland National Trust, operating under the stewardship of an independent philanthropic foundation advised by the best environmental biologists and zoologists he could hire. But Brooke-Carson was calling it a landgrab and a rich-men's hunting park.

Dolly loved to extract meaning not only from what was being said, but also from inflections, tone of voice, shrillness, all of it a sort of oral body language she could read better than most people. Professor Brooke-Carson was a conceited ass. She also read sheer envy in his tone of voice. Had he been selected by the foundation to advise it, he would have toadied to her husband. Laslo had once told her that Brooke-Carson was a good, intuitive ecologist, but his insufferable arrogance and Green religion eliminated him as a candidate for the foundation's board or staff.

Professor Brooke-Carson was also not above making specious arguments. It was true that state politicians had forced the foundation to open the grassland to hunting, but that was only for show. The state game managers in Montana and Wyoming had no intention of issuing more than a handful of permits, and in any case the affected states had granted the foundation the legal power to close as much as eighty percent of its land to hunting in any given season. It was true that the foundation had caved in to tribal demands to harvest buffalo, but Brooke-Carson knew full well that there would first be a ten-year moratorium while the herd was built and range restored, and that the foundation had plenary power to limit or even stop the buffalo hunting in the event that tribal hunting, along with wolves and seasonal hunting all conspired to threaten populations. The deals between the states and the foundation had all been aired in public hearings.

Did that professor really believe that the foundation would spend so many billions of dollars on an unworkable project? That Laslo himself would have spent a dime unless he knew for sure that the restoration of the grassland would survive the controversy and passion and politics it had engendered? Did Brooke-Carson really believe that her husband would blow ninety percent of his wealth on a doomed enterprise?

Of course not. Brooke-Carson knew full well that it would work, that the compromises wouldn't affect the restoration much and that the National Grassland Trust would become a model and a beacon for the world. And that's why he loathed it.

There he was, saying the Grassland Trust was unworkable, howling like a wolf because—Laslo wasn't a true believer in Green religion, and therefore the Great Satan. She knew what this was about: religion. She smiled at Laslo, who was just then absorbing all that stuff about the board full of evil financiers. In Brooke-Carson's religion, God was the natural world, Nature, unsullied by man the Satan, and Christ was the federal government, the only door to salvation, and the devil and all his minions were civilization, business, free Americans settling their homesteads and making their livings and fulfilling their dreams. And the high priests were academics, powerful arbiters of good and evil, sin and virtue, anathematizing demons such as the Nichols family, or heretics like Laslo.

She chuckled suddenly, seeing no horns growing from her husband's noble brow or poking from that long hair that scandalized financiers and bankers and Republicans.

"What's so funny?" he asked.

"Horns," she said.

"Buffalo horns?"

"Yours, dear."

He laughed with her.

The professor's diatribe spun down and the tape stopped. Dolly was aware, suddenly, that a shrill and invasive force had departed from Laslo's comfortable den, and a subtle relief spilled through her.

Laslo sprang up to flip the tape. "It's just rhetoric," he said. "I don't see any need to reply. I'll send copies to the board and see what they think of the Ayatollah Carson."

"Never underestimate the power of a religion, or its effect on true believers," she said.

He smiled. He often communicated with her in smiles. He had a whole vocabulary of smiles. This one said he agreed, and she was a smart cookie.

"Do you think the politicians will pay any attention?"

"I think the pols are grateful a private foundation's doing this. It's not their hot potato. The federal bureaucrats itch to take over the whole project, but itching's all they can do when they lack the scratch."

"Some will try to run it anyway."

He nodded. "They're trying," he said. "If they could regulate the ants in an anthill, they'd do it. That's one reason the foundation retains Hector Truehart."

The tape caught and spilled a new voice into the room, young and plaintive, leaking surliness even though its owner didn't know it.

"Well, he doesn't sound a bit like his parents," he said.

They listened quietly, and not unsympathetically, to a story of childhood loneliness in an isolated place where life meant struggle, and defeat came more often than victory. Martin Dudley Nichols carried scars wrought by loneliness and parents who probably should have been more alert to his loneliness, all of it now enflamed by Green religion.

Martin's assault on his parents as spoilers and agribusiness demons shocked Dolly, even though she had been expecting something like that from the young man.

"Cam and Sandy must be feeling very bad," she said. "Especially Cam."

"I feel sorry for the kid," Laslo said. "You know, he's making my case for me. The High Plains never had enough water to sustain human populations for long. It's not home for us—for people. I wish I could recruit Martin; we're not so far apart on things. He's probably a fine young man, but it'll take a few years to grow out of this stuff."

"No, he's not a fine young man," she said. "A few decades ago he would have joined a cult, maybe a robot-control, brainwash one. Now he's got the new religion. It's either Green religion or New-Age versions of Native American religion—spirit helpers, vision quests, sweats, all that. What they have in common is a sense that Nature is God."

He smiled again, this time the variety that said, if-you-say-so, dear. Early in their life together, she had let him know that she was a serious woman with serious ideas drawn from broad reading. She wasn't always sure how he took that. His mercurial intellect often reached conclusions without knowing how he arrived at them. But she connected and analyzed and collated life, and often her comments steadied and inspired his genius.

"He's alienated. Other young people have a bad time growing up—divorce, alcoholic parents, poverty—but they don't turn sour like that one. Listen to him! It's not all whine, but it's a lot of blaming. Poor Sandra."

"Maybe she was the cause of it. She's a drinker, Dolly. She was pretty well sauced that night. DeeAnn bailed her out and brought her back to the table and she had the grace to sit quietly and smile, but she was out of it. The kid's probably had to cope with that for years."

"I admired Sandra Nichols. Do you know what I saw that night at the dinner table? A brave woman. A woman in love with her man, so in love that she was enduring a place that tortured her, a lonesomeness she couldn't express to Cameron for fear of sounding disloyal. She wasn't made for that isolation, but by God, she's trying. He's quite a man. Did you take a look at him?"

Laslo's grin mocked her.

"Weathered nut brown, creased by wind and rain, the back of his neck turned to brown crepe, his hands work-blackened. But there he was in a tan cashmere sport coat and custom-made white shirt—you know the kind, with big collars, looking like Gary Cooper. And a smile that started slowly before it burst, and an intent look—I can't quite say it—he was really interested in me—and wolves, and . . ."

Laslo was full of mischief, his eyes dancing. "Interested in you, eh? I'm going to ditch that tape and put on something better," he said, cutting off Martin Dudley Nichols at the knees. "So you took to Cameron, eh?"

"I'm just saying that Sandy does, and it's killing her. She's a beautiful woman, and not just because she has that crown of red hair."

He opened a door that revealed scores of tapes. "I never did like the music we grew up with—you know, Beatles and Elvis. How about some big-band stuff? You up to dancing?"

She was enjoying this swift turn.

"Here. Glenn Miller, Artie Shaw, Les Brown, Tommy Dorsey, Harry James . . ."

"Perfidia" blossomed from the speakers, which she thought was appropriate. He took her in hand and effortlessly glided her around his den. She loved it, and relished what would come next, when he would dance her toward their bed.

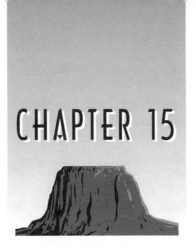

CHAPTER 15

Dudley Nichols loaded his old deer-hunting rifle into the back of the vintage green Jeep, along with a box of shells and a paper sack containing a beef sandwich, an apple, a can of Pepsi, and some Oreo cookies. He put binoculars on the front seat.

He eyed the sky, and decided not to wear his tan jacket. Dome-shaped clouds with flat, black bottoms dotted the heavens, and he supposed he'd take a soaking. Back in his house he exchanged the jacket for a flannel-lined canvas ranching coat with some warmth in it. Age had taken the heat out of his body, and he got cold fast now.

He didn't tell anyone where he was going. He never did. He jammed his old felt hat down over his wiry hair, slipped into the Jeep, which had a canvas top that would keep some of the weather out, and twisted the key that was always in the ignition. The old Jeep coughed into life, and he drove down the long lane and then north to the Antler Ranch.

He hadn't hunted for years. He had discovered that old men lose the taste for it, and once he stumbled across an article that said so. He had no sentiments about hunting one way or another. He raised beef destined for slaughter; death was a constant companion on any ranch. Calves and foals died of scours, cows and mares died of prolapsed uteruses, bred heifers died birthing, steers died because they felt like it. But the taste for hunting had fled him, and he ascribed it to his own impending death. He simply liked to see living things, their eyes bright and their flesh young and sound, full of the breath of being.

But this day he would hunt.

He drove an hour down dirt roads, the ancient Jeep shaking and rattling under him, until he needed to urinate. He stopped, stepped into the wind, smelled the scented spring air, turned his back to the breeze, and tried to make water. Relief came slowly now. He'd wrestled with prostate trouble for a decade; benign enlargement at first, and then they gave him one of those PSA tests, which rang up a seven when four was the sign of trouble, and they told him he had cancer and they would cut him apart and take it out, and it would be a rough operation with a long recovery.

He hadn't liked that one bit, especially the part about losing his manhood. So they told him they could probably save that because Johns Hopkins had a new kind of surgery that kept the nerve intact, but he didn't like that either. He didn't know why the hell he wanted to keep his virility intact; he was an old man, and Mabel had been gone for decades. But he did, and they told him about a new radiation treatment that involved planting radioactive seeds around the cancer area, so he flew out to Seattle and they did that, and his PSA dropped to three. They put him on some new hormone treatments, too.

He rode through a shower and welcomed it because the spring had been too dry, and no dryland rancher in his right mind ever complained about rain. The brief deluge muddied his windshield, and the wipers smeared the mud, but that was all right. The clouds cleared off and morning blossomed into a sunny April day.

He got to the Antler and avoided Joe Hardy's place. This was going to be a private hunting trip, and not one other soul would ever know about it. He didn't know exactly where the carcasses were. Hardy had taken Cameron and the rest out there to the northeast corner of the place, but that was all Dudley knew. That was all right, too. That country was fairly flat, but laced with drainages that gave shelter to wildlife. Some cottonwoods or box elders or willows or chokecherry brush crowded the coulees. The Antler had some gravelly patches that supported nothing but cactus, but it was a good ranch anyway. Old buffalo wallows pocked it. The country had a sameness about it that might have confused a newcomer. It was vast, but he knew it well. This had been one of the earliest of the Nichols ranches, and he had ridden cow ponies into every one of those shallow draws.

He paused on a likely ridge that gave him a sweeping view of many square miles, and pulled out the binoculars. He was going to find those wolves and kill them. Cameron would disapprove, but so what? Cameron had to watch out for the reputation of Nichols Ranches, especially now. And watch out for his own hide, because the act of killing a protected wolf could cost him a few years in a federal pen, and tens of thousands of dollars. But Cameron would never know. And Dudley didn't care. If they found out and sent him up the river, what difference would it make? It'd be worth it to kill the wolves.

Patiently, Dudley glassed the country through the unzipped window of the Jeep, focusing on the coulees where animals might shelter or rest. The country quivered under the sun. He saw nothing. Maybe the wolves had left. Cameron had instructed Joe Hardy to move the breeding stock close to the ranch house, where wolves would be less likely to kill. That probably had been accomplished. At least Dudley saw no sign of a Hereford in the sea of lime-colored spring grass.

All that was all right. This open country would yield the wolves if he kept at it. He started the Jeep, bounced another mile over ungraded dirt road, and tried again, spotting nothing. A light airplane drifted over and vanished behind a ridge to the northeast. He drove another step and parked below that rimrock ridge, which blocked his view of a shallow basin that marked the northern extreme of the Antler Ranch. He would have to hoof it to see what lay in that direction, so he clambered out, flexed his stiff legs, hung his binoculars from his neck, unzipped the rifle bag and extracted the old Remington, threw a handful of cartridges into his pocket, and started off. Ten minutes later, after scaling the precipitous slope, he topped the ridge and cut down its far slope far enough to cut the west wind, and there he glassed the open plains. He knew how to use binoculars, studying one area at a time, like a map grid. He saw several moving creatures that he thought might be the wolves, but the glimpses had been tenuous, and the targets elusive, and he finally gave up and ate lunch. When he topped the ridge and started for the Jeep, he discovered the light aircraft on the dirt road just behind it, and two men awaiting him. He guessed what that was about, and bristled.

They lounged beside his Jeep, no doubt having observed its contents thoroughly. One was a hippie, wearing a ponytail and those little rimless glasses. The other was burly and dark, probably the pilot. They were dressed in woolen shirts and opened jackets, but he didn't doubt they were either Montana Fish, Wildlife and Parks men, or else feds, and they'd flash badges if they felt like it.

"You two lost?" he said, poking his rifle back into its carrying bag.

"No, we were just wondering what a man with a rifle might be doing this time of year," said the hippie.

"I'm Dudley Nichols; this is my ranch. Who are you?"

The hippie smiled. "Sanford Kouric, United States Fish and Wildlife Service, and Tom Bainbridge, ditto. I'm a wildlife biologist."

"Well, you're trespassing. Just because you're bureaucrats doesn't give you the right to trespass."

"I met your son a few days ago," the hippie said. "We were looking at wolf kills. I think we have permission to be here; at least he okayed what I had in mind, which was collaring a wolf in your pack here—we're calling it the Antler pack—so we can let you know where it is at all times. He thought that'd be helpful. It's one thing we can do for you.''

The man had a fancy camera with one of those zoom lenses as long as a bull's equipment hanging on his chest. Dudley felt certain the film contained images of himself carrying that rifle.

Kouric seemed to read his thoughts. "We've been photographing the pack," he said. It's over that ridge. Seven, two more than I thought. No pups, as far as I could see. They've killed another of your cows, I'm afraid. But mostly they've been taking mule deer.''

"Where's the cow?''

"Oh, two miles east and a bit north. They got her before your manager pulled the cattle out of here.''

"That's registered breeding stock, and probably another two thousand dollars donated to your zoo," Dudley said. "It puts another hole in our program.''

Kouric wasn't smiling. "I'm sorry about it. If it weren't for the executive order requiring us to cooperate with the Horoney Foundation, we'd be moving those wolves out. We don't want anyone to be hurt. We'd move this pack, and the pack over on your North Ranch, too. We think we could relocate them in the Missouri Breaks without causing anyone much trouble.''

Dudley glared.

"You been hunting?'' asked Bainbridge.

Kouric interrupted. "Let it go, Tom.'' He turned to Dudley. "I know how you feel, but it's not a good idea.''

"Mr. Kouric, I don't care about me. I'm old and played out, and if they put me up the river and threw away the key, it wouldn't make any difference to me. And that goes for the fines, too. None of that even slows me down. I have a family, good citizens, working hard, a son and grandchildren and now some great-grandchildren, DeeAnn's kids, and it's for them. We have the right to defend ourselves. Go tell that to the bureaucrats back there in Helena, or Billings, or wherever.''

"It's still not a good idea," Kouric said. "Your son asked me what to do, and I told him to raise buffalo. They've been here since the last glaciation, maybe thirteen thousand years—came from Asia on the Bering land bridge—and know how to defend themselves against wolves. The meat's better for us—less fat in it. The demand's unquenchable. It's catching on. The profit margin's better. Buffalo's going up and hides sell for plenty, and so do the head and horns.''

"I'm a stockman," Dudley said.

Kouric shrugged. "It's just a thought, Mr. Nichols. There's a downside, too. Fences."

That put it mildly. Fencing two hundred twenty thousand acres of ranch land with buffalo-caliber fences would break the company. "That's going to be Horoney's problem, not ours," he said. "If his buffalo break down our fences, or our cattle stray, or his wolves eat our beef, he'll wind up in court."

"I tried to tell your son something about wolves. Did he pass any of that along to you?"

"No. It's just propaganda. Next thing you'll tell me is that they're nice doggies that don't touch beef."

"No, they're predators, and they'll kill cattle and sheep and domestic dogs if they have to, and sometimes do what we call surplus killing, especially of sheep. They're also shy, steer clear of ranches and homesteads, and prefer the prey that they've been conditioned over millennia to hunt. Cattle and dairy farmers in Minnesota get along with wolves in their backyards. That's because the wolves prefer to go after the deer there. They're not dogs. But they're an important part of the system that existed before civilization disrupted it, even valuable to other species because the weak are culled."

"Propaganda."

"I'm a wolf biologist. I'll send you the literature if you want."

"I don't."

"Let me ask you something: Back in the tough winter of 1997, a lot of cattle died off. Two hundred thousand in the Dakotas, twenty thousand more in Montana. Nichols Ranches lost one hundred sixty-seven. That's because they weren't sheltered adequately. They froze to death on open range. Wind chills running minus eighty. Ranchers shrugged it off. The big kill-off didn't inspire anyone to build shelters, put in open-sided sheds, anything like that. Tough winter, that's what they all said. Did your company build sheds, put in windbreaks? No. Now my question is, why do ranchers shrug off a massive cattle kill like that, caused by their own neglect, but get all steamed up about wolves? What's in your values, your beliefs, that says twenty thousand frozen cattle are a part of ranching, but a wolf kill isn't? How many wolves would it take to kill off twenty, twenty-five thousand cattle?"

"Look, Kouric, we can't control nature, and we can't afford fancy sheds."

Kouric was grinning, and Dudley knew it hadn't been much of an answer. That kill-off had hurt Nichols Ranches badly. Kouric was pointing to a cattlemen's tradition, a set of values Dudley had embraced all his life, and that made Dudley itchy.

Kouric stared at the open range a moment. "If you're going to kill wolves and get yourself into a jackpot, I can't stop you. But I hope you'll think twice."

He motioned to Bainbridge, and they climbed into the Cessna. Dudley watched the propeller turn over slowly, and then vanish in a blur as the engine caught. The light plane vibrated while the pilot went through his preliminaries. Then Bainbridge wheeled it into the wind and gunned the throttle. The Cessna buzzed along the dirt road, kicking up debris, and lifted.

Dudley watched it go, and then rubbed his eyes. A man wasn't even at home on his own land. He had lived too damned long.

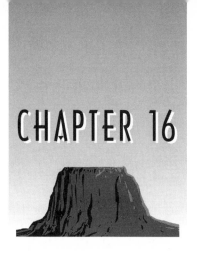

CHAPTER 16

Cameron moved his Herefords out of the two wolf-burdened ranches, resettling them on his southernmost outfits, which were his worst and most abused. Their soil was thin and gravelly, their clay didn't nurture life and turned into a vicious gumbo in the spring. Dry lakes, brimming with alkali salts, ate the land and seemed to expand year by year. Pasturing the Herefords there meant opening up all the land he had put into his range-recovery program. Years of restoring range were out the window but he had no other options. This was turning out to be another dry spring, and he needed all the grass he could get.

The whole business irked him. Nichols Ranches had two stock semis, but they weren't enough to move two thousand cattle fast, so he contracted the job. Two calves and a heifer died in the transfer. Moving all those cattle bit into his operating funds, and he had no guarantee that the wolves wouldn't appear the next day on the southern ranches. He left a few common horned cattle on the North Ranch and instructed John Trouble to keep close track of them. He wanted to know how they fared against the wolves compared to dehorned cattle. But the Antler Ranch no longer carried any livestock. He supposed, in a way, that all this constituted a major range-recovery program for both ranches. A lot of good it'd do him.

He kept his managers in place, asking them both to work on improvements and upgrade fences. Several stock dams had eroded and needed work. Two windmills needed a rebuild. He would keep his managers busy somehow.

It all made him angry. A thundercloud of trouble hung over Nichols Ranches, souring his life, threatening the corporations, scattering his breeding program, his dreams, to the four winds.

He heard nothing from Martin, and didn't expect to. His son had cut the ties. When the first of May rolled around, he corralled Sandy. They had a decision to make.

"Do we send Martin his check or not?"

"Whatever you think is right, Cam."

"For God's sake, this is something for both of us to decide."

She had deteriorated all the more, he thought. Drinking furtively, wandering through her life, no longer even bothering to sit in front of Oprah. They needed to take a vacation, get her into some sort of social swing that would lift her spirits. Meet new people. The thought of that subdivision returned to him. Bring people in. Pretty soon the whole area would become a big zoo, and people might enjoy ringside seats, lots bordering the National Grassland Trust where they could watch the buffalo. Then she'd have friends. But he'd have to deal with his father on that one.

"He's our baby," she said.

He knew how to interpret that; he'd been interpreting Sandy for thirty-some years. "I'll send it. We'll see him through his degree. But if he's got any balls, he'll return it. If he thinks our money's tainted and not good enough for him, he has a moral choice to make. All he has to do is send the check back, and I'll respect him."

"Martin's such a boy," she said. "I wish I'd paid more attention."

"We did all we could. You drove him everywhere. Future Farmers of America. Little League. All that. That stuff about sitting on the school bus hours each way, that's not true. He had a long ride, over an hour, and it must've seemed like two to a boy. But he should grow up, forgive and forget. He's got a whole life ahead of him."

She smiled at him gently. She obviously relished every bit of conversation they had, and he vowed to spend more time with her each day. She was starved for company. Odd how a crisis clarified things.

"We'll weather it," he said, touching her.

That touch did something to her, and she fled. He wished he could understand her better.

He cut a check for Martin, and penned a note in his stiff, angular hand: "Son, your mother and I will see you through your master's degree. Love, Dad."

Then he hiked down to the mailbox through a chill Mayday morning, plucked up the day's mail, raised the red flag, and posted the letter. Gus War Shield, the contract rural carrier, would pick it up in the morning.

He stuffed the *Billings Gazette*, the *Western Livestock Reporter, Newsweek* and catalogues under his arm and studied the first-class mail. A letter from Julie in Denver. Some feed bills. An accounting bill. A letter from the United States Fish and Wildlife Service. He dreaded to open it, the way he dreaded to open IRS letters. But he did, and read it on the spot, holding it at arm's length because he hadn't brought his glasses. It wasn't a form letter. It was signed by a deputy assistant something or other in Helena.

It informed him that the USFWS was going to hold hearings shortly about extending the Yellowstone Park wolf-habitat designation to include all of the National Grassland Trust territory, now that wolf populations have established themselves in the area. A provisional designation, effective June 1, would include private property within the confines of the habitat area. It explained that inasmuch as wolves had been recently discovered within the area, and historically the area provided habitat for the threatened species, the Service would designate Nichols Ranches and other property as a Threatened Species Habitat, subject to public hearings in ninety days at Miles City and publication in the Federal Register.

As of June 1 all modification of the land and its existing uses would be forbidden, upon pain of stiff fines, imprisonment, seizure and forfeiture. The proscribed changes included erection of buildings or their removal, tree-cutting, tree-planting, mining of any mineral including gravel and clay and rock, well-drilling, fencing, road-building, earthmoving, seeding, alteration of springs or riparian areas, plowing of untilled land, alteration of land from one use to another such as subdividing it into lots, weed or pest control, rodent control, sagebrush removal, burning, spraying defoliants or insecticides . . .

The list went on and on. It effectively removed control of his own property from him. Nichols Ranches might own the land, but it could no longer control what it owned. The ranches had become essentially the government's. The letter appalled Cameron. He hurried back to his home, scarcely aware of the joyous spring zephyrs, and headed into his den.

He called his attorney, Bob Rockwell, in Billings, and managed to reach him without wading through secretaries or voice mail.

"Bob, I'm going to read you a letter from U.S. Fish and Wildlife," he said without preamble, and he did so.

"What does this mean?" he asked. "Can they do this? To my own land? Family property?"

"Yes they can," Rockwell responded. "Cam, fax me that letter and let me make a few calls. I'll get back to you in an hour."

It took two hours. Cam paced his den furiously, and was exhausted by the time Rockwell called back.

"You're not entirely up the creek, Cam. I've been on the horn with some attorneys who've dealt with this stuff. The federal laws empowering the feds to do this are ambiguous and somewhat contradictory. Without question, they can impose habitat restrictions on federal land, but whether they can do it on private land is a gray area. Remember the spotted owl controversy out in California? The feds initially imposed habitat restriction on a wide variety of private property out there, ranging from virgin forests owned by lumber companies to homes and lots and acreages owned by private citizens.

"But there was a question: was this 'taking'? The Constitution forbids government from taking private property without just compensation. When property owners lose control of the property nominally in their possession, is that taking? The Supreme Court's been friendly to property owners on that issue. It's saying yes, that's taking. As a result, the feds have been picking on small-time property owners in the spotted owl habitat area, but no one with deep pockets who could take the issue to the Supreme Court again. Maybe we can roll 'em back on this one—but I think it'll be a tussle. If you want, I'll run up to Helena and see."

"Yes, do that," Cam replied. "I can't afford to carry a suit clear to the Supreme Court, but you can rattle the sword."

"They're pouring on the heat, Cam. It probably doesn't matter to Fish and Wildlife whether it wins or loses; they just want to pry you out of there. It may be a private foundation that's setting up the National Grassland Trust, but Horoney's got federal teeth. That executive order did it."

"The wolf's not a threatened species. Tell 'em that. A wolf biologist told me Yellowstone Park's got two hundred fifty now, and that's just for starters."

"The spotted owl isn't either. They found a lot more than they thought they had, and the owls were flourishing in second-growth land, too, much to everyone's surprise. But that didn't slow down the feds any. Once endangered, always endangered, that's how they figure it."

"Should I do something to test them? I've been planning a new windmill and a new stock dam down on the Twin Butte Ranch. I'll damn well start them, and we'll see."

"Ah, I'd hold off. It ain't an even playing field. That could cost you the ranch. Let me talk to this bozo in Helena, and I'll know a lot more."

"This is my home and my life, Bob."

"Sure it is, but I'm afraid you're in for a lot more harassment. Maybe we'll have grounds for some action but it's hard to sue the government."

"They were just waiting for the wolves," Cam said bitterly. "For seventy years no wolves around here, and now it's wolf habitat."

"That's a weakness in their argument that I'll certainly exploit. Cam—have you been looking at alternatives?"

"What do you mean?"

"I mean it's hard to fight the bureaucrats because they hold all the aces. Right now, without your meaning to, you're probably in violation of a few dozen federal regulations. How about pesticides and herbicides? You use both. Here's one for you—how about archaeological sites? You ever poke around in an old Indian burial ground on your ranches? Dig up arrowheads? Any of your managers change the oil in an engine and dump the old oil up the gulch? All I'm saying is, when they want to find something against you, they usually can . . . Think about it."

Cameron boiled. "Are you telling me to quit?"

"No, we'll fight this together and we'll get our licks in, and I'm sure we can beat 'em back. Meanwhile, cover your ass."

CHAPTER 17

Martin Dudley Nichols rehearsed what he wanted to say to Professor Brooke-Carson, but nothing seemed adequate and he didn't know what the protocols were. Well, he'd think of something.

He had cashed his father's check, feeling relieved. He had always known they wouldn't ditch him. There were other resources lying around a university, such as becoming a teaching assistant, but he didn't see why he should waste his valuable time on that stuff, or apply for some loan he'd be paying off forever.

Brooke-Carson was waiting for him in his oversize office, which he had wangled even before the new building was complete. Unlike Dr. Kazin, who operated out of a messy warren piled high with papers and books, Brooke-Carson possessed a spacious desk with a glass top, worktables with a few neatly stacked piles of papers and journals on them, enough shelving to house his formidable library, and a large window commanding a view of the snow-covered Spanish Peaks southwest of Bozeman.

"How good of you to drop by, Martin," Brooke-Carson said.

Martin admired the man. He was the very essence of a distinguished professor, wearing a navy turtleneck under a white shirt, under a raffish sport coat.

"Yes, sir, thank you," said Martin awkwardly, settling into one of the plush leather chairs that the professor had wangled from the housekeeping department.

"I thought the rally went well, didn't you? You know, it got the attention of the Green Coalition in the Senate. They're talking about legislation that would eject Horoney, pay him something, of course, but get him and his financiers out. They've done a little national polling, and the whole idea of a National Grassland is very popular. Running ninety percent favorable, you know. People from one end of the country to the other like wolves and buffalo and wilderness and kicking out agribusiness."

"Yes, sir, it went well."

"You certainly did your part. Admirable. It took courage to break with your family, Martin. You've won a lot of friends here, faculty people. If there's anything we can do—"

"I'm all right," Martin said, fidgeting.

Doctor Brooke-Carson eyed him restlessly. "I'm sure you have something in mind other than the rally."

"Yes, sir. But I don't—I fear I might be stepping on toes, sir. Getting into trouble."

Brooke-Carson smiled. "I think I know, but just for your own comfort, whatever you say here will be in strictest confidence. Count me as your ally."

"Well, sir, it's my advisor, Professor Kazin."

"Ah! I was right."

"I don't—ah, I'd like another faculty member for my advisor."

"That's perfectly understandable. But hard to arrange."

"I was afraid so. If it's a problem—"

"It's delicate. Is there some difficulty?"

"Oh, not exactly. We just don't see eye to eye. I have the feeling he's skeptical about my thesis. He keeps wanting to tone it down."

"He's a gifted man and a fine scholar, Martin. Maybe you should be paying attention."

"Yes, but he's not sympathetic."

Brooke-Carson stared a moment. "Could you be more specific?"

"He keeps reminding me that nature prior to the arrival of white men was no Eden. What he's really trying to say is that we've not really done much damage, an idea that outrages me. He keeps talking about taking the long view, avoiding what he calls trendy ideas—which means he's opposed to everything that the Environmental Movement is trying to do."

"Ah, Martin, that just isn't the case. His field, you know, is the impact of man's activities on ecosystems, and he's done a great deal of good work, detailing the damage, the alterations, the extinctions."

"Yes, but he doesn't want change. And you know who's funded his projects. Chemical companies that make pesticides. Defense industries. Seed companies. That taints everything he does."

Brooke-Carson leaned back in his plush swivel chair a moment. "Science is science no matter who or what funds it," he said. "If it's good science, the results can be replicated by others, and the work endures. Can you fault any of Dr. Kazin's work?"

"I could if I had the research money."

"Maybe you could. There's a certain reality about accepting research grants from such companies. The conclusions usually end up supporting the company. Perhaps some of Kazin's work might support those who've funded his research. Maybe you'll be the one to discover the errors."

"I've vowed that I'll accept only public funds, or funds from Green groups, like the Sierra Club. That way I'll be independent. I'll never accept a dollar from business. You know what my dream is? Working on behalf of the Sierra Club or the National Wildlife Federation."

"You're an idealist."

"I'd rather starve than give business some false leg to stand on. I'd never go around the country giving speeches about friendly environmentalism to Optimists Clubs and Stockmen's Associations, either."

"Well, that's an ideal that becomes you, Martin. The reason I accept grants only from the government is to retain my scientific integrity. I know that my results will be useful only to one or another agency, help them regulate things better, and of no use at all to polluters or businesses. When the government funds my projects, I'm certain not only of my independence, but also my security. There might be politics about whether to make the grant, but once they make it, they leave me alone. I'm proud to say my work's been of great value to the Fish and Wildlife Service, the United States Biological Survey, and even the United States Geological Survey—when I did the report on the effect of saline soil caused by irrigation on wild-game forage. As a result, the BLM was able to sequester several hundred square miles from the ranchers who wanted it for their cattle. In fact, I pride myself that my research has enabled the government to recapture hundreds of square miles of land and to improve the regulation of every ranch and mine in the United States. It's catching on abroad, too. Of course the money's nothing compared to what I could get from corporations, but I have my standards."

"I see corporate funding as a primrose path, sir, and that's one reason I'd just as soon change advisors. I—I simply don't want . . . let me put it another way. While I don't have control of my advisory committee, I do hope that my problem can be quietly discussed and some changes made."

Brooke-Carson mulled the matter for a moment. "This is difficult. You might just walk in and tell Dr. Kazin you'd like another advisor. Just cite personal reasons. No need for accusations or unpleasantness.

He'll understand. These things happen. Call it chemistry. Some people rub each other wrong."

Martin felt disappointment. "I was hoping to avoid that. Isn't there any other way?"

"The manly way is to ask him. He's a sophisticated man, even if he doesn't seem so. He's a veteran of academic life, and he'll swiftly understand. He'll no doubt disagree with your choice, but he'll surrender graciously. We all like to think we're guiding our protégés toward the best thesis, the best science, the most compelling hypothesis. And let me suggest that you might well take Dr. Kazin's cautions to heart."

There was no way out. This wasn't going to be done for him. He knew he would have to screw up his courage and ask old Kazin to resign. "All right," he said.

"Does that do it, then?"

"Ah, one more thing. About getting the advisor I want. Would you—"

"I'd be delighted. But I'm terribly busy. You know I'm advising four doctoral candidates right now, on top of my research load. And all of them are doing straight biological studies—my field—rather than your cross-disciplinary work. But let me give some thought to it. I'll come up with just the man."

"Yes, sir; thank you, sir."

Martin retreated, twice disappointed in the interview. With Brooke-Carson as his advisor, shaping his thesis, he'd have no trouble getting work. With Kazin as his advisor, he'd be lucky to get an offer from Monsanto or Du Pont.

He hiked through the twilight to his room on Willson Street, hoping Mary Lee would be around. He needed some hugging.

He found her in the clawfoot bathtub in that scabrous little student den, reading a Sandra Prowell Montana mystery.

"I'm in a bad mood," he said.

"You're always in a bad mood."

"I had a rotten day."

"When have you not had a rotten day?"

She tucked the flap into the book to preserve her place, and stood, rivering water. "I'm going to go to the library," she said.

"What for?"

"To be by myself."

"What's the matter with my company?"

She stopped rubbing her hair and stared at him. "You have too many needs."

"I'm sorry. It's just that I'm trapped. I can't get rid of old Kazin."

"I think I'm moving out, Martin."

That hit him hard. "Why? What do you mean?"

She pondered that a while, as if framing her thoughts. "Let's replay this scene," she said. "You came in and told me you were in a bad mood. You didn't ask me how I am. You could have smiled. You could have told me how nice I look. You could've brought me a doughnut or something. You could've asked how my day went. You could've kissed me. You could've—I'm just tired of you and your needs."

He watched her dry herself and dress. She never dressed casually, and even now, after a day's toil as a teaching assistant, she put on a white blouse and her gray suit and some good pumps. Then she pulled a soft-sided carry-on bag out of the closet and piled some things into it.

He didn't know what to say.

"I'm going to stay with someone I know," she said. "I'll come back for the rest tomorrow. You owe me for half the rent. We'll split the phone and gas and electricity later."

"Someone you know?" Jealousy pierced him.

"She's a friend," Mary said.

"But this is our home."

"We never had any home. We had sex and a shared bathroom."

He watched her go, and then stared around the empty little dump. She was right; it wasn't home.

CHAPTER 18

Anna Garwood Nichols eagerly awaited her family. They would gather this day at the Pioneers Nursing Home in Miles City to discuss the future of Nichols Ranches. Technically, it would be a meeting of the directors of the corporations; actually, it would be a family powwow.

She loved to see her family. She wasn't far away from them, but there were long stretches when no one came. She wished she didn't have to live in such a place, but she could no longer control her bladder. And she took more pills each day than she could count. She had lived a long time, since January 10, 1907, and sometimes she wasn't sure she liked this lingering.

Still, she was better off than all those *old* people who'd lost their minds and just stared blankly at a wall; better off than all the ones in wheelchairs, or the bedridden ones, or the ones with oxygen tubes in their noses. Much better off than the sad ones who cried all the time, or the ones who never received a visit. When Dudley brought her here she had despaired at first, but then she decided that as long as she was alive, she'd just have a good time. So she spent her hours visiting with the lonely and cheering up the desolate and mothering the nurses.

Her mind was crisp. She knew it and was grateful. Maybe that was because she refused to live in the past. She read the papers and magazines, and some books, too, although her eyes troubled her. She watched television, and liked the Discovery Channel the best because she learned about all the things that her family would discuss here today in the meeting room they had reserved, a dreary place painted an institutional green.

Dudley had told her they were facing some major issues. They had until June 1 to sell to the Horoney Foundation—or not. Now they faced wolves in their two northernmost ranches. She marveled at that. Not even as a girl had she ever seen a wolf. They were fascinating creatures, and no doubt played a role in nature. She had privately approved the reintroduction of wolves into Yellowstone Park, but hadn't said anything to Dudley about it for fear he'd think she'd gone batty. But times changed, and she had changed with them, and the more she marveled at the future, the more she embraced it.

She wondered who would come. Dudley was the only one of her three children still alive. But there were some grandchildren—Cameron's sister Eloise Nichols Joiner, who lived in Seattle, and Nicholas Nichols III, who lived in Oakland. Maybe her great-grandchildren would come. She could hardly remember the names of them all, but of course Deirdre would come with her children, and maybe Julie would come up from Denver. And Martin from Bozeman, although Dudley said he was currently very hostile toward his family. Still, he owned Nichols stock; he had been given some each year, as much as the tax laws permitted, and all the young people had shares.

A little before noon she headed down the long hall, using her antler-handled cane, and patting all those poor empty-headed old people as she passed. She reached the private meeting room just before her family walked in, and she saw at once that not many had come. Dudley, Cameron and Sandy, Deirdre and her husband whose name she kept forgetting—Cassady, Mark, that was it. But not Julie or Martin. And none of the West Coast people.

"You're looking grand, Anna," said Sandy.

They always said that, told her she was looking younger and younger. She figured about the time she died they would be telling her she looked twenty. But she didn't mind. Her old body was pumping along somehow, and when death came she wouldn't mind. Indeed, she was curious, and sometimes filled with yearning to know what lay beyond. She was fairly sure something did.

They all hugged her or squeezed her hand, and it was good to see them, see Dudley's eyes in his granddaughter Deirdre, listen to Cameron's inflections, which reminded her so much of the voice of her long-gone husband Nicholas, bless his soul.

They were served a rather insipid chicken meal—the food was one thing about nursing homes she didn't like—but no one noticed. She had always loved to cook, and loved to spice things well with onions, or saffron, or pepper, or the herbs in her cabinet. But it didn't matter. She gazed at each of her family, absorbing them. These were her treasures, and for all she knew she would never see them again, so she lived for the moment. There was Cam, the one grandchild strong enough to keep a dryland ranch company going, weathered brown yet urbane and worldly in his own way. And Deirdre, the one who would keep it going in the future; the one who hadn't fled, the way the rest had fled, but had made a home in a lonely corner of the world. Beautiful girl. Now that Anna was very old, she discovered beauty everywhere. The whole world glowed with beauty.

And her dear son Dudley, stiff, proud, too proud, but strong, too, and her heart went out to him. He was a good son, and she took a mother's joy in him.

They finished, sipped coffee—Anna preferred tea—and then Cameron rose. He would conduct the meeting. Because these were corporations, certain procedures had to be followed. Sandy pulled out a notebook and uncapped a pen. She would take the minutes. There would be recorded votes.

Anna was glad that Cameron would conduct the affair. She loved Dudley, but he was not one to stand before his family and conduct a stockholders' meeting.

"All right," Cam said, "a board meeting of the Nichols Corporations is being called to order. A voting-share quorum is present. Attendees will be listed in the minutes. Let's get on with it. You have some financial sheets before you.

"We have crucial matters before us. We are faced with the question of whether to proceed with Nichols Ranches, or dissolve the companies, or choose some middle ground.

"The Horoney Foundation has informed us it'll withdraw its offer to buy our land at the historic market price on June one. That's rushing toward us. We have a generous offer, twenty-five million for the land alone, plus technical help if we wish to resettle and ranch elsewhere. The obvious reality is that if we decline to sell, our land—deep within the proposed National Grassland Trust—will be essentially unmarketable, illiquid, whatever its worth. The foundation would still buy it, but at its depreciated market price.

"Within the past few days a new complication arose. The United States Fish and Wildlife Service has designated all of our land as wolf-habitat area, and that essentially freezes development. We can't so much as drill a well or fix a fence without permission. The penalties are draconian if we do not comply. Bob Rockwell's been gabbing with the bureaucrats in Helena. He reports that they're committed and serious, and won't admit to a weak case even though wolves have been absent from the area for seventy years. He believes the purpose is to pressure us to leave—to accept the Horoney offer.

"And thirdly, of course, we have the wolves. Two packs, protected as a threatened species. These have already made serious inroads in our stock, and forced us to move cattle to the southern ranches at a cost of eighteen thousand dollars, including shipping loss. There's no guarantee that the wolves won't move south and further destroy our stock. The Ag Department's Animal Damage Control people won't offer us much help, other than to report where the packs are. We will be able to get a partial repayment from that Defenders of Wildlife outfit, but their limit is two thousand per animal, and some of our better breeding stock are worth more.

"The options, as I see them, are basically these, although I am sure you'll add many more before this is over. One is to sell out and divide the proceeds. If we did that, federal and state taxes, capital gains, would take about half. Another is to sell this land and resume ranching elsewhere, which would be less costly in terms of taxes because the corporations would enjoy some protection if the transactions are done properly. Another is to continue as we have, and try to weather this. Another is to sell some of the land, but not all of it, which also has tax consequences. I've prepared a financial analysis of a hypothetical sale of two of the ranches, the North Ranch and the Antler.

"Another is to sell off our livestock and wait to see what the future brings. That also would involve a terrible tax liability, as you can see. Invested conservatively at six or seven percent, the remaining capital would provide our families barely adequate livings and pay the property taxes on two hundred twenty thousand acres. But it wouldn't suffice to keep our employees on hand, nor would it go far toward purchasing a new herd in better times. We would have to let the Troubles, Hardys, and the rest go—which would be one of the most painful things we've faced. Another—proposed by an intelligent wolf biologist I talked to— is to raise buffalo, which are selling well, earn good profits, and are better equipped to fend off wolves. There are tax advantages, but that has a downside. They're wild animals and can't be easily herded. They're hard to manage and dangerous. We would have to carry much more liability insurance. We would have to invest a great deal in adequate fences and new equipment, such as steel squeeze chutes and pens able to handle them. Some estimated costs are before you. Joe Klug did these cost analyses, by the way. I'm not sure we can fence or add equipment without USFWS approval, so that's a dubious proposition at best. That's it in a nutshell. There might be other options, such as leasing our pasture to the foundation, while retaining title to it. But I haven't approached the foundation about that, nor have I run that one past our accountants. I'll open the discussion for comment, and I'd like to start with our principal shareholder, Anna."

She was glad she was first. She summoned her thoughts, which had a way of skittering away from her these days. "When we came, it was the land that fevered our minds. So few people in all of history had land, and here was all we could ever want if we found the courage to take it. This became our land.

"I don't know about the rest, but I hope we keep our land. Storms come and go, but the land is forever. The land is what I want my great-great-grandchildren there, in Deirdre's lap, to inherit. I'm not thinking about me; I think only until tomorrow where I'm concerned. But I'm thinking about our babies. If we give up the land, we'll never get it back. The world is filling up and land is costly. I can go along with anything—but not selling the land. I'll listen to you all now, because you may have better ideas. But the land is our true wealth and our salvation."

She slipped into silence and studied their faces, wondering if the wisdom of the pioneers, of the early days, was still wisdom in their minds. She wondered how Dudley would vote her trust shares, which comprised the bulk of two of the three corporations. If they really wanted to sell out, she thought she would bow to that. It was their world now; she would not impede them.

By common consent, the next shareholder to speak would be Dudley. She knew about what he would say, and he didn't disappoint her.

Dudley began stiffly. "I'm against selling out. Why turn everything over to the government? Taxes and all that. It's time to fight. We've got lawyers; let's put 'em to work. Sue the feds. Sue Horoney. Sue the Ag Department and its worthless Animal Damage Control. Lobby in Washington. Those politicians listen when the Nicholses talk. If we have to, we can sell livestock to finance this. Rebuild later after we've kicked the last wolf out of the state."

That was Dudley, all right, she thought. Unbending as ever, but admirable anyway because he was a tough and honorable man. She wished Mabel had lived to soften him a little over the years.

Then it was Deirdre's turn.

"Mark and I have sure been thinking about this. We just hate to sell out," she said. "We like to think of this the way you think about a storm or a long winter, endure and it'll pass. We call the ranch our home, and that means a lot to us. We don't mind the isolation very much. I guess we're saying that we'd oppose selling the land, but if we have to sell off stock, or even raise buffalo, we'd prefer that. We love the place. Especially in the spring, like now, when the wildflowers are popping out and the cottonwoods are leafing. I sort of feel the tug of my ancestors, too. I want to think they're all here now, reminding us that they struggled through times worse than this to give us our inheritance. So, to sum up, we're against selling out, but we know we'll have to be flexible."

Anna loved that child.

Cameron smiled. "I heard from Julie. She asks that I vote her shares along with the majority. She'd like to sell her shares back to the corporation and build a house in Littleton. I guess we're all pretty much agreed not to sell out to the foundation, but to try to weather it. I haven't heard from Martin. Well, I have to put this to a formal vote for our minutes. First, all those in favor of selling out to the foundation?"

No one responded.

"All those in favor of restocking with buffalo—if the government lets us?"

More silence.

"All those in favor of dealing flexibly with circumstance—such as removing stock for a while, or shifting stock away from wolves, or whatever it takes?"

This time they agreed.

Sandy wrote it into the minutes, in a language more formal than the actual voting.

"All right, I'll write Laslo Horoney," Cam said. "Is there any other business?"

There wasn't.

"Before adjourning, I'll just say we're in for some bad times, and we'll be a lot poorer no matter what we opt to do, mostly because of taxes and declining land values."

Anna wondered what the future would bring, and knew she would not be around to see it. This afternoon heartened her. These were Nicholses, as tenacious and courageous in their way as she and Nick had been when they started so long ago.

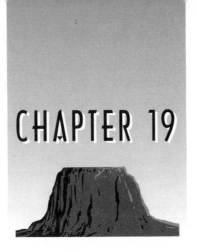

CHAPTER 19

Sanford Kouric stopped at John Trouble's place to let the ranch manager know he'd be on the property again. He had been doing that for weeks, dividing his time between the North Ranch and the Antler. He'd gotten to know Trouble and Joe Hardy pretty well, just by passing the time of day with them for a while before he drove toward the wolves.

He was monitoring both packs. They mystified him. He still had no line on where they came from. Using a small USFWS helicopter, he had netted and collared a wolf in each pack, so he now had radio telemetry to help him. The North Ranch pack had yielded a big scarred male with a limp. The Antler Ranch pack had yielded a beautiful pregnant female, probably an alpha. In each case the wolf had furiously fought the net that dropped over it. Kouric had sedated each with a jabstick, a hypodermic containing two effective sedatives, mounted on an aluminum pole. Then he had drawn blood, collared and ear-tagged the wolf, photographed it, injected it with a drug that neutralized the sedation, and waited around until it recovered.

There had been no DNA or other correlation between these wolves and the Yellowstone Park wolves. Wolves had to come from somewhere, and he kept wondering where and how, and why they weren't normal kin-oriented packs.

Trouble opened the door.

"Morning, John. I'm just stopping to let you know I'm on the place."

The big Cheyenne yawned. "Sure. Say, you mind if I come along? I haven't much to do these days."

Kouric shrugged. "Why not? Bring a lunch. You got binoculars?"

"No, but I got Injun eyes."

They laughed. Trouble wore glasses, like most Indians. On the reservations, glasses were ubiquitous.

A few minutes later Trouble emerged from the house in a thick jacket, and settled in Kouric's pickup truck. Kouric headed north on a two-rut ranch road. Ever since the cattle had been removed, most of the gates were open, so they made good progress.

"I didn't know they were over here," Trouble said.

"This pack's been drifting west. I should be able to pick up the telemetry in a few miles. They're hungry, John. They're trying to make a living on newborn antelope and fawns. Over on the Antler, they killed a couple of pensioned horses. But they're going to drift because they can't make a living around here. The muley and antelope populations are too thin."

"Lousy range," Trouble said.

"Deer are browsers and don't eat grass unless there's nothing else, but the bad range affects the antelope. For the life of me I don't know why wolves are hanging around here. It's not natural habitat."

"Why do you say that?"

"Because the range is more or less ruined, and that means there are few ungulates—hooved mammals like buffalo—for them to feed on. It was perfect habitat in the buffalo days, when wolves had only to follow a herd and pick off the old and weak and newborn. But what's left for them? A newborn antelope has no more meat on it than a cat. A healthy muley can usually outrun a wolf. Adult antelope have horns and a bad temper, and they can run, too. So this wolf pack's drifting out, and I expect the one on the Antler will, too. They're moving five to ten miles a day, driven by hunger, probably heading for some river bottoms where they'll do better on small game."

"Pretty soon they'll be out of here?"

"Yeah, I'd say so."

"And we can bring back the cattle?"

Kouric suddenly went cautious. "I don't know about that, John. I'm not going to tell Nichols to put them back on until I get a better line on these wolves."

They topped a bleak hill, and Kouric stopped. He stepped out, into the wind, and turned on a slick little radio receiver that would give him a fix on the wolf with the radio collar. He rotated the receiver in an arc, catching no signal, and then rotated it again. He had lost the pack, at least temporarily.

The tan soil under him was almost naked of vegetation. It had been raped generations ago, and now supported little life other than an occasional yucca or prickly pear, and some sagebrush. There wasn't much grass. He doubted that this pasture produced ten percent of the biomass that had existed here when the pasture was virgin prairie. Grazing had destroyed the marvelous root systems of the buffalo grass and wheat grass and other native grasses—systems that enabled these bunchgrasses to endure sharp droughts and recover, and to endure sharp grazing by passing buffalo. He knew bitterly that the wastes under his feet were the ultimate reason that this was not wolf habitat.

Even by the Soil Conservation Service's lax standards, this would be considered poor pasture. But those standards were a joke. Range categorized as good or excellent could have only a third or so of the biomass of virgin prairie. He returned to the pickup, thinking maybe the wolves were doing Nichols Ranches a favor if they drove off all the cattle. This range needed a ten-year rest.

"Not around here," Kouric told Nichols, as he started up and headed down a long grade.

"I haven't heard them at night. I like to hear them."

"I do, too. They've got a whole language. I like it best when they're just having fun. Scares a lot of people, though."

"Not me," said Trouble.

"Wolves are your brothers, eh?"

Trouble slid into deep silence, and Kouric knew he had stumbled into one of those pockets of difference. The tribal mythologies generally honored wolves. Kouric didn't know of any plains tribe that hated or feared wolves the way Europeans did.

"No," said Trouble. "They get the cattle. I don't want 'em around."

Kouric didn't really believe that. He topped the next ridge and got out again, hoping to pick up the telemetry. They weren't far from the northern border of the North Ranch. He picked up nothing. The pack had traveled some distance. He might have to fly to catch up with it. For some reason, the range here was better. A thin carpet of wheat grass and needle and thread greened the slope, interspersed with a few juniper and random rock. He glassed the country, seeing some antelope on a distant rise, but nothing else. The antelope were grazing, with a sentinel on a hillock, looking out for them. Probably no wolves around. Small puffball clouds plowed shadows across the land. Gnats and horseflies swarmed him, and he was glad he'd brought some repellent.

He stepped into the truck and made a U-turn. "No wolves around here," he said.

"Where'll you try next?"

"They've been drifting west. We'll go west when we get back to that turnoff."

"Yeah, that's where they're at," Trouble said.

Kouric wondered how the Cheyenne knew. "This is pretty good range around here," he said. "Not like back there a way."

"Yeah, we rested it and it came back some. We put in some stock dams. Lots of mallards on them. Lots of mosquitoes, too."

"The Nicholses work at it."

"The younger ones do. Old Dudley, he didn't. In the fifties, he ground this down to dirt."

"Times change. They've got a program now."

"It wasn't times, it was survival. When you got no grass, you call it quits."

"How do you feel about the Grassland Trust?"

Trouble shrugged.

Kouric maneuvered around a pothole full of crusted mud, and headed down the two-rut road again. It was too dry. They shouldn't be kicking up dust in May. He remembered growing up on a hardscrabble mountain ranch in southern Wyoming, around Encampment. His father had pushed the land hard, not out of greed but because he had to feed and shelter his large family. Kouric regarded the ruination of the plains as unintended tragedy, not as some sinister fruit of agribusiness governed by greed. That was one of the things that separated him from so many of the Greens he knew. They had conjured up an enemy, agribusiness, ascribed greed and profit hunger to it, and looked at it as the serpent in Eden. It was so easy to hate and scorn. But Kouric didn't hate, and he figured that if anything good were to happen, it'd be with the help and enthusiasm of folks like the Nichols family.

There were other things the Greens hadn't thought much about. This agribusiness they despised so much had produced one miracle after another: cheap, plentiful food, varieties of plants that yielded magical harvests, new cholesterol-free products like canola oil, some of which was produced here from rapeseed crops. Agribusiness had staved off world famine in spite of population growth. Agribusiness had evolved ever more efficient ways to grow food and fiber. It had produced miraculous disease-resistant grains, crops that grew in salt-poisoned soils, catfish farms producing tons of high protein food, better and cheaper beef and chicken, new nuts and fruits and vegetables. Diets had been diversified. Seasonal foods were now appearing year-round. Protein intake improved. Famine had been all but eliminated. Americans spent less of their income on food than any other people in history. At the beginning of the new millennium Americans remained the luckiest people in the history of the world, and the primary reason was, in his estimation, agribusiness. No, you would not catch Sanford Kouric condemning one of the nation's least appreciated and most profound miracles.

But he didn't much like what had happened to habitat and topsoil and dwindling animal populations. Laslo Horoney's great enterprise had intrigued and excited him from the start, and he wished it success because it offered a peaceful resolution. With some nurturing, these tormented pastures would spring back, and with the grasses would come wildlife, and big hooved mammals like buffalo and elk, and then the wolves who would serve their own vital role in the health of those ungulate herds. A pasture the size of West Virginia! And, ultimately, a grassland the size of New York State! He could scarcely imagine such a thing, but there was that madman Horoney, making it happen.

They rattled down to the bottoms of the Rosebud, and Kouric tried to monitor the wolf pack once again. He parked under a giant cotton-wood in new leaf, turned on his handheld receiver—and got no response.

Trouble watched, smoked, waited nearby.

"Nothing," said Kouric. "Maybe that pack's left the country. Or maybe someone's shot it."

"No one's shot it."

"How do you know?"

"Just do."

These mysterious pronouncements intrigued Kouric. "Where are the wolves, then?"

"Looking for a meal. They don't got any around here."

"You're right. And I'll tell you something more. They've got a female ready to den. They're looking for a place with enough food for the pups. Don't ask me how I know it. I just do. I've a wolf brain after all these years. I'll tell you something else. These wolves were brought here. They didn't migrate. They aren't packs. Don't ask me how I know that, either. I just do."

"How come the Fish and Wildlife says this is wolf habitat?"

"It's politics, pressure on your employer. Wolves are flexible animals. They're at home anywhere—alpine and subalpine, tundra, foothills, plains, desert. What defines wolf habitat is prey. Where there's prey, wolves are at home. That and wilderness. They don't like to be anywhere around humans. Very shy animals."

"This isn't wolf habitat."

"Not yet. When the foundation gets cranked up, and there's bison and elk here, that'll make it habitat."

Trouble grinned. "Those Fish and Wildlife guys, they're really saying Nichols cows makes it habitat."

Kouric grimaced. "You may be right. And forget I said that."

They ate their bag lunches there beside the sluggish creek, fighting off whining mosquitoes and flies, enjoying the timid warmth and the cheerful sun, watching blackbirds and mud hens and some noisy crows. The monotonous prairies redeemed themselves in these secret bottomlands that teemed with vegetation and life.

"Do you admire wolves as much as I do, John?" Kouric asked after demolishing an apple.

Trouble smiled and shrugged.

"When nature's put back in order, the wolves'll come," Kouric said. "They're the missing link. You should see Yellowstone now. The elk herd's smaller but healthier. Ditto for deer and bison. One of the biggest changes is the real estate. Grass. Browse. All radically improved. There's even some evidence that wolves are helping the grizzly population recover. The big bears are getting much more meat. They'll wade right in on a wolf-kill carcass and chase off the wolves. It's a sight to see. The grizzly birth rate's up sharply. The park has fifty more than it did five years ago. It's not proven, but I ascribe it to the wolf reintroduction. We're rescuing another endangered species. You'll see them out here someday. Grizzlies and elk used to live on the Great Plains. Once the foundation gets going, no reason they can't move in here."

"And I'll be out of work," Trouble said.

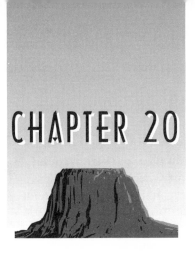

CHAPTER 20

DeeAnn stood on the corral rail, watching her silent father and Mark injecting combiotic into calves. Ever since the meeting in Miles, her father had folded into himself, hardly speaking to anyone, the remoteness masking a cauldron of emotion. She had never seen him like this before, and sensed that he was at the point of snapping in two. He had coped with drought, low beef prices, death, disease, government intrusion in his life, and a lot more. But not the things that were ganging up on him now.

Mark pulled the lever of the squeeze chute, and a blatting calf bolted out of it and raced toward its bellowing mother. Her father pulled the tip off the next hypodermic, and waited for Mark to haze another sick calf into the chute. The rear end of this one was dripping with green slime. They were having trouble with scours, bovine diarrhea, this year.

They could deal with scours. It was the things the Nichols family couldn't deal with that was upsetting her father. She understood the burdens he carried, and she ached for him. Like everyone else in the family, she felt utterly helpless to deal with the looming changes around them. The one thing they all had agreed on was to hang on to the land. That was their inheritance and their life. But beyond that, the family was splintering. Her grandfather was going to raise beef, and he'd be damned if he'd try anything else. And that's where she and Mark were parting company with him. The more she and her husband talked about their dilemma, the more they leaned toward raising buffalo. Tear out the fences, let the Horoney herd roam—for a price, or an agreed-on share of slaughter animals each year. It made economic sense. Buffalo meat had become a hot item.

But she didn't control the ranches; Dudley did. She knew it would be futile to try to change her grandfather's mind. There were other options

she and Mark had been talking about, things that would help her father—and maybe her mother.

Cameron cursed, having lost a hypodermic needle on a writhing calf.
She had scarcely ever heard him cuss, beyond a hell or a damn. He had
never slipped into the vice of profane language, which was so common
among ranching people. She took her father's slip for what it was, a man
at his wits' end, trying to move the earth with a short lever. Her father
was running a doomed enterprise, had a wife sinking into serious alcoholism—indeed, Sandy was unreachable most afternoons and evenings—
and was trying to cope with wolves and a whole new array of bureaucrats,
all of them with agendas.

The men injected the last of the calves just about at the nooning, and
she gathered up her courage. She intended to talk to Cameron about
something she and Mark had thought about. Her father gathered up the
veterinary supplies and started silently for his house. At this moment he
didn't look like a man who controlled millions of dollars in land and
cattle. His brown duckcloth pants and jacket were dripping with green
scours, his boots were caked with corral muck and manure, and his face
was smeared with mud.

"Dad?"

He turned sharply, unsmiling.

"Could we talk? Mark and I have some ideas."

"I've got to go check on your mother."

"I'm glad you do. Please come over for lunch."

He stared silently at her. She swore he was not far from tears, though
his face revealed nothing. Then he nodded curtly.

A few minutes later he did show up at her kitchen door, scrubbed and
changed. She set out a bowl of potato salad and some ham sandwiches,
while Mark served coffee. They ate quietly, and she sensed that his mood
was softening a little. She and her dad got along well, and she knew he
enjoyed her company.

He finished, sipped coffee, and settled back in his chair. "You had
something to discuss?" he asked.

That was a good sign, she thought. He wasn't dodging her.

"About the place," she said. "Would you trust Mark and me to run
it?"

He said nothing, and she could not even guess what was passing
through his mind.

She backpedaled fearfully. "I don't mean you wouldn't have control.
I just mean, you wouldn't have to be here all the time."

He seemed to be forming sentences in his head, and finally spoke in measured cadences. "Of course I'd trust you to run it. You know the business as well as I do, and I was about your age when I took over from my dad. But we're in big trouble, and I don't think you or I or anyone else can get us out of it."

She smiled. "We were thinking you might enjoy some city life or some travel. Southwest? Sedona? Albuquerque?"

"I don't know what I'd do with myself."

"Live there, fly here now and then."

"This is for your mother," he said, suddenly aware.

She nodded. "And for you. No one can talk her into drying out or even leaving here. It's tearing you to bits. That's plain to Mark and me. We can't do anything about the Buffalo Commons, or the wolves and bureaucrats, but we can free you up. Mom'll just drink herself to death here; in Arizona or someplace, she might at least think about drying out."

"What would you do different, running this?"

She and Mark glanced at each other. "Everyone's agreed on keeping the land. The question is what to do with it. Grandpa's a stockman, now and forever. I guess you are, too."

"I guess so." He smiled. "I sure riled him up when I suggested putting in a subdivision."

That emboldened her to proceed. "Mark and I would like to raise buffalo."

That did surprise him. "That's not possible," he said. "We can't throw out generations of Hereford breeding. Or override your grandfather."

"We know that. We can't buck grandpa. We'd run the ranches just the way you have. The only difference is that you'd take Mother out of here and see what happens when she's among people again."

"She's among people," he said stiffly.

"None of us knows why she drinks. Maybe there are no reasons. Maybe she just likes to. But it's just going to get worse here, and it might get better in Arizona."

He sighed. "It's too late. She's gone. Have you ever smelled an alcoholic? Her whole body gives off a smell; it's trying to get that stuff out of her system. I can't even describe it to you, but that smell—it's like formaldehyde. She's embalming herself. I don't see how moving will help that. She just sits there in front of Oprah, or *Jeopardy'*, or Tom Brokaw—it doesn't matter. I've lost her."

"No, you're not a widower. And she's not lost."

He straightened in his chair.

"You've had a good marriage."

He nodded.

"Your marriage has been so good, you and Mom love each other so much, that it's been a model for me—for us." She smiled at Mark. "Pure love."

"It was good," her father said. Past tense.

"We just wanted you to know we'd like to take over, and we hope you'll consider making some changes in your life."

"I'll think about it," he said. "It would have to be voted on."

All that was good. He wasn't rejecting the idea out of hand, as she feared. "Mark and I can talk to Grandpa, if you think you would like to try this."

"I just want to think about it," he said. He turned to Mark. "What would you do about the wolves—and bureaucrats?"

Mark grinned. "Raise buffalo."

They laughed. It was good to see her father laugh. He hadn't laughed in weeks.

"When I took over from Dad," Cameron said, "I sold off three hundred horses. It pretty near killed him. What would you do? Sell off the Herefords?"

"Raise llamas. They're plumb mean. They'd chase a wolf into the next county."

A crinkle of amusement built around Cameron's eyes. "I hope they have the same instincts about bureaucrats," he said.

That's how it was left. Cameron and Mark took the truck out to fix a windmill that was chattering in the wind. She put away the remains of lunch, content with the way things had gone. She and Mark had put an idea in her father's head. He didn't have to shoulder all these troubles. He might be able to do something about Mother if he was freed from all the burdens of the ranch. That's all she could do for him, but it could be a great deal.

She dried her hands, stepped into a brisk afternoon, and headed across the flat to the old ranch house, intending to visit with her mother if that was possible. By one or two in the afternoon it often wasn't. She knocked, headed for the den, but her mother wasn't there. The television wasn't even on.

She found her mother out on the veranda, where she sat in an ancient rocking chair absorbing the spring sun. She wore her down parka as if it were very cold, though it wasn't.

"It's a good day for some sun," DeeAnn said.

Sandra nodded.

"I haven't seen you for a while. We've been so busy with scours and things."

"You haven't seen me because I've been too drunk."

That startled DeeAnn.

"See this glass? There's nothing but Schweppes in here. I'm holding off today because I feel like it. The sun is nice. You're here to talk to me about my drinking and how I'm hurting myself. You don't have to tell me again."

"No, you're not just hurting yourself. You're hurting Dad. And us."

Her mother stopped rocking.

"Mark and I are trying to talk Dad into getting out of here and letting us run the place. He could take you to Arizona."

Sandra looked away. DeeAnn waited for a response and got none.

"Mom, what do you want?"

"Want?"

"If you could have any wish come true, what would you wish for?"

"Just to be here with your father and you."

"Please don't play those passivity games!"

Sandra started to get out of the chair.

"Just sit a minute. We're going to do some root-canal work. Do you want to live—or die? We can't help you if you really just want to fade away. But if you want to live, you can help yourself, and we all can help you. It's up to you. You're tougher than you think."

Her mother shrugged and then sipped the tonic in earnest.

"That's what it comes to," DeeAnn said. "You're a slave. But you still have a choice. You can stop being a slave—if life is worth anything to you—or not. It's up to you."

Sandy nodded, and in that small nod DeeAnn saw her choose.

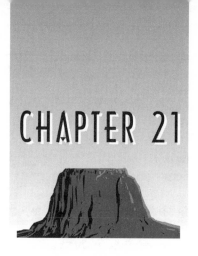

CHAPTER 21

J. Carter Delacorte had reason to celebrate. The Nichols ranches had been declared wolf habitat by the government. He relished that. If he had not planted the wolves, the Fish and Wildlife Service could not have done it. Surely this was monkey-wrenching at its most sublime. It would only be a matter of time now before the Nichols empire toppled, and along with it the remaining small fry, and then the largest wilderness preserve on the American continent would bloom to life.

He was going to celebrate this triumph with a very private dinner party tonight. There would be only one guest, Monica Zettendorf, the chromium-plating heiress, she of the jade eyes and jet hair and pneumatic figure. They were old friends and lovers who shared certain viewpoints.

Delacorte had made sure that this would be a special evening. He had dismissed his help, so that the eight-thousand-square-foot peeled lodge-pole lodge northeast of Jackson would be his alone this evening. Last to leave would be his dog man, who cared for the forty-nine sled dogs two hundred yards distant. J. Carter—the J stood for Jason—would do most of the cooking himself, making a meatless tempura from ingredients left by his cook. That and some fine New-Age California wine called Pisces Ascending, and some delicious conversation with Monica about certain things, and the Walker-Bean hot tub, and the heated Sherman waterbed with wave control, all added up to a banner evening.

J. Carter was a man of means. He had never been poor, thanks to the steady success of Delacorte Latex Products, a small New Jersey company started by his late father. But with the advent of AIDS in the eighties, the company had grown at a dizzy pace, and a flood of wealth had landed in J. Carter's coffers. It pleased him that at any second of any hour, his product was in use all over the world, preventing AIDS and babies, slowing down the population explosion. Such was the genius of the company's managers that they had steadily generated new lines, new colors and textures. Recently they had added a hot new product for underendowed males, marketed as Roosters, a concept that had won national marketing and advertising awards for the company, and tripled its sales. No one had ever realized how many men needed Roosters.

He could scarcely imagine a more humanitarian business. His net profit per act of love was about twenty cents, and it enchanted him to turn all this seminal wealth over to good causes in the form of seed money. Of course he never used the company products himself, because he found them annoying and also he didn't belong to any of the social strata who were at risk.

Good works, yes, that was it. He belonged to every known environmental group, which he regarded as the salvation of the world: the Sierra Club, Friends of the Earth, Earth First!, the National Wildlife Federation, the Audubon Society, the Northern Plains Resources Council, the Elk Foundation, and many more, including the new High Plains Foundation, a group totally dedicated to steering the Horoney interests in the right direction.

He had been particularly active in his opposition to clear-cutting of national forest. Clear-cutting was the concentrated felling of timber, and it usually left ghastly scars upon the mountainsides, monuments to the rapine and greed of profit-making commerce and the venality of the Forest Service. Thanks to a series of lawsuits largely seeded by Delacorte, the Forest Service had curtailed its logging contracts, and was now virtually shutting down timber harvesting on public land. He regarded it as one of his great triumphs. But there had been an unexpected side effect of shutting off the national forests: the rapine had been switched to privately owned forest, where trees were falling like bowling pins. So Delacorte was fostering legislation to prevent the slaying of private forests in the U.S., hoping to drive timber capitalism north to Canada, where there were abundant forests waiting to be chainsawed.

Monica had once complained to him that around twelve thousand lodgepole pines had died to construct his lodge, and she was right. J. Carter had felt deep remorse, and to atone he had bought a Honda Civic so he would use fewer of the world's precious resources thenceforth. Now he took pride in driving the Honda, and considered ostentation a vice. Monica was his conscience, and that was all the more reason for the pair of them to celebrate tonight.

He decided to dress up this chill Saturday night in May, because great moments required formal clothing. Summer had not yet penetrated the alpine reaches of Jackson Hole. He chose a Robert Redford–style velour shirt of sky blue, and his best prewashed, prefaded designer jeans, and

Gucci loafers. About his neck he hung his treasured rose quartz crystal, which had kept him in good health and spirits for a long time, almost a year. At first he had been skeptical about the claims of the Hungarian scientist, Miloslav Rakosi, who had discovered that crystals worn on the body affected auras, somehow absorbing and rectifying dissonant harmonics. But after reading the scientific literature, Delacorte decided to try the crystal, and was stunned by the beauty he was experiencing. Later he discovered there was an extensive eastern European folk literature about religious observance that employed crystals as the mediating force between harmony and sin, which was disharmony. Crystals made life very sacred. His New-Age California friends had been right. Spirit and holistic healing and love would conquer the world, and he was into them all.

Monica would be late, of course. She could never get her little buns to function on schedule. It was in her horoscope. She was a Libra, and whoever had known a Libra to be on time? So J. Carter busied himself with the vegetarian tempura, which he was spicing with morels and truffles, while a tape that emulated the sound of surf provided a soothing and spiritual background.

He heard the hum of her Hummer, then the hiss of her recycled-tire huaraches on his huge redwood plank deck, and wiped his hands.

"Jay, dolling," she said, letting herself in. They hugged madly. He touched her cheek and ear tenderly, with socially significant gestures intended to establish harmonics, while she kissed his earlobe as a promise of what the evening would bring. He and she had a sensitized understanding of each other's gestalt, which they had undertaken through videotape therapy and sex counseling and watching the tapes of Bill Moyers interviewing Joseph Campbell.

"What a trip," she said. "All that traffic. It's only May, but Jackson's simply packed."

"It'll get better," he said. "Tourism's declining because Jackson's getting too expensive. Price is the best way to get rid of undesirables, I always say. And the average building permit around here's for a two-million house. Pretty soon Jackson'll be its old self."

She poured herself a glass of the nonalcoholic chardonnay, and perched on a stool while he donned his Friends of Wildlife biodegradable apron, and set to work in earnest on their dinner.

"Have I got something to tell you!" he said. "Something big. The biggest thing I've ever done to save the Earth."

"A vasectomy?"

They laughed. How they loved to laugh. If only Monica weren't so opposed to committed relationships they could be enjoying life together.

He'd proposed an earth-union, performed by a hip Shoshone medicine man with a blue jewel in his earlobe, but she had turned J. Carter down, saying it would violate her spiritual independence and that it would resonate poorly.

"I'll tell you after dinner," he said. "It's so sexy you'll go mad."

He cooked the tempura in a special maple syrup and tofu broth, while she smiled at him. Then he added the ground peyote, and carried the dish to the dining table, where there was a splendid view of the federal elk reserve below, and the Tetons beyond it, looming in the last light.

They ate and smiled, and got up from the table feeling a little hungry because that was the health-oriented thing to do, and he swiftly slid the few dishes into the washer. Then he led her out to the hot tub, enclosed in a glass-covered redwood deck where they could sit and soak and watch meteors and the moon, and watch the headlights of cars on the artery between Jackson and the south gate of Yellowstone Park. It was heavenly.

And so was her bod, especially the mother glands. She slipped into the purling water, and he followed, leaving his designer clothes in a heap because he did not want to appear anal-retentive.

"Tell me," she said, once she had sunk into the heat of the tub.

"All right! I will! I've done the best thing of my life. But first you must swear—I really mean this, Monica—swear by all that's sacred in your soul—never to say a word to anyone. I really mean that."

She smiled.

"You've got to say it," he insisted.

"Okay, I swear. This better be good."

He touched her cheek and earlobe to reestablish harmony, and then sprung his surprise.

"I've single-handedly won the day for the National Grassland Trust," he said. "You won't believe it."

"Tell me," she breathed.

"I did the wolves."

"Uh, what?"

"I monkey-wrenched the Nicholses."

"Uh, Jay, I'm not on your wavelength. We've got to match auras here."

He was patient. Libras required patience. "I put the wolves on the Nichols ranches. Two trips. I got them from a trapper in Alberta and brought them in as sled dogs."

"You did? Why?"

"Because wolves are protected. Up until 1998 they were listed as experimental, so Fish and Wildlife could kill or remove them even if ranchers couldn't. But now they're a protected species. There isn't anything the Nichols family can do about them. If they shoot the wolves, they go to the federal slammer. The wolves took to beef like they'd been born rich. Once they got the hang of it, those packs each killed and ate three or four cows a week. They still are. And when they produce pups, they'll wipe out the whole Montana beef industry. It's the biggest blow against agribusiness since health-food stores."

"So?"

"So, the Nicholses will go into the red. They can't fight back. That's maybe two hundred thou a year in dead loss."

"I'm missing something, Jay."

"Monica, the feds had wolf biologists crawling around there for weeks, and now the feds have declared the whole area wolf habitat. Don't you see? That's doom for any private owner, any holdout. Once an area's habitat, it's like a glacier landed on it. All the holdouts can do is pack up. They're toast. Then we're back to wilderness and bison."

"Wow! Jay! You thought that up yourself?"

"You bet. It took some doing, too, and lots of risk. I did it all myself. I sold off some sled dogs in Alaska and then picked up the wolves this guy trapped. Boy, it was scary, going through U.S. Customs, but I did it. I had it all down. They hardly paid attention. Some guy comes along and shines his light in the kennels, but he wouldn't know a wolf from a poodle, so it all went fine. I drove the truck down from Canada and let the wolves loose. The first batch went on the Nichols North Ranch, and the next on the Antler, and no one has a clue how they got there. I can just imagine all those wolf experts scratching their beards and tugging their ponytails."

He laughed.

"Did you know the government would declare the area habitat?"

"Well, ah, I sort of guessed they might, and it worked! It's the most important thing I've ever done to help the Earth. We are all brothers—and sisters."

"Wow, Jay," she said, and snuggled closer to him to share the heat. "You're almost Jesus."

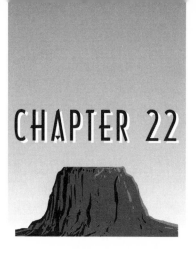

CHAPTER 22

Bad news. Hector Truehart read the letter, grunted, and phoned Horoney. There was a lot of bad news, and Truehart decided he had better talk to Laslo in person. Horoney had a quirk: he didn't take bad news well over the telephone, and when he got it that way he usually spewed ill-considered, impulsive instructions, which Truehart had learned to set aside until his client had a chance to quiet down and reconsider. But whenever Truehart could present the bad news personally, things went better. Truehart sensed that his presence was a steadying influence on the man.

A half hour later the maid ushered him through Horoney's Arlington home to a favorite lair of the shopping-center magnate that overlooked a private garden to the rear. It didn't look like the heart of one of the world's great business empires because it wasn't an office. It looked like a library, which in fact it was, but equipped with leather wing chairs in conversational groups.

"Hector, come in," Horoney said. "You must have bad news. When it's good, I get it by disembodied voice or writing."

"You're looking chipper," Truehart said, neutrally. He dug into his attaché case and extracted the letter. "You'd better see this," he said.

Horoney donned his spectacles and read it.

The brief letter, from Cameron Nichols, said, simply, that the Nichols family had weighed the final offer from the foundation, and declined it. They would continue to ranch as always.

"Roots run deep," Horoney said. "It's not rational. They're letting sentiment override their good judgment."

"I suspect Cameron didn't have the votes," Truehart said. "His father and grandmother rule that roost."

"It'd be better for that family if they moved. That decision cost them a fortune."

"Maybe not, Laslo. What would that land be worth if it's a window on the greatest zoo the world's ever seen? The greatest wildlife resort in the lower United States?"

"Zoo! Hector, sometimes you sound like a real estate tycoon." They laughed. "I see. Yes, it could be worth a lot in the hands of shrewd entrepreneurs. That is, if U.S. Fish and Wildlife doesn't freeze development by calling it wolf habitat."

"It may, but they're on thin ice. I'll go into that when you have time, or do a memo. Now look at this." He handed Horoney a copy of the *Western Livestock Journal* in Billings, which carried a lead story about the Nichols family decision to stay put. "My colleagues FedExed a copy to me. The word's out. The Nicholses aren't budging."

Horoney read it swiftly. "This puts a big hole into the west side of the National Grassland Trust. Why don't things ever go right?"

"It's going to cost us a lot more than two hundred twenty thousand acres, I'm afraid," Truehart said. "Those ranches aren't contiguous. They're interlaced with private, federal and state land. Years ago, the Nichols family did a big land swap with the BLM that consolidated the holdings of both, but there's still a lot of loose land, some ours, some federal, that we're going to be locked out of. There's also isolated state school sections inside Nichols's holdings, which the state's turned over to us—but we won't be able to use them. Nichols can't either, so they'll be fenced squares of public land out of reach. The foundation won't be in the business of herding buffalo through land we don't own to get to land we own. So, effectively, the Nichols decision denies us about four hundred thousand acres. That's around six hundred square miles of land—for starters. And I suspect the small fry will start hanging on, too, inspired by the Nichols decision."

"What do you suggest, Hector?"

"I'll write 'em and say that the foundation still wants the land, even though it can no longer guarantee the former market price. Keep the channels open."

"Yes, good, do it. They made their choice, and they'll have to live with it. That land'll drop like a rock, once we launch."

"Don't count on it, Laslo. We've been fighting speculators and sharks from the start. The ones who are hanging on to their land are betting its value will rise—or at least, they're betting the foundation will pay more to get them out of the trust lands, which amounts to the same thing."

"We won't do that. Never. Let 'em stew in their own greed."

"My reading of the Nichols family is that greed hasn't a thing to do with it. They've fought that dryland for generations, it's rewarded and wounded them, it's an old love-hate thing. It's the devil they know, instead of the devil they don't know. They have troubles now, but that's been a family with traditions and roots. That's more than my own assessment. I got that from half the Montanans I talked to."

"You're right, Hector. Write me a memo, not only on how much this bites into our grasslands, but what it'll cost. We'll have to build buffalo-proof fence, keep the herd off Nichols land, and that'll cost over a million. I'll look into it." He jotted a memo to himself. "Also give me options. Can we rent the land from the family? Is there room to deal? Can we just pull down fences and use the land—for a fee?"

"I'll probe it with Cameron. Now, Laslo, there's more stuff floating in."

"I'm not sure I want to hear it. I've had enough for now. You want a drink?"

"No, nothing with a mule kick. But some iced tea . . ."

Horoney spoke into a speaker phone, ordering two ice teas. "All right, what's next on your gloom sheet?"

"Lawsuit. Thirty plaintiffs, all small ranchers, factory owners, residential owners in the proposed grassland, suing the foundation on multiple grounds, alleging injury to business, to property values, to access, to the right to live as they choose . . ."

"We anticipated some of that. Tell me, is it to hold us up for a big settlement, or is it to drive us out?"

"Actually, as I read it, they want to get us out. These people don't like the National Grassland and want to go about their lives and businesses—ranching mostly, but there's a plant that turns rapeseed into canola oil, a pet-food processor, two seed-grain companies, and the town of Ekalaka, demanding fenced, paved access to continue, along with all services. They don't want a buffalo herd blocking the highway."

"All right, deal with them one by one, settle if you can, litigate as a last resort. We knew we'd face it, and actually there's been less than we'd expected. That's because you've been up there, dealing kindly with these people, allaying their fears, looking into any question of damage, being fair and flexible. That's what you're so good at, and why I'll always be grateful to you, amigo. Putting this together's mostly diplomacy. Anything else, Hector?"

" 'Fraid so."

The tea arrived, delivered by an erect, friendly looking woman with the bearing of an army officer.

"Thank you, Betsy," Horoney said.

Truehart sipped. He liked a good sweating glass of iced tea on a blistering day. "Seems that that Bozeman rally a few weeks ago got some results," he said. "There may be some hearings in the Senate about the whole project, and about us—the foundation. And you. The chairwoman of the Interior Committee, Elsie Drogge, is pretty much in the middle of the road, but she's being pressured by the Green coalition, with Senator Dennis from Oregon as point man. She's basically leaning toward a hearing and putting him in charge of organizing it. They're going after us."

"On what grounds?"

"It's private. It's a rich man's theft of public assets."

Horoney looked startled. "We're buying private land for a public purpose."

"Laslo, remember where this is coming from. First and foremost, the Greens don't care about property rights. It's all habitat and ecosystem to them. That's why the EPA and Fish and Wildlife keep expanding their regulatory reach—trying to control land that isn't theirs, without buying it from private owners. They'd like nothing better than to federalize all the loose land in the West and then run it, or have their anointed run it. So when you wander in, buying private land and winning the cooperation of the states and feds, they don't like it. You're on their turf. I mean that. They regard private ranch land as their turf."

"What'll happen?"

"They may compel your testimony and mine. We'll face a lot of grandstanding, some of it hostile. A lot of rhetoric about rich men's takeovers, the sinister landgrab. Abuse of ecology and disdain for the environmental movement and its experts."

Horoney laughed. "What'll come of it?"

"Bills in the hopper to pay you off at ten cents on the dollar and turn the feds loose. But enacting a ten-billion-dollar program that would evict law-abiding citizens from their homes and ranches and businesses is another matter. The Greens don't have the votes, so they'll try to drive you out by harassing you."

"I'm naive, Hector. When I started all this, I thought I'd have allies among those who want to restore a major chunk of real estate to wilderness."

"You do have allies. The ones who aren't ideologized. In fact, you could say the serious people, including the best biologists around."

"Hector, can you think of anything we've done—as a foundation— that might get us into legal trouble? Will some sort of criminal charges arise from this?"

Hector stared into the garden. "Years ago, I could answer a question like that confidently. Now I can't. There are certain lean-and-hungry-Cassius types, mostly in my profession, who've succeeded in criminalizing ordinary conduct, including the conduct of foundations serving good ends. People bent on hurting you'll find ways to do it. They've learned how to abuse class-action litigation to bleed their victims. You may face it. That's my gloomy crystal ball-gazing."

Horoney didn't reply for a moment. Then, "I've invested, so far, nearly four billion dollars into what has become a life's passion. I've three-quarters of the National Grassland, but right now it's as full of holes as Swiss cheese. Before I'm done with phase one, I'll spend three billion more and take a billion loss on my real estate just to keep the grassland project funded. It's not liquid, commercial real estate, and to move it, we've had to offer choice properties at well below appraisal, mostly to the Japanese. I'm doing this for the public good, for the good of besieged creatures and plants, and for the sake of a biological renewal. I sense it'll settle the restlessness of our times and heal man and nature. Each to his own home.

"But the people who ought to be most enthused see little good in it because it doesn't fit their conceptions. I have no intention of quitting, and I'll finish what I've started if it's within my power to do so. I just want to know what drives my critics."

"You're not a member of their church," Truehart said.

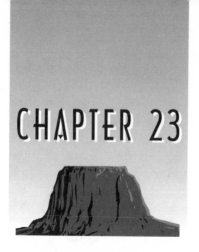

CHAPTER 23

John Trouble didn't use horses much because the all-terrain vehicle was handier. He hadn't used the geldings at all this spring, but now he intended to ride one. He hiked into a paddock near the ranch house, carrying a pail of oats and a halter. Without the bribery he couldn't catch them at all anymore.

Some ranch hand, he thought to himself as he hiked painfully through tender new grass to the old quarter horses standing nose-to-butt at the farthest fence, their tails lashing at the vicious black horseflies that tormented his stock. It was always that way. Why couldn't a horse be close when he needed one?

He would ride the bay today. The steeldust tended to be too spirited in the early spring. The horses sidled as he approached, but the bribe did its work, and in moments Trouble had the halter over the bay and was leading it back to the ranch. It would be a great day to ride, with a fresh breeze rippling the young grasses, and puffball clouds riding an azure sky. At the pens he brushed and saddled the bay, wiped it with repellent, added a saddlebag that would carry his lunch and binoculars, tied a yellow poncho behind the cantle, and then hung a sheathed rifle on the near side.

He led the horse to the stock trailer, and had trouble loading it until he bribed it with more oats in the manger. Then he slammed the rear door and dropped the heavy steel latch.

Kouric would not be here today. The Fish and Wildlife man had said he'd be out of the state for several days, and then he'd be over on the Antler looking at that other pack. Trouble liked the wolf biologist. Kouric didn't act like most white men. He didn't act like an Indian, either. Different, that's what he was.

Trouble drove slowly north and west, along rutted ranch roads, through open gates, dodging miry puddles and stretches of gumbo left from some welcome showers. After an ominously dry spring, the fickle rains had come in a rush, and the ranch ached with green. He drove into rougher country, sandstone ridges separated by swales, with slopes dotted with juniper and ponderosa. He liked this country. He knew every cranny of it after managing the North Ranch for seventeen years. That's what separated him from Kouric. He watched antelope scatter at the onslaught of his outfit, and saw some muleys on alert, but they let him pass. He was climbing, actually, toward a dry divide separating the Rosebud and Tongue River drainages.

From the divide he could see forever, the undulating prairie stretching into white haze fifty miles distant. Once the air had been cleaner. Now the haze was permanent, except a few days a year when the wind blew down from Canada, and those days so lifted his spirits that he often drove to this vantage point to look at the distant Rockies to the west, or to look into his spirit, which he saw with clarity from the ridge.

He parked the outfit there and backed the gelding out of the trailer. It sniffed the fresh air, snorted, and stood restlessly while John Trouble mounted. Trouble felt uncomfortable in the saddle, and wondered whether it was just because he was out of shape after a soft winter and idle spring, or whether he was getting old—or both. The horse seemed eager, and he let it move along at something less than a trot that kept him comfortable and didn't pound his butt.

He rode two miles toward a gash in the rough country that seemed only a blue shadow at first. But as he drew closer, the wind-eroded sandstone escarpment presented detail to him. When he reached its south lip, he dismounted and tied the horse to a juniper. The fresh wind, out of the west, would carry his scent east, away from most of the gulch.

He pulled out his bagged lunch and binoculars, extracted his rifle from its sheath, and settled against a sun-warmed slab of sandstone, partially concealed by juniper. He liked this moment and the day. Gradually he glassed the gulch, looking for the wolves. He was pretty certain the collared female was denning here, and the reason Kouric wasn't getting any signal was that she was holed up in any of several dens Trouble knew about, eight or ten feet into the ridge and well above the floor of the gulch. There would be massive amounts of rock blocking the signal.

He saw no wolf but didn't expect to. A hawk hunted the gulch. Some magpies jabbered far below, probably about the hawk. He focused on a badger hole, and then on a small den under some sandstone caprock. The pack was probably well aware of his presence, even though he had chosen a downwind route and had left the truck far behind. Kouric had told him things he didn't know about wolves: that the pack would feed and protect the female and her litter, bring food, watch over the whole birthing and infancy of the pups, instinctive guardians of the whole wolf clan. He studied the gulch again, looking for anything—movement, carcasses, the flight of crows, whatever. But he saw nothing. That was all right. Since the cows had been taken off the ranch, he hadn't much to do.

He opened his paper bag and unwrapped a thick beef sandwich Mavis had made for him. He liked beef. He hadn't told her where he was going. Sometimes he did, sometimes he didn't, whatever suited him. He had left her sewing on a star quilt she wanted to have ready for the powwows and fairs later in the summer. He polished off the sandwich before the flies ruined it, ate some commercial chocolate chip cookies, and drank a Coke. He didn't much like vegetables, so she hadn't included any. Then he wrapped up the debris in the paper bag and jammed it into the roots of the nearest juniper. Ranch-style recycling.

When he glassed the gulch again, he spotted four wolves sunning themselves under the north rim. So they were here. He set down his binoculars and examined the wolves through the scope of his rifle, which had better magnification. He examined that area closely, and decided the den was two or three hundred yards upslope and east, in a place he knew about. Once he had gotten out of a storm there in one of four or five hollows eroded into the stratified sandstone. All of the hollows contained evidence of animal habitation, including some lion scat.

He enjoyed the sight of the wolves in his scope. He was too distant to make out the details, or give them identities. But they were there. Others were no doubt out hunting. There was prey here if they knew how to get it. The Rosebud bottoms, three miles west, always had mule deer and sometimes whitetail, too. But this wasn't good antelope country. They depended on open land and speed to defend themselves. Still, there had been several antelope less than a mile back, before the land was too broken for them. And the wolves would know about them.

He backed off, having seen what he wanted to see, mounted the bay. He did not sheathe the rifle, choosing to carry it across his lap. The bay twitched as horseflies crawled its ears. Then he rode the way he had come, upward and eastward toward the grassy divide, looking for the antelope.

He found them where they had been, mostly sunning on a warm south-facing slope, with their sentinel on the ridge above. A horse, even one ridden by man, was less alarming to antelope than a vehicle or a man on foot, and the sentinel allowed him to come within two hundred yards of some of the grazing antelope. That would have to do. He sensed they would bolt at any second. He slowly dismounted, rested the rifle on the saddle to steady it, picked out a large animal in the crosshairs, and fired. He had never been a good shot, and now he waited curiously for the result, if any. The animal stood a moment, and then crumpled. That was fine with Trouble. He ejected the shell, watching the rest of the antelope race over the ridge and vanish. On second thought, he dismounted, picked up the shell, and stuffed it in his pocket.

Then he sheathed the rifle and rode back to his outfit, wondering why he had done that. And why tomorrow he would drive to the Rosebud drainage and shoot a mule deer if he could. There were some things, like religion, that one just did.

Then he drove back to the ranch house and put away the horse and trailer.

"I'm going to Busby," he told Mavis.

She eyed him curiously, and smiled.

He stopped in Ashland for a carton of Camels, and pushed across the res, through rough country whose beauty made his heart ache, through Lame Deer, and finally into Busby, where he felt the layers of responsibility peel away from him.

It was suppertime, and he debated what to do, finally deciding not to worry about it. David Gray Wolf would see him, no matter what the hour. Trouble did not know the young man, except by reputation. The man's name, Gray Wolf, sent a certain tremor through him. It was all coming together.

He found Gray Wolf's house where he knew it would be, on the north edge of the town. A weathered canvas lodge stood behind it, bleached white by years of sun and wind and snow. The house itself wasn't much, one of those minimal frame cubicles built by the government allegedly to give Indians a piece of the American Dream. It, too, had weathered until its tan paint had faded into a nondescript shade that made the house at last blend into the landscape. This would be a tribal house, and Gray Wolf was an employee, of sorts, of the People.

Trouble knocked, and was met by an unsmiling young man dressed in jeans and a blue denim shirt. The young man had parted his straight black hair severely and wore it in long glossy braids, the old way. He eyed Trouble patiently, no doubt knowing who had come visiting.

"Keeper of the Hat, I am John Trouble and I have come to see you," Trouble said, handing Gray Wolf the carton of Camels, the traditional tobacco gift. Gray Wolf was the current keeper of the Sacred Hat, one of the ancient and sacred relics of the tribe. It was a job no one wanted because the keeper could not leave the bundle, hanging in the lodge, and thus was chained to Busby by sacred obligation.

Within, Trouble could see faces staring. A wife, two half-grown children. He saw no sign of food.

Gray Wolf nodded, and stepped aside to let his guest in. The family smiled shyly and fled into the some other corner of the tiny house.

"I know nothing about the old ways," Trouble said. "I don't even know my own tongue."

Gray Wolf nodded. "There are others, dreamers, who could teach you more than I. You know who they are. But you have chosen me. Let's go outside," he said. "I have a place." He paused to collect a leather pouch, made of buffalo calfskin, and led his guest to a place not far from the ancient lodge.

Gray Wolf lowered himself into the grass, and Trouble sat opposite him. The young man slid an old pipe from its leather case—it was one of the Cheyenne sacred pipes, though Trouble couldn't say which. He'd ignored that stuff for thirty or forty years. This one had been carved from the red pipestone that came from Minnesota, like so many of the Plains pipes, and had a long hardwood stem. The bowl was unadorned.

Gray Wolf tamped tobacco into the bowl and lit it with a match and sucked until the tobacco caught. He did this leisurely, silently, and with a certain dignity that did not escape John Trouble. Then Gray Wolf lifted the pipe to the heavens, lowered it to the earth, and offered it to the four winds, all according to ancient ceremony. Then he smoked it and handed it to Trouble, who did the same thing. After that they jointly smoked the charge of tobacco in utter silence. When the last coal had died in the bowl, Gray Wolf slid the pipe back into its sheath.

"Today I shot an antelope to feed the wolves," Trouble said.

"There is not enough meat for the wolves?"

"Nichols took the cattle off. I was afraid the wolves would go away."

"You have come to see me," said Gray Wolf.

"Why did I do that? Shoot the antelope?"

"Kinship, maybe?"

"I don't know, I don't know none of that stuff. I make a good living."

"But you want to know why. The wolves will take your good living from you."

"I just felt like it, is all. What I want is . . . I want to learn about the old ways. I don't know anything."

"It takes years. You are in a rush. Maybe you shouldn't try to walk the path backwards."

"Maybe I shouldn't; I don't know."

"I'm not an elder and I shouldn't instruct you. But if you wish, I can take you a way down the path, and then you can go to a grandfather. Three live close. First, we will have a sweat and then we will talk, and then we'll plan the trip to *Noahvose*, Bear Butte. You must go there with three elders, a party of four, to listen and pray, and learn about Sweet Medicine and what was given to him."

"I don't know if I want to get into this." Bear Butte, the sacred mountain of the Cheyenne and other tribes, was clear over in South Dakota, just north of the Black Hills. A long way.

Gray Wolf nodded slightly and waited.

"I haven't had a sweat since I was a boy. When I was maybe twenty I said the hell with that stuff; it's another world now. But maybe I was wrong. The buffalo are coming and the fences are going down and the white men are leaving. Maybe we are at the end of the white men's time and going back to our time."

Gray Wolf gazed quietly.

"Long ago they gave me the winter-keeping robe, and I got it out a few weeks ago. Mavis, she thought I'm crazy. No one kept a winter since the 1930s, so I put in dots for missing years and named this the Winter of the Wolf and painted in a wolf head. Then I rolled it up again."

"Maybe it is a new time, maybe not," Gray Wolf said. "First we'll sweat. I hope you're not going anywhere."

"I'm here," Trouble said.

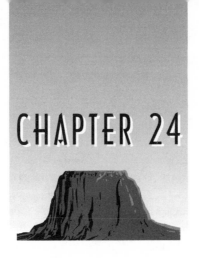

CHAPTER 24

Cameron stared bitterly at the carcass of one of the horned cattle he had put on the Antler Ranch after the registered stock had been hauled south. Joe Hardy had summoned him that hot morning, and he'd driven right over.

But this time things were a bit different. Fifty yards away lay a dead wolf with a large puncture wound just behind its rib cage. Flies gorged in the wound. Cameron photographed both carcasses, then shot a close-up of the brown-stained horn of the brindle steer, and then shot more close-ups of the puncture in the wolf.

"I figure these are holding off the wolves a little," Hardy said. "This here's the first, and we've been running 'em a month almost."

Cameron grunted. "I can't afford one a month. Get that extension agent down from Miles, and get this certified. Defenders of Wildlife should pay the whole ticket; this old steer wasn't worth more than seven hundred."

"They'll be paying a lot more if this keeps up, I guess," Hardy said.

"They'd better. They swore they would."

"Least this one killed him a wolf."

"That's not very promising. So they get a wolf now and then. So what?" Cameron was in a proddy mood.

"So, them horns work, I'm thinking," Hardy said. "This old brindle, he swung a horn right into the gut of that old wolf and probably lifted him ten feet into the sky. What you oughta do is run a thousand of the horned cattle, mean little scrubs, around here, and then you've got two things going. Every time a cow gets ate, bill the Defenders of Wildlife for it, and meanwhile maybe they'll kill a few wolves with those horns. This steer did before the pack got to him."

Cameron forced a smile. "I'm glad you're thinking. I need all the help I can get. We don't make money on scrub cattle, that's the problem.

You get the government, and see what they say, and I'll get out of here. I sort of like your idea of sticking it to Defenders of Wildlife."

Hardy laughed, and called Miles City on his cellular phone.

Cameron drove overland half a mile until he hit a two-rut ranch trail that would take him out of the Antler. He hoped he hadn't treated Hardy badly. Joe had been with him for a decade and was a solid, conscientious man with a family.

Cameron knew he wouldn't stick Defenders of Wildlife. The outfit was actually trying to help, in its own way, and Cameron had a grudging admiration for any bunch of Greens who'd back their ideals with hard cash. Most of them just denounced corporate America and propagandized. But that outfit was trying to build a bridge and make things work.

The truck rocked and lurched along the road, raising a plume of dust behind it. The ranch looked bad. Why hadn't the grass come up? Cameron stopped, got out, dropped a wire gate, went through, got out and hooked the loop over the post, closing it again, and headed west. He would go through three more gates before he hit the gravel road. Why did the goddamned ranch look like the surface of the moon?

He'd been in a lousy mood for days, and every time he entered his house and saw Sandy, it got worse. She'd absolutely refused to go to Billings for help, and he'd finally thrown up his hands and quit pushing. You couldn't force someone, you couldn't kidnap someone. You could only watch helplessly while the one you loved destroyed herself.

But he'd been toying with a new idea ever since DeeAnn and Mark had talked to him about taking over. What if he bought a condo in Billings, or a house, and they moved there? He could commute by air, twenty-five minutes, still run the ranch. Maybe Sandy would snap out of it once she got to town. Start some social life. Join some clubs. He'd encourage her. Maybe it'd work if she wasn't too far gone. Maybe it'd help a little, slow her boozing, something like that. There would be plenty to do there; she wouldn't be bored out of her mind.

The catch was money. He didn't know where he could get his hands on a hundred-twenty or -fifty thousand dollars. The old Nichols instinct to avoid bank debt flowered in him when he thought of the mortgage. Bank debt had sunk most of the dryland ranchers he knew; avoiding bank debt was the single thing that had enabled the Nichols family to survive out there.

The ranches might be worth millions, or they were until Horoney withdrew the offer, but they never earned much. Talk about rich ranchers with big net worth—that was a joke. His share of the meager profit from Nichols Ranches, along with the manager's wage the corporations paid him, came to thirty or forty thousand in a good year, twenty or less in a bad one, with housing thrown in. Two hundred twenty thousand acres for that. And what it came to is that he'd have to scratch hard, maybe cash an IRA, if he and Sandy were to move to Billings. But by God, he'd do that. He'd do anything to help her, take some risks if that would help.

He'd always consulted Sandy about everything, and he planned to talk the Billings house or condo over with her after he thought it through a little more. He could do it, somehow, even if he spent weekdays at the ranch and weekends in Billings. She'd perk up in town. Lots of interesting people there. And if she didn't like the social life, she had her pick of classes she could take, or even jobs she could work if she wanted. There was even a Junior League if that stuff interested her.

But now he wasn't so sure he should consult her. She'd been elaborately passive lately, deflecting all decisions and responsibilities back upon him in self-destructive—and maddening—ways. He decided he'd talk to her about the house—he'd always do that, treat her as a full partner, a competent adult, even when she no longer was. It pained him to think that. Well, by God, he'd offer to move, and by God, he'd do it anyway if she begged off. That begging off was a way of pouring sand in the gears, stopping their domestic life cold.

He hit the gravel road and cut south, heading for the Rimrock Ranch, which snugged along the northern border of Custer National Forest, its boundaries tortured and twisted like a wind-blasted pine above the snow line of Granite Peak. He hadn't talked with his manager there, Leon Hopper, the only bachelor among his managers—and the only college graduate, although most had had some ag schooling.

The Rimrock was entirely a steer operation, drawing its stock from other of the Nichols ranches. It lay in rough country, guarded by a lot of sandstone ridges, but it was also the most beautiful of all the ranches, with little green valleys watered by springs, and hidden gulches. It supported flocks of ducks in its marshes, Canada geese, weasels, badgers, meadowlarks, coyotes, and so many jackrabbits they sometimes robbed him of good grass. It was also loaded with ponderosa, which eliminated cow-calf operations. It wasn't good breeding ground, and they had learned not to run heifers on it because there were too many hiding places. Its one disadvantage was the presence of lions, and the big cats cost the ranches several steers a year. But better a steer than future breeding stock.

Cam loved that ranch more than the home ranch, but it was one of the most isolated of the group, and had been even before the neighbors cleared out and the foundation moved in. He left Leon pretty much alone; the man was reliable, and never needed prompting to rebuild some fence, or put out stock salt or mineral, or feed hay, or check the windmills, or vaccinate, or turn a sick steer into the pens beside his log house, or drive a steer into Broadus for help if a vet was needed.

Cam could never figure what inspired Leon, or how the man endured his lonely life. He didn't seem to miss women—at least as far as Cam could see. But he did take two weeks off every fall, and never said much about where he'd gone. Hopper was shy and taciturn—except on his favorite topics, and then he was garrulous. One of these was Indian relics. He'd turned himself into an anthropologist, and had collected astonishing materials from various sites, which he sifted through with all the skill and knowing of a trained archaeologist. That was all illegal now, but Leon probably excavated anyway, because the collection of potsherds, bone and stone tools, skulls of man and beast—including part of a jaw of a mammoth—that filled shelves in his log home, kept growing. Heaven knows, the Rimrock was proving to be an archaeologist's dream. Cameron had never seen Leon pick up so much as an arrowhead, and had never said a word to Leon about the law.

Leon's other passions were horses and traditional ranching. He would have nothing to do with an all-terrain vehicle, even less to do with a visored cap or athletic shoes, or artificial fabrics. Leon's accoutrements included the best-configured quarter horses he could find, a sheepskin coat, a weathered Stetson, high stitch-patterned boots with his jeans tucked inside, and a handlebar mustache with waxed points. Leon wouldn't have an iron squeeze chute or a gas-fired branding iron heater on the place. And he vaccinated only because Cam insisted on it. But Cam enjoyed all that. Each to his own.

Cam would have called ahead, but Leon wanted nothing to do with newfangled cellular phones, which the rest of his men carried outdoors, when riding or herding or haying or fencing. And the chances of catching Leon in his house during the day were about nil. But Cam intended to look things over, visit with his company recluse a while, and talk about the future. For some reason, Cam had always shared more information with Leon than with any of his other managers, except DeeAnn and Mark Cassady. He didn't know why; there was simply something about Leon that inspired candor.

Cam arrived at the ranch house late in the day. It lay on a tiny creek, Starvation, that bubbled out of the national forest to the south. He discovered Leon shoeing one of his lean quarter horses under the shade of a majestic cottonwood.

He watched silently while Leon worked amidst a swarm of green-bellied flies and a few black and biting horseflies, deflecting business until his manager had nailed shoes on the forefeet of the restless fly-besieged gelding.

"I guess that's enough for today," Leon said, stretching an aching back. He plucked up the old shoes, bristling with twisted nails, and checked the area for more nails. Then he put his gear into a wooden tote box. "I try to save me a flat tire," he said.

"Anything new?"

"Well, yes. Just this morning some bureaucrats came by. EPA fellows. I'd gone out to the hill to pick up a humped-up steer—he's the one in the pen—and they were here when I drove in."

"What did they want?"

"Oh, they were taking pictures of the pen and the creek running through it. I guess maybe they'll make you move the pen so the cowshit don't get in the water."

"I don't think so. There's thousands of pens like that in Montana, and we're pretty well grandfathered in. Did they ask permission to look around?"

"No, they were just poking around here. They were pretty decent fellows. I asked what they wanted, and they said I'd probably have to stop running springwater into the cabin. Seems I'm not supposed to drink that water. I'm supposed to have a deep enough well."

"How'd they know you've got springwater piped into the house?"

"Darned if I know. The pipe's buried from the house to the cliff. The drain goes into the creek. It just runs all the time unless I shut it off."

"You think they went into the house?"

"I expect they knocked and I wasn't there so they stuck their heads in."

"They can't do that."

"They must have done it. They had a bunch of little flasks with water samples in them."

Cameron sighed. "I think we're in for some trouble. The place has used that spring ever since it was built in the teens, but that's not going to help us any."

"I expect you're right, Cam."

"What did they say?"

"Oh, not a lot. But they were sure doing a lot of writing in a note-book."

"It's trouble. I just stopped by to see if you needed anything. Lose any steers?"

"No, it's quiet. Those wolves haven't arrived here yet."

"They killed some of the horned cattle I put up on the Antler. I just came from there. But you know, Leon, one of those wolves paid for it with a horn through his gut."

"Well, that's good news. If I were you, Cam, I'd be selling off the Herefords and running longhorns instead. Those horns, man, have you ever thought about what those pitchforks would do to a wolf? Or what a bunch of longhorns, circled like an old wagon train against Indians, could do to protect their calves?"

"Longhorns!"

"Yeah, they're a breed now. A whole association bred them up, put some meat on those long frames, but they're still the old devils from the open-range days. You ever read old Frank Dobie's book about long-horns? He says they're the only cattle that are up to snuff when it comes to dealing with lobo wolves, and that they'd just get themselves in a circle, those horns lowered, and hold off the wolves. He says they're as good as buffalo at dealing with wolves. Cam, how'd you feel if you were a wolf and you had to wade through a wall of those horns to get your meat? Man, Cam, that'd be a sight."

"Longhorns!"

"Yeah, you can maybe make money at them now they're bred up. Better carcass weight, but the good thing is you can sell every pair of horns you raise, for anywhere from twenty-five to fifty an animal, depending on those horns. People lap them up."

"By God," said Cam, "maybe you're onto something."

"Cam, I don't think there's enough loose longhorns around to stock even one of your ranches. And the ones you see today are bred different, not so ornery. Maybe you'd better experiment first."

"Not much time for experiments," Cam said. "But I'll try anything."

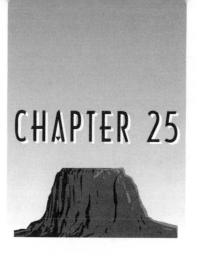

CHAPTER 25

Deirdre walked over to Dudley's house, along with Mark, as her father had asked her to do that June evening. Something was up, but Cameron hadn't said just what. It would have to do with the crisis that was lowering over the Nichols ranches.

"Evening, DeeAnn, Mark," her father said.

Dudley grunted something and sipped bourbon on the rocks. "Pour yourselves a drink," her grandfather said.

Neither of the Cassadys took him up on it.

"What's up?" she asked.

"Maybe a way out. Let's see what you think," Cameron said.

A way out sounded just fine to Deirdre.

"All this began a few days ago when Joe Hardy called me to report a wolf killing—one of the common cattle we have up there now. But the thing was, that steer killed one of the wolves—drove a horn through its gut."

Cameron described the whole episode, while DeeAnn listened skeptically. So a wolf died. So what?

"I talked to Leon on the way back here. He had an interesting idea. He said longhorns can fight off wolves. It's all in J. Frank Dobie's classic, *The Longhorns,* so I read it and made a lot of calls around the state—and the whole country—before I was done.

"The old Texas longhorns were ferocious around wolves. They'd form a ring around their calves, lower those horns, and dare a pack of wolves to take that calf. Those horns typically ranged four feet, some oxbowed, some corkscrewed, some just cockeyed, some pointing up, some straight out, some forward. The biggest horns ran over eight feet. They were so heavy the beast could hardly lift his head. Horns on steers ran larger than horns on bulls and cows. They were so big it took a lot of feed just to grow the horns, but the result was an animal that could flourish in the wild, handled wolves and even bears."

"Cameron," said Dudley, "we can't go back to longhorns. They're all bone, no meat, and take forever to grow—three, four years, I think. We'd go broke."

"Well, that's the downside of it, Dad, and there's more. There aren't many longhorns around. It's an exotic breed, mostly bred for fun and to sell the horns. They're tough to ship because of those horns. Can't get 'em into a cattle truck unless you twist their heads half off. Same with cattle cars. And once you crowd 'em all together, you end up with puncture wounds. The same horns that fend off wolves are a menace to people and horses. And you can't run them through the usual squeeze chute, either. Not only that, but there's some question about whether a modern longhorn, which has improved blood in it, would be as feisty around wolves as the skinny, mean, wild beasts that had grown up in the brush of Texas. In other words, maybe the old-time longhorns did fend off wolves, but there's no saying that the modern ones would. The breed pretty near died out, but the government preserved a few, and a few remained in Texas and Oklahoma that some folks who wanted to preserve the breed used as foundation stock.

"What do you think?"

"We'd have our own zoo in the middle of Horoney's zoo," Dudley said.

DeeAnn detected some pleasure in her grandfather's voice. He was a cattleman more than anything else, and if it took longhorns to keep on going, he'd go for longhorns.

"What are you proposing, Dad?" she asked.

"Trying it. Stocking the North Ranch and Antler with longhorns. Maybe they'll drive off or even kill all the wolves in the neighborhood."

"Not very likely," Dudley said. "I read Dobie fifty years ago; grand book. Guess I'll reread it. Where do we get longhorns?"

"In small quantities all over. It'll mean selling off some Herefords."

"Is this a losing proposition?"

"More'n likely. They need maybe three years on pasture before maturity, more than double the time it takes us to raise a feeder steer. We'll have trouble selling them as feeders. We'll have trouble selling them to stockyards—all for the same reason. The horns. The problem of hauling them. The veterinary bills. We're going to have to customize our stock trucks to load animals like that. And forget about modern ranching, squeeze chutes, all that."

Dudley grinned. "Well, if the Horoney Foundation wants to yank us back a hundred fifty years, we can join 'em."

Deirdre wasn't so sure. "What good is it if we lose money?" she asked. "We've got to make money or get out. We've always depended on the best ag science we could find, not history books about mythical Texas cattle. Grass management, water management, upgrading stock."

"Well, there's some new angles," Cameron said. "The horns sell—that's a premium. And if the horns are unusual, a good corkscrew, an odd unbalanced pair, or just plain big, they command big bucks. Someone'll want 'em to put in their den."

DeeAnn remained doubtful. "What good would this do if the government gets rid of the wolves, as we've asked?"

"That'd be temporary. Once Horoney's foundation finishes rolling up wire and resting the land and taking down buildings and buying buffalo, and once the government reintroduces elk and bear to the plains, the wolves'll be back—either reintroduced, or drifting in."

"You think maybe the longhorns are our only option."

"I'm not saying that. Maybe J. Frank Dobie's stories are more legend and myth than reality. Maybe modern longhorns have been bred into docile, fat cattle. Maybe we'd take a real beating, selling prize Herefords for some longhorns. Maybe we should raise llamas or elephants."

"They sure are pretty," Dudley said. "Brindles and blues, and blacks, and duns, and mottled, and red-browns, and every other earth color. Look at one and you think it's the ugliest, most misshapen thing you ever saw, with big shoulder hump and skinny butt, but look at a herd, and see all those horns, and all the color, there's no sight like it."

"About all we could count on is higher shipping costs, beef that takes a long time to raise, a lot of horn injuries, and we'd need more manpower to wrestle down an animal if we don't have chutes anymore," she said.

"If you want an in-law's opinion, I'd like to try it," said Mark Cassady. "But maybe just one ranch at a time. Maybe the Antler first."

"They'll put us into the hospital. What happens if someone like Joe Hardy gets gored?" she argued.

"They'd all have the choice to stay on or not," Dudley said. "I'd guess someone like Leon would be tickled half to death to run a longhorn outfit."

"One step at a time," Cameron said. "If it's no good, we'll back out. Do we agree?"

No one disagreed.

"Longhorns!" exclaimed Deirdre, and the others laughed.

"You're an old-time cowgirl now, DeeAnn," her grandfather said.

"Running guided tours across our ranches to keep from going under," she replied. But something about the old Texas cattle tickled her.

"I've something else to talk to you about," Cameron said gravely.

They settled back in Dudley's gaudy cowhide chairs.

"I'm going to be buying a place—maybe a town house—in Billings. It's become necessary. We'll move there. I'll be around, fly over here and keep on working, but I'd like to turn most of it over to you, DeeAnn and Mark. I plan to keep the ranch house, maybe stay in it weekdays and fly or drive to Billings weekends."

DeeAnn watched her grandfather draw into himself, which was how he dealt with anything unsettling to him. The news didn't surprise her. She and Mark had been hoping for something like this, as much for her father's sake as for her mother's.

"Will it do any good?" she asked.

"I don't know. Nothing else does. I tried to take her to the dry-out place, and she stonewalled that. She's bored and lonely here—especially since we've lost our neighbors and everything's fallen apart. I think that even if she got dried out and counseled and all the rest, she'd slide right back into trouble if she came back here. She's a city gal, and she's braved the country all her life, did fine until recently. I think moving's the only out." Cameron turned to Deirdre. "You and Mark up to running this outfit?"

"I thought you were going to fly here."

"I am. I'll be here constantly. But I'll still be more and more of an absentee manager. I'm not quitting, and I'm not asking the corporations to find someone else—not now. But I've got to do something about Sandy before there's nothing left to do."

"Dad, it's a good idea. Mark and I'll help any way we can."

"Dudley?"

Her grandfather nodded abruptly. He was the sort of old-timer who couldn't bear to air dirty linen, and now he had the look of a man itching to change the subject.

"I can do a lot in Billings," Cam said. "Close to the stockyards."

"Does Mom know?"

"No. I thought I'd make sure you've no objections first."

"Would she resist?"

Cameron nodded sadly. "Yes, but it'd be the charade she's been doing for years. It's really what she'd want, but she'd never admit it to me. All she ever says is that she's a Nichols, and everything's fine. But I'm just going to go ahead and do it."

DeeAnn saw a helplessness in her father's face. She had scarcely ever seen despair in a man she admired as one of the strongest and most courageous and thoughtful she'd ever known. Impulsively, she gripped Mark's hand and squeezed hard.

"What'll you do in Billings?"

"Entertain. Your mother loves company. That's all I can do for now."

"What if she—you know—drinks too much at these parties?"

"I'm sure she will at first. We're facing some embarrassments. She'll blow the cooking, blow everything. We've so many friends in Billings, and they'll be patient. I believe your mother's a strong and courageous woman, and I think that she'll heal herself when she finds herself out of the trap she's been in for so long. Someday soon she'll awaken to the fact that she's not isolated; she can live the life she wants."

"You don't really believe that. An alcoholic—"

"I believe it. Your mother's special."

There was something in the way her father said it that brought DeeAnn almost to tears.

"Luck," she said, wishing she had her father's faith and optimism.

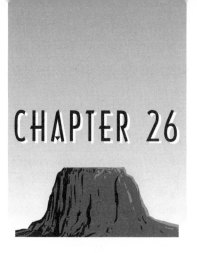

CHAPTER 26

Day by day, Dolly Horoney watched Laslo wrestle with a territory that, when both phases were complete, would be as large as the country of his birth. She had always had her doubts about pouring such a fortune into the desolate High Plains, and could not help but wonder what good would come of it.

If she was a convert now, it was only because she had educated herself and had listened to Laslo's corps of experts and enthusiasts. Almost every schoolchild in the nation ached to see a National Grassland Trust full of buffalo and elk. For most Americans, the project seemed almost miraculous. Some saw it as a way of preserving the past. Others saw it in pure ecological terms. Still others saw it as a vast petting zoo full of nice animals. A few hunters saw it as a place to safari for Boone and Crockett trophies, better than the African savannas. Some saw it as a way of preserving and restoring precious topsoil. A very few who knew a great deal about the fortunes of nations, knew that a country's real wealth was grass, and the nations that nurtured their grasslands into thick healthy turf were the nations blessed to prosper.

Some others, the alienated and the people-haters, rejoiced in a wilderness that would soon be beyond the reach of capitalism and commerce and human greed and the Chamber of Commerce mentality they despised. A few others thought that perhaps it would all become Indian lands, and the tribes would restore their ancient ways of life in that vast territory that lay adjacent to several reservations. Weird Californians had opined that the grassland would emanate a great spirit of tranquility and healing that would affect the psyches of all the world's family, and achieve psychic unity and peace so everyone would become brothers and sisters.

Dolly had become aware of all these strands of thought and belief whirling around Laslo's great enterprise. Her instincts had always been to help people, not nature. At her prompting, a decade earlier Laslo had invested five million dollars in a pilot program for the homeless in Los Angeles. She had considered that the wisest and kindest employment of wealth—until their project collapsed upon the rocks of reality. They had acquired an old hospital building, renovated it, hired a staff, and opened their doors to the homeless, who could find within it shelter, food, clothing, job training, psychiatric and medical care, counseling, job networking, family assistance, and more.

But it never worked properly and its success rate was dismal. It was ultimately crushed between two millstones. On the one hand, the federal, state and county bureaucracies harassed the project with regulations that drove costs into the stratosphere. Politically correct bean counters insisted that the facility abandon its effort to serve whoever walked in, and serve only a proper mix of homeless based on gender, race, ethnicity, age, and sexual orientation. That was especially tough because there were virtually no Chinese or Japanese homeless. The result was to leave the facility half-empty on any given day to placate the bureaucrats and their quota system.

On the other hand, many of the homeless preferred their way of life, resisted employment, medicine, counseling, and detoxification, using the facility only for a flop and a meal. Matters weren't helped when police prowled the place looking for rapists and burglars, while on the other hand some of the homeless victimized others, attacked nurses and counselors, sold narcotics in the halls, and otherwise abused their succor. After a flurry of lawsuits, insurance hassles, bad publicity, bureaucratic ukases and licensing threats, and revolving-door staff turnover, Laslo and Dolly had quietly shut it down—which made half of Los Angeles furious and caused the newspapers to condemn the callous rich.

After all that effort, they had permanently helped thirty-seven people find new lives—Dolly treasured thank-you letters from three of them—and had randomly fed and housed and medicated several thousand people for the three years the foundation had wrestled the scourge of homelessness. That was a small harvest for an expenditure that ultimately reached thirteen million. Religious groups operating on a shoestring had done better, and she and Laslo had spent hours at such storefront centers, watching faith and love and belief in the healing power of God do more than all his dollars and experts could do.

The experience had left Dolly and Laslo feeling burned-out and discouraged as well as cynical about the "helping professions." Both believed that massive bureaucracies and foolish ideologies were gravely impairing the genius and generosity of the nation. They had also discovered the perversity of human nature, and the futility of trying to help people bent on self-destruction. It had turned Laslo toward Christian religion, which he pursued sporadically and tenderly, as the only truly healing force, while Dolly, the agnostic, mostly argued with herself and wondered why she could come up with so few answers to life's puzzles.

The National Grassland Trust had turned out to be only slightly less controversial, and quite the reverse of what she had expected. Most of those who had sold their properties to the trust were grateful for an easy escape from an unwelcoming and cruel land, while those who most desired a national buffalo commons had become the most vocal critics of the foundation. Not in a million years, she told herself, would she expect that.

She came to the vision of a restored High Plains reluctantly, finding the restoration of barren land and buffalo herds less soul-stirring than helping people. And yet she gamely kept up with Laslo, listened to his skilled agronomists and biologists, until their vision had nested within her, and she had absorbed Laslo's passion as her own. His odd leap of logic—or leap of faith, really—that a restored grassland would somehow heal some of the derangement of American society, eluded her.

One day she found him studying a Bible, as excited as a child. He had her sit and listen to what he was discovering: that both testaments taught a doctrine of stewardship, of resting the land, of leaving some of the harvest for the poor and for wildlife, of fertilizing trees and plants. He had found not a word that might justify unbridled exploitation of the earth, and had concluded that environmentalists erred in blaming a Judeo-Christian ethos for the damage done to the natural world. If the damage had been done by nominally Christian businesses and families, it was in direct contradiction to the precepts he was finding in both testaments.

Laslo had shared his insight with his colleagues, and it had become another strike against him among those adherents of Green religion for whom the natural world was Good, and man was Evil. Curious about his discovery, she had done her own research and come to the same conclusion. Biblical texts ranging from Mosaic law to Christ's parables denounced exploitation and favored stewardship. Why did the Greens demonize the dominant religious belief in America? Was the idea of stewardship itself suspect?

The news that the Nichols family had decided to hang on, and that their decision was influencing scores of landholders within the proposed trust boundaries, had discouraged her as much as it had Laslo. She had become, almost by osmosis, the foundation's spokeswoman, and now she wrestled with public perceptions of the foundation's failure, as well as Laslo's frustration. She finally issued a simple release saying that the National Grassland Trust was disappointed but would continue to develop the grassland regardless of the choices of other landholders.

"Laslo," she asked at dinner one evening, "why don't you just put the bison on? I think once the herd's grazing, everything'll fall in place."

"Legal problems," he said. "Hector's working them out one by one. The oil companies want their oil patches fenced and want fenced easements. We're opposed to fencing the easements, but we'll fence the oil fields if we have to. Some of the electrical co-ops in the area want to take down transmission lines before we stock the grassland. But the biggest thing now is that suit. Their attorneys have asked a Montana court for a permanent injunction prohibiting stocking the grassland."

"Oh, Laslo . . ."

He shrugged. "I know, but we'll get past all that. Hector's opposing the injunction, but he says the district judge's not a bit sympathetic to the foundation or the project. We'll probably have to appeal."

"Can they tie it up?"

Laslo grinned. "The buffalo, maybe, for a while. But meanwhile the land's getting a rest, and we're rooting out sagebrush and Russian olives and planting bluestem. We've planted over ten thousand acres of former wheat farmland. Some of the pasture's had a two-year rest, and some one year, but we still have twenty percent of the land to acquire and work on. And the proposed injunction won't stop the state from reintroducing elk or bear. And we've a long way to go before we roll up all the barbed wire and dismantle the last building."

"It's another delay, though. We'll be old before we see the dream become real."

"If I die, the work will continue. I've drawn up the papers."

"You're young."

"Who's to say what tomorrow will bring?"

"Do you think if the Nicholses pulled out, the rest would fall in place?"

"I think so, except for some commercial problems, like the oil patches and utilities."

"I'd like to invite Cameron and Sandra Nichols to La Jolla for a weekend. Send the Gulfstream up for them."

Laslo paused over his medallion of beef. "I don't know how they'd take it. Cam Nichols is an angry man."

"That's for them to decide. Let's invite them. I like them."

"What about Sandra?"

"She's a gracious woman who'll offer no trouble."

"What do you expect will come from it?"

"I'll surprise you. Not what you think. A friendship."

He grinned. "And of course a nudge or two in the direction of the grassland?"

"Only if they bring up the topic and talk about it."

"Let me see if I'm free."

He was; they could entertain any weekend in July.

She called, wondering which one of the Nicholses would answer, and whom she should ask. She got Sandra.

Dolly introduced herself and worked past the weather and the preliminaries.

"I'm calling to invite you and Cameron to La Jolla for a weekend. Lovely weather there, always is. We'll send the plane for you."

"Oh," Sandra said. Dolly could almost hear Sandra's mind whirling.

"We enjoyed your hospitality and would like to share ours," Dolly said.

Sandra mumbled something. She probably wasn't very sober.

"Ask Cameron," Dolly said. "Or I will, if you'd like."

"He's in Billings," Sandra said. "He's been there all week, doing things. Who knows what he does?"

"We'd love to fly you to La Jolla on Friday June thirtieth, and return you Sunday, the second. Would you let us know?"

"Yes."

"Would you write down our private number?"

Sandra repeated it back to Dolly, her voice only slightly slurred.

The next day Dolly heard from Cameron. "We'll come," he said. "I had to talk Sandy into it. It'll be a great weekend, and we'll enjoy your company. I'm eager to hear about what you and Laslo are going to do."

"We're just hoping to get to know you and Sandra, Cameron. You have so much to teach us and share with us."

"Well, that's certainly mutual. You make the arrangements, and let us know, and we'll be at the airport."

Dolly hung up, feeling she had set something good in motion.

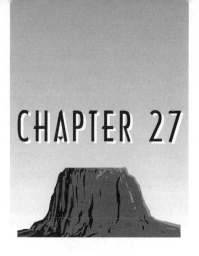

CHAPTER 27

Professor Peter Andrew Brooke-Carson had been looking forward to this little tête-à-tête a long time. He lamented that Bozeman hadn't a decent restaurant. This would be an important meeting, and he wanted all the edge he could get.

The formidable lady across the table from him held some of the keys to success. J. Shirley Thorn was a deputy director of the Environmental Protection Agency and headed its Montana field office in Helena. Professor Brooke-Carson vibrated with the thought of being so close to such power.

"So good of you to come," he purred, after they'd ordered. "We've so much to talk about. You're a most accommodating woman, driving all the way over here just to talk to an ecology professor. I must say, you're simply radiant. Your job must agree with you."

"Cut the bull," she said.

He laughed gallantly. "Right to the point. Very well. I want to talk about the Horoney business."

"Everyone does."

"I, ah, have been both encouraged and dismayed by it all."

"Why?"

"Because, well, it's such a grand idea, swiftly going haywire."

"How?"

"Well, that's a long story. Perhaps we should tackle these Caesars first?"

"I didn't come to Bozeman to eat salad."

"Well, first I'd like to say that the EPA is doing a brilliant job. Thanks to you, I think the High Plains'll be rescued from a century of abuse. It's plain that Horoney's foundation couldn't do it alone and needs the muscle of the federal government."

"Is that why you invited me to lunch?"

"Well, partly. I think grateful citizens should thank federal officers who are making a dream come true."

"Odd, but I've thought all along that Laslo Horoney's vision of a restored High Plains is what's making it come true."

"Well, his instincts are mostly good, but of course what he can achieve can't ever meet our goals."

"Whose goals?"

"Our goals." Brooke-Carson smiled amiably. "An entire restored ecosystem."

"Whose goal is that?"

"The goal of every American worried about environmental catastrophe on our little spaceship Earth."

"It's not the EPA's goal, Professor."

That dumbfounded Brooke-Carson. "How could it not be?"

"EPA's not in the business of restoring ecosystems or wilderness. We're not in the business of managing land, or removing American citizens from their ranches and homes."

"But of course you'd like to. It's only because a benighted Congress won't grant you the means."

She smiled for the first time. "Professor, our mission is to create a clean, safe, nontoxic environment to protect citizens from pollutants; and to help the U.S. Fish and Wildlife Service to protect endangered species and their habitats."

"Well, we're on common ground after all. Now, confidentially, I want to tell you that the federal classification of the whole proposed National Grassland area as wolf habitat was a stroke of genius. It'll drive out the last of the diehards, like Nichols Ranches. It'll restrain what the Horoney industrialists can do with the land."

"I opposed the designation. It was imposed on that area from Washington over my objections."

"You opposed it?"

"It's a clumsy, heavy-handed way of making life unbearable for good citizens, like the Nichols family. It's based on the flimsiest imaginable rationale. One is historical. Wolves once populated the High Plains. The other is just as weak: two packs of wolves have recently been discovered on the Nichols ranches, supposedly making them habitat. Where does that give the government the right to ruin a productive ranching enterprise by taking the control of its property?"

Brooke-Carson could hardly believe his ears. "But it stops agribusiness from damaging the range; it helps the foundation consolidate—"

"Nichols Ranches aren't ruining their range. They've worked with us for years. Before they began spraying to eradicate sagebrush they consulted with us. Their grazing land is in better shape than it was a decade ago."

"I question that, Ms. Thorn. You mustn't trust the work of county extension agents when it comes to evaluating rangeland. They're paid to help agribusiness."

"That's not the point. The point is, the EPA's been damaging itself because of an excess of zeal. There have been some highly publicized cases in which the EPA's trampled on the rights of citizens, and the agency is determined to stop it before Congress cuts us off at the knees."

"Well, of course, some abuse is always going to occur, but that shouldn't deter your agency from its mission, which is to save the planet."

"Professor, we're not in the planet-saving business. The Supreme Court has rebuked agencies like us for taking control of private land without compensating the owners. The Constitution clearly prohibits the government from taking private land without just compensation. And the courts have consistently ruled that when we impose habitat restrictions on private landowners, effectively denying them their rights as owners, we're taking their land from them, and they must be paid or we must back off. That strikes me as a valid argument, even though most of my colleagues disagree."

Brooke-Carson stabbed at his salad, feeling himself suddenly in the hands of a typical bureaucrat more interested in rubber stamps and office politics than in the things that would rescue the world.

"I'll tell you something else," she continued, relentlessly. "The wolf biologist who's been looking into the wolf packs on the Nichols ranches, Sanford Kouric, has completed a report that is now circulating in EPA, USFWS, ADC, the Forest Service, Park Service, and Ag Department. It's an internal document so I can't show it to you, but I'll tell you what's in it—in confidence, of course.

"Kouric makes several points: one is that wolf habitat must be defined by food supply, and there isn't enough game—mostly wild ungulates—in that area to support very many wolves, and that the area can be defined as habitat only by including domestic cattle as prey. If U.S. Fish and Wildlife insists on making its temporary habitat designation permanent, it'll be sitting on a time bomb. What would the public think of that, professor? A habitat designation based on cattle as wolf meat?"

Brooke-Carson knew Kouric, and didn't trust him. "Well, of course, that's one man's opinion. His background is agricultural, you know, a bias there."

"I grew up on a ranch in Idaho. That makes me biased."

"Well, don't read anything into my observation that isn't there, Ms. Thorn."

"You didn't really answer my question: what would the public think of a federal habitat designation that depends on domestic livestock to justify itself?"

"These things can be kept internal."

She laughed shortly. "There's more. Kouric's studies of both packs led him to the belief that the wolves were planted there, and didn't migrate. The packs are odd, atypical, the age and sex mix is wrong, and appeared at first to be without clear alpha males and females. The DNA patterns of the two collared wolves don't relate to any Yellowstone or Glacier Park wolves. Kouric believes the packs were smuggled in from Alberta, probably by a wealthy environmental activist—it takes big bucks to smuggle live wolves."

"Who is it?"

"You'd like to know, of course, so you can warn away someone who's maybe contributed to Green causes. But no, that's not for you. My point is otherwise. If the wolves on the Nichols ranches were planted, that makes the federal habitat designation even less supportable. I suspected something like that from the beginning, but was overruled, and now it looks like the EPA and Fish and Wildlife are setting themselves up for trouble in Congress and the courts because of their stupid, impulsive, opportunistic attempt to drive out the Nichols family."

"Well, of course, those are technical difficulties. But no one needs to know about them. As you say, this is an internal document. And Kouric is just one voice."

"He's the best wolf biologist in the federal government."

"But he's not—really dedicated to saving the environment."

"And you are."

She said it with such irony that he laughed uneasily.

"Now, just suppose that Sanford Kouric were to leak his report to the press," she continued. "It'd get him in trouble with his superiors, but he's man enough to endure trouble. I admire him. He's a relentlessly honest scientist. Or suppose that he testifies as a private citizen against the permanent habitat designation at the forthcoming hearings in Miles City. Just suppose he lets the world know that Fish and Wildlife, along with EPA, have more or less fabricated the wolf-habitat designation out of tissue paper. Then what, Professor?"

"I see. Yes, we'd all be damaged. But you can prevent that, I'm sure. USFWS could promote him. You could get contradicting opinions—"

"I don't wish to prevent it. I'm encouraging my superiors to abandon the wolf-habitat proposal."

"But if you do, the diehards won't leave the grassland."

"That's an interesting point. The diehards won't leave their land unless the government ties up their property and renders it useless to them—all with an essentially fraudulent habitat designation."

"You make it sound worse than it is. It's simply a minor expedient to benefit an ecosystem that's so besieged, so devastated, that serious people doubt that it can ever be restored."

"I'm talking about rights. The rights of ordinary citizens in their unending struggle against government excess. Rights guaranteed them by a millennium of English and American common law including the Magna Carta, the U.S. Constitution and Declaration of Independence, rights guaranteed them by subsequent judicial interpretation of that law, and rights guaranteed by the constitution and law of Montana."

"Coming from you, that's quite a surprise, Ms. Thorn."

"Professor, do citizens have rights or don't they?"

"You have to put things in perspective. Of course they do, but the world is falling apart. The planet's being incinerated. Species are vanishing, never to return. Habitat is vanishing. Unless the government makes some severe moves soon, there won't be anything left—no rights to worry about. All I'm saying is, we have to put first things first, assign some hierarchy to the various desired values. And right now, some abstract eighteenth-century ideals are just about at the bottom of any serious thinker's list."

"The rights and freedom of Americans are high on my list. Unfortunately, not many people in EPA agree with me."

Something about the witch annoyed Brooke-Carson almost beyond endurance. She was not only a classical rubber-stamp bureaucrat, but she lacked vision. And she was subverting the mission of her agency. He thought he'd finish up this miserable lunch and then get word to the alleged wolf smuggler to cool it.

"Well, what I really wish is that the population of the world would decline by ninety percent," he said tersely. "If it were ten percent of what it is now, I wouldn't worry about rights. Maybe AIDS will do the job; I hope so. But with the planet so crowded, and extinctions occurring daily, and global warming, and oxygen depletion, and the destruction of the biosphere, I hardly think that scruples about archaic rights amount to much."

"That's what separates us, Professor. I've been assigned to this field office to curb excesses. For several years, the EPA's been in hot water because of its penchant for abusing citizens. The administrator finally put several people like me in key slots for a very important reason. Congress has put us on notice that if we continue to abuse citizens, we'll have our wings clipped. I don't want that. Our biggest problem is people like you egging us on. I accepted your luncheon invitation to let you know."

Brooke-Carson stared at her, full of loathing. How did they let such a creature in the door? He could see that the Environmental Protection Agency needed radical reform.

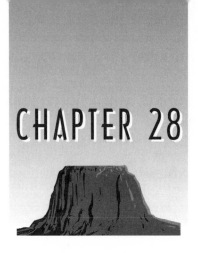

CHAPTER 28

Finding a house wasn't easy. Finding a pleasant neighborhood wasn't easy either. Billings was a misbegotten city that managed to make itself as ugly as possible. Cameron knew where he would like to locate; the area snugged under the rimrock on the northwest side of town was comfortable, sunny, and had a view. But it was also the most expensive.

Prices shocked him. What he thought might be a seventy-five-thousand-dollar house would be tagged at two hundred. He didn't know how he could manage. He had lived much of his life in a Nichols corporation house, and had no home equity. The Nichols family was theoretically rich, if one looked at the value of the land, but the dryland ranches hadn't ever yielded much income, and he hadn't saved much. His story wasn't much different from that of all the other ranchers in Montana: they all struggled to survive, fought off debt, rolled with the punch when bad weather or low beef prices or grasshoppers hit, and then retired rich when they sold off their outfits for a million or two or three and headed for Sun City.

After consulting various real estate brokers, with names like Floyd and Donny and Sissy, he retreated to town houses. These turned out to be more pleasant than he thought, and he eyed one just off Poly Drive that looked good: two bedrooms, a den, an island kitchen, a fireplace, built in 1995. He could summon fifty thousand by cashing most of what he'd set aside for retirement, and run a seventy-five thousand mortgage. If the bankers would let him. He wondered about that.

Even more did he wonder how Sandy would react. Or not react at all. He dreaded the shrug, the passive surrender, the "whatever you want's fine with me, Cam." He wanted her to take back her life and manage it. He wanted her to make a home, and he worried that the small town house—it was only a third the size of their rambling ranch house—wouldn't seem home to her.

She had grown up among the elite of Butte: power-company executives, railroad men, Anaconda's moguls back when Anaconda was still an imperial enterprise that bought and sold legislatures. But that had long since vanished, when Anaconda had been swallowed by an oil company and became little more than a footnote in its annual reports to stockholders. Even so, Sandy had been part of Butte's elite, if such a thing existed in a place where every window in town opened onto an ugly headframe of a mine, and rich and poor neighborhoods were jammed cheek by jowl, and labor-union executives were richer than some poor power-company official like her father.

How would she react to an anonymous town house, that lacked individuality, that offered little chance for her to stamp her self, her tastes, her essence, upon it? Sandy needed a *home,* and he wondered if this would suffice. He crawled with doubts, and made one last prowl through older neighborhoods near the university, off Virginia Lane. There indeed he located a spacious home for a hundred forty-five, built in the fifties, maple floors, high ceilings, lousy old kitchen but a fine dining room ideal for entertaining. The place begged for renovation. She might like that better. He asked the broker to hold it for forty-eight hours.

He drove up to the airport, cranked up his Cessna, ran through the preliminaries, got clearance, took off into the westwind, circled south over Billings, and then pointed the plane on a heading of ninety-five degrees. He was going to be doing a lot of flying from now on—if Sandy agreed to move. But what if she didn't? He felt so helpless. He couldn't give her a life if she didn't want to live one. He couldn't give her a home if she wouldn't make one. He couldn't give her will if she had abandoned will. And yet . . . if she could not or would not respond, he would do what he could, regardless. He would bring her to a place where she had friends and they could make new ones. He would entertain, even if she didn't participate. He would engage her in a continuous round of activities—music, plays, movies, charities, speakers, golf, whatever it took. Maybe, somehow, he could awaken whatever had been buried in the placid isolation of the home ranch.

A half hour later he throttled down, pulled back the yoke, and settled the Cessna on his carefully scraped dirt runway that topped a ridge above the ranch. He tied down and headed through a silent, glowing summer afternoon toward the house.

He found her watching a soap opera, or seeming to. An empty glass stood beside her.

She smiled, absently, and he knew intuitively she was too drunk to respond coherently. But he had to try. He zapped the TV with the remote and settled on the couch, opposite her.

"Sandy, I've been house-hunting in Billings."

"Nice," she said.

"I'm hoping we can move to Billings."

"Whatever you say, Cam."

"I don't think you're hearing me. Would you like to move to Billings? A new home? Old friends and some new ones?"

"If you think it's a good idea."

"Sandy. We need a social life. It'd be good to get off the ranch and be with friends again. I've worked it out—I'll fly over here. Billings is just a commute."

"Whatever you say, Cam."

She maddened him. He could hardly bear to hear that. "Please don't say that. I want to talk to you about the house. What would you like?"

"It's up to you."

"Sandy! It's not just up to me. We're in a partnership, and we're talking about your happiness."

"I'm happy."

He quieted himself down, feeling defeat roil through him. "If you could have a house in a city, would you like something small and simple and easy to keep, like a town house, or would you like something larger and more traditional?"

This time she didn't answer at all. She reached for the glass and swallowed the residue of ice in its bottom. Then she smiled.

"I've been looking at a house that might remind you of your family's house in Butte. It's old, and needs repair, but it's got some comforts."

"Our house in Butte went into the pit."

A lot of Butte, including some of its most historic districts, went into the huge Anaconda pit on the east edge of town. Then the company stopped mining in Butte altogether, driven out by low copper prices and astronomic labor costs, and the pit began to fill with water. Now it was nothing but a great, polluted hole.

"You loved that old house, Sandy. Would you like something like it now?"

"Whatever you want."

"Would you like to go see the one I'm looking at?"

She stared out the window for so long he wondered whether she had heard him.

"If you'd like to show it to me," she said.

His spirits rose. That was the first sign of something, anything, and it filled him with hope. "We'll fly over in the morning," he said.

She didn't reply. Instead, she stood, steadied herself, and headed for the kitchen and the bottle.

He sat desolated. What a long downhill slide it had been for her, and for him. He blamed himself: he should have seen it long before, and figured out what had been eating her. Now it was too late.

He retreated to his office and continued his other project—finding enough longhorns to stock just one of his ranches. He needed a thousand, and he would take whatever he could get: bulls, cows, steers, bred heifers, calves, yearlings. And he was going to have to sell blooded Hereford stock to do it. And he was going to take a beating no matter what he did, because shipping longhorns from all over the West in whatever trucks and cattle cars could handle them would not be cheap. He spent the night on the phone, running down a list of names provided him by Willis Parker, head of a longhorn breeders' association down in Texas. He dickered for cattle sight unseen. He wanted horns and horns and horns, and maybe a little beef behind the horns. That night he lined up a hundred fifty more, and got a line on an Oklahoma hauler who could carry them in single-deck stock trucks with rear gates that swung wide open.

"We haul anything, including them longhorns, Mr. Nichols," the man said. "And we'll take care of them horns. Tape a rubber ball on each tip, stuff like that."

Cam had never heard of that, but it suited him, so he closed the deal.

The next morning he hurried Sandy into the Cessna before she had a chance to get into her bottle. She exuded a stale odor these days, the smell of a body trying desperately to expel the gin she poured into it. She seemed rather excited, and smiled at him, and he prayed her brightness would last as he warmed up the engine and began his preflight routine.

An hour later he stopped before the house he was thinking about. The real estate lady, Sherry Somebody, was waiting for him. "This is the place I'm looking at, Sandy," he said, aching for something to light up in her.

He was rewarded. "Oh, Cam," she said, her gaze running over the generous house, its second story, the big oak front door, the small lot with mature plantings, lilacs and a big cottonwood. He saw some animation in her, fleeting but real, something alive in those dead eyes. It vanished when they got out, but he had seen it and his heart thirsted for that look in her face.

The house stood empty. He ushered her into a foyer and living room. A bay window offered a view south and flooded the room with sunlight. She wandered through it all, the dining room, a den, a screened porch at the rear that would be pleasant during Montana's brief summers, the old and worn and inefficient kitchen, a pantry, a downstairs half bath, also archaic and bordering on the intolerable; three bedrooms upstairs, a full bathroom to serve them all, the larger bedroom not much bigger than the other two; all of them lacking much closet space. She eyed them all, and he caught her every glance, aching for some sign of life, of delight, of renaissance.

"Would you like it?" he asked.

"Whatever you say," she said.

"Would you like to see the town house I'm looking at?"

"I don't think so."

That, in its way, was a choice. "Sandy, I'm doing this for you, for us. Do you like this house? If you do, we'll buy it. If not, we'll keep looking."

"Whatever you think."

He pushed aside the maddening need for something, anything, from her, and focused on that brief moment when he saw something in her face. It would be a leap of faith, an act of desperation—but at least an act. He smiled at the real estate lady.

"Let's run down to your office," he said. "I'll make an offer and put some earnest on it."

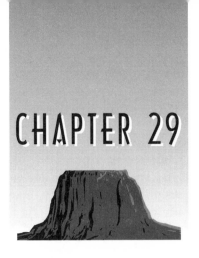

CHAPTER 29

Martin Dudley Nichols shut down the computer. He had been trying to correlate human population densities in rural areas to declines in various game populations, without much success because the data were skimpy and contradictory, and most of his material was anecdotal. The research had gone sour, and he wanted only to escape it into the summer sun. He didn't know why the hell he'd chosen a cross-disciplinary topic, when he could have been making a name for himself in pure environmental science.

Everything had gone haywire. He was stuck with that old fossil Leonard Kazin, guaranteed doom for anyone wanting to get anywhere, and he was stuck with an ill-advised thesis that didn't interest him anymore. And he was stuck in Bozeman on a fine June day when the whole world sang and green grass grew at the foot of snowcapped peaks. Angrily he paced his little cubicle on Willson, aching to get away, go somewhere. But he had his regular appointment with his advisor, and in ten minutes he'd have to cut across to the west edge of the campus and go through the ritual again.

Only he just couldn't. He felt trapped. Brooke-Carson wouldn't take him, and wouldn't even help him. He scorned his father for sending the check every month, making him a slave. He hadn't been home since the big rally in the field house, and hadn't even spoken to his parents or his sisters. And yet the check came, and he despised it, despised them, loathed himself, feared the university, and dreaded his loneliness.

That was it, mostly. He had never been so lonely. He had chucked his family and had no home. He'd driven out Mary Lee by being self-centered and gloomy. He had isolated himself from everyone in the Environmental Sciences Department. He had hidden in the library pretending to do research, but mostly just fantasizing about the future, about girls, about being some big-deal ecologist and spokesman for some Green group.

But nothing worked. He tried drinking one night and quit in a fury. He was eating junk food, just because he felt like it, the sweeter the better: candy bars, colas, ice cream, donuts, and sugar cookies.

Wearily he gathered up his material and plunged into the sun—and suddenly knew he wasn't going to Kazin's office, and he wasn't ever going to finish the thesis, and probably was going to go to hell. He had some vague sense that he was cracking up; that it had been all downhill ever since he kissed off his family; that they were laughing at him by sending him money and watching him cash the checks. Damn them! They spent generations tearing the world apart, and now they were tearing him apart.

The hell with Kazin.

At the curb he got into his beat-up Subaru—he wouldn't be caught dead in a Detroit gas-guzzler—and started it up. He knew where he was going. He pulled hard into Main Street traffic, heading west through light traffic. The city seemed different in the summer, with ten thousand students out of its belly. He stopped at a 7-Eleven on the west side of town and bought some Coke and a plastic-wrapped sandwich that would taste like cardboard.

He drove west to Four Corners and then south, toward the Gallatin Canyon, past places that built log homes, past the old Gallatin Gateway resort, rococo splendor that, oddly, made him feel good. It was a relic of the old days when the Milwaukee Railroad brought people into the Wild West, that being Bozeman, and stuffed them into the resort for some scenic views and trout fishing and tennis.

He found the gravel road he was looking for a mile or so into the canyon, and turned onto it, climbing over foothills and then, suddenly, into a lovely secluded valley. A discreet sign said Turner Ranches, and another warned that there would be bison loose, and that they were dangerous. He was on a public road leading to a Forest Service campground—a road that cut through the famous Flying D, now stocked with three or four thousand of Ted Turner's buffalo.

He drove several miles into the place, marveling at its beauty. Emerald foothills vaulted upward, layer upon layer, toward the Spanish Peaks. Pines blackened the upper ridges; aspen in new leaf clumped on slopes; and June wildflowers rioted at every turn. Turner's ranch was one of the most beautiful in the world, perhaps the reason it had been owned by a succession of very rich men before Turner bought it. Martin had never seen such verdant grass, which seemed untouched by any grazing animal.

How different this lush pasture was from the starkness of eastern Montana, with its silvery sagebrush, its thin bunchgrasses, weeds, and barren brown soils. He wanted to believe this was nature in purest form, but he knew that wasn't the case: knapweed and leafy spurge were ruthlessly attacked here, along with other noxious weeds.

He followed the gravel road as it wound through the foothills, and then, around a corner, there they were, thousands of buffalo blackening the slopes, more than he could count, big, shaggy, noble animals so numerous they formed a black blur as they grazed peacefully. This was a sight few living mortals had seen, beyond anything they could imagine. Here were the carefully nurtured progeny of a handful of survivors, a few dozen buffalo that had, at the last split second, been preserved in the late nineteenth century to keep the American bison from extinction. No one knew for sure how many were actually left; some said just ten or eleven of the northern herd, plus an unknown handful in Canada. Others said forty or fifty. Whatever the case, the noble animal was rescued—but not entirely. The southern herds were entirely wiped out, and with them went a lighter-colored and smaller buffalo not found in the north.

He stopped the Subaru, rolled down the window, and watched, hoping this awesome sight would lift his spirits. He wanted it to. He'd hit bottom. He sat quietly, studying the animals, noting the old bulls who isolated themselves, and the newborn calves, red and blocky in the glowing sunlight. The bison was a remarkable animal, ungainly looking, with enormous chest and hump, small, weak eyes, woolly face, short, curved, useless-looking horns. In spite of its awkward form it could run faster than all but the fastest horses, maneuver on a dime, and defend itself better than any other ungulate. In the old days wolves had followed the great herds, but only to pick off the sick and old and isolated; rare indeed was the calf that fell to a wolf pack. The lordly buffalo ate more efficiently than cattle, requiring less fodder. It sustained itself on a wider variety of grasses and browse, too, thus resting the pasture and placing less strain upon it than cattle. Its small, sharp hooves worked the soil, driving seed into it, naturally harrowing it in ways that evoked good pasture.

Now there were buffalo breeders everywhere, and even annual conventions and stock sales, in which the breeders, ever mindful of the limited genetic material from which modern herds had been built, traded and bought bulls and cows, often from distant places, to nurture the genetic strength of an animal that had come within a whisper of departing forever.

Martin watched the herds undulate across the hills, constant restless movement. There were, actually, seven or eight groups, all within sight of the other groups and yet distinct, as if this giant herd had divided itself into precincts. This is what he wanted in eastern Montana, herds like this, nature rampant, untrammeled by the hand of man. Except that he was romanticizing. This ranch was carefully run; the numbers of buffalo held to its carrying capacity. There wasn't even a fly around. Somehow the thought depressed him after his initial elation. He wanted to see a world not run by mankind, but this was not it. These buffalo had all been handled, vaccinated against brucellosis to protect surrounding cattle. They could not be herded, at least not the way cattle could, but they could be driven, penned, doctored, injected, dealt with by rough means.

The thought made him morose. He'd never see a virgin world. Even this throwback to a virgin world was carefully orchestrated by a wealthy man whose crew was capable of spraying spotted knapweed, restoring pasture, planting seed, culling animals, erecting or tearing down fences. This was a man-made Eden, not a wilderness. He sat for an hour and had seen enough; not even several thousand bison with hundreds of bright calves could lift his broken soul.

He ate the miserable sandwich, not even knowing what was in it, and sucked the Coke absently, cardboard food for a cardboard man. Then he drove back to Bozeman, with the gates of his mind wide-open to all the thoughts he'd pushed aside driving out there to that oasis. This day he had crashed. This day he had quit. This day he had abandoned years of work, thrown out a dream, walked away from a master's degree.

He drove back into Bozeman, past a new sprawl of business on the west edge of town, past gaudy car dealers, past model homes, past a bank with welded iron elk on its lawn, past the old Baxter Hotel, and then down to his room. What would he do? Maybe he'd just start hitchhiking, digital express, all over the place. It was the beginning of summer, and nothing is better than Montana in summer. Maybe he'd scrape together some camping gear and go up in the mountains, maybe climb some high ones, up above timberline. He didn't want to talk to anyone. He was going to have a summer alone, total silence, doing whatever he felt like doing. He'd read a little, but he didn't like books and he was sick of print and computer screens. He didn't know what he'd do—what did it matter?

The red light on his answering machine was blinking when he walked in, but he didn't feel like running the message. It would be Kazin, asking what had happened and when could they get together. He let the light blink and threw the cellophane and junk from his lunch into the waste-basket, saving out the Coke can for recycling.

He slumped back on the bed. What was going to happen when his parents found out that he wasn't working on his degree? The checks would stop; he'd have to get a job. What could he do? Bag groceries? What good was a degree in biology with a minor in sociology? What would it command in the marketplace? Two cents.

He felt bad. He wanted to do what was right. He shouldn't be taking his father's money under false pretenses. He should let his old man know. Then he should support himself if he could. He didn't want to be a parasite. He knew he would like himself much more if he were making his way in the world. But good jobs were hard to find and he didn't have much to offer an employer.

But maybe that was negative thinking. He remembered all the things his grandfather had taught him, the goodness of work, the seriousness of life, the value of friends, the need to master a trade, acquire skills. Those were all good things. His grandfather was right. The recollection of the old man filled Martin with courage.

He sprang up and played the message. It was Kazin, all right—no one else called him now. He had growled everyone away for months.

"Martin, I'm sorry to have missed you. Did we get our meeting mixed up? Please stop by anytime—I'm quite free this summer."

Martin thought maybe he would in the morning and let his advisor know he'd crashed and burned.

CHAPTER 30

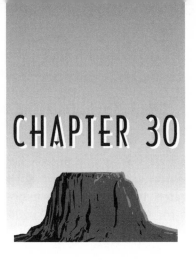

So the young man was quitting. Leonard Kazin eyed the sullen youth, wondering how many times, over how many years, he had received such news. Outside, the blue mountains shimmered in the June sun, and he wished he could open the window to let the breezes in. But the new building foiled him.

He wouldn't lecture. "Well, Martin, I'll miss you."

Martin squirmed, eager to escape.

"Would it help if you had another advisor?"

Martin looked startled, as if a guilty secret lay naked on the desk between them.

"Oh, I know how young people feel sometimes, especially about some superannuated professor who probably should've retired years ago. I can arrange it if you'd like."

"I just want to bail out. I wasn't cut out for this."

"What do you want to do with your life?"

"How should I know?"

Kazin knew he had touched on a tender area. They were all so scared at that age, feeling that every decision, every failure, was fateful and couldn't be redeemed. Life had never been so competitive, and the gulf between the educated and privileged, on the one hand, and the hoi polloi, on the other, so stark. The awesome strides in science and technology had done it: you either mastered them or worked as a drone.

"You don't need to decide now. Take the summer off, that's what I'd do." He looked at Martin with a certain understanding gleaned from decades of dealing with students. "You know, if you do want to keep at it, I can arrange a teaching assistant job. Maybe scrape up a scholarship. Help you with a student loan."

"I'll think about it," Martin said.

He looked ready to bolt, and if he did, his life might take a very bad turn.

"You know, Martin, I'll probably never see you again. I'd like to take you out to lunch, visit a little if you'd like. In fact, Bozeman's getting me down. Let me take you over the pass. I know a nice pasta place in Livingston where we can say farewell. You've been a good student, worked hard, and it just would please me to take you to lunch."

Astonishment spread across Martin's face, and for a moment the hostility faded.

"If this is a bad time, how about coming to my house for dinner? Mrs. Kazin's always looking for an excuse to break out the china."

"For dinner?"

"Sure, come on over and let me bore you with a few reminiscences. Let me check with Dorothy."

Martin looked paralyzed.

"Let's do both," Kazin said. "Let's go for lunch now, and we'll plan on dinner tomorrow."

Martin nodded, words failing him. But Kazin sensed a great softening in that hard edge. The professor led his silent protégé out to his Olds and drove into a glorious summer day. As they topped the pass and descended to Livingston, the young man's edge vanished altogether.

When at last they were seated and dipping thick, moist chunks of bread into olive oil laced with red vinegar, Kazin decided simply to talk. Martin wasn't in the mood for it.

"I'm going to retire next year," he said. "I've been at this too long."

"What'll you do? Go to Arizona?"

"I'd like to do what I've always loved most—speak at various groups about how Mother Nature works. I like to think I've done some good, doing that."

Martin retreated into himself.

"You know, I've been in academe for forty-odd years now. When I started, in fifty-nine, it was biology. No one except a few professionals talked about ecology. That came later. As it happened, I did some studies that were pretty unusual for their day, mostly about the impact of human activity on ecosystems. Did one on how feedlots—they were often built right on the riverbank in those days—polluted rivers, the Yellowstone, actually, every time a heavy rain came along. I showed what happened to all the life-forms in the river when they were subjected to repeated exposure to that. Did the same with precious metal mines, and then I did the same with pesticides and agricultural spraying, following the effects up and down the life chain. Primitive stuff now, but it got me a reputation as a comer back then."

He paused to let the waiter take their orders—both chose the buffet—and then continued.

"Those were good days. I loved my work and I loved the future. Rachel Carson had just published *Silent Spring,* and it was finally reaching the public, this worry about a crumbling world."

"Who's Rachel Carson?"

Martin's response utterly astonished Kazin. How could he be in biology and not know? So young, so very young. "Rachel Carson? A marine biologist who wrote a book that changed the United States. That was 1962. She wrote mostly about what pesticides—DDT, especially—did to various species."

"I guess I heard of her somewhere."

How could the boy be working on an advanced degree without coming across Carson? Kazin had to remind himself that the youth across from him had been *born* more than a decade after Carson's work transformed biology. "Well, I tell you what. Without Rachel Carson, you probably wouldn't be studying in this field, and I wouldn't be heading something called a Department of Environmental Sciences. She wrote sensitively, lyrically, about the natural world and the threats it faced, and she reached laypeople in ways that the old naturalists didn't." He refrained from telling Martin to read the book, that it was unthinkable that he should get an advanced degree in this field without knowing that book. But he held his tongue.

"I just like to keep up with what's new," Martin said. "Everyone tells me that new research turns over our field every two, three years. So the past's a waste of time."

Kazin decided not to get into an argument with a youth on the brink of ditching the field. So he turned to his reminiscing. "Well, there was a certain amount of law against polluting then, but it wasn't what we have today. So I just got out on the lunch-bucket circuit and the rubber-chicken dinner trail, and I talked to nice people around the state. Rotary clubs, Kiwanis, Cow Belles, 4-H Clubs, mining conventions, petroleum engineers, stockgrowers associations—met your parents several times at those. I had a slide show and some charts, pretty old-fashioned stuff, but I showed 'em what happened to birds exposed to DDT, what happened to trout, what happened to bees that were needed to pollinate various crops—I had it all, big flip charts, a wooden pointer, slides. And you know, I got some results just by jawboning. Some of those feedlots pushed back from the river and built catchments and berms to hold the sludge; a few farmers took a closer look at what they were doing when they sprayed for grasshoppers or weeds. I urged them to leave some ground unplowed, belts of brush, habitat. Well, they still like me to come back and tell them what's new.

"It's different now, of course—they're all scared to death of the EPA, and Fish and Wildlife, and penalties, and lawsuits, and edicts that make no sense to them. Sometimes they get conflicting rules from two federal agencies—do this, do that, and they're caught in the middle. They're scared to put some gravel in a puddle in their driveway. So my task's different now. I go on out there and tell them how to avoid getting into trouble, what's good practice, what's cheap and effective, what protects habitat and what hurts it. I've been going out for four decades now, and I guess those people need me more than ever because they keep asking for me."

Martin dipped bread into the olive oil, silent and angry again.

"Around the department they call it consorting with the enemy," Kazin said, a big laugh building in him. "They've got the world polarized between good guys like ecologists, and bad guys like—your folks."

Martin stared.

"So, it's up to the old bad boy Kazin to bridge the two camps. I like to think I've done a lot to keep Montana green, just by getting the word out."

Kazin devoured some lasagna and dabbed at his lips with the linen napkin.

"I'm thinking that you need a new advisor—if you come back, of course. My way isn't very popular around the department anymore, and it might even compromise you in some of those high-flier circuits. I've always believed that the young have the right to create their own world, and shouldn't be hamstrung by some old fogeys wagging fingers and pointing to rules. I guess what I'm saying, Martin, is, if you'd like another professor to oversee your graduate work, I'd not only understand, I'd do my best to line up someone you'd like to work with."

"I don't know; I'm just out of it. You want an answer right away?"

"Before the fall term starts is soon enough."

Martin smiled briefly.

"You want to talk about your plans?"

"I don't have any."

"Want to talk about what's bugging you?"

"No."

"Well, whatever you decide, Martin, is fine with me. It's your life."

"Yeah, that's what I tell myself."

"The universities aren't so much fun anymore. Big factories now."

"Look, you can't just haul up the past and tell me it was all great back in the old days. What good does that do?"

Kazin paused. "Sorry. I'm indulging myself. Academia began to change in the seventies, and I never got used to it."

He picked up the tab and stood. He won some, lost some, and probably would lose Martin Nichols. But they sometimes came back. They needed a year or two just to find out what they wanted. Most of them were so afraid that if they followed one avenue they'd close off other options, that they spent their twenties trying to run away from committing to anything.

He rebuked himself for being judgmental, remembering what it was like to be young, with a whole life ahead.

"Thank you, sir," Martin said.

"My pleasure. Good to get out. We'll be seeing you tomorrow evening for dinner?"

"I guess so, sir."

"Good. We're always at home if you ever need a home."

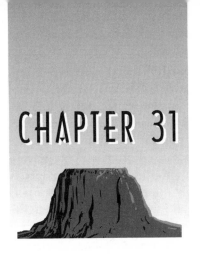

CHAPTER 31

Laslo and Dolly Horoney waited quietly for their guests to arrive at their little La Jolla casa. A few hours earlier, their gleaming white Gulfstream V had picked up Cameron and Sandy Nichols in Billings. They had landed in San Diego a half hour earlier, and were being chauffeured to La Jolla for a leisurely weekend.

He loved this place, just as he loved his others. Long ago, he and Dolly had thought about what sort of life they wished to live, now that they could afford anything money could buy. They both hit upon these little hideaways, comfortable but not ostentatious, rented or owned at places they loved, including La Jolla. This house, high above the shimmering Pacific, had low ceilings with a wall of glass overlooking the sea, a radical architecture that was derived from Frank Lloyd Wright concepts about uniting interior and exterior, and a special intimacy in its conversational groupings and dining arrangements. This was just the sort of place to get to know people. And he intended to get to know the Nicholses very well, and intended that the Nicholses would get to know him just as well. There were large matters to deal with, if the Nicholses wished to deal with them. If not, it would still be an amiable weekend with new friends.

He wasn't particularly worried about the possibility that Sandra Nichols might be drunk. He and Dolly could deal easily with that. Mrs. Nichols would be no problem at all compared to the swine they had dealt with—cocaine-sniffing movie stars, shadowy entrepreneurs who arrived with tacky mistresses, fat, mean politicians, murderous generalissimos from swagger-nations, vacant-eyed nouveaux riches who considered it de rigueur to despoil their hosts' furnishings, blackmail artists, decadent Riviera jet-set shipping tycoons, and even munitions dealers. He and Dolly had dealt with them all, and would find Sandy Nichols a pillar of courage and beauty no matter that she sipped too many gin and tonics.

He heard the purr of the white stretch limo, and met the Nicholses at his front door, Dolly beside him. Cameron Nichols shook hands a little warily, a certain caution in his sun-stained face. Laslo had expected that. Nichols certainly looked prime and fit, graying at the temples, lean, a rancher's roughness smoothed down by an open white shirt, sport coat, and casual slacks. Only the man's polished boots betrayed a way of life. Sandy looked drawn and worn, the bloom faded from her face, but she seemed more animated than she had in Montana. She wore a blue suit straight out of the sixties, a Coco Chanel sort of thing that would have looked right on Jackie Kennedy. She, more than Cameron, seemed a little nonplussed in the company of such wealthy and celebrated people—something Laslo and Dolly well understood and dealt with in a practiced way.

"Come see our view—everyone loves it," Dolly said, leading the Nicholses into the wedge-shaped living room with its wall of glass overlooking the sea.

Laslo listened patiently to the exclamations, the trip in the Gulfstream with all its subdued and elegant appointments, and the ride from San Diego Airport.

"What'll you have to drink?" he asked.

"A glass of tonic," said Sandy.

"Add some gin to mine," said Cameron.

That pleased Laslo. He served them himself. He and Dolly traveled with two middle-aged servants, a couple they'd employed many years, but on this occasion it'd be just a foursome, and Dolly would cook, as she occasionally did, in fits and when the mood struck her.

The conversation faltered along, and Laslo let it, knowing that the taciturn rancher wasn't at home here, and would be happier talking cattle or rangeland or the price of beef. But Sandy shone, maybe glowed was the word, surprising and at ease, in her element. What an odd match, he thought, odder than his own with Dolly.

A lull in the small talk arrived, and Laslo deemed it an appropriate moment to say something:

"I'd like you two to set the ground rules for the weekend. If you'd like to talk about the foundation and its work, we'll talk about it. If not, we've some delightful adventures planned—some fishing, the San Diego Zoo, Old Town, all sorts of things."

Cameron didn't miss a beat. "I don't know about you, Sandy, but I'd like to see the area. Maybe fish."

"Whatever you say," Sandy replied, and Laslo caught a flicker of sadness in Cameron's face.

"We could take you on a little cruise down the coast, along Baja, if you'd like," Dolly interjected. "Nothing but blue sky, sun, some deep-sea fishing, and sunburn."

"You have a yacht?"

"Actually, immediate access to one."

"You know something?" asked Sandy Nichols. "I'd like to learn everything there is to know about your vision of the National Grassland."

Astonished, Laslo eyed the woman closely and found pain in her face along with courage. She wanted to talk about the grassland; Cameron didn't.

"I'd be glad to. Perhaps you'll join us, Cameron?"

"Maybe tomorrow, Mr. Horoney."

"Tomorrow, then," Horoney said.

He wanted to discuss the grassland. He wished they could arrive at a deal, and he could sit down and write out a check for two hundred twenty thousand acres. And he wished he could invite Cameron to become one of the directors of his foundation. The man was wise in the ways of the High Plains and its people. If that place was home to the Nichols family, then perhaps the rest of the High Plains would be, too, if Laslo could persuade Nichols to see it that way.

That afternoon and evening progressed uneasily, in spite of Laslo's best efforts. Cameron Nichols sat warily, and Sandy finally subsided from her small talk and did the same. They were adversaries, and not even Dolly's rare skills, including a raconteur's gifts, failed to ignite any warmth. They dined lightly on Dolly's quiche Lorraine and French vegetable dishes, and then settled into a long, slow evening carried by Dolly and Laslo's restless conversation. Laslo wondered if it had all been a mistake.

Cameron Nichols did talk a bit about the ranches, and Laslo learned, to his astonishment, that the Nichols family was starting to stock one of them with Texas longhorns, a breed apparently capable of fending off wolves. And Laslo also learned more about how the family businesses were set up: Cameron's grandmother and father held the cards. Most of the stock was in a skip-generation trust for tax purposes. Cameron's grandmother was still controlling some of the stock as she saw fit from her Miles City nursing home, and after she died, Cam's father, Dudley, would be voting all those shares in addition to his own and the trust shares.

Quite early in the evening, barely nine, Sandra asked for a nightcap. "I need one to sleep," she explained.

"Shall I make it?" Laslo asked.

"I will."

He watched her fill a glass half-full of gin, and add some ritual Schweppes and a bit of lime. No ice.

"I guess I'll go to bed," she said.

The forthcoming weekend stretched longer and longer, and Horoney decided he would take time tomorrow to work on his ever-present business load, while making himself available to the Nicholses. He wanted to review the foundation's progress toward cleaning fences and buildings off the land, and also his legal staff's progress. Northwest Energy, a Denver outfit, was exploring a large potential field down near Bay Horse, Montana, near the Wyoming line, and was demanding assurances from the foundation about easements, access, and liability. He wanted to read the proposed contract. He wanted to look at a report from Truehart, who was trying to quiet the suit filed by unhappy ranchers. A gas-pipeline company whose easement ran through the grassland wanted a variety of things, including the fencing of its surface facilities with a buffalo-proof chain-link barrier, and some indemnification guarantees. The Bureau of Land Management was demanding indemnification in the event that any of its land, scattered through the trust, was damaged. Headaches.

Dolly looked uncomfortable.

Maybe it was a trick of light, but Nichols looked more and more like the weathered rancher he was, his face and body chastened by wind and rain and sun, hard work, broken bones, bad moments on a horse or sailing off of one. The lamplight had turned his flesh the color of chestnuts. Horoney noticed the man's battered and scarred hands, which had no doubt suffered from rope burns, horseshoe-nail punctures, various bone breaks, and plenty of contact with dirt, manure, blood, and rock. The man's sport coat looked too soft, almost a scam. Nichols exuded anger that slapped the room smartly.

"Let's talk," said Nichols.

Horoney nodded, actually relieved. The evening had hung like a thundercloud that couldn't discharge its electricity. He eyed Dolly, who nodded slightly. But Nichols surprised him.

"I'm sitting here not being a good guest, and we'll leave in the morning. This was a mistake. You know why. Your foundation's driving my family to the wall. Thanks to the trust, on October 1 we'll be in a new county without schools and road repair and even without its own sheriff. Fire protection stops. Trash and landfill services stop and we'll pay to haul our trash out—somewhere. But we'll still pay taxes because we won't be in a privileged class, like your foundation. We'll stop getting rural mail delivery on September 1, and we'll have to drive to Ashland to get it. Thanks to your outfit, the co-op that supplies our power is turning line-maintenance over to us. If we want electricity, we pay them to do it. Thanks to you, the phone company's ditching us unless we maintain thirty miles of line. We've got cellular, but so what? We'll be paying extra to have propane and ranch gasoline delivered. All we wanted was to be left alone, wrestling with our world as best we could. Oh, sure, it's all for a good cause, or so you say, and it's all very enlightened, and maybe that's true. But my family's being torn to shreds. Just for starters, switching to longhorns will put us deep in the hole this year. We're trading topflight cattle for scrubs, paying tough prices for shipment, getting lousy prices for the prize Herefords we're selling to do this—a major setback we didn't ask for."

"I understand."

"I'm not sure you do. There's my beef. What's yours?"

This was a Cam Nichols that Horoney had never seen—hard, abrasive, angry.

"We've gone out of our way to make you whole—generous offer, resettlement help. We've done that for each of the owners we've dealt with. If you choose to stay and endure the loss of services, that's your privilege. It's your choice."

Horoney knew he was talking to a stone wall, but he continued.

"The foundation has a few complaints of its own. One of our beefs is that you're actually tying up four hundred thousand acres, not two hundred twenty. You've got federal and state land mixed with yours—and while the governments have given us the use of that land, we can't reach it."

"I can't help that."

"You can't use it and we can't either." He smiled wryly. "But at least something is accomplished. That pasture gets a rest. Actually, we'd like to do some land trades—you consolidate your holdings, the BLM consolidates its, and we consolidate ours. And if the state wants to get into it, we'd like a four-way trade. Among other things, it'd save us about a hundred eighty miles of buffalo fence."

"We like our ranches just as they are."

"If you can't or won't sell, we'd like to lease your whole outfit, all the land except what you want to reserve around your home base. We'd fence that for you and pull down the rest of the wire. You'd make plenty, with no care in the world."

Nichols was silent, which Laslo took for a good sign.

"I've started the work that culminates a lifetime," Horoney said quietly, "and can't back down now even though I know it hurts good people like you. I'll spend ninety percent of what I've accumulated on it. I'm giving back to the country what it gave me. For me it's the salvation of our world and our nation—it's that important to me. The reasons are complex and difficult to explain. Someday, if we can still be friends, I'll tell you how it came about. It's all about homelessness." He smiled. "My logic eludes Dolly, and it sometimes eludes me, but that's what it's about. Now, I can't back away from something I'm so committed to, but how may I help you and your family?"

"You can't," said Nichols. "Thank you for asking. I apologize for my conduct. If you don't mind, we'd like to return to Montana in the morning."

"As you wish," said Horoney, sadly.

CHAPTER 32

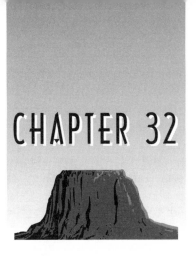

Dudley Nichols saw lights in the big ranch house and crossed through late-summer twilight to see about them. Cam's white Chevy was parked in front.

Dudley walked in without knocking. He did that now that Sandy wasn't around. He discovered Cam in the kitchen, slathering peanut butter over a slab of bread.

"You're back early. What happened?"

"I lost my temper and we left."

"You've been doing that a lot lately."

"Maybe I should do it more often. I'm afraid I offended Horoney."

Dudley grunted disapproval. "You didn't work out anything."

"No. I told him what we faced, and he told me it was our own choice. He's right."

"It isn't our choice. I don't know why you say that. This came on us."

"We had the chance to get out whole, into a better place, with a net gain in worth."

"This is our home."

"That's what I told him."

"What happened then?"

"They flew us back this morning."

"How was Sandy?"

"She did fine. She didn't touch the sauce until bedtime, and then she poured a stiff nightcap and vanished."

"She in Billings now? How's that going?"

Cam shrugged. "Too soon to tell. She's drinking, if that's what you want to know. But she's brighter, and pretty soon she'll get out in the world, or I'll bring people in."

"She's not a Nichols."

Cameron glared at him. "She's as much a Nichols as you and me."

Dudley grunted his disbelief. He'd always believed the marriage was a mistake.

"Dad, she could've gotten out of here long ago—spent winters in Scottsdale, gone off to the cities for all the things she likes. But she stuck it out here, being a mother and a sweetheart. That's class."

Dudley knew enough to keep his trap shut. Cam filled him in on the trip, La Jolla, the Horoneys, the luxurious flight in the executive jet.

"I'm glad you're back. I've got stuff to go over with you."

Cameron downed his bachelor meal and headed for the den, where he had traditionally wrestled with the ranch and its troubles. He turned on a light and dropped into the leather swivel chair, while Dudley settled into the couch. The room felt close and Dudley felt his armpits dampen. There had been some lightning, and a hint of mayhem in the turgid twilight.

Dudley had some news. "Three weeks ago I asked Bob Rockwell to find out some stuff, and he put some shavetail in his firm on it. I wanted to know how much land Horoney's foundation's bought and recorded. So this kid spends days in every courthouse that's affected, and comes up with some calculations. The foundation owns only fifty-odd percent of the grassland. That means there's a lot of people out here, like us, hanging on."

"It'll be more like seventy or eighty percent if you include done deals that aren't closed or recorded at the courthouses, Dad."

"Yeah, but it's still nothing. Horoney hasn't even got a handle on this frying pan yet. We can fight him. I know who to call, who'll write checks."

Cam stopped eating and knocked back a Coke. The house was hot and close.

"We fought all that years ago. Horoney came to the legislature and we fought it. Stockgrowers, sheep people, wheat people, two hundred grand, trips to Washington, trips to Helena and Cheyenne, full-page ads. We lost."

"No, Horoney's losing. No one's caving in."

"Most will. He's been generous. He's not the sort to screw anyone."

"Let's take it to the courts. Tie him up. We can back him off. Big bucks don't always win."

"Who'll pay? We're bleeding."

"It's worth it."

Cam was sweating. Dudley wished they had headed out to the front porch.

"Dad, so far, no one's gotten very far in court. For one thing, this grassland is now national policy and has been ever since the president issued an executive order saying so and requiring the bureaus to cooperate. Same for Montana and Wyoming. Creating this grassland's the official policy of Montana, and there's a pile of legislation authorizing it and freeing utilities from certain obligations. And that's not the half of it. The foundation's been generous. Whenever Truehart's people go into court and show that they've offered to make anyone whole and then some, the plaintiffs don't get very far."

Dudley nodded. "You know," he said sadly, "there was a day when a stockman was a valued man in Montana. A day when a Nichols could go into the legislature and sit down before an agriculture committee and get a respectful hearing—and usually some legislation out of it. I used to go with my father. Then I did it myself. Fifties, sixties. Walked in there with a stockgrowers' proposal on livestock taxes and got it through in a week. I got brood-stock depreciation through. I always stopped to see the governor. I'd just walk in and he'd say, 'How are you, Dudley?' and I'd say, 'As good as it rains.' Then I'd go shake a hand with the lieutenant governor, the secretary of state, and all the rest. I always stopped to visit with the brand inspectors—they'd been stuck in a lousy office and I always told 'em I'd try to get 'em something better. We were real people then—stockmen—and the state hadn't become the yuppie capital of the world, full of hippie left-wing novelists and movie stars."

Cam grinned. Dudley grinned, too, though he didn't know why because the estate of stockmen had never been lower.

"Yup, and don't forget the food fascists who've been telling us that beef's bad and stockmen are killing off good Americans."

"The hell we are! Beef's good for us. It's been proven."

Cam was grinning at him, which ticked him off.

"Peanut butter," Dudley said.

"Speaking of Helena, there's something I want you to do there."

"I don't know anyone anymore, Cam."

"I want you to just go talk to some people about services. We're going to be paying taxes in this new Buffalo County, same as before, but they're going to cut off services. I want something for our taxes—access to schools, trash pickup, scraping our road at the least. This is a raw deal for all of us staying on in this Big Empty."

"What good would I do? I don't know who to talk to."

"We'll get some names from Bob Rockwell."

"I haven't met a governor for fifteen years."

"Well, it's time you did."

"Used to be I could walk in there. Now they'd think I was a crank or an assassin."

"Would you try?"

Dudley nodded, in defeat. Helena would be hell now. "Don't get old, Cam. They don't know you anymore."

"You're not old. Seventies isn't old."

"I was talking to DeeAnn the other day about old movies, good movies about real people, not this trash where Schwartz—what's his name—blows everyone up. Good movies. And she'd never heard of Ingrid Bergman."

"Should she?"

"Ingrid Bergman was the woman who made the century worthwhile."

Cameron didn't make a joke, and Dudley was glad he didn't. Ingrid Bergman and Greer Garson, those were his two. Almost like Mabel. He blinked back something he didn't want Cam to see.

"Will you go?" Cam asked.

"I suppose, but a lot of good I'll do."

"I've another item. Would you mind stopping in Bozeman?"

"Martin?"

"Martin. Just stop by. He'll welcome you. He's not mad at you."

"He's mad at all of us that ever put a cow to grass."

"Well?"

"He'll think I'm snooping."

"Let him. It'll send a message."

"I knew his advisor, Leonard Kazin, some, stockgrowers' meetings. Nice young fellow. Not so young now."

"Why don't you see Kazin?"

"I wouldn't be caught dead walking into the Environmental Sciences Department."

"Meet him for lunch. Get some news about Martin. He's your grandson."

"That's debatable."

"I'm going to bed. We're getting three hundred longhorns tomorrow."

"Used to be we raised beef, not horns. They eat all day and what does it make? Horns."

Cameron was grinning.

"All right, I'll come watch. Skinny no-good things."

"Bring your camcorder."

"We used to have cameras. When I'm gone are you and DeeAnn going to keep this place?"

"We're going to try. No one's giving up."

Dudley abandoned his son and walked into a soft, starlit summer night, with the warmth of the sun rising from the earth. He liked the feel of his own land under his feet. The family land, Cam's, DeeAnn's, and then the great-grandchildren's. Maybe. Maybe it wouldn't be a ranch, though. Maybe they'd raise beef in big metal barns the way they raised pork and chicken these days, bringing in all the food, letting the manure drop through wire floors, out of the way. Fluorescent lights but no sun, a stink that spreads five miles. Maybe Nichols Ranches would be nothing but a bunch of metal buildings full of livestock in ten years. If the Food and Drug Administration didn't outlaw beef. There were aspects of this modern agribusiness that bugged him, and that was all the more reason he was glad he wouldn't be getting too far into this new century.

He thought he'd put on the tape of Frank Sinatra singing "In the Wee Small Hours of the Morning," but he didn't because he longed for that world too much, and he wondered what it would have been like to kiss Ingrid Bergman.

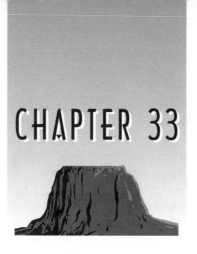

CHAPTER 33

J. Carter Delacorte always looked forward to July as the peak mood-level in his annual cycle. In that blessed month he held his annual Delacorte Condominium at Blackwood, a small, elegant hostelry north of Jackson, set on a ridge top with a glorious view of the Tetons. The word, condominium, meaning "joint dominion or sovereignty" was his intention exactly, and thus he called his meetings condominiums.

The Delacorte Condominium was, of course, by invitation only, and his guests were treated to the most advanced thinking on the planet. This year they would be tackling cosmic issues, breathtaking in their scope: The Limitations of Science, and The Triumph of Universal Spirituality.

He could scarcely imagine topics more charged with energy. Maybe this would be the event that would transcend science once and for all. He had engaged remarkable thinkers who would demonstrate that any discipline that didn't consider anecdotal and spiritual and other forms of evidence, including auras and extrasensory perception, was fatally flawed, and could not explain the mysteries.

Oh, it would be the best one yet, and he'd put on seven so far. This year the condominium would feature Dr. Peter Andrew Brooke-Carson. The man radiated ideas like a cloud shooting out lightning. No one knew more about nature, especially the High Plains. Last year Dr. Carson had also been a Featured Sharer, along with equally eminent students of Nature. And of course the man had been invited to every one of Delacorte's Condominiums because his sheer genius shot bolts of insight through the proceedings.

Now, in moments, they would be arriving in vans for the opening gathering at Delacorte's lodge. He loathed stand-up cocktail parties, a relic of the world he wished to transcend, so he intended that this group would begin with a unifying ritual. In that fashion, introductions—so painful for most—could be dispensed with, and bonding would follow of its own accord. No last names were ever employed at his intellectual condominiums because they were so invidious. Just nicknames, to put people at ease. They were free to call him J, just J, and to call Brooke-Carson "Pete." That removed all unseemly vestiges of rank and stature, and let people meet in an arena where all ideas were equal and none were to be condemned.

The only person who didn't really measure up was Monica Zettendorf, but he always included her because she wielded her checkbook in gracious ways, and because these conferences always generated tensions in his gonads, which she cheerfully drained each night. In that, at least, she was as formidable as any of the attendees were in their specialties. But of course that's what these condominiums were all about: crosswinds, carrying brilliance from mind to mind, like pollen on the wind.

He watched the vans from Blackwood wind their way toward his aerie, and felt the excitement of the moment. These were planetary thinkers who transcended culture—especially the archaic, dying culture of Western Civilization. He had selected them with precision to obtain just the right balance of race, ethnicity, gender, age, and spirituality. Among them were people from the Ivory Coast, Argentina, Iraq, Bosnia, Mongolia, Ecuador, and Pitcairn's Island, all flown in at his expense.

This would be a formal affair, of course, and he had dressed in a white turtleneck under his black dinner jacket, his gold necklace and crystal at his chest; stone-washed designer jeans, and Birkenstocks. He had urged his guests to dress for the occasion, to celebrate the spiritual importance of the condominium.

He opened the door to welcome them to his rustic living room, which would absorb all forty of them with room to spare. There, amid peeled-log furniture, third-world wicker, Persian rugs, Hudson's Bay blanket decor, llama-hair curtains, and acres of exquisite old-growth redwood flooring, decking, and trim, they would get to know one another. As each entered, he flashed his thousand-watt smile and grasped the outstretched hand between both of his.

"Peace and love," he said. "You're Alphonse—no last names here. Call me J."

One by one they filed in, Wally, Maya, Olga, Antonio, Pericles, Armand, Osa, Mariel, Salome, Gregorovich.

"Peace and love, Tanya," he said. "No last names now, and titles are abolished."

"Peace and love, Monica," he said to his companion of spirit and body.

"Mostly love," she replied.

He turned to Brooke-Carson. "Peace and love, honored sharer," he said, clasping the professor's paws between his. "Do come in."

"I want to talk to you later," Brooke-Carson said.

"Yes, of course, Pete."

Carson grimaced.

At last they were assembled, studying his shining and well-lit digs, and waiting for his leadership.

"Now, my dear colleagues and friends, I always begin these condominia with a little ritual to bring us together. Please form a circle and hold hands."

They did, rather reluctantly. He clasped the hand of Gregorovich on the right and Solana on the left.

"There now. Feel the power. Feel the electricity flowing around this circle of humanity," he said. "With this circle we are bound together. Feel the ideas and auras leap from hand to hand, mind to mind, an endless circle. I've brought you here because you're the finest thinkers in the solar system. From here, the ether will be charged with light and knowledge. And from here, the world will receive its luminous future. Now then, peace and love, and help yourselves to snacks and beverages."

The circle broke up, and "these homo sapiens species," as Delacorte liked to call them, drifted to the lavishly encumbered table of health food and naturally grown snacks, provided by Bliss, Servicer of the World, a New-Age Jackson caterer.

Brooke-Carson poured himself some Pisces Rising and nodded J. Carter Delacorte out onto the twenty-yard-long color-matched redwood deck, where they could have some privacy.

"Lots to talk about, and now's probably the best time," the professor said.

"Yes, I can hardly wait for your keynote speech on the collapse of science—"

"It's not collapsing, but it does need some broadening and a new set of rules. Now that I have you in private—there are things happening on the grassland front."

"Oh, good!"

"Not so good. I had lunch recently with J. Shirley Thorn, the EPA's field director in Helena. Frankly, she alarmed me. I've always suspected there were bad eggs in EPA—people not truly dedicated—and now I know there are several. The Environmental Protection Agency is on the brink of being captured and gutted by bureaucrats and reactionaries."

"Well, Pete, we have to expect some of that."

"This woman frankly told me she is not totally committed, and was put in place by superiors in Washington to ride herd on alleged EPA abuses and excesses."

"Such as?"

"Violating the constitutional rights of citizens."

"We need a new constitution. I hope we'll address that in this condominium. We can write one. This is a new age."

"Well, what I'm getting at is some full-page advocacy newspaper ads—you know the type—alerting the Green movement to the problem, so something can be done, pressure some congressmen, build up some heat. This Thorn woman should be explicitly named. A thorn in our side, if I may say so."

"You want support. Yes, of course. A page in the *Washington Post*."

"That would be a start. And we need somehow to fund an alert; direct-mail everyone. Montana's particularly sensitive because of the grassland project. It's awful to have the Montana EPA in her hands."

"I'll look over my funds, Pete. I always like to help."

The professor smiled. "Knew I could count on you. There's some other stuff. I did manage to worm some things out of the woman, all of it valuable. Here's one: the Nichols family isn't budging. And because they aren't going to sell out, a lot of other ranchers are going to hang on. Horoney's grassland has more holes than Swiss cheese."

"They can't hang on. No reason to. They can't keep stock on the place, not with wolves."

"But they are. And that's another point. The feds have figured out the wolves were planted there and didn't migrate."

"How do they know that?"

"Abnormal packs, no DNA match to Yellowstone wolves, no history of migration—that is, wolf kills in between known wolf habitat and the plains. Things like that. Fish and Wildlife has a crackerjack wolf biologist, Sanford Kouric, tracking the new packs. He's a great biologist, but not very reliable, if you know what I mean."

"How do they think the wolves got there?"

"They don't know or aren't saying."

"Well, it's a mystery. Wolves are remarkable."

"I think maybe you know."

"Who, me?" Delacorte winked.

"I thought so. You're the only one with enough money. I got more from Thorn. At least she didn't clam up, the way so many feds do. She doesn't think the U.S. Fish and Wildlife's preliminary wolf-habitat designation's going to stick. It's not habitat if it lacks adequate wild prey for wolves. I got wind of an internal memo circulating through the EPA, Fish and Wildlife, Park Service, and all that. Kouric wrote it. It says that the only way the High Plains could currently be declared habitat is to include domestic cattle as prey. Obviously an explosive conclusion, and that's why it's all hush-hush. But I have my sources in EPA, and I heard about it. Haven't seen it, though. They're trying to draft an Environmental Impact Statement for the permanent habitat designation that slides around Kouric's paper. Of course, that won't come up in the Miles City hearings."

"Does this mean corporate agribusiness can keep on wrecking the plains?"

The professor shrugged. "We'll know in a few weeks. After Fish and Wildlife's done with the hearing. Looks like Nichols Ranches'll win this one. Which is why we've *got* to get the federal government to take over this project from that prick Horoney and kick out the corporate revanchists."

"That's the perfect word."

"That's where you come in, Carter. You could be the Hinge of Fate for the National Grassland—for the nation. We need to find a way to drive out Nichols. Once they've thrown in the towel, the rest'll bug out."

"What did they do about the wolves?"

"Moved their Herefords to other ranches, I hear. They've got more land than they know what to do with."

"Well, we have to do something. I'll think of something, Pete."

"I'm sure you will, Carter. Maybe it's time to get rough with them. Hire an investigative firm. See if we can get them audited. Run some adverse publicity about corporate agribusiness. Or continue with whatever you're already doing."

"I think I can do that," Delacorte said, thinking of one more trip to Alberta.

"Sled dogs," said the professor.

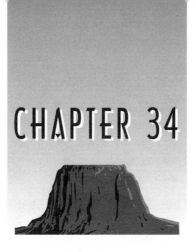

CHAPTER 34

John Trouble returned to Busby four nights later, again carrying a carton of Camels as the ritual gift for David Gray Wolf. They had smoked that first time, and then talked of many things, none of them involving Cheyenne tradition or the old beliefs. Gray Wolf's ancestors had come up from the Oklahoma captivity along with Trouble's. Maybe that was why he sought out the young man. Maybe it wasn't. Who could say? He hardly knew why he behaved as he did.

This night, Gray Wolf was waiting for him, and again led him outdoors for a smoke close to the lodge that housed the Sacred Hat bundle. Trouble went through the ritual impatiently, not really feeling traditional, and not even feeling Cheyenne. But it was something he wanted to pursue.

At last his young mentor knocked the dottle out of the old pipe, put it in its pouch, and set it aside.

"Sweet Medicine is a good place to start, but not the best. The oldest stories are best, but that would take many evenings."

"Okay, Sweet Medicine."

"He might have lived, maybe not. We have only the stories, oral tradition handed down to us. Fortunately, they've been recorded now and won't be lost."

"John Stands in Timber," Trouble said.

"Yes. And others. Among them Fred Last Bull, who kept the sacred arrows when they were up here in the nineteen fifties. But we'll get to that later. There are similarities between the Sweet Medicine story and the white men's stories of Jesus and Moses. But we don't call Sweet Medicine a god. No one knows how old the stories are, but they go back before eighteen hundred, before we had contact with white men."

Trouble listened skeptically while Gray Wolf described the conception and birth of the great Cheyenne cultural hero. A Cheyenne girl, only child of middle-aged parents, conceived a child after hearing the voice of Sweet Root in her dreams, saying he would come to her because she was young and clean. Her parents were embarrassed by her condition, and hid her until her time had come. When she gave birth, she did so alone, in brush beside a river. Then, after birth, she abandoned the baby in the rushes. But it was discovered by an elderly woman who was there to cut grasses, and she took the child, Sweet Medicine, to her lodge and raised him, little knowing that Sweet Medicine would become a lawgiver and spiritual guide to the People.

"That sure sounds familiar," Trouble said. "You sure this story was floating about before white men showed up?"

"It is certain," Gray Wolf responded patiently.

Sweet Medicine did some youthful miracles, which Gray Wolf related, but was exiled in his youth for failing to heed the instruction of an old man who wanted the hide of a yellow buffalo calf Sweet Medicine had killed during his first hunt. He escaped in a cloud of miracles, and was exiled four years, during which the Cheyenne fell upon bad times. But the exile was to be portentous because Sweet Medicine eventually arrived at Bear Butte, *Noahvose,* the sacred mountain of the People, north of the Black Hills.

Trouble knew this part of the story very well. Any Cheyenne did, even in the Year Two Thousand. When Sweet Medicine arrived at Bear Butte he was welcomed into the lodge of the gods, and taught all the things he was to teach the Cheyenne. And then he was given the Four Sacred Arrows, two for hunting, two for war. He learned many ceremonies and laws associated with them, and was warned to keep them covered in a special lodge except during the ceremony of renewal. Whenever any Cheyenne murdered another, the arrows had to be purified. And so Sweet Medicine returned to his people, taught them the arrow ceremonies and laws, and organized the tribe, giving it forty-four chiefs, and establishing its first warrior societies, the Swift Foxes, Elks, Bowstrings, and Red Shields.

He stayed with the Cheyenne many years, teaching them all their ways, and when at last he felt his time had come, he had them construct a hut of bark and rye grass, and had the people carry him there. But before he died, he gave them a prophecy: short-haired strangers called Earth Men would appear among the Cheyenne, light-colored and powerful and capable of clever things. The buffalo would die, but another animal would replace them—the new animals would have split hooves and long tails and would become the food of the people. And another shaggy-necked animal with round hooves would come, and the people could ride these creatures and go much farther than they could on foot. The people would abandon their ways and religion and quarrel with each other and forget the good things and become mad.

"Well, that was Sweet Medicine's prophecy, and it all came true," Gray Wolf concluded. There was a question in his face, and Trouble dodged it.

"Something to think about," he said.

Gray Wolf nodded. "There is much more to teach—all the old ways. And you have a trip before you."

"Don't know that I want to get into it that much."

"You'll go to the sacred mountain?"

"Maybe. Right now, I've got some work. The first of Nichols's long-horns are arriving, and I've got to get them settled on pasture and check the gates and keep an eye on 'em for shipping fever and all that. Should be interesting."

"Longhorns?"

"Because of the wolves."

Gray Wolf nodded. "I will see you soon," he said.

Trouble wondered how the man could be so sure of that, or sure that Trouble would be driving to South Dakota on a pilgrimage to an ancient holy place.

Trouble drove home through the long summer twilight feeling torn. The Sweet Medicine story tugged at him, even though he knew it was only ancient tribal myth, once employed by the elders to give the Cheyenne people a set of laws and ideals. There had been good in all of Sweet Medicine's teaching. To this day the Cheyenne avoided feuds and violence, and murder among them was very rare.

But they weren't really Cheyenne anymore. He was driving a Chevrolet pickup truck, the product of European genius. In his home he and his wife enjoyed television via a satellite dish, and convenient food, and appliances. Gray Wolf had given him a taste of his heritage, and he liked that, but that was old and this was a new century, and maybe a new era. Funny how the wolves had inflamed this thing in him, and before that, the buffalo commons.

He felt itchy, and uncertain about his future.

Mavis was waiting for him when he returned. "Well, you going back two centuries, or forward into the next one?" she asked, kindly, enjoying his sudden absorption in the past.

Trouble shrugged.

"Maybe both," she said. "We don't have to be whites. We can keep our ways and still be Americans."

"We'll see," he muttered.

"You're all tore up," she said. She set aside her star quilt and came to him, hugging him robustly in her way. He liked that and hugged her back.

"If you want to go back to the old ways, I'll go with you. If you want to stay here, I'll stay with you. I like them both," she said.

"I like the wolves."

"Maybe this is a new time. Maybe the whites will fade now."

"Hardly likely."

"Every culture has its turn. Then it dies. Theirs is over but they don't know that. They think all their technology'll get them ahead, but they've lost their heart and spirit."

"Maybe some of it. Religion's dead, I think. They mostly hate their God. He gets in their way. But I'm not going to trade in my truck for a pony."

He slept uneasily that night, but the next day everything was all right.

Cam Nichols arrived before the stock trucks did. He wanted to see what the longhorns looked like. These were coming up from Texas and Oklahoma.

"How are you, John?" Nichols asked. He wore his oldest jeans and his battered hat, ready for all sorts of dirty work.

"Same as ever."

"Are the wolves around?"

"Just the same. I hear them sometimes. I got so I like the sound of them at night. Talking about where there's prey, that's what they do."

"Grass looks good."

"There's been nothing on it all spring now."

"All the gates shut?"

"Yes, but I'm going out to check after these arrive."

"Good idea. They'll hang around here for a while anyway."

The trucks rolled in around nine, one after another, each hauling a single-decked stock trailer with a rear gate as wide as the truck. The big Peterbilt Kansas rigs lined up in a row, waiting to unload, while the lead truck backed into a chute that Trouble hoped was wide enough for cattle with an average horn spread of four feet.

"You go down there and look at these?" he asked Cam.

"No, I bought by phone. It's mixed stock—bulls, cows, steers, heifers, calves, the works. I think I bought a lot of horn."

A couple of the truckers dropped a combo gate and ramp at the back of the truck, metal clattering onto the chute and into holding pens. And then the longhorns began to drift out, one by one. They fascinated Trouble. They looked like prehistoric cattle, bone and sinew, strange hollows in the flesh, long and massive and thin all at once. The colors dazzled him. Every animal was different: brindles, reds, blacks, tans, splotched colors, spotted and striped animals, browns and blues. The horns were just as fascinating. Some curved up, some out, some corkscrewed, some hooked in unexpected directions.

"I think I bought about two dollars' worth of horn for every dollar's worth of meat," Cam said tartly.

"They're sure different."

"I guess we'd better look 'em over." Cam began to study the brutes as they drifted into the chute. An occasional plaintive bellow erupted from the herd, mixed with the blatting of calves.

"Look at that one," Trouble said, eyeing a red cow with the most murderous-looking horns he'd ever seen. Those horns rose heavy out of her skull, weighing down her head, flared outward and then forward into lethal spikes. "I sure wouldn't want to be some damn wolf around her."

Nichols grunted.

"There's one got blood on it," Trouble said. A heifer had been stabbed by a horn, and her flank was caked with brown blood. "How we gonna work these?"

Nichols grinned. "I never ask anyone to do something I wouldn't do," he said. He opened a wooden gate and slipped inside with a lariat. The cattle let him pass. He maneuvered the heifer toward a gate.

Trouble hastened in that direction, opened the gate, then stepped back as far out of sight as possible. So far, his boss hadn't been gored, but the whole thing was pretty close. Gently, Nichols drove the heifer into the narrow aisle and Trouble closed the gate behind her.

"Easier than I thought," Nichols said.

"Doctoring won't be, though," Trouble said. "We've got to give her some combo antibiotic and maybe clean out that wound."

Nichols entered the aisle and between them they pinned her into a corner.

"Well, let's see," Trouble said. He pulled the cap off a throwaway syringe and eased toward the heifer, who turned and faced him. Those horns looked like a barbed-wire prison fence to him, but he slipped in beside her and nailed her just as she trotted off. He got the combo in just before he lost her, and Nichols sprayed the wound with purple antiseptic.

Cam sighed. "I don't know about all this," he said. "You were lucky. Those horns—she wouldn't fit in a squeeze chute."

"Well, Cam, maybe we'll just have to return to the old ways," Trouble said, wondering how Nichols would understand that.

"Look at this stuff," Nichols said as he surveyed the bawling mass of cattle. "Is this the beginning of a new century?"

"For some," Trouble said.

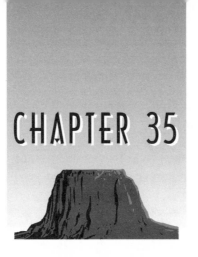

CHAPTER 35

Sanford Kouric heard about the longhorns through the Fish and Wildlife grapevine. Some of his colleagues thought that Nichols Ranches had found a legal way to kill wolves, and were angry about it. Some were even talking about fining the Nichols family if some wolves got killed; it was just wolf-killing with a new weapon, they said. But Kouric had never thought that way, and as much as he loved wildlife, he wasn't hostile to ranchers. The idea of longhorns utterly fascinated him, and he itched to see what would happen. Maybe, just maybe, Nichols Ranches had worked out a way for wolves and ranchers to live together on the same turf. If so, the world would be a better place.

He had thirty-eight wolf packs to keep track of in Montana, and hadn't been over to Nichols Ranches for several weeks. But now he set aside his other observations and opened up a week-long window in his schedule. He wanted to be there long enough to see an encounter. He wanted to observe, firsthand, what happened when wolves jumped some longhorns. He sensed the moment would be historic.

He drove over from Helena, rented a motel room in Ashland for a week, and then drove out to talk to Nichols himself. He liked to make sure people knew he was on their place, and what he was doing. But Cam Nichols wasn't home, and neither was Dudley. So he turned to the daughter—what was her name? DeeAnn, over in the house a half mile back.

He found her there, in the yard, that hot July day. She was quite a gal, he thought, angular, open, forthright, plainspoken, Western to the core, dressed in jeans and a Western-cut shirt and boots. If she didn't like him, he'd sure hear about it. And if she did, he'd hear about that, too.

She eyed his federal truck, reading a lot from it as he got out.

"I'm Sanford Kouric, a biologist with Fish and Wildlife. Actually I was looking for your father, Ms.—"

"Mrs. Cassady."

"Yes, we've met but I didn't remember. I just wanted to make sure you knew I'd be around, and make sure it'd be all right to look around your north ranches."

"You're the wolf biologist."

"Yes."

She eyed him long and somberly. "You want to see the longhorns. Probably don't like them."

"No, I particularly like them."

That certainly piqued her. In fact it left her speechless.

"Let me tell you something. If your longhorns work, and they're a way for ranchers and predators like wolves to live together, I'd celebrate. I've always had this war in me. Wolves belong in nature and perform important functions. But I come from a ranching family in Wyoming, and I know how it is."

She scuffed a boot toe in the dust. "Dad's in Billings with my mother. My grandfather's in Helena. I'll let them know you're here."

He took that for acceptance. "I expect to be here for a week and I'll tell you why. I want to see an encounter. You've done something good, putting those longhorns out there."

She smiled wryly. "What you'll see is a pack of killers go right around those horns and pull down a longhorn we just bought for a thousand dollars."

"I hope not. But whatever I see, whatever I figure out, I'll let you know, okay? Maybe I can help."

"You don't sound like U.S. Fish and Wildlife Service."

"No, I guess I don't," he agreed. "Were those longhorns tough to bring in?"

She smiled again. "We're bleeding red ink, and they were bleeding red blood. We had fifty punctured animals. You can imagine. You know, I sort of like them. We've one with a seven-foot spread. My God, I'd hate to have one of those horns coming at me. That old steer's carrying so much weight he can't lift his head high—those big horns are just aimed out in front of him."

"Wolves'll respect those."

"From the front," she said dourly.

"I hope they work for you."

"If they don't, we'll try something else. My grandfather says we're just pumping grass into horn instead of meat."

"I guess the horns sell, though."

"They'd better," she said. "The hides'll bring something, too. All those brindles and splotches and odd colors—just right for Western furniture and rugs."

"I'd better get going. I've got a camcorder with a high-powered telescopic lens. I may have something interesting to show you, if I get lucky."

"I'm not sure I want to see it, Mr. Kouric."

"Well, I'm not sure I do, either." He laughed, and she warmed up to him.

He left her and drove out to the graveled county road, through choking heat and dust, and then north toward Trouble's place. Mrs. Trouble told him that John was out with the new herd, looking it over, and gave him directions. He drove west, past several wire gates that he carefully closed behind him, and spotted Trouble's pickup on a ridge.

Trouble appeared from behind the ridge, carrying binoculars.

"You looking for wolves?" he asked. "I was just watching them."

"They're here? We've lost radio contact."

"I'll show you." Trouble led him over the ridge, and Kouric found himself staring into a deep, narrow gulch walled by sandstone. Heat shimmered the land.

"She's denning in there. I haven't seen pups, but she rarely comes out. They feed her." Trouble pointed at a distant cavity in the yellow rock wall.

"That's why I can't pick up signals," Kouric said.

"They're here," Kouric said. "Eating antelope."

"I see you've got longhorns on the spread."

Trouble grinned. "Word gets around."

"Truth is, I came to see this. This is prime-time entertainment, John. I'll be spending the week here and on the Antler, hoping to see an encounter."

"What are the odds, you think?"

"Oh, maybe two to one, longhorns."

"It'd be a sight. Cam says some history book's got stories about wolves and longhorns. He also says Nichols Ranches'll be raising more horn than meat."

Kouric laughed. "This is important to me, John. I have high hopes. I think Fish and Wildlife'll like it, too, once they get the idea that it's a way for wolves and ranchers to coexist."

Trouble grunted. "Maybe those old stories aren't true. Maybe the longhorns are bred different now."

"I hope to find out. My guess is that the acceptance of Horoney's project—at least by its neighbors—depends on this."

Trouble went silent, as he sometimes did, and glassed the gulch for a long time. Kouric did, too, seeing nothing.

"We won't see any, you and me talking like this," Trouble said. "But I come here sometimes."

"What're they eating?"

"Antelope. Deer if they can get one."

"You know of any kill sites?"

Trouble looked uneasy. "They're around."

"I'd like to see one or two."

Trouble silently retreated from the gulch, Kouric following, and drove eastward to a flat barren plain baking under a brassy sky, stopping at last a mile or so from the gulch.

Trouble led the biologist to the scattered remains of an antelope, mostly bones and hide, and a head with pecked-out eyes.

"Not much to see," Trouble said.

Kouric didn't agree. The gut and haunches had all been eaten out, not only by wolves but other predators, bones scattered. But the throat area remained—untouched. Kouric poked around with a boot. "Don't know how they got this one," he said. "See any more?"

Trouble shook his head, and Kouric sensed the man had slid into his own world again.

"I think I gotta go check the herd. Shipping fever, things like that."

"Where is it?"

"Two, three miles east of here. It's pretty interesting. You want to see it?"

"I will on the way back. Right now, I want to look for wolves."

"See ya," said Trouble, heading for his pickup.

Kouric watched him go, and then hunted the plain for more kill sites. He found another only a hundred yards distant, this one as old as the other, but with something that caught his eye: a puncture in the antelope hide, over the ribs. He flipped the remains over with the toe of his boot, and found a similar puncture on the other side. Maybe a bullet. And no evidence of punctures by canines at the throat this time, either.

Was someone feeding the wolves, and could that someone be John Trouble? The thought disturbed him. Maybe it was something for Montana's Fish, Wildlife and Parks people. Maybe shooting antelope to feed wolves could be defined as poaching. He decided just to let it ride. If Trouble was feeding wolves, why?

He drove part of the distance back to the ridge, left his four-wheel vehicle some distance from the gulch, and edged in for a closer look. There wasn't much wind to give him away. He settled at last in some scrub juniper for shade and a concealed place where he could glass the wall of the gulch. He tried a radio fix, and got no signal. The alpha wolf was denning within that rock, or else her collar had gone dead, as they often did. A horsefly found him, and he slapped at it.

Two long, hot, dull hours later he spotted a lone wolf carrying something—probably a hare—glide up the gulch, and then bound upslope to the stratum that apparently held the den, and vanish. A few minutes later two wolves emerged, and suddenly his portable radio was beeping softly. That was her, taking some air, leaving her pups for a time. She trotted downslope, squatted near the bottoms, and then returned to her den. The radio signal vanished suddenly.

Later in the afternoon another wolf emerged, this one carrying no prey, but holding its head in a way that suggested it would feed the pups by regurgitating food for the pups to eat. Wolves had a unique way of nurturing the pups in a pack, by regurgitating food directly into their mouths. The family solidarity of wolves was something that intrigued Kouric; in some ways wolves were so like human beings. Even in this motley pack—brought here from somewhere by someone unknown— the instinct to nurture the pups had inspired concerted effort to feed them. The pickings were poor, and this pack was scouting far and wide for meat.

He shot some footage with his telescopic camcorder, watched until the dinner hour had passed and he himself was half-starved, and then slipped out of there, satisfied with a hot day's work. On the way out he detoured over to the new longhorn herd. Trouble had long since gone.

What a sight! The low sun glinted off of horns that looked like dark swords, scimitars, corkscrews. The sun lit the flanks of gaudy, lean animals, red, blue, roan, black, tan, brown, white, cream, speckled, blotched, striped. Big and small, chaos on the hoof, some with horns so heavy they walked with lowered heads. They watched him idly, not really concerned by him. They grazed pasture that had been allowed this year to reach maturity, grass just starting to brown during Montana's harsh, dry, late summer.

Nichols's riposte. Kouric liked it. He thought Defenders of Wildlife would like it, too, once they thought about it. He hoped his colleagues would like it, too, but knew they wouldn't. They wanted everything to be tidy.

On impulse, Kouric decided to camp there while daylight played out. If anything was going to happen, it would be right about where he waited. He backed off to a low rise, settled down on scorched earth beside boulders radiating heat, and hoped to see something not ever seen—at least for a century.

CHAPTER 36

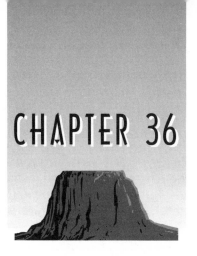

One by one, five wolves appeared, single file, out of the southeast, a direction Kouric hadn't anticipated. But he should have; they were downwind of the longhorns. Three were slate gray in the twilight; two lighter-colored. He tracked them through his lens, which magnified the light.

Kouric found his pulse climbing. He was going to see what he had come to see, and on his very first night in the field. The cattle grazed, oblivious for the moment. The wolves circled, counterclockwise, examining the 150 longhorns scattered in clumps over a vast pasture. He hoped they wouldn't get out of range. He desperately wanted to tape all this. He started his camcorder, focused the eighteen-inch-long tele-photo lens, and followed the stalk.

They paused, sat on their haunches, and watched. Then, mysteriously, in some way no wolf biologist understood, they settled on a target. In short bursts of speed, punctuated by moments of lying motionless in the grass, they approached a cow with a black calf sucking. The wolves, work-ing in some sort of remarkable unison, scrambled and darted to within fifty yards—pouncing distance. Several longhorns stopped grazing, sens-ing something was amiss.

Then, again in unison, they leapt toward the calf. The cow saw them and bawled, lowering her horns. The calf scurried back behind his mother. Her bawling set up a roar from the other longhorns, who saw the danger and raced toward her, but not as fast as the wolves, which were streaking like greyhounds.

She swung her horns, not a particularly large set, and headed toward the lead wolf, which veered out of range at the last instant. Another wolf got by her and reached the calf at the same instant a big, angry longhorn arrived and hooked a giant horn at him, lifting and tossing the wolf ten feet.

Kouric watched, mesmerized. The wolf lay stunned a moment, and scrambled to its feet, out of the fight but apparently not fatally gored. Three other longhorns, including a bull, arrived and began to build a circle around the blatting calf, their horns lowered into a spiked wall that for the moment deterred the wolves, which dodged around, looking for a way to kill the calf and get out. But still more longhorns arrived, forming the ring, more horns lowered, like a wagon train circling against an Indian attack.

The silent wolves darted, circled, feinted, crawled, and finally sat on their haunches, frustrated by the horns. And then trotted off, defeated. It hadn't taken long. Kouric's meter showed a little over four minutes including the stalk. The wolf who'd been tossed limped away with the others. Kouric could see no puncture or blood, but there might be internal injuries from a blow like that. A minute later they had vanished, chastened by prey they had never encountered before.

Kouric stopped recording, shaken and breathless. In all his years as a wolf biologist he had never seen anything like this. He felt elated and yet drained, glad the injured wolf hadn't been fatally gored, oddly pleased the longhorns had deflected the pack, privileged to have witnessed something he considered terribly important, something that would help bring social peace to a state torn by polarized opinion and gut-wrenching anger. He knew that this tape would soon be shown from one end of the country to the other, and that its effect would vary. For some, it would only prove that wolves were vicious killers. But others would see this encounter differently, as evidence that a large segment of a state could be sequestered, restored to ecological balance, and yet be contained as an island in a busy world that needed to raise food.

Quietly he packed up his gear, loaded it into his four-wheel, and drove back to the ranch road through some welcome eddies of cooler air. He needed headlights now. The lingering light told him it was about ten o'clock in this northern clime. He wouldn't get to Ashland for another hour. His sweat-caked shirt clung to his body. He felt starved, but that didn't matter. Because of all this, Laslo Horoney's National Grassland project was several steps closer to realization. It pleased him.

The restaurants were closed, but he found a Conoco station with a convenience store, and managed to assuage his hunger, if not his hope for a civilized meal. He gnawed a sawdust sandwich with the vision of what he had witnessed dancing through his mind, the sleek, gifted wolves, squirming and squirting toward striking range, and then their hell-bent race to clamp their canines around the windpipe of that calf. The longhorns, primeval cattle, something out of America's romantic past, bone and muscle, mean and feisty, utterly unlike the placid Scots and English breeds, had formed a defense that no English cattle would even have thought of, and rescued a calf from a formidable predator. The whole episode had poetry, drama, darkness, beauty and brilliance in it.

Actually, he thought, the episode settled nothing. The wolves were going to get an occasional longhorn, and not just the sick and the old. And he didn't doubt that the longhorns would gore an occasional wolf. He wondered whether the Nichols family would settle for that loss, and doubted it. For generations, they and other stock growers had lived in a world virtually free of predators, a world they dominated by eliminating wolves, reducing eagle and coyote populations, and even killing the rare mountain lion. That made it a false world in the continental United States, although a normal enough one in the British Isles, where the Scots and English cattle—Angus, Hereford—had been nurtured for hundreds of years. Would stock growers settle for an occasional loss, especially in hard times, with people eating less beef and prices at rock bottom?

But what if stockmen throughout the western United States switched to longhorns? And what if longhorns were bred up to carry more meat? Wishful thinking. A fantasy in an age when cattlemen, with the technical help of university ag schools, kept improving cattle, tampering with genetics, decreasing the amount of time for a calf to mature, increasing the efficiency with which beef cattle converted feed to flesh, and breeding to improve carcass weight. Those were the bottom line: faster, cheaper, heavier. Where would longhorns fit into decades of serious effort by breeders and ag scientists?

The next days, Kouric hunted the Antler Ranch looking for the other pack, but he found nothing and got no signal through radio telemetry. He talked to Joe Hardy, who had not seen or heard the wolves for weeks. He studied the colorful horned cattle spreading out on the dust-caked grasses of what had once been the Nichols nursery ranch, and found no sign of restlessness or wariness. They grazed peacefully and didn't spend time studying every slope. He knew he would need to overfly the whole country, searching for the Antler pack. They had probably migrated toward country that offered more prey and full bellies.

He returned to the North Ranch for one last day, and spent it watching the pack feed its denning alpha female. One wolf limped but was learning to get along on three legs. That encounter with the longhorns, plus perhaps more unseen by mortal eyes, had steered this pack toward other game. He talked a few times with John Trouble, who seemed enigmatic and unreachable, especially about the wolves, and finally gave up.

He made one last call at the home ranch, and found Cameron Nichols about.

"I heard you've been on the ranches," Nichols said.

"I'm leaving now. But before I do, I'd like to run some tape for you. In fact, if your daughter and father are around, I'd like them to see it, too. I think I can show you something valuable."

"My father's in Helena, but I'll get DeeAnn. The only valuable thing you can show me is the death of every last wolf, Mr. Kouric."

That wasn't very promising, but then again, this family was bleeding because of those wolves and faced an uncertain future because of events beyond their control.

Ten minutes later, Kouric plugged his cassette into the VCR in Cameron Nichols's ranch house, while Nichols and his daughter watched.

"This is the North Ranch," he said. "It happened last Monday."

They saw it all, stony-faced. The twilight stalk brilliantly engineered by skilled predators; the sudden rush, the agitated cow, the onslaught of other longhorns, the frightened calf, the wolf hooked and catapulted ten or fifteen feet—which brought audible gasps from his viewers—and the formation of a wall of horns circling the helpless calf. They watched while the wolves retreated, tried to penetrate that fortress, sat on their haunches, and finally trotted off into the deepening evening, one limping badly.

"Please play it again," DeeAnn said.

Kouric did.

"At least that answers some questions," Nichols said.

"But it doesn't settle anything," DeeAnn added.

"We can't make money raising bone and horn," Nichols said. "And we'll lose cattle anyway."

Kouric didn't respond to that, but he did have a bit more news for them. "The pack on the Antler's vanished, and I suspect it's migrated somewhere. I'll have to do a flyover to find them. It looks like that herd isn't going to deal with wolves."

"That's a relief." Nichols's tone had softened. "I'm glad you stopped by and showed us. Could we get a copy of that tape?"

"I'll dub one when I get back to Helena. It belongs to USFWS, but I'll slip you one. It's historic."

"Yes. I never dreamed I'd see anything like that. Well, those horns are good for something more than looking pretty in someone's den."

"Mr. Nichols, you'll still lose a few animals, and you'd better figure that into your calculations. Wolves are smart, and they understand weakness—sickness, old age, and isolation. They'll surround an isolated animal and kill it. In fact, their real genius as predators is to isolate prey and attack a lone animal. Horns don't help much when several wolves are attacking from the rear. On the other hand, wolves drive away coyotes. But that would affect a sheep man more than you."

Nichols smiled wryly. "We'd prefer coyotes."

Kouric recovered his tape and headed for the door. He liked these people and understood their strain, and the bittersweet nature of what they had just witnessed. "There's something I want to tell you," he said, tentatively. "When the hearings come up—the ones about turning the provisional wolf habitat into a permanent one—I'm going to testify against it."

"You are?"

"I'm going to say that this country hasn't supported wolves in a century, and the only way it can support wolves is by listing cattle among the prey—which'll be a nice hot potato coming from a wolf biologist. I'm going to get into trouble, since I'm with Fish and Wildlife, but I'm free to speak my mind as long as I make it clear I'm not talking for the government."

"Mr. Kouric, you're a man with a mind of your own. We appreciate that. We're going to fight it, one way or another. We have the right to the control of our own property."

"Yes, you do. That habitat designation was hasty and I didn't like it."

They shook hands at the door. It was a good handshake, a hearty handshake, the type of clasping of hands between men who respected each other.

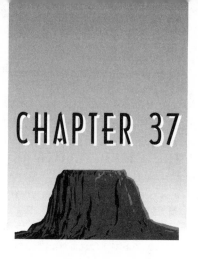

CHAPTER 37

Dudley Nichols checked in at the Colonial, where he always stayed in Helena. He was tired. Driving wasn't so easy anymore, now that he had to stop frequently to relieve himself. It was maddening what an enlarged prostate did to a man. Helena hadn't grown much, not like Bozeman, and he felt at home there, snugged into mountains that defined the edge of the Missouri River valley. It had been a gold town once, but now its business was government.

He drove over to the capitol, and that was familiar turf, too. The flowers still bloomed, the equestrian statue of Governor Meagher still collected pigeon droppings, and the impressive dome still lorded over the lower city, even though the true imperial power lay within the anonymous confines of the federal building up Last Chance Gulch.

He began, as he always did, with a courtesy call on the governor. This one was named Magruder, and he hadn't met the man. But of course any governor would know of the Nichols family. He entered at the rotunda, where his footfall echoed hollowly, made his way east to the governor's suite, and entered.

A gorgeous blond receptionist greeted him.

"I'd like to speak with the governor, if I may," Dudley said.

"Ah, have you an appointment?"

"No, I always just stop in. I'm Dudley Nichols. Nichols Ranches. He'll know who I am."

"Mr. Nichols?" She paused a moment, undecided, and then rose. "Just a moment, please."

She returned a few moments later, bearing something. "Sir, he's tied up at this point in time. Did you have business with him?"

"Yes, always. A few things about the National Grassland, of course."

"Well, what I'll do is have you give him a voice-mail message. If you'll just pick up that phone over there . . ."

"Voice mail? I want to speak to the man."

"I'm sorry, sir. We just can't—"

"Nichols. Nichols Ranches."

"Governor Magruder values your opinion, sir, and you're very welcome to leave a message. He cares deeply."

Dudley felt old. Voice mail now. That's what it came to. Disembodied voices. "No, thanks, I'll be on my way."

"Well, Mr. Nichols, we're so glad you stopped by. The governor asked me to give you this signed picture of him, and of course our Montana Visitor Kit. And we'd be pleased to have you sign our logbook."

Dudley felt ice water pour through his veins, and turned away.

"Thank you for stopping by," she said.

He had met every governor since he was a boy in the forties. But now he was an old fogey wandering the marble halls in shiny, ancient boots.

He returned to the rotunda, where a uniformed guard scrutinized him, and then hunted for a rest room. Maybe he'd go over to the legislative wing, just to reacquaint himself with one of Charles Marion Russell's greatest works, which hung there. But he thought better of it. They'd nab him for an art thief. He found the rest room and waited patiently for his constricted bladder to empty. But he didn't really want to go out there again. The rest room he understood; the world out there he didn't understand.

He hung in the rest room, aware of some sort of reluctance to leave it. Maybe go home. But he summoned his courage. He'd visit the secretary of state. He knew this one, Lester Rooney. The man had been secretary of state forever, just like his predecessors. Montana secretaries of state stayed in office until they croaked, and then a year or two after that, for good measure. Dudley wanted to see him, anyway, find out how the new county would be shaped up, and how his family could obtain services. Rooney had to be the guy. He'd known Rooney for decades, so this would be easy. Rooney didn't have much power, but he could still do some things, such as making sure the new Buffalo County took care of its handful of citizens. Heartened, he sallied back into the great, hollowed halls of the capitol, past another guard.

"You lost, fella?" the guard said.

"Do I look lost?"

"Well, the man at the rotunda said—"

"I am not lost."

"Where you going?"

"To see the secretary of state."

"He expecting you?"

"He's an old friend."

"It's that way." The guard pointed.

"I know. I've been going there since before you were born."

Seething, Dudley tramped toward Rooney's bailiwick, and bulled in the door and confronted an elderly matron in a miniskirt.

"Mr. Rooney, please. Dudley Nichols calling."

"I'm sorry, sir, Mr. Rooney is—"

Rooney appeared. "Dudley!" he bawled.

The guardian of the gate retreated behind her *Helena Independent Record*.

Rooney led him into his handsome chambers, and swung the door shut. "You're not looking a day older, Dudley."

"I've lived longer than I want, Lester."

"How are things out there?"

Dudley laughed. Dreary eastern Montana was "out there" to people who lived in the mountains. "Well, that's what I came to talk about. You're the only live body a man can talk to anymore. Everything else's voice mail, recorded messages, and press five if you want further assistance."

"Well, Dudley, you'll always have a friend here," Rooney said. "What's on your mind?"

"Services. We're going to be paying taxes to this new county, but we're losing all services. I've got great-grandchildren going to start school. Where'll we find a sheriff if we need one? What'll happen to our trash? Lester, we're paying taxes, and as long as we are, we've a right to be treated like other citizens."

Rooney stared at the cowboy art on his wall a moment. "You know, Dud, they're trying to drive you out. They wouldn't say that, of course. Just pull the rug out from under you. The feds are doing the same thing—wolf habitat, freeze everything you do. You and all the other holdouts. State policy, federal policy, to depopulate that land. Biggest theme park in the world. The new county will have almost no tax money. The foundation's land is exempted, but the foundation will pay half a million a year in lieu of taxes so the state can administer the area. As for police, the highway patrol has jurisdiction and that'll be your recourse."

"What about schools?"

"Oh, something can be arranged, I suppose. The children on your ranches will have to be schooled in Rosebud, or Ashland, or Miles, or some place, but the new county would have to pay something to the outside districts for them. No buses, though. It'd break the back of a small district to send a bus seventy miles for two kids."

"What about trash? Landfills?"

"Won't be any."

"Maybe we can dig our own, one for each ranch. We've a backhoe."

"Not without permits from the Health and Environmental Conservation Department."

"Well, then we'll fill some gulches with junk, just as every ranch in the state did."

"No, those are drainages, and the water-quality people won't allow it. You'll have to haul it out."

"Haul it out where? Neighboring counties won't take it—it's not their trash."

"That's a tough one, Dud."

"Our taxes should be cut if that's the deal."

"I agree—but it's not in the enabling legislation. You're stuck. But let me talk to some folks. I can't promise anything . . ."

Dudley simmered. The taxes on Nichols Ranches and its stock would be the same as ever, but now there'd be nothing returned. "We didn't ask for this. We just want to be left alone to ranch and be good Montana people."

"I know, Dud. Things happen. It's a different world. But let me scout around. Maybe something'll work out. They know Nichols Ranches."

"That's what I'm afraid of. Just say nothing, Lester. They'll just find more ways to plague us. They're not driving me out. Not from my land. The only way I'm going out is feetfirst."

Rooney nodded. "Probably broke, my friend, if they start fining you for dumping trash. They don't even have to go to court anymore. Just slap it on you. There's some around here that'd love to do that."

Dudley wrestled down his temper. "Well, thanks, Lester." He stood, feeling old again.

"Sorry I couldn't help, Dud. You might go over to Environmental, or go up the gulch and talk to the EPA."

Dudley drifted out of the capitol building feeling like a relic. He ached to quit, but wasn't a quitter, and he still had time to bother more bureaucrats. Maybe he'd get some answers in the Health and Environmental Conservation Department.

Twenty minutes later, having threaded the Cogswell Building labyrinth, he found himself at the bullpen desk of a solid and hazardous waste bureaucrat named Billy Stortz, who looked to be about fifteen and yet to shave.

Dudley introduced himself and swiftly reviewed the dilemma Nichols Ranches faced. "The new county will have no landfill and no trash collection. Where do we take our household and ranching garbage and trash?"

"You'll have to get rid of it. You can't just leave it around."

"Yes, where?"

"To a licensed landfill."

"Where would that be?"

"I'd have to consult the register."

"Can we just bury it on our ranches?"

"Not without a permit."

"How do we get a permit?"

"Go through the landfill-licensing process. We need water-table information, percolation tests, site topography, things like that."

"Does the state do that?"

"No, the operator does. It costs a few hundred thousand dollars, and of course is subject to further modification."

"Well, every ranch in the state has some gulches where trash was dumped. I guess that's what we'll do."

"That'd be extralegal, sir. A gulch is a watercourse. You could talk to water quality over there. He'll give you a copy of the regulations."

"Well, I know what we'll do. We'll truck it all right here and unload on your doorstep."

"That'd harm the environment, sir. And it's a felony now to threaten public officials."

"Young man, Montana's environment can't be harmed any more than it is right now by people like you, and I'm in the mood for felonies. Good afternoon."

Fuming, Dudley escaped into the hot afternoon. Helena's invisible spiderwebs choked him and he needed to escape. He'd have a high-cholesterol medium-rare T-bone and in the morning he'd see whether he wanted to stay in this nest of vipers and talk to a few more, or go back to civilization.

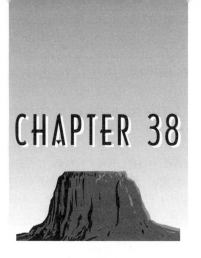

CHAPTER 38

Dudley Nichols fled Helena with the first light, glad to get out. Once, long ago, he had loved the old mining town. But that was back when he was a sovereign citizen in a sovereign state. People were powerless now; the federal bureaucracy had won. No wonder no one voted anymore. He didn't think he'd vote again.

The trip to Bozeman, through stark winter-wheat country, didn't take long. The wheat was approaching harvest, fading from green to yellow, and looked good. The Gallatin Valley was choked in smog now, and it troubled him. Where did all those people come from?

He barely recognized Bozeman; it had almost tripled itself in fifteen years, and was bidding to become the largest city in the state. But he sure knew where to find the university, and where to find Martin's quarters.

He turned south on Willson and pulled up at an ancient frame building that probably dated to the 1920s. Parking was going to be a hassle. He found a slot a block away and hiked back. Willson had once been lined with grand homes, but now it had decayed into a nest of student warrens. He remembered that Martin had been living in an efficiency carved out of the back of the old building, so he hiked around to the rear, found the door, and knocked. No one responded for so long he was about to give up, when suddenly the door opened.

Martin, in skivvies, confronted him owlishly. It was almost ten, but the young man hadn't started his day.

"Martin?"

"I suppose they sent you to spy on me."

"Your dad asked me to check up and see how you're doing. Are you up to breakfast?"

Martin stared, nodded, and stepped aside. Dudley entered a dark, dank, close place that exuded the odors of unwashed clothing, unwashed dishes, and sweat. Martin wasn't much of a housekeeper. The kitchenette was stacked with plastic dishes; piles of laundry formed mountains in corners.

"You should've called first," Martin said.

"We live the way we choose," Dudley replied crisply. "It's your life."

"Why is it that when I'm around my family, I get lectures?"

"I'm glad to see you."

Martin didn't reply. He headed into the bathroom, and Dudley heard the sounds of ablutions. That was good. Martin was in need of ablutions.

Dudley unearthed a chair, removing books, a canvas tote bag, old tennis shoes, and tee shirts, and settled into it. A worktable lined one wall; a bed another. A junk dresser and junk chairs completed the ensemble. A poster of a howling wolf hung on one wall; another poster, of a herd of buffalo, occupied space over Martin's desk. A third poster of wolf cubs, looking like nice puppies, was tacked on the wall behind Dudley. A fourth poster, this one in elaborate type and rainbow colors, announced that Wilderness is the Salvation of the World. A photograph of a buck-naked woman stood on the desk, half-hidden behind some paperback books.

Dudley supposed he should mind, but he didn't. He'd been young once.

Martin emerged from the bathroom, still unshaven, his stubble two or three days old, his unwashed hair caught in a ponytail. He wore a tee shirt with a howling wolf imprinted on it, and grimy jeans. Dudley suddenly regretted inviting his grandson to breakfast, not because of the tee shirt, but because he was not clean and groomed. As far as Dudley was concerned, anyone who didn't groom and civilize himself was just yelling to the world about his own worthlessness. In his day, young people wore clean and pressed clothing, the girls in flowery summer dresses, the young men in chino pants and cotton shirts. They were shaved, combed, groomed, and attractive. What had happened to young people? Why were they so indifferent to their own mortal selves?

"Perkins all right, Martin?"

The youth shrugged. "They all serve empty plastic food full of herbicides."

"I don't think so. But let's go. It's a fine day, and I'd enjoy hearing how things are going."

"So you can report."

"Your parents want to know how you're doing. You could call it caring."

Martin didn't reply. They walked through a golden morning, climbed into Dudley's pickup, and headed west on Main Street. In Perkins, no customer paid attention to an odd couple, an old man in a sharp-pressed Western-cut suit, with shined boots and a disciplined haircut, and a young man who looked like a street bum.

Martin ordered oatmeal, tea, and an apple. Dudley ordered a second breakfast, this one French toast. He always stayed slim, and didn't much care, at his age, whether he ate too much fat or not.

"Well, son, how's your work coming along? The paper?"

"It's not. I quit."

"Taking a summer break?"

"No."

"You've abandoned it? You'll go back in the fall?"

"I crashed."

"What does that word mean? I don't catch the modern slang."

"Crashed. Like a wreck."

"Ah, what're you going to do?"

"Nothing."

"Ah, was there a problem?"

"Lousy advisor."

"Who was that?"

"Leonard Kazin. Doesn't know his left hand from his right."

"Kazin?" Dudley started to say he knew Kazin, but instinctively clammed up.

"Look, just tell my parents I quit. They'll quit sending me a check and that'll be that, okay?"

Dudley thought back to his salad days. He'd been so busy, first in the military after the war, and then in school, with a bride to care for, and only the GI Bill for support, that he'd never had time to worry about where he was heading. But Cam had bounced a few times before settling down. Quit once, returned to the ranch, returned to school, drifted one summer.

"Martin, it's okay. It's hard to find our bearings. I don't think your folks will worry much, as long as you don't make drifting a way of life for long."

"Who says I'm drifting?"

Dudley sighed. "Poor word. Now that I have you here, there's something I'd like to do. I'd like to see the Flying D."

"You would?" Martin looked startled.

"Sure would. I've been there once. That was when one of the Kleberg family owned it. Texas people. I think it's just about the most beautiful outfit I've ever seen. What I want to see is the buffalo Turner's put on there."

"You can't always see them. There's only that one public road, and the rest are blocked off."

"Let's go," said Dudley. "I've had a hankering all my life to see a pasture black with buffalo."

He drove out to Four Corners, and then south past Gallatin Gateway, thick now with suburbia, and into the canyon. Martin directed him onto an unmarked gravel road, and shortly they found themselves in green-clad foothill country, with the blue Spanish Peaks bolting into the southern horizon. They entered the ranch, drove three miles more, and then, suddenly, there were the bison, spread like a black carpet over slopes and around horizons. Dudley stared, awed, marveling at the odd, explosive sensations he felt, things he couldn't explain to himself.

"There's supposed to be three or four thousand," Martin said, all sullenness gone from his voice.

Dudley discovered an animated young man beside him, whose face had transformed itself.

"They tore out all the interior fencing," Martin said. "Now it's just wilderness."

"Not quite. We're sitting on a nicely scraped gravel road. I hear Ted Turner's fought spurge, knapweed hard. He has a regular crew."

Martin looked annoyed again. "Let's go. Now you've seen them."

"Let's watch, Martin. I'm enjoying this."

"You're just seeing it as another ranch with exotic stock."

"How are you seeing it?"

"This is what the world should be. Without humans in it, except in cities."

Dudley didn't reply. He parked the truck, turned off the engine, and let the spectacle permeate him. The black carpet moved in fits and starts, often stalling entirely, and then mysteriously eddying over lush grass. It wasn't wilderness—it was really a well-managed ranch, a rich-man's private zoo. What was Martin seeing in it, and why did Martin resent any suggestion that all this was intensively managed?

"Had enough?" he asked after a while.

The young man nodded, and they drove silently back to Bozeman. Dudley didn't know what to say or do: his own grandson had become a sullen stranger, someone literally opposed to the human race. But if human beings were the enemy, what about Martin himself? And if Martin thought white men and European civilization were the particular demons, what about himself? It didn't make sense to Dudley.

"What don't you like about Professor Kazin? Maybe I can help," he said.

"He's not with it."

"Is he the reason you're quitting?"

"You spying on me?"

"Trying to understand."

"Well, don't." Martin stared at traffic a while. "Kazin's trying to make me write things I don't believe," he said and went silent again for a while. "Like Indians. He says Indians were part of the ecology. He just doesn't understand what wilderness is. He's been around cities too long. What he's really saying is that white men are part of nature. We're not. We're just despoilers, wrecking millions of years of evolution."

Dudley listened, wanting clues, understandings, and not getting them. He waited for more, but Martin had slid into his sullenness again, which ballooned with every block as they penetrated Bozeman.

They pulled up at Martin's place on Willson, and Dudley found himself at a loss. He wondered if he'd ever see his grandson again.

"Well, I guess you're done spying on me," Martin said.

"Why don't you decide what I'll say to your parents. I'll tell them I saw you and you're in good health. You tell me what else. Do you want me to tell them you quit your work on a graduate degree?"

"You'll tell them anyway."

"No. You decide and I'll abide by your decision."

Martin looked stricken. "Tell them what you feel like."

"Should I tell them you're happy?"

"No."

Martin looked ready to bolt. "I'd like to see you again, son. Mind if I come over in the fall?"

"Whatever suits you."

With that, Martin fled the pickup truck. Dudley watched the miserable youth hike around the corner of the house and vanish. The boy was as alien as someone from Mars, he thought. What had wounded him? What had happened to the world Dudley once knew?

Dudley couldn't make sense of any of it, especially Martin's alienation from the society that had nurtured him. This was more than just a nest-leaving rebellion against parents. This was a rejection of his very civilization, its science and religion, its values, beliefs, sacred traditions.

He turned his truck onto Main, heading for the interstate, feeling he had lived too long. He was getting that feeling all too often these days.

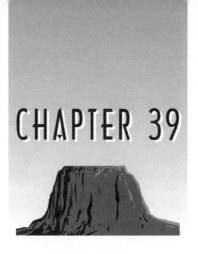

CHAPTER 39

Sandy Nichols toyed with a perfectly delicious dinner at the Rex, wanting another drink. She and Cam were dining with old friends from the Hereford Association, Arnold and Phyllis Bjorn, who had sold their ranch and retired in Billings. Cam had put this together. Ever since they'd moved to the new house, Cam had resolutely taken her to lunches, even breakfasts with their many friends there. But never dinner before.

Poor Cam! He was trying so hard. A wave of helplessness and pity overwhelmed her as she watched him eat, and maintain their end of the conversation because she just couldn't. All she wanted was another drink, but she was damned if she would. Not when Cam wanted so much to help her. He'd moved here, to this ugly city, from his beloved home—for her.

She fought back tears. The Rex was such a lovely place; the finest in Billings, and she should have loved it. She should have rejoiced to be here, away from the boredom and desolation of the isolated ranch. Instead, she felt as taut as a cello string, unable to release herself or enjoy the talk. Cam assessed her now and then, his concern seen only by her as she nibbled at the garlic-roasted filet topped with cognac dijon mustard sauce.

They were talking about the wolves, and she heard a tinge of anger and bitterness in Cam's voice. She heard that constantly now, and knew her hot-tempered husband was under pressures he had never before experienced, like a plugged volcano ready to blow. That bad moment at La Jolla with the Horoneys drifted across her mind: Cam choking back his anger, the weekend ruined, the gulf between two fine men unbridgeable. Now she heard that tone of voice all the time, and knew she was contributing to his agony.

"I think I'll go to the powder room," she said, not really knowing why. She just needed to escape, be by herself a moment, compose herself because she was on the brink of tears.

"Sure, honey," Cam said, and she felt his gaze follow her as she threaded her way across the crowded room and down the stairs to the ladies' room. She was fleeing, running, desperate for something to release her. Within, she found a booth, sat clothed, and buried her head in her hands as tears came. She wept hotly, hearing people come and go, hearing snatches of conversation. Then she dried her eyes and sat desolately, afraid to return because her face would tell her tale. She had done well this evening, actually, just one double gin and tonic when drinks were ordered.

The thought ushered a great sadness into her soul. She loved Cam; he loved her. Theirs was a match made in heaven—except that she couldn't bear his isolated home, and he couldn't live anywhere else. She'd been a good wife, bringing up the children, finding company in that isolated place, nurturing him . . . a good wife until the last two years or so, she thought guiltily. That's how long it had been since they made love. She was too crocked every night, and he just pulled into himself, sometimes just hugging her while she lay there. Once she had desired him more than she could say in words. He fulfilled something in her. A wave of guilt flooded her, and she buried her face in her hands again. Poor Cam. It was her fault, really. No, no, it was no one's fault. It was just a star-crossed love—two people rejoicing in each other, torn asunder by things neither could control. She loved him so, ached with love for him. Ached for the moment she could be happy with him.

She needed to go back to the table. She could do it. She was tough. Anyone of any class who grew up in the mining town of Butte, Montana, had a resilience and good humor and tolerance of weakness in others, and she wasn't any exception. She thought about rowdy Butte, the pit now half-flooded with poisonous water, the dowdy old downtown on a hill, the skeletal headframes on top of the town, the hard-bitten humor. Oddly, she had no desire to return; life had transformed her, and she would be as uncomfortable there as she had been on the ranch. Maybe, maybe Billings . . .

"Sandy?" That was Phyllis's voice.

"I'll be out in a sec."

"Cam sent me. You stayed so long he was worried."

"I drink too much."

"Well, you're fine. Let's go."

Sandy rubbed her eyes and emerged from her sanctuary, hoping Phyllis wasn't too observant, and they made their way back through the restaurant.

She found Cam's tender gaze following her progress, and then it was over. She smiled, ordered dessert, drank decaf, and listened to the talk. She gathered courage, defended the Horoneys from Arnold's vitriol, fought back the need to order an aperitif, drew out the somewhat subdued Phyllis about how it was to leave a ranching life behind, and found courage when she thought she lacked it. The last of the evening went brightly.

Cam drove her home quietly. She drew one of his hands to her, and held it, squeezed it gently.

In their house she drew him to her and hugged him and wept, and he hugged her for a long time. She ached to say things, but couldn't.

"Don't ever leave me," he said.

She puzzled that, and then knew what he meant. She had already drifted from him into her boozy world.

"I won't," she whispered. "I'm tough. A Butte kid." She laughed unsteadily.

The next days went a little better. Every time Cam could, he took her out, as often as possible with company. Some she knew; others she met for the first time. He was introducing her to the world she had been starved for out on the ranch. But it would be up to her to continue with it, invite people to dinner, join groups, widen her social life. She drank, but in a more controlled way now, disciplining herself when she was with others, which was, oddly, hardest of all.

She never imagined her drinking was a "sickness." That was the mythology of the helping professions, as they called themselves. She knew what drinking was: a weakness of character, and she hoped she'd have enough character to control it. She didn't like the idea of demonizing alcohol, which she regarded as a blessing to a hard-pressed world. She would not make a devil out of it because that was to give it powers it lacked. She knew exactly what she needed to do: control it, control herself, say no when she needed to say no. But that was so hard.

Cam seemed distant. He flew out to the ranch, sometimes stayed two or three days, and flew back again. Once in a while he drove. He had planted her in better soil and was quietly waiting to see whether she bloomed. She desperately wanted to bloom for him. He was so strong, and she felt so helpless. He was looking drawn and worn these days with the ranches hemorrhaging money.

Her thoughts turned to making him comfortable, easing his burden, and she found ways, however small, to help. Flowers appeared in their house. She stayed off the liquor enough to cook good dinners, and came to anticipate his phone call from his cockpit when he was approaching Billings, telling her over the roar that he'd be home soon. It delighted him to sit down to her meal, and sometimes she found him gazing at her, his eyes alive with things he couldn't voice.

Then Dudley came, stopping by after his trip to Helena and Billings. Cam was at the ranch. She welcomed her father-in-law and urged him to wander through the place. He had seen it only once, just as they were moving. He strode the formal old rooms stiffly, poured himself some bourbon with a glance at her, and seemed at a loss for words.

"How did it go, Dudley?" she asked.

He sighed. "Magruder's the first governor I've not met. Times change," he said. "They wanted to give me a signed picture of him." He laughed dourly.

"Did you get anywhere about the ranch?"

"Oh, Rooney's looking into it, but he says it's a lost cause because the state's committed. We've got police protection from the highway patrol—even if they're fifty miles from us when we need 'em. As for the rest—I told some twerp in one of those environmental departments that if they won't take our trash, I'll unload it on his doorstep."

She laughed. "What did he say?"

"He said it was a felony."

Her heart went out to him, to Cam, to DeeAnn, the three struggling so hard to save the Nichols ranches. But she craved other news.

"Did you see Martin?"

"I did. He's well—sort of. He's one unhappy young man, though."

"He always was. We tried so hard. But not hard enough, I guess."

"You and Cam did a good job, Sandy. Martin's just a lost young man, the kind that didn't grow up."

"How's his work?"

"It isn't. He's quit, just drifting. I get the sense that it's not just for the summer, either."

"Oh!" She felt pierced by failure.

"He didn't care one way or the other if I told you and Cam. I took him to Perkins—he looks like some hippie. No, he looks like a street bum, and his room smells worse than a feedlot. Piles of laundry, life lived by poster. Does he ever think an independent thought?"

"He was rather neat in high school. Did he say anything about us?"

"We steered clear of that. We went out and looked at Ted Turner's buffalo on the Flying D. He thinks the world should be all buffalo and no people—except himself and a few environmentalists, I gather. That's truer than it sounds, too. Those people want to recapture the West and drive the rest of us out."

"Cam's still sending Martin a check."

Dudley stared into the sunny window. "My first instinct was to throw the kid out. That'd be rash. It's up to you, of course."

"I don't want him to become one of those dependent boys." She paused, her spirits fading. "I guess it's up to Cam."

"No, Sandy, it's up to you both."

"Cam'll know what to do," she said, dully.

They talked a little more, and he left. He was always a bit stiff around her, and never more than now, in this house, off the ranch. She felt her own failure engulf her. Martin throwing his life away, sour and unhappy. What kind of mother had she been? Drinking, ignoring her youngest child, piling burdens on poor Cam just when he needed a strong woman.

She headed for the kitchen and poured a triple, if that's what it was. Mostly it was gin with a splash of tonic.

CHAPTER 40

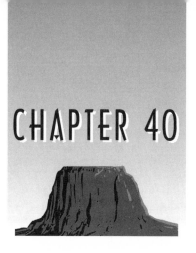

The message dangling from Cameron's fax machine turned out to be from Laslo Horoney.

"Dolly and I deeply regret the unfortunate events of last month, but we understand your feelings, and our esteem for you and Mrs. Nichols remains unchanged. We hope you feel the same about us.

"I will be spending two days doing helicopter overflights of the grassland project. There is room for more in the helicopter. Perhaps you and your father will join me, if only to educate yourselves about the project. And of course, Dolly and I would like you and Mrs. Nichols to join us for dinner in Billings.

"Let me know. Schedule and information attached. Laslo."

Cameron liked the idea, but squirmed at the thought of meeting the man he had abruptly abandoned. Maybe it was he who owed the apology. He'd been so short-tempered and angry for months that he felt barely civil. Well, he'd manage that, he thought. He was man enough to apologize. The overflight would be fascinating, and whatever he could learn about Horoney's project would help Nichols Ranches cope.

Promptly at eight the next morning a formidable white helicopter settled on his lawn, and he and Dudley clambered aboard. Horoney was accompanied by Hector Truehart and two aides, notepads in hand. The introductions were a bit stiff. Cam shook Horoney's hand firmly, in a way that sent a message without words.

"We're doing the southern part today, northern tomorrow," Horoney said above the roar of the ascending chopper.

The pilot swung the machine southward over ponderosa-forested slopes interlaced with brown valleys, and the deafening rumble settled into a low hum, permitting conversation.

"Here's a status map, showing what the foundation owns and the parcels it doesn't," Horoney said, passing a collection of county plat maps. "Federal and state lands are marked. The foundation now owns or has commitments for seventy percent of private lands in the target area. We'll probably end up with about eighty percent. The remainder of the freeholders, like you, will continue as they have."

Cam stared, fascinated. What appeared an empty prairie, an under-populated plain to academics and visionaries, was actually country rife with the marks of development: railroads, paved and gravel roads, power and phone lines, grain elevators, railroad tracks, factories, warehouses, coal and gravel and bentonite mines, oil and gas fields, on and on.

"Not exactly a nineteenth-century wilderness," Cam said.

"We can live with all these things," Horoney said. "That's what sep-arates us from the Edenists, as we call them—the purists who want every last trace of civilization removed. Mostly federal wildlife people and their Green allies."

They crossed a vast, empty land under a brassy blue sky. The seasonal dry of late summer had cured the grasses to tan, making the world below seem earth-colored. The ridges were vegetated by juniper, which looked like black pennies from above, or scattered jack pine, while the dry wa-tercourses often ran through buffaloberry and chokecherry and willow brush that remained green or red. And in some places they passed over a sea of silvery green sagebrush, a predator that devoured good range and was the devil's tattoo of overgrazing. This would be good buffalo country, all right, an endless sea of prairie and dryland forest, as myste-rious and hostile now as it had been to the early settlers.

The helicopter arrived at a ranch under demolition by one of Horo-ney's crews. Below, Cam could see that a metal building was being dis-mantled.

"We dismantle the metal ones, and either burn or blow up the other structures," Horoney said. "See that pile? That's several tons of barbed wire. We're shipping tons and tons of scrap barbed wire to Colorado, where it's being recycled. We're pulling up metal fence posts, but leaving the wooden ones to rot."

They overflew a wheat ranch, with its alternating rows of cropland, half-fallow, half-planted in any given year. The wheat below them had turned golden rather early and was nearing a not very successful harvest because of drought. Metal sheds and a neat white ranch house completed the holding.

"They're hanging on," Laslo said.

To the west, as they approached the Wyoming line, they could see a huge coal operation, where a thick seam of low-sulfur coal was torn from the earth by giant clamshell scoop-shovels, and eventually hauled off by unit trains, with hopper after hopper of coal in them, destined for the Midwest.

"They're outside our boundary," Laslo said. "But we've some oil patches down here that'll be in the grassland. Part of what we're doing today is looking at them. Everyone's worried about access, and we're offering easements but not roads. It'll be up to businesses within the grassland to maintain their own roads. The federal government's especially touchy about that. They want maintained roads to their BLM and Forest Service land, but nothing in our enabling legislation requires us to maintain any roads at all, when the purpose is to restore wilderness. So it'll be up to them."

"You have trouble with them?"

Horoney grinned. "A great deal. That's a long story."

Truehart pointed at country that had once been a wheat ranch. "That was replanted this spring with bluestem—buffalo grass," he said. "From the air we can still see the old wheat plantings, but from the ground that bluestem looks pretty good. That's one of the foundation's minor successes. We put the seed in early enough to take hold before it got too dry—but there've been some disasters, too."

Cameron studied the place, noting the blackened foundation of a ranch house that had once been the home of some family, the place where it lived and dreamed and hoped and maybe died. He felt a sadness envelop him. This grassland project was the death of so many dreams, and maybe his own and his family's, too.

Quietly he and Dudley listened and watched, as Horoney examined one problem area after another: a pipeline company with an isolated gas-cleaning facility worrying about access; an oil field that could be hurt by buffalo; the ranch of a man who was suing the foundation for reasons not made clear to Horoney's guests; a federal highway that posed fencing and animal-migration problems; an isolated piece of Custer National Forest that the Forest Service wanted to sequester because of archaeological finds on it. Cameron found these diverse problems awesome in scope, and marveled that Horoney and his foundation didn't just abandon the whole project. Truehart took notes; one of the aides took photographs; the other kept files and data at the ready.

They lunched in Gillette, Wyoming, and then overflew another segment of the grassland near the Black Hills. Late in the afternoon, over South Dakota, Horoney called it a day and instructed his pilots to head for the Nichols ranch.

"It's coming along," he said. "Slowly, in its own way, mostly because we stay flexible and try to accommodate people. Our biggest problem is the government."

That piqued Cameron. "I thought this is what they want—the creation of a High Plains wilderness or something close to it."

Horoney laughed, this time cynically. "Well, let's talk about that. They have an agenda, but along comes this rich man Horoney with another plan, and they don't like it."

"An agenda?" Cam asked.

"Sure. Among themselves, they're perfectly frank about it. You sit down with any bunch of Fish and Wildlife or Park Service people, and most Forest Service and BLM people, and you'll hear it. But not the public. What they want is to change the face of the West, restore it to wilderness and habitat for all sorts of species from grizzlies to wolves and buffalo. And how would they do that? By systematically driving out ranching in particular, and agriculture in general. Since Congress won't give them money to purchase land, they're doing it by other means, mainly regulation calculated to undermine ranching."

"Such as?"

"These fellows aren't your county extension service, Cam. You're in their crosshairs."

"Whose crosshairs?"

"The Park Service, Fish and Wildlife, Interior Department, BLM, Forest Service, Army Corps of Engineers, their allies at the state level, the Green groups—all of them except perhaps the Nature Conservancy—and academics. The feds have virtually bought all the environmental departments in Western universities. Not with grants, but with research contracts. And somehow or other, all that research just happens to support the federal wildlife policies the bureaucrats were planning all along. And it fattens the universities and faculties. That's one thing about my foundation. We've hired the best independent biologists we can find, people still committed to serious science wherever it may lead them. There are some, you know."

Cam peered down at the passing landscape, his beloved country, the stretching infinities of the plains, along with its abrupt ridges and hidden refuges for man and animal. The shadow of the helicopter needled through a herd of Angus cattle, a fleeting eclipse of sun upon a ranch. These plains had become the prize in a struggle that reached the core of reality: was mankind good? Was mankind's dominion over the earth good? Was mankind's desire to make the earth bloom good? Would it be better for the world if people didn't exist upon it? Negative answers to these questions lay at the heart of Green religion. Ancient Jewish and Christian religion had positive answers to all of these things, settled ideas that had animated his grandfather and father. Tend your gardens, they would say, whether the bloom is daisies or beef. But now it was all being questioned again by people who wished to destroy their own culture.

"Reestablishing habitat is half of it," Horoney continued. "The other half is federal ownership. They want to repatriate most of the rural West, make it all public land, but so far, Congress won't fund such a thing. That's why we're facing these activists."

"What about food? How'll this country eat?" Dudley cried.

"They haven't even studied the matter, other than to recite the mantra, beef is bad. And wheat? Who needs wheat? If they can't have land, they want control, so much control that it becomes uneconomic to ranch or farm—too many restrictions. Then the rancher or farmer quits, beaten out of his own land. That wolf-habitat hearing coming up—what do you think that's about? Wolf habitat? Only in part. It's about making it impossible for people like you to hang on."

"Why are they opposing you, Laslo?"

"They wanted it for themselves." He smiled. "Turf war."

"Yeah, our turf," Dudley growled.

Horoney turned serious. "That's right, Mr. Nichols. Your turf and ours. We're a private entity without any more status in law than you. We can't and won't force our will upon anyone. You can live with us. You'll have trouble living with a bureaucracy that has police powers and can arrest or fine you for violating arbitrary rules. Put it this way: we're neighbors, the government isn't. We'll respect your home and ranch—the bureaucrats won't."

Grudgingly, Cam Nichols acknowledged the truth in it. He didn't like the foundation; he liked even less the government bureaus that intended to turn the Nichols ranches into wilderness.

"Where do you stand on the wolves?" Cam asked Horoney.

"I wish they weren't there, at least for now. We need ten or fifteen years to build the buffalo herds, but with wolves that may be impossible. Let me tell you something: the wolf advocates say that wolves kill the old and sick, thus purging and improving the herd. That's true—as far as it goes. But wolves really prey on the defenseless young, and so successfully that prey populations decline because what biologists call the recruitment rate falls below what's needed to sustain the population.

"Here's a tragic case. In 1970, there were twelve thousand of the rare woods buffalo in Canada's Woods Buffalo National Park. But that year, the Canadian government stopped its wolf control program, and now there are a little over three thousand of the buffalo, the population's declining, and the woods buffalo faces extinction—all because of wolf depredation."

"You're opposed, then."

"Not entirely. A carefully controlled pack or two would be desirable, if only to cause the buffalo to stampede now and then. Stampedes cause the prairies to rebound." He smiled. "It's not wilderness. It's management we're talking about."

The helicopter settled gently to the grass before Cam's home, sending DeeAnn's blue heeler howling off. Cam unbuckled his seat belt and turned to find Horoney's hand awaiting his. He shook it solemnly, and so did Dudley before they stepped down to their own ground.

CHAPTER 41

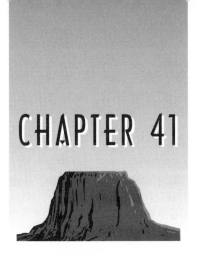

It was time for a pilgrimage, a spiritual journey. John Trouble had felt the need for days, and had mixed feelings about it. Gray Wolf had instructed him about Cheyenne tradition, the old ways, and awakened something in him, a yearning for the past. Odd how it all began with the Horoney Foundation's effort to restore the Great Plains to its original condition. That had awakened powerful feelings in a lot of Cheyenne, not just him. The memories of buffalo, grasses bending in the wind, the sacred land, the origins and laws of the People, had been coaxed to life by this white man's project.

Sometimes Trouble saw himself on a spotted pony, wearing a breechcloth, painted for war—and knew the vision was ridiculous in terms of modern reality, though it might hold some sort of profound spiritual meaning for him and others of the People. Maybe something good would come of all this; a way of life carefully insulated from the modern world. But was that good? Would he prefer to get his body healed by a medicine man, or a doctor? Would he like to surrender his pickup truck for a horse? Would he take up the old spiritual beliefs of the people, Sweet Medicine's law? He didn't know.

"I guess I'll take a few days off," he said to Mavis one evening, after supper.

"Bear Butte," she said.

"I guess so."

"Maybe you'll return to the old ways. Then I will, too."

"I don't know. Maybe."

He had no camping equipment but borrowed a modern nylon tent with an aluminum frame and a cooking kit from his friend Bill Running Deer on the res, told Cam Nichols he was taking a few days off, and left one dawn, just after Labor Day, for Sturgis. The timing was good. All those tough leather-jacket motorcycle people had left after their annual debauch. The summer heat had moderated. It would be a quiet time, a chance to find out who the hell he was.

He drove down to Ashland, got onto Highway 212, and headed southeast through country he loved so much it made him ache, piney ridges at first, finally giving way to grassland that leapt toward distant horizons where the future seemed to lie. What was it about the sky? Nowhere else on earth was there such sky, mysterious, vast, filled with portent. All this was the heart of the new buffalo grounds, and now it lay deserted. Even this road was doomed. Later, toward the South Dakota border, the country turned hilly and rough and wooded again. He passed through Belle Fourche, an area blessed with beauty and water and grace, and on down to the interstate. From there it was a short hop to Sturgis, all in the shadow of the Black Hills, land sacred to his people, the Sioux, the Arapaho, and others. He turned off on the road that led north of town, passed old Fort Meade—built in 1878 in the shadow of Bear Butte to control the wild tribes—and found himself staring at the huge, isolated black rock that jabbed electrically into the transparent sky. He felt an odd stirring of his energies whirl through him. Something mysterious, almost sacred, radiated from the scowling dark rock. He saw images, faces, peering down at him. He entered the state park, passed wandering buffalo, fine shaggy beasts that eyed his truck passively, and parked at the modern, rustic headquarters.

This was a holy place, this rock.

Beyond the usual curio shop he discovered a fine, sensitively wrought exhibit, some of it dealing with Bear Butte's unique geology, but most of it about its spiritual meaning to several tribes. Here the Cheyenne had received their sacred arrows and the wisdom conveyed to the people through Sweet Medicine. But here also the Sioux had received their wisdom. The rock was a dwelling place of lesser Sioux gods and myth-figures, though the Sioux believed in Wakan Tanka, the One Above, similar to the white men's idea of God. The Kiowa, Arapaho and Apaches considered the place sacred, too.

He read the signs sternly announcing that this was a holy place. The state was making an effort to respect Indian belief and tradition here, and he liked that.

He asked the clerk where he could camp. "I am Cheyenne," he said.

She looked him over, decided he qualified—the special camping area for Indian worshipers was not intended for white people in RVs—and steered him to a flat south of the towering rock, near a jagged arm that extended outward toward the east. It was especially not open to hip New-Age white people who were making a cult of Indian religion, running around having sweats, seeking medicine visions, reciting Indian prayers, and ridiculing the Christian faith of their forefathers. Trouble had always been amused by such people and such antics—hollow white men he called them. People without a sense of their own spiritual inheritance. He found the place, parked, noted three other tents—apparently all occupied by Indians—and set up camp, trying to understand the surges of feeling that coursed through him with every glance at the mysterious, looming mountain.

He felt at one with the history of his people. Now and then the tribe's medicine men returned to the Holy Mountain, as the Cheyenne called it, to renew themselves in the place where Sweet Medicine received the arrows and his wisdom from the gods. Cheyenne had fasted there during World War I, and in 1945 four others went to the sacred place. In August of that year, the sacred arrows were brought up from Oklahoma for a ceremony there, and in 1948 they were brought there again. The bundle protecting the arrows was opened and the arrows were shown to white men. In 1965, within Trouble's memory, a Cheyenne party including Albert Tall Bull, Alex Brady, Charles White Dirt, and Arrow Keeper James Medicine Elk had gone there, received a holy vision, and predicted the imminent end of the Vietnam War. One of that party, Willis Medicine Bull, was making his fourth pilgrimage.

Many Cheyenne who went there fasted because the holy mountain was said to bless those who fasted before it, and to give them the power to heal the sick. But John Trouble had come just to feel things out, let his spirits run, stretch his soul, kindle a sense of self and being. The Cheyenne never held ceremonies on top of it, unlike some of the other peoples. That place was too holy, too much the home of the gods. But he would walk up partway, not high enough to give offense, but as far on the sacred trail as he could go.

He spotted one of his neighbors, a thin youth in traditional braids, who had emerged from his tent to chop some firewood. But the other tents exuded silence. He decided to hike up the trail that very hour and eat later. It would take him two hours to reach the top, but he would stop short, and return in the summer dusk. He passed the usual signs warning that the trail was a sacred road and that the prayer ribbons and bundles left on the trail were to be respected. Well, he would do that.

The trail turned out to be steep and unrelenting, and it winded him fast. He felt his heart race. He passed bright-colored ribbons and prayer shawls tied to limbs. They seemed like Oriental prayer objects to him, things he had seen in Vietnamese temples, cloth oblations to mysterious unknown powers. If it was true that the Peoples were Asian, he could see-the resemblances here. He paused for breath beside a clump of pine, and then started up again, traversing the east side of the holy mountain, and then curving around to the north, where he was given vast views of the plains. For an hour more he struggled up the trail as it wound around the north face, and then upon the west, where, it was said, lay the cave in which Sweet Medicine had received the sacred gifts. He found a rock ledge from which he could watch the plunging sun. He had come far enough, in more ways than one. There he emptied his mind, settling into a profound quietness.

He was not a prayerful man, and didn't pray, because he didn't know who or what to pray to. But he was an open man, and could let the tendrils of thought play through him. Below him stretched much of Creation, the plains sacred to his people, their home ever since they had migrated out of the northeastern forests. He didn't really know where his people had come from, but the anthropologists said they were once forest people. That was fine with him. After that they had become buffalo people, their lives focused around that source of meat and fat, bowstrings, weapons, tools, trunks and parfleches, robes, wool, and much more.

A man in jeans and a blue shirt, his jet hair in braids, quietly passed him. They nodded. That one was a Sioux, he thought, not knowing why he thought it. He had some primordial way of recognizing other peoples.

He returned to his camp at dusk. One worshiper had built a fire and was cooking. Trouble had a small propane stove, and cooked some hamburgers with beef from his Styrofoam cooler, all the while wondering why he had come and where this was leading him. After that, in the velvet darkness, he tried to make sense of his first hours beside the natal place of the plains Cheyenne.

He wasn't surprised by the direction his mind took, as he sat in the warm quietness, utterly comfortable on his sleeping bag, against a portable backrest. He thought the old ways were largely superstition. He didn't believe that he would receive a vision if he cried for it, or that he would acquire a spirit helper, some creature whose wisdom he would imbibe, some animal who was supposedly wiser than he, a mortal, who would empower him beyond the designs of his own intelligence. No, all that was a stew of ancient mythology of a people trying to find some sort of dominion over a mysterious and unpredictable world.

He wondered, amused, what his Cheyenne people would think of that sort of thought. Actually, they would accept it easily; each person would follow his own road, and that had always been the way. His way was not to tap the powers in eagles or foxes or deer or turtles or otters—or rocks or the moon or sun or any of the physical world. No. That might have been a part of his people's past, his own past, but that was not a usable past and it had not led the people to any particular insights about the world, or science, or nature, or anything else. It was nothing more than the evoking of mysterious nature, and it gave the Cheyenne no special powers at all.

Did he consider the traditionalists and their belief insincere? No, not at all. He respected them all, including his mentor David Gray Wolf. The young man had inherited a long and deeply believed tradition. David had taught him about the keepers of the Sacred Hat, from about 1900 onward. The keepers had included Coal Bear, and his sons Sand Crane and Head Swift, and then Wounded Eye who lived between Busby and Kirk; and then Black Bird got in about 1920, and Rock Roads, and Sand Crane's brother Head Swift alone, and after that, in the 1950s, no keeper could be found for five years, so Swift's daughters kept it. Then Ernest American Horse kept it, and Henry Little Coyote, and then Henry Black Wolf after 1965, and now Gray Wolf.

Did it mean anything? Yes, it was good. For memory's sake. But did the Hat convey powers and blessings upon the Cheyenne? He didn't know.

He stared at the emerging stars, enjoying the way they popped out of the twilight. Did he believe God was in nature, that nature was God? No, he didn't believe that. Nature was nature, not something divine. He liked the idea of a Creator better, the omniscient, omnipotent God of the monotheistic people, the Muslims, Jews and Christians, who separated Himself from what he had created. That made more sense to him. That seemed plausible, real, powerful. Nature had no spiritual powers; rocks, crystals, amulets, medicine bundles, animals had no powers because they were a part of the natural world. But a Creator did. That made sense.

John Trouble sighed. His first encounter with his own people's spiritual beliefs and history had led him toward something different and more beautiful: God, however a Creator and loving guide to mortals, might be defined by the different faiths. Many white men had abandoned this great spiritual insight, and he couldn't understand why. They were saying the universe had been fashioned by happenstance, random chemical and physical forces, and there was no Creator, no God. For Trouble, that was appalling. Life was wondrous. Even an ant was wondrous. And the work of design, not a few billion years of chaos.

He wondered where it would all lead, and crawled into his sleeping bag, pleased with his voyage of discovery and all its unexpected turns. He might be a Cheyenne by blood, but not by ancient belief. He would stay a day more and go back to Mavis and tell her who he was. The pilgrimage had gone in an unexpected direction, but that was fine with him.

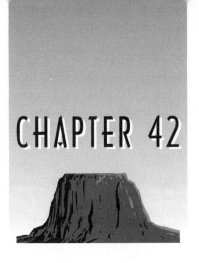

CHAPTER 42

Dr. Peter Andrew Brooke-Carson pondered the forthcoming wolf-habitat hearings, and wondered how he could best influence events. He was, after all, the foremost man in the field, and his word would weigh heavily upon those U.S. Fish and Wildlife Service officials who would decide the matter.

Moreover, his prior work had been directly related to the question raised by the hearings: the desirability of extending the Yellowstone wolf-habitat designation to the Great Plains. He was working on an almost identical topic just then, a research contract from the Park Service dealing with the environmental effects of turning the Horoney Foundation's grassland project into a new Grassland National Park. He had completed two other research contracts for the Park Service: one on the ecological impacts of expanding Yellowstone Park boundaries, and the other on the impacts of expanding Teton National Park boundaries. These three-hundred-thousand-dollar contracts had been awarded to his little corporation, Western Research Associates, and he had done quite nicely supplying environmental services and expertise to the government. His company simply utilized grad students to do the nuts-and-bolts research, and he was always careful to list them as research fellows in the end notes, and note their contributions. He didn't pay them, of course, because he was their faculty advisor and they were doing the work in pursuit of their doctoral degrees at the university. They got prestige out of it. There were always more students wanting the cachet of working for him than he could use. That gave him ample low-cost labor and increased his company's profits. The cash had always been his solace for an abysmal paycheck. His income was nothing, of course, compared to the obscene salaries and bonuses and stock options of corporate executives, but federal funding of his company was all very nice, and even gave him a few pleasures, such as his new Lexus and trips to the Caribbean.

His findings had supported the Park Service, but that was to be expected. His proposal to extend Yellowstone Park boundaries north forty-five miles into Montana, westward twenty miles into Idaho and Montana, and thirty to forty miles eastward into Wyoming, would ensure grizzly, wolf, and other habitat currently endangered by the Forest Service's disastrous multiple use concept, which had even allowed cattle to wander through country that should be a wilderness. He had particularly delighted the Park Service by proposing, for sound ecological reasons, that the park boundaries be roughly tripled rather than doubled, and that Teton's boundaries be quadrupled with the purchase of a vast and important high plateau to the west, prime elk and future wolf ground, partly held privately.

But now he was researching the most exciting thing of all, the proposed Grassland National Park, with a half-million-dollar research contract. He was going to report that the whole plan was desirable from every biological angle, and that the proposed new national park encompass much more of the High Plains than Horoney had envisioned; indeed, most of eastern and central Montana, with the Indian reservations either islands within, or adjacent. The proposed park's headquarters should be placed right on the Nichols Ranch home base, a beautiful corner and just the spot to provide park visitors a window on a unique natural world.

The foundation, of course, was the perfect stalking horse for the Park Service, achieving its goals without stirring up much more opposition after the bitter legislative fights of three or four years previous. The foundation was wildly popular among American people, even including some Greens, unfortunately, and would have to be dealt with carefully with well-orchestrated objections, such as the rally in Bozeman the previous spring. But with some lobbying from Green groups, the Park Service would ultimately prevail.

For the moment, perhaps, it would be necessary to assist the foundation in its initial effort to drive out ranchers and farmers and small holders. And that's where this wolf hearing came in. Crucially important. A permanent wolf-habitat designation would freeze all those ranchers and farmers in their tracks and prevent further ruin of the plains.

Brooke-Carson intended to prepare a text, rather than speak extemporaneously, because a prepared statement would be precise and focused. But he didn't quite know how to deal with opposing arguments. He needed something dramatic, powerful, overwhelming, some bit of science that would justify the permanent habitat.

One could argue, he supposed, that the grassland would be a perfect wolf-breeding and -marshaling ground, from which wolves could disperse into Wyoming, Colorado, Nebraska and Kansas. He could make a sound case for it. But it would be politically risky. Far better to capitalize on the nation's current love affair with the wolf. The High Plains should be declared wolf habitat simply because it would be the place where people could come to see wolves. Yes, that was it. If national parks were zoos of a sort, the proposed grassland park ought to be a wolf and buffalo zoo, the place where citizens could see nature raw in tooth and claw, from observation blinds such as one might find on an African safari. In fact, that was the whole thing: the grasslands should offer the safari experience to Americans, something like the African veldt, where tourists, their pulses rising at the spectacle of blood and death, watched lions at work on ungulate populations.

All this could be justified by sound ecological reasoning, of course, and he imagined that even the Horoney Foundation would accede to it. Montana would be the safari state, restored to wilderness as far as possible. It would mean removing some of the natives—he called them Montanoids—but that would be no problem with the government's power of eminent domain. A few of them could become licensed Park Service guides, who would drive people out to the killing fields in Land Rovers or something similar, to give visitors a sense of the romance of nature.

Yes, he would testify that the grassland should not merely be wolf habitat; the High Plains was so perfect a home for the gray prairie wolf that the area should be the official incubator for the species. That would get good press.

Disciplined man that he was, he completed his ten-minute statement in a week, just ahead of the hearings. Then he drove to Miles City two days early, no matter that the fall term was beginning and he should be on campus. Students didn't matter. They were a necessary annoyance, the cross professors bore. He kept his distance from them.

He wished to examine firsthand the area he was working on; it would certainly help to be able to say that he had walked the ground, so to speak. And, of course, what he would see would only confirm his thesis. Thus he checked in at a motel on the interstate that September day, and then drove his Blazer along endless gravel roads, deploring the condition of the range, noting the extent to which sagebrush and cactus and yucca had damaged pasture, enjoying the fading warmth of the sun, and keeping an eye out for scenic locales that would be good observation points in the proposed national park.

Surely this had to be Nichols Ranches land. Only giant corporate agribusinesses would brazenly abuse rangeland the way this had been abused. He consulted a map, and discovered that he was still far north of the northernmost Nichols ranches, and that some other shortsighted and stupid rancher had done the damage he was looking at.

He drove twenty more miles along the lonely road, seeing not so much as an oncoming car or pickup, growing faintly uneasy at the thought of his utter isolation. The awesome sky oppressed him. The vast land made him feel uncharacteristically small. He plugged in a cassette, one of those therapeutic tapes intended to soothe the soul, this one the sound of surf crashing on a rocky shore, with the cry of seagulls as a leitmotif. God, how could any mortal live in such a place? The farther south he penetrated, the rougher the country, the grassland surrendering to rocky slopes crowned with ponderosa and juniper. This appealed to the eye more than those naked wastes he had traversed. And here, indeed, he came to the first of the Nichols ranches, marked with a discreet corporate logo on a sign.

Well, that sign would tumble down soon enough. He found himself in rougher country, with ridges and draws and grassy bottoms. He had never been in this area before, and had relied on topographical maps, photos, assorted reports and papers to generate his forthcoming research report for the Park Service. Research material—that's what teaching assistants and grad students were for, and he had put six or seven of the slaves to good use.

He happened upon a wire roadside gate with a No Trespassing sign posted by Nichols Ranches, and decided to examine this country off-road. No one was about, so it wouldn't matter. He had trouble unhooking the loop that held the wire gate shut, but eventually he did, drove through, and then fastened the gate behind him. He negotiated a vague, two-rut path that carried him over a ridge and dropped him into a grassy valley, still faintly green in spite of the time of year. He saw little sagebrush here, but that didn't acquit the Nichols family. For too long had ranchers raped the plains.

Twenty minutes later he discovered cattle, but these weren't a familiar breed. They certainly weren't the red-and-white Herefords the Nichols family raised. These were rangier, horned, thinner, taller, and multicolored. Some were even gaudy. Probably common cattle. Maybe wolf fodder. Yes, that was it. Now that wolves roamed here, the family had populated this range with the cheapest cattle it could buy. He stopped to photograph a few, using his fine telephoto lens to zero in on several of the odd creatures.

After photographing the cattle, he started his Blazer. The engine fired, coughed, sputtered for a few moments, and died. Alarmed, he cranked the engine until the battery began to fail, without result. Only then did he discover he was out of gas. The knowledge punched him hard. He was twenty or thirty miles from help, on an isolated ranch pasture, and without food or water. His mind whirled through options, but the reality was that he would have to hike out. He consulted his Geological Survey maps, but they weren't detailed enough to steer him toward human habitation or help. There he was, no phone, no radio, no services, and God only knew how far from any traveled road. He found himself both hungry and thirsty, and rued the moment he had driven this way without proper preparation. He might die here! The world might lose the most eminent man in the field! He might suffer!

And yet, all wasn't lost. Those cattle had to water somewhere. He would follow them.

He slumped in his seat, paralyzed and witless, not knowing what to do, fearful that any course of action might be a fatal one. Then he grew angry. How could this happen? There should be emergency services everywhere in the United States, help immediately available. Cars should be equipped to send out mayday signals at the press of a button. Detroit had failed him. He examined everything he had brought with him, a suit and sport jacket, slacks, a turtleneck, custom shirts on hangers, tasseled casual shoes, a trench coat. Thank heaven for that. It would be a chill night.

He couldn't imagine what to do, so he sat there, staring at the cattle, waiting for them to take him somewhere. When they moved, he would, too. Water! He needed water. He sat sweating, as much from fear as from the afternoon heat. One hour, two hours dragged by, and nothing happened. No one came. The cattle didn't wander. His throat felt parched. His heartbeat had accelerated. Why had he ever come to this godforsaken place? It appalled him that people lived so far from civilization and safety.

The Blazer ticked in the afternoon sun, another hour crawled by, and still Brooke-Carson sat, unable to make himself leave the safety of the vehicle. And then a miracle happened. A battered blue pickup truck topped a ridge and rattled his direction. The driver halted across from Brooke-Carson's sports vehicle. The professor waved frantically.

"Need help?" the man asked.

Brooke-Carson surveyed the driver—probably a Native American. "I'm out of gas. And I could use a drink."

The man got out of his truck, reached for a jerry can in his truck, and was soon pouring gasoline into the Blazer, five gallons in all. Then he handed the professor a warm can of Mountain Dew. "Stock tank right over there," he said, pointing to a metal object a hundred yards distant.

The professor stared, chagrined, and then cranked the Blazer. For a while nothing happened, but at last the engine caught. He felt a flood of relief.

"Thank you; I'll pay you," Brooke-Carson said. "I'm glad you came." He guzzled the fizzy soft drink, which was unbelievably delicious. He downed it all, handed the can back to the rawboned man, and itched for another can.

The Native American shrugged. "I guess you got permission to be here." It was more question than statement.

"Ah, no, just looking around. I'm Dr. Brooke-Carson, Montana State University. Just taking some pictures. Some research. This is public land, isn't it?"

"Nichols Ranches. North Ranch. I guess it's all right. Those long-horns are pretty interesting."

"Longhorns?"

"Old breed, out of Texas; almost extinct, except some folks raise 'em for fun and the horns. Now, those horns, they sometimes get seven feet wide, though most are around four. They're the only breed that can defend themselves. That's why Nichols put 'em on here. Just the other day, one of these got him a wolf—horn right through the ribs."

"Really?"

"Want to see the wolf? We got a regular wolf biologist comes around here checking, and I was going to show this to him. Follow me and I'll drive us over there—if you're still interested. Looks like you're in a hurry to get out of here."

"Oh, no, show me."

Moments later Brooke-Carson was staring at a decomposing carcass of a gray wolf. Predators had eaten out its gut and flanks, but the hide remained.

"This looks shot. Someone shot it."

The Indian kicked the carcass over with his boot. "No, one of them horns entered here—hole six inches wide."

The professor stared, somehow loathing what he saw. "Ah, how many wolves have these cattle killed?"

"Just this one. They injured another one. That biologist, Kouric, made a tape of it. Really something to see."

"Have the wolves killed any of these longhorns?"

"Not yet, but they will."

Hastily, the professor shot numerous photos of the carcass.

"This is an endangered animal, you know. Putting that sort of cattle on here's like holding a gun to a rare and endangered species of wildlife."

"Well, they don't see it that way. They figure it's a way to keep on going with the ranch."

"I think these cattle should be prohibited on this future National Grassland."

"Well, sir, this is private land, not National Grassland."

"Well, details. Tell me—I didn't get your name—"

"Big Trouble."

"Ah, very good. Big Trouble. I admire the humor of your people. Ah, will it work?"

The Indian shrugged. "Looks like it might if the longhorns are profitable. They get extra for the horns and hides."

"This'll kill wolves. This isn't right."

"Likely they will, some anyway. I think maybe they'll drive out the wolves. That's all we need. Depends. No one knows."

"This throws a new light on everything. Agribusiness always wins in the end. Killer cows, resurrected from the past."

Trouble's face settled into somber neutrality.

Suddenly Brooke-Carson itched to return to Miles to do some research on primordial cattle and rewrite his testimony. He held all the aces now.

"Ah, thanks for the gas," he said.

"Thank the Nicholses," the man replied.

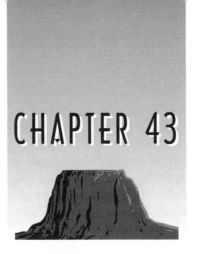

CHAPTER 43

Dudley Nichols didn't want to go to the wolf-habitat hearings in Miles City, but Cameron and DeeAnn wanted him to. What was the world coming to? A man had to go defend his right to control his own land from wolves. Who were these people?

He fumed as he dressed, wondering what the hell had happened to the world. What was the matter with raising beef? Were these people all alfalfa eaters? A bunch of damned rabbits?

He dressed carefully, intending to let the world know who he was. He put on his best Western shirt, the one with navy piping on a sky-blue ground; he put on his best Western-cut gray woolen suit. He spit-polished his good Nacona boots until they glowed. He collected his 5X beaver gray Stetson from the shelf, a hat almost virginal in its splendor. If anyone might ask him whether he was making a statement with all this, he would have said "Hell, yes." He was a stockman, proud of it, one of generations of stock growers, one of those who had made Montana a legend and a model. People who wanted to plant wolves on his land and prevent him from controlling his ranches or killing the predators were flat-out nuts. For generations, his family had worked with the ag people at the university, with the Soil Conservation Service, with the breeders associations, with the county extension agents, with range-management people, weed-control people, stock-dam builders, feedlot operators, cattle-truck operators, and many more. Worked with Montana's Department of Fish, Wildlife and Parks, building shelter belts that had become the refuge of deer and small animals, building stock ponds that had watered antelope. And now some wild-eyed fools were planting cattle killers on his land and telling him to sit there and take it.

Let them eat wolf.

Cam drove the three of them to Miles that morning in a brooding silence. He was going to testify, using material prepared in part by Bob

Rockwell. None of them supposed it would do a bit of good. The day of the American rancher had passed. There'd be beef around, raised in giant feedlots in Nebraska, with all the fodder trucked in. But ranchers in the High Plains were an endangered species.

They arrived early, had a late breakfast, made their way to the community-college auditorium and found the place almost empty. No one gave a damn about a habitat regulation that would strangle every landowner in the area. Dudley stared balefully at the motley handful, spotting that wolf biologist Kouric among them. He snorted. This was a Fish and Wildlife circus, and Kouric was their paid clown. Some young hippies—Greens, probably—who'd sweetly testify that wolves were really family people, like humans, and deserved lots of tender loving care. DeeAnn always grumbled at him when he called them all hippies, and said there weren't any and hadn't been any for decades. So just to get even he called anyone under thirty a hippie. That's what they were, including Martin. He exempted DeeAnn, but kept her on probation.

Six, count 'em, six bureaucrats filed in and settled on folding chairs behind a long table on the stage. Dudley snorted. It took six bureaucrats to do the work of one. Six salaries paid by taxes laid on the backs of regular people. They tested their recording equipment—this whole she-bang was going to be taped and transcribed—and then waited self-importantly for the hour of ten.

Some goofball from Washington arose.

"Good morning, people, I'm Lowell Flowers, deputy director of Fish and Wildlife. May I introduce, from my left, Ms. Wallmann, Mr. Bullwer, Ms. Dechutes, Mr. Danig, and our recorder, Ms. Bierstadt.

"We're here today to receive public opinion about our plan to make our provisional wolf-habitat designation permanent. You've received maps and texts. We have eleven people wishing to make statements, so we'll hear six this morning, five after lunch, and we will receive comments from the floor after that. Thank you all for giving us your valuable input."

Valuable input. Dudley snorted. The whole thing would be a charade, the sort of procedure that bureaucrats conducted to give a democratic veneer to their imperial designs. This deck was stacked. He spotted only one other person who looked like he might testify against the permanent habitat. The fellow had dirt under his nails, and wore battered Western boots. But the next one in the turtleneck and tasseled Gucci loafers with a crystal dangling from his neck would be for it, and that fat hippie girl would too, and that row of professors in tweed jackets would, and that bearded mountain-man type in fringed buckskins would, and the Jackson

Hole sporting type in designer jeans would, and that long-haired, soulful, anemic-looking girl who hadn't bathed in a month would.

Sure enough, the Jackson Hole one, with fifty-dollar mirror blue sunglasses jammed in his wavy brown hair, turned out to be a big-shot Green man; indeed, the voice of the Green outfits. He was all for wolves, and wilderness, and habitat, and the preservation of the world, and the poetry of unviolated Nature.

Dudley fumed his way through that; he was good at fuming. That fellow hadn't done a lick of work in his life; he could tell. He lived on inherited money and pestered productive people.

Next was Sanford Kouric, the wolf biologist. Dudley prepared to fume at him, too.

"I'm a wolf biologist with U.S. Fish and Wildlife, but I am testifying today strictly on my own, as a private citizen, and nothing I say should be construed as the viewpoint of the bureau I work for. This is my personal opinion, drawn from my experience as a biologist with a dozen years in the field, most of it spent on wolves."

Dudley glared, only to be surprised by Kouric's opening:

"I am speaking today in opposition to permanent wolf-habitat status in this area," Kouric began.

Dudley wasn't the only one surprised by this sally. Assorted Fish and Wildlife people looked astonished.

"Wolves are flexible and can live in many geographic circumstances, provided they have adequate prey. It is true that the Great Plains were once prime habitat, and could be again. Up until settlement, wolves preyed on buffalo, deer, antelope, elk, and smaller species, all of which were present. Some are no longer present, or present in reduced numbers. There are few, if any, elk on the plains; deer populations are dense in some areas, very thin in others; buffalo are not present except in domestic herds.

"I've been responsible for tracking two packs in this area, which arrived mysteriously and are abnormal. I suspect they were brought here. There's no evidence that they migrated; no trail. One pack has vanished. The other survives south of us and is engaged in feeding its half-grown pups. The pack that departed—we've lost it temporarily—appears to have left because game was thin in the area where it was first discovered, the Antler Ranch belonging to Nichols Ranches. I believe it headed eastward, toward the Black Hills, but until we do aerial radio surveys, we won't know for sure.

"Antler Ranch is poor deer habitat, almost entirely grassland, with little browse for deer. North Ranch is better deer habitat because it includes riparian areas along the Rosebud River that nurture prey. But none of these sites could be defined as wolf habitat because prey is inadequate—unless one includes domestic cattle as prey."

That certainly stirred the pro-wolf people, and pleased Dudley. That fellow Kouric might be a wolf man, but he was a smart wolf man, equipped with gray matter.

"Shortly," Kouric continued, "the Horoney Foundation will introduce bison—five thousand is the figure one hears. And Montana Fish and Wildlife intends to reintroduce elk. These populations, fragile and thin, would be heavily eroded by wolves, even one or two packs, and might not recruit adequately enough to expand as intended, especially if they are hunted as well. I believe there will be an eventual role for wolves on the proposed National Grassland, but they should be introduced only after ungulate populations are well established. Say, twenty thousand elk, fifty thousand buffalo. Until then, wolves should be captured and removed from this region."

Kouric sat down amid a shocked silence. A *Billings Gazette* reporter scribbled furiously on a notepad, and Dudley knew Kouric's offhand comment about including domestic cattle as prey would make the front pages of many papers around the West. Kouric was a brave man who had put his job on the line. Dudley knew what the man's superiors could do to him—probably banish him to a pencil pusher's desk.

Next came a young lawyer from the Horoney Foundation, who testified that the foundation would just as soon not have its land tied up as wolf habitat for the near future, and probably not ever. Among other things, it would needlessly interfere with range-reclamation and -restoration projects, the reintroduction of other species, and the removal of the remnants of civilization. He also questioned the legality of it.

He was followed by two oil company lawyers who strenuously objected to a designation that could prevent them from drilling new wells on oil-bearing properties, or doing secondary recovery on existing wells, or even maintaining passable roads to the oil fields.

Dudley thought that maybe the hearing wasn't quite the pro-wolf party he had anticipated.

Cameron was invited to speak next, just before noon. Dudley watched his strong, lean, weathered son walk quietly to the lectern, pull on his glasses, and begin to read. His was largely a legal and historical argument: Fish and Wildlife had never been given authority by Congress to establish habitat areas on private land, only on federal land. To do so was "taking," a violation of the Fifth Amendment, which said, "nor shall private property be taken for public use, without just compensation." In recent years, Cameron explained, the Supreme Court had applied that measure to efforts by public agencies to deny property holders reasonable control over their own properties, ruling in favor of the owners several times. In this case, the habitat rule would prevent Nichols Ranches and other private holders in the designated area the right to manage their holdings, and thus render them worthless, depriving them of the value and use of their own land without just compensation.

It was all familiar to Dudley, and he thought the case was powerful. But he doubted that the Greens present gave it a second thought, because their thinking didn't run that way, and the protection of the civil rights of citizens didn't interest them.

Cameron turned to history, noting that the area had been without wolves for most of the century, and that an area without wolves until recent months could scarcely be labeled habitat. It was a quiet, dignified performance, Dudley thought as Cameron sat down amid a deep silence.

Next, and the last one that morning, was a flashy Bozeman professor in the de rigueur tweeds and shiny loafers. This fellow, a Professor Brooke-Carson, let it be known that he was eminent in his field, and a consultant to the Park Service as well as informal counselor to several federal agencies. He said he would favor the extension of the Yellowstone wolf habitat to include the High Plains.

"Wolves are so critically important in the fabric of wildlife, and the food chain, and the maintenance of balanced populations, that wolves should be protected at all costs, and wherever they're to be found, including ranching country. If wolves are present in ranching areas, that is good, not bad, and will help nature redress the abuse it has suffered by overgrazing. If this means the death of a few cattle, that also is good because that domestic species has for too long been privileged to live in an unnatural world without predators. The most desirable aspect of this proposed permanent habitat is that by reducing herds it will prevent the further ruin of range. If that makes ranching uneconomic, so much the better; the High Plains will no longer be raped by greedy ranchers."

Dudley listened furiously, a rage building in him.

The professor droned on, his language confident, cocky, and patronizing. He himself had recently completed research that would lead to an expansion of Yellowstone Park in order to preserve habitat, and now was researching that very topic as it applied to this area and the Park Service's plans for it.

"Unfortunately," he continued, "Nichols Ranches has introduced a prehistoric breed of cattle called the longhorn as an attempt to circumvent USFWS laws against killing wolves. This fierce breed, as rawboned and cruel as a Spanish bullring bull, has already killed a wolf and injured another right in this area. I myself have seen the wolf carcass and photographed it for the record.

"I've done some research. It seems that this was the primeval cow driven north in the 1870s and 1880s to rape virgin range. But it was swiftly abandoned in favor of more docile and efficient cattle such as Herefords and Angus. A man named Dobie wrote a book that obviously fabricated a mythology about the breed. The longhorn is a useless animal, all bone and no meat, raised purely for a hobby by a handful of Texas people. But there is anecdotal evidence that it is a lethal enemy of wolves, and that is what drew Nichols Ranches to it. My researches indicate that it also takes much too long to reach maturity and thus has no legitimate economic value as a beef animal. Therefore, the sole reason that Nichols Ranches has switched to these animals is to do with horns what they cannot legally do with rifles. And that ought to be the topic of federal inquiry and possible criminal investigation."

Dudley sprang to his feet. "No, by God!" he cried.

He couldn't remember what he intended to say next. Everything was confused. Everything turned light. He felt himself falling, puzzled by that. Where was Mabel? Frank Sinatra was singing "I'll Never Smile Again." Why couldn't he think? Where was he, and why did he—

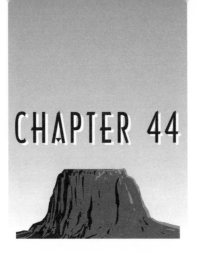

CHAPTER 44

Cameron waited desolately in the bleak fluorescent light of the waiting room, while DeeAnn called her husband. Cam knew his father was gone, no matter whether life still lingered.

It had been so fast; alive and angry, then a writhing body on the floor. The hearings had halted. Rescue arrived swiftly and paramedics wrapped Dudley and carted him off on a gurney. And that was all Cam knew. The lunch hour passed, DeeAnn thrust a cup of vending-machine coffee at him, which he held absently.

Then at last a graying, ruddy doctor in green scrubs appeared, and invited them into a consultation room.

"I'm Dr. Terwilliger, Mr. Nichols, ma'am. I'm sorry. Massive stroke. Your father's alive but his brain's full of blood. We injected an enzyme that helps reduce the damage." He sighed. "At this point it looks doubtful that we can do much, and he's too critical to send to Billings."

"How much damage?" Cam asked.

"Left side gone, but it's not over."

"Memory?"

"The chances aren't very good."

"He's better off dead?"

"That's a judgment you'll have to make."

"You think he won't make it?"

"He's failing fast."

"What would you do if it were your father?"

"Let it happen."

Cam turned to DeeAnn. "All right with you?"

She turned to Terwilliger. "What would my grandfather be like if he weathered this?"

The doctor lifted his hands, helplessly.

"I mean, would he know us? Even know he's alive?"

"One thing we can't do very well is climb into the brains of stroke victims. You might ask yourself this: what would your father—ah, grand-father—want?"

That did it. "He was a dignified man," she said. "He couldn't bear it, not having control of himself, his body functions." She turned to Cam. "Let it happen."

Cam nodded. "You can take him off—what do they call it? Heroic measures?"

"I'll need a signed release. Do you want to see him?"

"Yes."

Moments later they stared at Dudley, whose face had contorted into a grotesque leer. His eyes saw nothing. An oxygen clip at the nose fed his lungs. A plastic thing prevented him from swallowing his tongue. Wires connected him to monitors.

It wasn't Dudley anymore. Cam found a hand and held it. It felt cold, lifeless.

"How long will he last" he asked.

The doctor shook his head.

"All right, thank you," Cam said. "We're going to go over to the nursing home and break the news to his mother. You can reach us there," he said. "Then we'll be back." He stared at the doctor. "Thanks for all you've done."

The doctor nodded.

Cam and DeeAnn penetrated into a bright day and headed for the nursing home. He wondered what to say to Anna Garwood Nichols and how she'd take it. But it had to be said.

"How're you doing?" he asked.

DeeAnn smiled wanly at him.

"I'm sorry I talked my father into coming. That damned professor—"

"He killed Grampa."

"I don't know. Dudley told me a dozen times he was ready to go. He didn't much like this new world."

"But that wolf business, that was the stupidest accusation."

Cam smiled. "We hadn't thought of it that way, but I can see the professor's logic. Actually, Dud would have liked to kill the wolves."

"That professor called for a criminal investigation because we put longhorns on! That killed Grampa."

Cam retreated into silence. Dudley had lived an upright life for over seventy years. That accusation was like a sword to the heart. Maybe it did kill him. That and the crime of being a stockman. That accusation was a sad last memory to take to the grave.

At the nursing home they discovered Anna Nichols had finished lunch and was napping. Cam decided not to awaken her. He dreaded telling her. He and DeeAnn drifted to a café beside the inter-state, but neither was hungry, so they nursed coffee and then return-ed to their watch at the hospital only to discover that Dudley had died.

"Peacefully," said the nurse in charge. The doctor had gone to lunch himself. "It's best, we think. We're so sorry."

"You did all you could," Cam mumbled.

"We'll need instructions," the nurse said.

He felt alone. Both parents gone now. Dudley had been a good father, a model for him, a man of unbending rectitude. That part obsessed him. A man of rectitude being accused of criminality by some ass of a profes-sor, an accusation that felled a fine man. For the first time, a rage built in him. He was going to reply to that *Doctor* Brooke-Carson, who lived in a world populated only by wildlife.

They retraced their steps to the nursing home in a glorious September day. Not a good day to die.

Anna was up, sitting in the familiar chair beside her bed, watching a small television.

"Boring thing," she said, smiling. "How are you, dears? Speak up, I'm pretty near deaf."

Cam braced himself. "Grandmother, Dudley's gone."

She absorbed that and didn't ask that it be repeated.

"Well, I expected it," she said at last.

"This morning. At the hearings. He had a stroke. A bad one that took him in two hours."

She smiled. "I know. I saw it on TV."

That astonished him.

"They showed that professor and then they showed the medics wheel-ing Dudley out, and said he had a stroke."

"I'm sorry you got the news that way."

"I'm glad I did. That made it easier for me. He had a good life, except that he lost Mabel. We mustn't fear death, especially when it visits the old."

"Oh, Grandma," DeeAnn said. She held her great-grandmother's hand.

"I'm all right. We see death here about once a month. I'm doing fine, but who knows? What're you going to do?"

"Go to the mortuary, I guess. Look at his will. He had a lot of stock in the corporations, and I don't know how we'll be able to deal with inheritance taxes. But that's not for now. We'll bury him beside Mabel, Anna. Couple of days, I guess."

"I'll come if they let me out of here."

"Of course they will."

"Cameron?"

"Yes, Anna?"

"Pray for his soul. He was a good son and a good father."

Cameron felt tears well up in him, and fought them back. He wasn't one to cry, even if all the psychiatrists in the world told him he should. He nodded.

"I will, too," said DeeAnn.

"Now," Anna said, "you know what I'm going to do? Play some Glenn Miller. He loved that big-band music, and so do I. I'm glad I still can hear a little."

They headed out to the pickup, and Cam made some cellular phone calls, first to Sandy, then to his uncle Nicholas, then to aunt Eloise Nichols Joiner, then to his other daughter, Julia, who wasn't home, and finally to Martin, who wasn't home either. In Martin's case he left a message on the answering machine. The calls exhausted him.

DeeAnn called her husband, and then they stopped calling and stared at each other. A mortuary would be next. And some quick decisions.

"How should we do it, DeeAnn?"

"What would Dudley want, Dad?"

"He'd want to have the whole world say good-bye."

"Well, we'll do it. A big public funeral here, private burial out on our plot. I don't want the whole world to come to the ranch."

"He would have liked a simple memorial service better than a funeral, I think."

Cam smiled. "Granddaughters know grandfathers."

That afternoon crept by slowly. He set a time, arranged for a cremation, set up a memorial service at two o'clock in the Congregational Church, something long on eulogies and remembrances, and stopped at the bank, where they told him they'd need a death certificate before they'd turn over Dudley's lockbox to him.

He climbed into the pickup and stared blankly ahead. DeeAnn touched his shoulder.

"I'm glad you were here," he said. "I couldn't have done this alone."

"I'm glad I was here, too. Let's go home. Everything's okay for now. I'll drive if you want."

"I'll see. I might let you."

When they got home at twilight, they found the news had preceded them, and several of his company ranch managers and their wives had come by to help or at least express their sorrow. The whole thing had been on the evening news, including that professor's accusation, which had enraged them all.

He thanked them, left them to DeeAnn, and headed for his office. He collapsed in his swivel chair. The message light was blinking. He listened to several messages, including one from Laslo Horoney, genuinely kind and thoughtful. He wondered how the man could have known, and then remembered that two of Horoney's attorneys were at the hearing and had seen Dudley collapse.

The phone rang and he ignored it, but DeeAnn poked her head in. "It's mother," she said.

He picked up the phone.

"Oh, Cam," she said. She was crying. "I was drunk and I didn't get it. I'm coming home."

"No, Sandy, stay there. I'll get you tomorrow."

"I hate drinking," she said. "I'm coming. I'm all right now."

"No, Sandy—"

"Cam, there are things that happen sometimes that sober up a drunk in two minutes."

She hung up abruptly, and this time Cameron didn't try to stop the tears.

CHAPTER 45

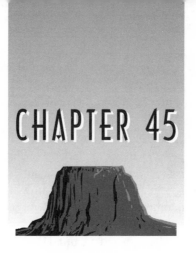

Martin stood at graveside, glad he had come. When he first heard the news on his answering machine, he had decided not to. But in the next hours, he knew he had to.

The Congregational minister, Mr. Stillman, radiated kindness, and knew intuitively what this family needed. They were doing all this in reverse, burying Dudley first, and then holding a big memorial service up in Miles in two days. Grandpa would have liked that.

Mark Cassady had dug the grave with the backhoe, after tenderly removing the layer of virgin prairie, so that it could be returned. The family had always treasured that bit of undamaged grassland. Now, most of the family had gathered, even Julie, up from Denver. And with them were the ranch managers and their families.

Martin liked the tall minister. The family was nominally Congregational, but the nearest church had been hours away and the Nicholses had largely been unmoored from their religious roots. Only Anna, who hadn't come here but would go to the memorial service, had kept up her contact, and had been regularly visited by the Reverend Mr. Stillman.

When Martin drove in, he wondered what sort of reception he would get, and was prepared to drive out again. But his father had instantly clasped his hand, held it long, not wanting to let go, with a silent smile, and Martin had fought back something he couldn't cope with. Cameron looked worn. The ranch crisis had aged him. Martin furtively eyed his mother, finding the signs of alcoholism upon her face. Her nose was venous, her eyes bagged, and her bold red hair was fading into gray. And yet, she was clearly sober now, and she had smiled tentatively at Martin, with a bright question in her blue eyes.

And so he had unpacked in his old room in the rambling house, the family traitor, and now he found himself listening to Mr. Stillman talk about the thing that mattered, death.

"It is the visitor who comes to us all," he said. "For those of us, like myself, who believe in another life with God, death is only a gateway to something so beautiful we can barely imagine it. God is always with us. But even for those who don't believe in a hereafter, death is the final blessing, the escape from our failing bodies.

"Dudley lived long and well, was honored throughout Montana for his pioneering work in stock raising. His voice was always listened to and respected. He lost his beloved Mabel early in life, but has joined her now. He carried on, raising his children to become fine people, living to see his grandchildren and great-grandchildren.

"Now we say good-bye to our friend and parent. We'll recite the Lord's Prayer now, as our benediction upon his soul.

Martin barely knew the words. He hadn't ever read the Bible, recoiling from it as if it were the book of gloom. Maybe he should. He should know something about the religion that had wrought his own Western civilization and had gone on to influence much of the world. He should know something more about his parents' faith. It would help him in his research.

Mr. Stillman finished the prayer, commended Dudley Nichols's soul to God, and was done. Martin stared one last time at the unadorned coffin that lay in its hole in the earth, lowered there by the ranch managers. Later, Mark and some of them would shovel in the earth and restore the sod. A gravestone would arrive soon, and his grandfather would be there forever, beside his Mabel.

Martin dodged the small reception at the house, knowing what all those managers thought of him, and fled back over the ridge, needing to escape into yellow rock and juniper and sagebrush and prickly pear, the harsh playground of his childhood. He paced through a chill September morning, hardly knowing what to make of the world. Something terrible disturbed and angered him. The man he admired most of all in this world, Professor Peter Andrew Brooke-Carson, had uttered the accusation that had stabbed Dudley.

The man had been grandstanding, rabble-rousing, not dealing seriously in his field or employing his expertise. He had been scoring points—against the Nichols family—instead of making sober comments.

Martin knew damned well that his family had not purchased longhorns to kill wolves, but to continue with their ranching in a new environment. But this flashy professor had found something sinister in it.

Nor was that the end of it. After the story broke and occasioned a storm in the press and on TV, Brooke-Carson had offered only the most perfunctory sympathy, and then denied that his comments had anything to do with the stroke.

"It's simply an accident of nature, the sort of thing that happens to people who eat beef," he had said. "Regrettable. But I stand by my observation: there was an ulterior motive in putting longhorns on land that was wolf habitat, and that deserves a serious investigation. It's just another example of the callousness of agribusiness, and its disdain for the public interest."

That was what the man had said. Martin had memorized it, and now he rehearsed it in his mind, over and over, between the image of his grandfather's coffin resting in the gray clay of Powder River County. He remembered, too, how casually the professor had dismissed him when he had sought help—unlike old Kazin, who might be out of another era, but who was a warm human being.

Brooke-Carson was a jerk.

He hiked over the familiar hills until he was tired. He was still angry, but felt helpless as he often did. He turned around, finally, and walked home, crossing pasture he knew well, grasslands where he had ridden horseback, herded cattle, hiked and hunted. The grass was lousy. Thin, weak, full of cactus and inedible little microflowers that flourished on the grave of a prairie. Why had his family wrecked it?

Maybe they hadn't meant to. Yes, that was important. What was known then wasn't the same as what is known now. His family was trying to bring it back, as an act of remorse, maybe. Dudley himself had probably done the worst damage back in the forties and fifties. Martin figured he had to forgive his grandfather, and wished he could have done so while the old man lived. Now it hung over him, unfinished business. His father had started the restoration. Not that it was enough, or did much good. Why the hell couldn't his family just sell its livestock, put the money into securities, and wait a decade? It'd be more profitable than ranching.

But to ask that was to answer it. They were part of a tradition, an inheritance. They would have had to let eight ranch managers go, some of them old friends, most of them with families. And they would have had to pay taxes on eight empty houses and their outbuildings. But most of all, his people were stockgrowers, and had to keep on going.

He walked into the kitchen from the rear door, discovered that the guests were gone, and found his family sitting in the airless living room, huddled together, even in silence. His mother smiled at him.

"I'm glad you came, Martin," she said.

"I'm glad I did, too," he said. He glanced at her, seeing her for the first time. He had been away for years, and now suddenly he was seeing his parents as people, not parents. He had never looked, really *looked*, at them before. His mother was wreathed in sadness, as if she were trapped but hadn't surrendered to her fate, and bore it because she had to. He had never noticed that.

No one asked him how he was doing at school, and he was glad. Maybe that would come after the memorial service. Maybe he could pack and get out of Miles right afterward and dodge the bullet. Coward, he thought to himself. He wasn't very proud of what he was becoming.

He talked with Julie for a while. She had always been a mystery to him because she was so self-contained, so absorbed in her music teaching in Denver. He hardly knew how to talk with her, except to ask polite questions, which he did.

He raided the sliced ham and buns on the dining table, suddenly hungry, and his father joined him.

"Are you staying for the memorial service?" Cameron asked.

"Yes."

"I'm glad you are."

Walls of politeness, veils over anger, civility papering over the grand canyon between them. But that was good. That's what civility is for, to circumvent pain.

"Want to look at the faxes and e-mail?"

"The what?"

"Condolences. It seems odd to receive condolences like that, instead of handwritten notes, but that's the way the world's going. Nothing wrong with it, I guess. People send their love one way or another."

Martin loaded up a paper plate and followed his father into the familiar old office, redolent of leather, decorated with trophies, photos of beloved horses, but also full of the best office machines his father could buy. His father never sat on tradition.

"Mother looks all right," he said.

"I hope so. The house in Billings is helping. She knows she has a whole world outside her door."

"Do you think it'll help?"

"I just hope and pray. Alcoholism is a demon each person fights alone, even when there are friends and counselors around."

Martin read through an amazing array of faxes, most of them torn from the machine in long strings. Former neighbors, old family friends, ex-governors, legislators, old Army buddies, Mabel's relatives, beef-growers' associations, over fifty faxes. They admired Dudley, called him a man of courage and character and integrity, called him the last of the pioneers, called him the cattleman who saw the future, called him a friend. It all amazed Martin. He had never realized how widely known his grandfather was.

There was more. Some friends had faxed news clippings and editorials. A few editorials, including one in the Billings paper, praised the lifelong Montanan for his progressive views and contributions. Martin grunted. "Progressive" meant forward-looking in business, and not what the term meant in college. A few had faxed clippings about the habitat hearing, the accusation, the collapse—and had expressed their outrage in the margins.

He turned to the computer and read through a dozen e-mail messages sent to the family. More of the same, but somehow more intimate than faxes. Lots of friends, and in the forthcoming weeks the family would receive the handwritten notes as well. It touched Martin that his grandfather had been so loved and admired. Why hadn't he known this?

"I wish I'd known him better."

"One of the things your grandfather treasured was his visit with you last summer. Seeing the buffalo. He told me he was awed by Ted Turner's herd, and he told me something else, son. He saw you come alive when you saw those big dark animals blackening the slopes over there. He came back here and told me about it, how something in you rejoiced at the sight. Whatever it was, and however much you and he disagreed, he loved that moment when he saw the joy in you. He loved you. We're glad he stopped to see you."

Martin turned away, but was unable to hide.

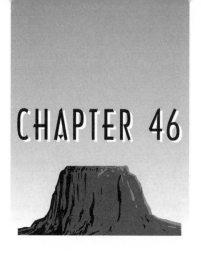

CHAPTER 46

J. Carter Delacorte followed the wolf hearings closely, devouring every scrap of news. He could scarcely believe what he heard and read. He called his old pal Pete Brooke-Carson at once, wanting the inside scoop. The papers never got anything right anyway.

"What's this about the longhorns?" he asked over the phone.

"Nichols Ranches have a herd on their North Ranch. It's killed one wolf. I saw the carcass myself. I got the story straight from the ranch manager."

"And injured another?"

"That's the story."

"They can't do that!" It irked him that his wolves were threatened by those exotic cattle.

"They're going to get away with it. No one at Fish and Wildlife wants to touch it because of the public reaction."

"You sure caused a stir. Old Nichols getting a stroke."

"I didn't do it. He did it to himself. Anyone who eats beef all his life, that's his fate. Sorry he died, of course, but that's not my problem."

"Absolutely. You were simply pointing out the truth. What can I do to help?"

"Distribute the transcript of the hearings to people on our side. There's good stuff in there. Our people will see just how furiously the commercial interests, oil companies, will fight this. And then there's Kouric. I always knew he wasn't solid. But I understand that'll be handled by Fish and Wildlife, but don't say anything. I got that confidentially."

"How'd you find out about the longhorns and the wolves?"

"On-site research. I'm a scholar, remember?"

"Who told you about the dead wolf?"

"Native American named Trouble. He manages that ranch."

"Trouble. That's a crock."

"Where'd the longhorn idea come from?"

"There's a romantic book about them—nothing scholarly of course, all anecdote and bits of history."

"Yes, Old West mythology."

"Well, that relic of history blindsided us. I never knew there was a breed of wolf-killing cattle. Say, Carter, I gotta run."

"Sure, Pete."

Delacorte knew what he had to do. He called a certain trapper in Alberta and left a coded message on the answering machine. This was going to be expensive, at five grand a wolf, but two more packs planted on the southern Nichols ranches, where there were no longhorns, would swiftly drive them out of business. No one knew how Fish and Wildlife would rule about permanent wolf habitat—they might cave in because old Nichols died—but Delacorte had his own ways.

His sled-dog rig could carry sixteen, and this time there would be no sled dogs on board. Two eight-packs of wolves. He had to plan. He'd need to collect some gold—Canadian maple leafs of course—and line up all the rest of it. But he was an old hand at that. First, though, he had to drive through the southern Nichols ranches and locate drop-off points. Everything had to be done right.

He spent the next two days roaming the country between Ashland and Broadus in his Bravada, his camera at the ready, the wildlife photographer at work. But he barely saw a soul. It was all empty country, largely owned by the Horoney Foundation. He selected two good sites on Nichols ranches, one on a branch of Otter Creek, the other in an obscure corner of the Powder River valley. He timed his access and photographed the area so that he could find his drop-offs even in bad light. The nights were growing longer now, and would cover him.

Then he waited for word from the trapper, Jacques Bouleau, in Alberta, and one day in late September, headed for Canada with his empty sled-dog rig and eighty thousand in gold bullion which was well hidden inside aluminum tubing and would not be declared.

He made Lethbridge that night, after crossing at Sweetgrass and Coutts. The next day his passage took him through the breathtaking glaciated mountain scenery of Banff and Jasper National Parks, where his journey went unremarked by the last of the year's tourists, and finally up to rough-and-tumble Hinton, where he lodged in a log motel. His trapper pal lived forty miles out of town, at the end of a long, twisty two-rut road in the midst of a lonely wild. Bouleau would supply him not only with sixteen *canis lupus* but also a bill of sale for sixteen malamutes from a known sled-dog dealer outside of Edmonton, and a Canadian veterinary certificate from the same city. Malamutes were the sled dogs that most resembled the gray wolf.

Bouleau lived alone in a solid, warm, log home built of peeled lodge-pole pine, set on a creek in a clearing. As Delacorte rattled in, the trapper emerged from within, wearing his usual red-checkered woolen shirt and high lace-up boots. Carter found himself staring into that dour, wolfish, gray-bearded face once again.

"Ah, Delacorte, you turkey, we meet again, eh?"

"So we do."

"Maybe we are destined to meet again and again and again, eh?"

"Maybe, Jacques."

"You want maybe some coffee or hot chocolate? Cognac? Fat Cuban cigars you can't get down there? A little powder up your rich nose? A woman, maybe?"

"Sure, later. Just now I want a look at the malamutes."

"All business, you turkey. Nothing but mean dogs that tear the throat outa some poor Bambi. You must have a mean heart."

"This is important. So important that it's the most crucial act anyone in the entire environmental Movement could do. I feel honored to have been chosen."

"Chosen?" Bouleau's face suddenly turned into a mask.

"Figuratively speaking, Jacques. I mean I feel chosen by Fate to play a role in the destiny of the world."

"Well, damn, and I'm just a trapper son of a bitch. Yeah, come on back. I got them wolves, and they don't like being in a cage none. Maybe you should walk in and get a feel how they like it, rich turkey."

"You got any females?"

"Oh, sure, nice-looking ladies."

Delacorte followed the trapper out to a specially constructed pen built with stout posts and corrugated sheet-metal roofing for walls. It also had a woven wire ceiling. The pen had once been constructed of chain-link fence, but too many of Bouleau's wolves had broken their canine teeth chewing on that wire.

"There, climb up on the stump there and look down in," the trapper said. "Go in if you got guts. All they can do is eat you, and you probably would taste no good anyway. What do you do this for, you rich son of a bitch? You got my gold?"

Carter ignored the man. Every time he came up here for wolves, Bouleau insulted him. But the man took his gold fast enough, elaborately counting it out, as if Carter were going to cheat him.

Delacorte climbed up on a tall stump that afforded a view into the pen. The place stank. Most of the filthy wolves cowered under a sheltered portion of the pen. Out in the open, amidst stinking piles of dung, were half a dozen deer carcasses in various states of ruin. Bouleau probably fed them a deer as often as he could shoot one.

"They come into the flat to browse each night. So I shoot one when I can so I don't have to spend my maple leafs on dog food."

Muck clung to the pelts of these wolves. They scarcely resembled the proud animals that ran free in the foothills and mountains of western Alberta. They stared at him listlessly, all but one, which eyed him and paced back and forth endlessly, his gaze boldly on Delacorte.

"They sick?"

"Any wolf just caught, they think they're dead."

"There's only one that's moving."

"Too bad. You pay five thousand each or no wolf leaves the cage. Maybe I'll skin 'em and sell the furs. You want a wolf pelt?"

"Let's load."

"Show me your gold."

"You show me the vet papers and bill of sale."

Bouleau shrugged.

Delacorte followed him into the log house. It was surprisingly trim and clean within. Bouleau laid a thick manila envelope on the pine table, and gestured at it.

The bill of sale looked all right. Petersen's Malamutes and Sled Dogs, sixteen adult dogs, trained to harness, health guaranteed for six months or money refunded . . .

The veterinary forms looked even better. These were preprinted green forms with assorted typewritten X's in little boxes, all signed with an indecipherable hand. But rubber-stamped underneath was the name of an alleged Edmonton vet. Just for insurance, there were sixteen color photos of good-looking malamutes, each identified by a number that corresponded to the veterinary forms. Good job.

"All right. I've got two days of travel and an overnight stop this time. How do I handle them?"

"I made this little jabstick. Hypodermic. Stick it in this ampule, ten cubic centimeters for each. That first night, you jab each one and that puts them asleep if they ain't dead yet. Then open the cage door, put in meat and water and clean out the crap."

"What if one jumps out?"

"Then you lose five thousand dollars." He thought that was pretty amusing.

"Will they eat?"

"They think they're dead. That's how a captured wolf thinks. But they might lick up some water."

"Will they howl?"

Bouleau grinned. "You're sure scared, rich boy. I hope they howl right at old U.S. of A. Customs."

"I'm going through Del Bonita. I never go through the same port twice."

"Where's the gold?"

"All right. Half now, half when you've loaded them."

"All now, or go home."

Delacorte flashed his thousand-watt smile. "No problem, Bouleau. No problem. Peace."

He headed out to the kennels on his flatbed, and unscrewed a part of the framework, a long aluminum tube. Eighty thousand dollars of gold was almost more than he could carry, and he staggered into the house with it.

"All right, count," he muttered, easing it down on the table.

The wolfer lifted an end of the tube until the maple leafs slid out. He took one long glance at the fortune on his table. "Okay, okay, we'll load now," he said.

Amused, Delacorte followed him out and into the early-morning sun. From above, the wolfer tranquilized every wolf, one by one, enjoying himself, whistling as he worked. A while later he had lifted the last of the wolves into the flatbed kennels.

"Well, so long, rich Yank."

"Peace and love," Delacorte said.

He reached Del Bonita late that evening, and wished he had taken his beta-blocker an hour earlier, because his heart was going crazy again.

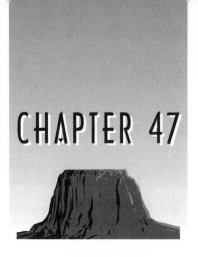

CHAPTER 47

J. Carter Delacorte eased his rig across the line and into the sleepy port of Del Bonita, on the Blackfoot Reservation. He had timed his arrival well, full night, hard for a Customs man to separate a malamute from a wolf, even in the white glare of the port inspection lights. He wouldn't have to wait. This port huddled on a lonely road, a roundabout route between Lethbridge and Cut Bank. From here he would go to Shelby, the town that once staged a Jack Dempsey fight, and then on down to the High Plains.

He wished he didn't get so nervous. His heart felt like it was about to fibrillate, but shortly he'd be plowing south through the tunnel of night.

The Customs man approached, and Delacorte rolled down his window. The beam of a bright flashlight surveyed the cab, settling for a moment on his hands. Delacorte stared up onto the face of a ruddy, fifty-year-old man with a black, questioning gaze that pierced through him.

"You an American citizen, sir?"

"Yes, sir. Live in Jackson."

"You bringing in anything? Declaring anything?"

"You mean for duty?"

"Yeah. What've you got back there?"

"Sled dogs. Malamutes. You want some vet papers, I suppose."

The officer nodded. Delacorte opened his tooled-leather portfolio and extracted the papers. "Here. All vaccinated. Bills of sale for all of them. I bought them in Edmonton, so I guess I owe some duty. Sled-dog duty." He laughed.

The man studied the papers and grunted. "Guess you better get out."

"Why, is there some trouble?" Delacorte flashed his thousand-watt smile.

The officer didn't reply. He ran his flashlight along the kennels, examining the contents of each. His breath plumed the night air.

"I'd better look at some of these. Let this one out."

"Let him out?"

"Yeah, let him out."

"But—he's settled down. It's hard to get them to travel."

"Let him out."

"He's a big one. Malamutes are big."

"Let him out."

"He doesn't have a collar yet. He'll get away."

"Well, get a collar. You got a box of stuff there."

"Ah, he might bite me. He doesn't know me yet."

"Get a collar and open the door."

Delacorte's heart was tripping fast. "Hey, man, it's just a dog."

"Maybe. You just go ahead and show me."

"Look, is there any way I can persuade you without risking loss of a dog?"

"Bring the kennel into a room here." He pointed at a brightly lit inspection area inside the door.

"Oh, I'll just open it," Delacorte said, his thoughts winging everywhere. Gingerly he opened the door. Nothing happened.

"I guess he's afraid of me still."

"Yeah, well drag him out so I can see him."

"He hasn't been handled. He might bite me. That's going to be my first step, handling these dogs until we're friends. It's a great breed, very affectionate."

"Mister, that's no malamute. Not like the one lives next door to me." He played the beam of light over the animal within, which cowered at the back of the cage, its slanted eyes fiery in the light. "You want to call it a wolf?"

"Oh, no, nothing like that. They told me they had some crosses, quarter-wolf but still dogs, you know."

"So you bought quarter-wolf sled dogs, is that what you're saying? Okay, either you get him out and show me he's a nice doggy, or we'll go inside and you can tell me why you're bringing sixteen wolves, an endangered species in Montana and illegal to possess privately, into the good old U.S. of A. And let's see some ID."

"Why do you say they're wolves?"

"I got eyes. And we were asked to watch out for wolves."

"Who asked you?"

The Customs man grunted.

"I haven't done anything wrong."

"These are fraudulent papers, maybe?"

"Well, all I know is what they gave me."

"Who gave you?"

"The breeders."

"Maybe the wolfer Bouleau, same as trapped the Yellowstone Park wolves when they started up the packs."

"Who's he?"

"Show me your ID."

Delacorte pulled out his driver's license.

"Delacorte, eh? All right, Mr. Delacorte, you have a problem. Sit there and don't leave. You're under detention. Close the kennel door and come in here."

J. Carter Delacorte, apostle of Green peace and love, walked into the dreary green room and settled gingerly into a hard wooden chair, enraged at the abuse he, an American citizen, was now suffering. The Customs man phoned someone and asked for assistance.

"We got him," he said. "The same m.o."

"Look, I can explain everything. I'm not killing wolves, I'm bringing them in, increasing the species, helping out."

"Yeah, well that's interesting. I should warn you that whatever you say can be used against you. Read this; it's the Miranda decision."

"Against me? As if I'm a criminal?"

The Customs man smiled gently. "Malamutes?"

Delacorte agonized. "I need to take a pill. My heart, you know."

"Let's see the bottle."

"Inderal." Delacorte pulled his prescription bottle from his coat pocket.

The officer read the label, pulled one out, handed it to Delacorte, closed the bottle, and returned it to him.

"What did you pay for these wolves?"

"Why, the bill of sale, right there, says four thousand for sixteen malamutes."

"How about five grand a wolf? It's a felony to lie to an officer."

"A felony?"

"How much did you take with you? Eighty thousand? You had to declare it, you know. Anything over ten thousand you have to declare. That's to stop money laundering. So that's another little problem. You're going to have a few problems with our friends on the other side of that line, too."

"My God, what are you saying?"

"Oh, three, four years, maybe less if you're a good boy."

"But I haven't done anything."

Two other Customs men drifted in, and then the questioning began in earnest.

"I want a lawyer. I'm not saying anything!"

"Sure, you're allowed a phone call. You want to get this over with? Then talk. It'll go easier on you if you just spill it. No one figures you for a big-time heroin smuggler, so just go along with us, and tell the exact truth, and maybe you can get out of it with a fine and a month or two. You want to clam up, make your jailhouse call, and sit in our holding pen while you wait for your shyster to fly up to nowhere, or do you want to talk, go before a federal judge in Great Falls tomorrow, post bond, and deal with it that way?"

"What are you going to do with the dogs? They need care."

"Fish and Wildlife guy's coming. Sorry, we're holding your rig. Equipment used in smuggling is seized. Maybe you'll get it back if they find malamutes out there."

"Do you mean that about talking?"

They looked amused. "Sure, talk. Right here, into this little recorder, okay? Now then, you've read the Miranda card, know your rights, you're talking voluntarily, and declined a lawyer, right?"

"Ah, yuh."

"How many times you bring these charming little animals across?"

That's how it went that awful night. He talked. He decided that if he could make his whole case public, there would be a rush of sympathy for him from one end of the country to the other. Everyone believed in environmentalism. So he talked, they listened, took notes, asked more and more questions. Sometime in the small hours of the morning, the federal wildlife guy arrived, pulled the kennels off the flatbed, and drove off with Delacorte's wolves. What had happened? Had that swine Bouleau betrayed him? The Judas!

"How'd you know about this?" he asked wearily.

"Both EPA and Fish and Wildlife have been looking into it," the youngest one said. "Why'd you do it?"

"Monkey-wrenching."

"You must like to pick on defenseless people who can't fight back. Those ranchers down there. They get into big-time trouble if they shoot a wolf that's eating their beef. You're such a nice guy, wrecking a legitimate business."

"That's what those ranchers deserve," Delacorte replied sullenly.

About dawn they took him to a restaurant where he ordered a soy-burger and salad, then handcuffed him and took him to Great Falls in a green federal sedan, while he suffered indignation, outrage, and bouts of exhaustion. He sank into a virtual stupor. He could barely grasp what was happening to him. They got his lawyer, Nina Tall Chief. Court, arraignment, bail, out, and a weary trip to Jackson, with his attorney.

The worst and most demeaning time of his life.

The press picked up on it. The Wolf Smuggler, the Jackson Monkey-wrencher, the condom heir with twenty-one counts against him, the deepest pocket among the Greens, caught with sixteen abused wolves, some of them half-dead.

He plunged into his bed and scarcely got up for two days, and then weariness laced him, and after that self-pity. Why was the world picking on someone who had only good intentions? Why him? Why not white-collar criminals and crooked ministers and corporate executives? Every-one turned against him. Old Pete Brooke-Carson wouldn't even return his calls. And Monica had decided a trip to France was what she needed just then. How could he ever hold his condominiums again?

He talked, plenty, calling in the press and giving them long stories. If he was going to be a martyr, he'd make the best of it. That's what he was, the Joan of Arc of Environmentalism. They might burn him at the stake, but he would leave his mark. He read the editorials and opinion columns with disdain. They were the work of ignoramuses who hadn't a clue about the condition of the communities of Nature.

Public opinion was important, so he issued a press release: "Mr. J. Carter Delacorte seeks only peace and love and the brotherhood and sisterhood of all animals. The introduction of an endangered species into an environmentally parched area was intended to enrich the global village and promote spiritual well-being.

"Mr. Delacorte regrets any inconvenience his activities may have caused, but continues to believe that Green organizations must press for the salvation of the world."

Then came a subpoena. The Nichols family was suing him for a million in actual losses and punitive damages. That appalled him. How dare the rapists of the plains do that to him? They were simply taking advantage of laws stacked in favor of plaintiffs. This was just another example of Corporate Amerika at work, and it irked him far more than the federal case.

In a month he would face that mean, jowly bald judge in Great Falls and face what his attorney had worked out in advance with federal prosecutors: Three years, sentence to be reduced to three months upon good behavior. Then probation, restrictions on his Green-related activities, and near-maximum fines on each count, running over a million dollars. That plus three hundred thousand in attorney fees.

That was a lot of condoms.

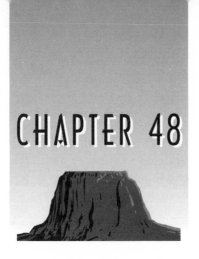

CHAPTER 48

Martin listened to the message on his answering machine. Professor Kazin expressed his sorrow at the loss of Martin's grandfather and invited Martin to dinner Friday night. There would be other guests, Tom Hornsby and his wife Bea. Tom was the paleoecologist over at the museum, a spellbinding man whose talk leapt eras and epochs.

Martin called his advisor and accepted. Old Kazin might be a fossil, but he was a good man. Martin realized he had been slow to grasp that; that people had many facets. Kazin was a kinder person than the flashy Brooke-Carson, whose callousness had probably killed his grandfather, and who had subsequently made light of it all in the press. Martin despised the man, no matter what sort of gaudy reputation he had among the Greens. Brooke-Carson was a hollow man, with no more soul than a werewolf.

Martin remembered how much he had ached to have the man as his faculty advisor, how bitter he was to be turned down. And now he was thankful that Brooke-Carson had been too busy to bother with a humble master's candidate like himself. Or any student. He couldn't remember Brooke-Carson ever helping any student in need. He collected sycophants, so that they might mirror his own glory, but never nurtured a sense of scholarship, a quest for truth, in any of them. Martin had been lucky. Maybe that was his grandfather's real legacy to him.

He didn't know what to do. The fall term had started, but it was not too late to take a few classes and pick up his research and writing. He stared into a golden day, still as lost as when he had quit. Things seemed all the more confused now, and he was less certain than ever about what to do with his lousy life.

The memorial service in Miles City had come as another surprise to him. He had been too absorbed in his own miseries to understand his family's roots in Montana. People from all over the state came to that service, and some of them rose to eulogize Dudley in words so kind that they sent thrills through Martin.

The minister, Mr. Stillman, had read a message from Governor Magruder; they heard from the state's congressman and two senators at that service. Several described Dudley as a pioneer, not in the sense of settling the frontier, but in the sense of turning cattle ranching into a progressive business employing record keeping, range management, skilled breeding, efficient feeding, and many similar advances. But they had admired Dudley for something else: his word was his bond, his handshake deals were better than written contracts, and his simple perception of himself as a member of a civic community made him an honored and loved man.

At the time, Martin had rejected it all as something out of the prehistoric past, yet there it all was, the attitudes of ordinary citizens, the ideals scorned on the campus. That bothered him.

Through his brief stay at the ranch, his father had never raised the issue of those monthly checks. But his father had drawn him into the office and showed him the accounts on the computer screen. Nichols Ranches were now losing a thousand dollars a week. This time, those figures meant something to him. Before, he had despised countinghouse talk—it was all part of the agribusiness he hated.

He reflected on his trip, glad he went to Dudley's services, glad he rediscovered his mother and father, guilty that he had abused their kindness. He had to finish up his degree—being paid for at such cost—or stop being a burden on the companies.

That evening he arrived promptly at six at his advisor's comfortable, battered old home east of the campus in an area that had gotten a little seedy. Brooke-Carson lived in one of those huge gaudy homes off Kagy Boulevard, but that shining monument to the man's ego lacked the warmth of Professor Kazin's homey home. Martin walked in to the heady scent of cooking beef.

"Ah, Martin, I'm glad you came, so glad. Come say hello to my wife. She's cooking a rib roast for ourselves and the Hornsbys, but we have a vegetarian meal for you. Just make yourself at home, and we'll have a good visit. I hope your family's bearing up."

"Yes, sir. My father's not doing so well—I can tell. But we're okay. Ah, would it be all right if I had some of the rib roast?"

Kazin registered that, vanished into the kitchen, and returned a moment later. "She says she'd be delighted; it's almost done. Smell it?"

Martin did. He couldn't imagine why he wanted meat: good, sizzling, tender, pink-centered, crisp-edged prime rib, just the way his mother once cooked it before he left home. Before he rejected the Nichols family and all its works so savagely. Now the smell whetted his senses, almost maddened him. He hadn't eaten beef for years, but suddenly he couldn't bear another ten minutes without it.

"We're going to have some good company tonight, Martin. You know much about Tom Hornsby?"

"No, sir, I guess I don't."

"Well, he's done pioneering work in paleoecology, along with his wife, Bea. They're both Ph.D.s from Columbia, I think. Quite a jump from New York to here. But they know more about prehistoric large mammals than anyone else in the country." Kazin eyed him amiably. "Might be some questions you'd like to ask that'd relate to your thesis. They spend much of each year at fossil digs, so we don't see them as much as we'd like."

Martin didn't respond. He wasn't sure he'd ever start on that again.

"You want to know about bison, they'll tell you," Kazin added. "The modern variety haven't been around here very long, did you know that?"

"I thought they've been here forever, almost."

"Nope. Recent ice age. But we'll ask the Hornsbys."

Tom Hornsby proved to be a compact, natty man, and Bea a compact trim woman, both armored with horn-rimmed glasses. And it swiftly became apparent to Martin that these people were true scholars, devoted to their quest, which was the understanding of the natural world in its previous manifestations.

"Martin is working on a thesis about the transformation of the High Plains from its preranching days to the present," Kazin explained. "I thought you'd enjoy meeting him. Maybe he'll pick your brains a bit."

"Why, Mr. Nichols, if we can help you with your work, we'd love it," said Bea.

"Well, ah, I'm not sure—"

Kazin interrupted. "Martin's taken a little break. Burnout. I wonder how many times I burned out putting my degrees together."

"Oh, then we can help," Hornsby said. "Maybe you just need to take a new tack. Why don't you tell us what you're up to?"

Martin reddened. He wished he could duck out. The heady aroma of the rib roast emanated from the kitchen. "Well, I don't know—"

"The Hornsbys can help ground you in the past," Kazin said. "Tom, I told Martin you'd talk a little about bison. He's particularly interested in the beasts."

"Why, certainly. You know, there was an ancient long-horned North American buffalo, but that one's extinct. Maybe killed off by Clovis people. A lot of large mammals vanished about then. But the modern buffalo's descended from two species that crossed the Bering land bridge—"

"The land bridge? When the ocean dropped?"

"Yes. The ocean dropped anywhere from eighty to a hundred thirty meters during the ice ages, when the ice caps built up as much as seven or eight kilometers at their domes. That turned the Bering Straits, between Russia and Alaska, into a temporary land bridge enabling migrations of stock between the continents. How all that happened is long and complex—read Pielou, *After the Ice Age*—but the effect was to populate this continent with modern bison beginning maybe eighteen thousand years ago. Two species, one with a double hump, gradually evolved into our present ones, the plains buffalo and woods buffalo."

"That's recent."

"Yes, and the Great Plains are even more recent. As the ice retreated, the plains were covered with swamps and forests, not at all hospitable to grazing animals like buffalo. We're coming to the end of an interglacial right now—speaking in geologic time."

"What about global warming?"

"Oh, there are always brief variations within a larger trend."

"How do you know all this?"

"Many ways. Fossil evidence, especially micro flora. Carbon-14 dating. Known and dated layers of volcanic ash."

Martin had always vaguely known that the Great Plains weren't eternal, but now, suddenly, he was discovering that the plains were always in flux. The Hornsbys led him through one period after another, the extinction of one species after another, an early little horse called the eohippus, sabre-toothed cats, big bears, mastodons, mammoths, all gone, mostly from altering climactic conditions, but also from the ruthless hunting of Clovis people and others who followed, such as the Folsom people.

Martin enjoyed it all. This was better than small talk, or politics, or Green incantations. This was information, and it was giving him perspective. He was taken by this man and woman who were so devoted to their field that they lived for little else. What stories they had to tell! Dating methods that didn't match. Controversy about what killed off species. The ability of primitive people to slaughter whole species with crude devices such as pitfalls, nooses, stampeding over cliffs, deadfalls, atlatls, employing geographical features to trap herds. It dawned on Martin that mortals had been a part of the ecology since the dawn of the species, and that it was foolish to think in terms of wilderness when there hadn't been pure wilderness at all.

Then they were called to dinner, and suddenly Martin found himself staring at a plate bearing a huge slice of tender beef. It was as if one of those moments of truth had arrived. Where had his ferocious vegetarianism come from? And what did it mean to abandon it? Had he hated his family and its business so much? One thing he knew: the health rationalizations, the cholesterol, the food puritanism, had nothing to do with this. That succulent, heady, juicy slab of beef would define him. He toyed with a Waldorf salad, ate fresh green beans sautéed in browned butter with sliced almonds, poked at a yam—and then gently sliced away a bit of fat, and took beef into his mouth.

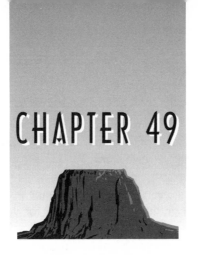

CHAPTER 49

Sanford Kouric knew he would pay a price, but he didn't know when or how much. The answers arrived sooner than he had expected. Three weeks after his Miles City testimony at the habitat hearings, his supervisor, M. Collard Cheeseman, invited him into the executive office of the Montana division of U.S. Fish and Wildlife.

That was all right. A man had to live with himself. In the end, his integrity counted for more than his status. He had seen a lot of junk science masquerade as public policy over the years. He had seen hidden agendas at work, especially in this service, and the EPA, BLM, Park Service and Forest Service, which, between them, wanted to recapture much of the American West. Some of their land, water and air regulations were based on shaky scientific foundations, something that the agencies piously denied.

At the appointed hour, Kouric sailed past Cheeseman's secretary and entered the sanctum. There was the head honcho himself, puffy, bulging out of his navy polyester, his shoulders flaked with dandruff. And there, too, were his deputies, Clyde Marks and Angela DiTruffo, personnel people. The pair of them were straight out of the sixties. The only reason they bathed and wore business clothing was that they couldn't get away with tie-dyed tee shirts and sandals in the office.

Witnesses. This was serious.

Cheeseman glad-handed Kouric, sweaty palm meeting cool flesh. "Ah, have a seat, Sanford. Yes, nice day. We have a little surprise for you. We're promoting you."

Kouric grinned wolfishly and said nothing.

"Aren't you curious?"

"Certainly."

"Why don't you explain it, Angela?" Cheeseman said.

"Yes, of course. Sanford, there's a position open that involves educating the public about wolves and other wildlife programs of the Service. It requires the utmost diplomacy because you'll be dealing with the public, especially children, the very ones we want to understand the importance of protecting the natural world."

Kouric nodded.

"We're going to make you deputy assistant information director in charge of wildlife programs. We've arranged for you to have your own private office here—you'll like that after years in the field, lots of comfort—and you'll be entirely on your own. What you'll do, basically, is respond to queries for information from the public. You'll send out our brochures, keep tabs on the number of contacts, report once a month to our public-relations supervisor. Quite a nice job, no doubt a relief after coping with harsh Montana weather."

"I'm a wildlife biologist specializing in wolves."

"Well, that's it exactly," she said. "We need a sensitive wildlife biologist in this slot. Now of course we'll establish the parameters, what you can say and not say. Written guidelines. Since you'll be in this sensitive position as our spokeshuman, we'll expect you to refrain from private comment because the public would become confused—you know, separating you from your role in the USFWS."

"This is a promotion. What will be my new grade and salary?"

"Ah, you'll stay the same GS, but you'll have a new title and important new responsibilities. That's what we meant by a promotion."

"What is the designated grade?"

"Ah, GS-18. Now that's below yours, but we feel this is a sensitive area and we expect to raise the designation in the future. And of course you'll remain at GS-34 pay."

Kouric grinned.

"Is there something amusing you?" Marks asked.

"Does this happen to have anything to do with my Miles City testimony?"

"Nothing whatsoever."

"It doesn't have anything to do with my statement that the proposed wolf-habitat designation is invalid unless domestic cattle are included as prey."

"Well, that didn't please us, but we respect your right to your opinion even when it goes against policy, and our tapes show that you did indicate that you were speaking on your own. But of course the public gets confused. Very regrettable. But we know that this sort of thing doesn't come under the Hatch Act; you have a right to express your views, and you did. We pride ourselves in our liberality," Marks said solemnly.

"Well, do you accept?" asked Cheeseman.

"Actually, no."

"Well, we may be forced to put you in that slot, accept or not. That is, unless you wish to resign. We feel you're not happy with the government."

"No, I'll not resign."

"Well then, we'll put you in that new slot. That's all for now. Angela will instruct you in your duties. You'll report directly to her for the time being, and we'll do some evaluations after a month or two. Glad to have you help us with such valuable work, Sanford."

"Crap."

"Inappropriate language, Sanford. We'll be forced to put that on your personnel file. Angela, take him to his new offices, if you will."

She led Sanford to the elevator, which they took to the basement of the Helena federal building, and there she hiked through concrete corridors to a place somewhere behind the boiler. His office, A-147892, consisted of a cell-like cubicle painted hospital green, a metal desk, a battered chair, in and out boxes, a phone, and nothing else.

"Hope you like it," she cooed. "Here's your key. By the way, we'll clean out your desk upstairs."

"Hope you enjoy it."

She smiled. Everything in his former desk would be scrutinized with an eye to doing as much damage to his record as possible. They would find a few things on his computer, lunch-hour letters mostly. They were experts.

They wanted him to resign but had no grounds. In one or two sentences, he had demolished their permanent habitat designation, intended less to protect wolves than to drive the last ranchers and wheat growers out of the Horoney Foundation's grassland. Those sentences had caused an uproar in the press and on TV, and had been quoted nationally, usually without Kouric's caveat that he was speaking as a private citizen. Then, to make matters worse, some idiot named Delacorte had been nabbed at the border with a load of wolves. He'd blabbed freely, admitted to bringing in the first two packs. USFWS hadn't gotten around to revoking the provisional habitat yet, nor would it. It was obviously just going to lie low for a year or two and then pick up where it left off—and Kouric was the problem.

He settled into his miserable swivel chair, closed the door, and stared at his green hell. The fluorescent lights glared whitely down at him. The green concrete walls closed in as if he were in a prison. He had heard of this room, this Siberia of the Federal Government, where its inhabitants lasted a week, a month, six weeks before resigning from their agencies.

Witnesses. The three of them would write up their reports of the encounter and file them. The paper trail would be redoubtable. He'd love to see his personnel record, and the stuff sliding into it just now, after years of excellent ratings. That's how they did it in government, insidious little knife cuts, all for the sake of power and none for the sake of truth. The government was spawned as an engine of force and it used compulsory taxes, law, incarceration, regulation as its weapons. And the climbers knew exactly how to whittle power away from someone and add power to their own arsenals. The USFWS was a police agency, and it was foolish to think otherwise. It could arrest, fine, prohibit, compel, seize, commandeer, and upset the lives of ordinary citizens. It had its cops, and it used them. Kouric was one, actually.

He checked the drawers of the metal desk. No paper, nothing. No typewriter or computer. He could stay here and do whatever he chose, bring in a word processor and write, take the money and run. If he was a whore. He knew he couldn't. He would stay long enough to find new employment, which was really what they had in mind. There wouldn't be many places that would want a wolf biologist except the government. Not that he needed to stick with wolves. A doctoral degree in biology with a specialty in mammal reproduction equipped him to deal with many things. Zoos employed many people with his background. But there was one potential employer he might enjoy, perhaps far more than his work with the USFWS.

Had it been worth it? He knew it had. Years ago, he had read David Riesman's pioneering work about the evolution of Americans from their origins as tradition-directed to inner-directed and then to other-directed. He knew himself to be an inner-directed person, relatively immune to the tugs of ideology and fashion and trend. He had never gone off looking for nirvanas, never hungered to be with-it or ride the cutting edge of the zeitgeist. He didn't connect himself to the world that way. He had preferred to be faithful to himself and to his values.

He had friends who were desperately "with-it," sampling New-Age nostrums, Zen, Native American religions, peyote, nihilism, and all the other things they had salvaged from the scrap heap of philosophy, science, and history and tried to resuscitate. Not a one of them owned himself or knew how to resist whatever was new and chic. He actually knew a number of pathetic types who supposed their beards or their clothing or earrings or a crystal dangling from a necklace was the expression of their uniqueness.

The things he believed and practiced weren't necessarily traditional. No one who believed in reintroducing wolves into the civilized United States could be described as traditional. He loved wolves and believed in their natural mission within ecosystems. But this was the twenty-first century, and the wolves would have to be carefully managed and kept to certain areas, and kept away from food supplies, which were coming under increasing pressure. He loved wolves because they improved the prey species, killing the weak and diseased, honing the genetic gifts of each prey species. And he loved them for themselves.

Maybe all this would be liberating. Now he could say all the things he knew: for instance that the foundation's plans to reintroduce buffalo, elk, bears, and other species to the Great Plains wouldn't work because of the political choices imposed on it—and the wolves. With wolves, hunters, and each of the tribes guaranteed a quota of buffalo, the reintroduction wasn't going to work; the buffalo recruitment rate would be too low, the foundation's plan to expand the herd to several hundred thousand animals would never happen. The foundation needed a twenty-year cushion at the least. No hunters, no tribal harvests, and no wolves— or at least no more than a single pack.

He felt the profound silence of his cubicle suffocating him. That was all right. He wouldn't be here long. He tried his key, found that it worked, headed to a canteen where he could acquire some vending-machine coffee, bought a Skye's West novel, and thus spent the day amiably.

At home that evening, he drafted a letter to the Horoney Foundation, inquiring whether it could use a good independent biologist. He updated his résumé and ran off a copy on his printer. He told the directors of the foundation that he was in broad agreement with their objectives. Then he donned a coat and mailed the letter at the main Helena post office late in the evening, and hoped he would hear soon. All this was good, and he knew he was his own man.

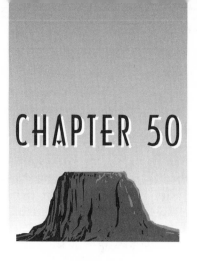

CHAPTER 50

In the quiet of his study, Laslo Horoney listened, thunderstruck, to Hector Truehart's news. His dream, his gift to the American people, was falling apart.

The Montana Supreme Court, Truehart explained, had on this Friday September 29th, declared unconstitutional most of the tax aspects of the new Buffalo County.

"Basically, Laslo, they left the new county intact but ruled in favor of Nichols Ranches and several other ranchers and oil companies that the tax arrangements were discriminatory and violate the state constitution's provision that taxation should fall reasonably equally on all within a tax category."

"Go over this again, Hector."

"Sure. First, they've ruled that landowners such as Nichols are entitled to full government services, and cannot be deprived of the fruits of the taxes they pay. That means the new county must maintain schools, law enforcement, waste collection, everything that existed before, even if only a handful benefit from them.

"Secondly, they've ruled that the property-tax arrangements worked out with the foundation for the new Buffalo County are invalid for the same reason; they don't apply elsewhere in the state. Therefore, the foundation's land is to be taxed at the same rate as anywhere else in the state."

"But we can't afford that."

"It gets worse. Montana imposes a personal-property tax on livestock. The court is ruling that this also applies to any buffalo owned by the foundation. In this case, the buffalo are not considered feral creatures, but livestock that can be bought, sold, traded, and herded. That means, in essence, that the foundation must pay an annual per capita tax on each buffalo." He paused, smiling a little. "Needless to say, this'll have a domino effect. Most states have constitutional provisions guaranteeing the equal imposition of taxes within categories. We can expect Wyoming and South Dakota to follow suit."

"What did we argue?"

"That buffalo are feral animals, and that apart from our initial purchase of a herd no one will own them."

"And what was the opposing argument?"

"They said that in fact we controlled the buffalo, prohibiting the hunting of them except by the tribes, and therefore they were privately owned."

"Where do Nichols Ranches stand now?"

"They're slightly better off. They now have a court-guaranteed right to all existing county services. Schools for the children of their managers. Fire and police protection. But no tax relief."

"And how did we argue the property-tax law?"

"That the nonprofit Horoney Foundation was exempt from property taxation in accordance with the enabling legislation, and we had agreed to an annual fee in lieu of taxation purely for state and county administrative purposes."

"It's not so small a fee, and it'll cost around a million a year, Hector. The foundation's got to be self-sustaining, and even that was as much as we could manage. Selling licenses to guides, and permits to deer hunters, is about the only income we'll derive from the grassland."

"Well, we're in trouble. Property taxes in Montana alone will come to around two hundred fifty million a year if we're taxed at the same rate as the surrounding ranches. We can expect the same in the other states."

"Can the Montana legislature help us? Exempt buffalo from the property tax? Create a property-tax category for nonprofit foundations that applies uniformly, statewide?"

Hector answered the question with a shake of the head.

"What are our options?"

"That's going to take some time to work out. But you can bet the Greens'll be enjoying this."

Horoney felt short of breath. A stone lay over him, crushing the life from him. "What's next?"

"Pay taxes, sell, or give it all away. Or start another campaign to get what we need from the Montana legislature."

"You think we have a chance there?"

"It was one thing for them to carve out a special county for us; it'd be quite another to ask them to repeal or equalize their taxes across the board to legitimize ours."

Horoney nodded. "Do we have any time?"

"No. The new county becomes a reality this Sunday, October 1. It's going to need money because it's required, in all fairness, to maintain full services. And it's going to tax us at exactly the rate that befalls Nichols Ranches and other private holdings. That's what the court ordered."

"I'd better cancel the buffalo purchase. We've scheduled delivery the first week of October. Maybe that's all right, Hector. Give the land more rest. One of the foundation's objectives has been to restore the range."

"That's not going to help with the taxes."

"Two hundred fifty million a year to Montana, a hundred million to Wyoming and South Dakota. We can't sustain that. I don't know what to do."

Neither man said anything for a while. Horoney sipped coffee, feeling empty, wondering whether he should return to commercial real estate and stop spending billions of dollars on foolish and grandiose dreams. Maybe he'd been a rich fool. Truehart paced, turning at the fireplace, rotating around the couch, pausing at the window to stare at Dolly's lush gardens.

"Sell to the federal government, or give it to them. Sell to the state of Montana, or give it to them. Or put it on the auction block and sell to ranching interests." He smiled. "The Greens would love that. You could expect a plague of lawsuits, injunctions, and bureaucratic harassment."

"What about turning it over to the Nature Conservancy?"

"They employ various conservation agreements with private owners. They own some land. But that land remains private and subject to normal taxes. It'd get the load off our backs—if you could persuade them to take it. But they won't, except for a small corner perhaps. They're not rich."

"I don't want the feds to get it if I can help it. This was intended to be a gift to the American people, not to the governing land agencies or Fish and Wildlife."

"The federal agencies will fight you for it. They're rejoicing right now, you can count on it. This came out of left field, Laslo, and no one expected it, but they see their chances. By this afternoon they'll be flying in asking you to turn it all over."

"As the giver I could stipulate certain things."

"When has a government bureau ever stuck to an agreement? They might while you live, but afterward it'd just be federal land to do with as they choose."

"I'd rather sell the land back to private ranching interests than do that, so it could be put to productive use again. What would you do, in my shoes, Hector?"

"Oh, I don't know. Give it to the state, with strong stipulations. That's probably your best bet. It'd become a giant Montana state park. Don't expect Montana to pay for it. But their land management bureaus would be far more responsive to the public, and to governance, than federal bureaus."

"Just give it to Montana?"

"With stipulations. That it remain open grassland in perpetuity. That it be managed to restore range to its original status as far as possible, and that the original wildlife be maintained on it. That existing private tracts within be respected, and their economic activities remain inviolate. That'd protect the people you've tried from the beginning to protect. Like the Nichols family, and people working the oil patches, and wheat farmers if they choose to remain."

"We could do that. What'll the reaction be?"

"The Greens will hate it. They want everything federalized, perhaps because then they get the chance to play God."

Horoney sighed. "We don't have much time, do we? Taxes are going to pile up."

"Not much time, Laslo. We could appeal the Montana Supreme Court decision to the United States Supreme Court, but I don't expect anything from the high court unless we can conjure up a major constitutional issue. I'll look into this, of course. Do some consulting. That's outside of my realm."

"Please do. I want the best opinion, and a detailed analysis of every option open to us."

"Will do."

"How'd this slip up on us?"

"The Montana Court scheduled it on an urgent basis because of the October 1 date for the existing legislation to take effect. We argued last week; they took only a few days to decide. The faxes came in about ten and I drove straight over here. They announced at eight-thirty, Mountain time."

"Are you satisfied that your people did a good job?"

"I'll review the record, but yes, so far."

"What about the Fish and Wildlife wolf-habitat plan?"

"Still up in the air. I think that testimony from their own man, Kouric, put a crimp in their plans. Not to mention the arrest of that buffoon who was smuggling wolves. My guess is they'll lie low and then, when the furor dies, stick with their plan. They still want to kick out Nichols. Those people don't give a hoot about the rights of private citizens."

"That's why I'd prefer not to turn everything over to them. Keep me posted—day and night, Hector."

"Sure, Laslo . . . I'm sorry."

Horoney nodded, and saw his right-hand man to the door, and then settled in a chair at his window. Whenever he needed to make great decisions, he needed to see blue sky. He stared into it, this warm autumnal day in suburban Dallas, wondering what he could do, where he might turn. He had no answers.

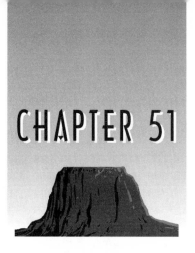

CHAPTER 51

Cameron stood at his father's grave, which he visited often. He had come to admire his father at the last, ignore his various rigidities, and appreciate his strength and courage and integrity. He had been a man of honor in a world without honor.

The prairie sod had browned this early October day. It had been carefully restored over the grave, this bit of virgin prairie. A simple unpolished headstone had been added, a name and two dates. DeeAnn had kept remembrances there for these several weeks—flowers while they still bloomed—now sprigs of evergreens.

Nichols Ranches had won a small victory, but one likely to bear bitter fruit. They would have county services. The Horoney Foundation's land and livestock—the buffalo—would be taxed at the same rate as elsewhere in Montana. And that was what worried Cameron. What would Horoney do? Either auction the vast prairies to private interests, or else give it to the government. Knowing Horoney as he did, Cam knew that the land would go to the government, so that the vision of the restored High Plains grassland might still live. And that meant that Nichols Ranches would be surrounded by federal land.

Well, Laslo Horoney, one of the world's richest men, might have more options than Cam could imagine, powers so sweeping that he might yet establish his foundation and his grassland dream. It was a good dream, really, as long as it accommodated people like himself who wanted to stay on, work their ancestral lands they had always called home.

He loved this burial place. He had been here countless times. This home ranch he had traversed on foot and horse and all-terrain vehicle so much that he knew its every cranny and secret corner and hidden gulch, its every animal den and hidden spring. He remembered where everything had happened: the place where Martin had sat down next to a friendly rattlesnake; the place where Julie had been thrown off her mare and broke an elbow; the slough where he had found a mammoth tusk. He wasn't a particularly sentimental man, but what held him here ran deeper than sentiment. He was bonded to this soil. If he were to move off of it he would be a different man, truncated and incomplete. These ranches were his dominion, or were until the habitat ruling froze his plans and turned him into an alien upon his own property. He could not so much as repair a stock dam now without the consent of the federal government. That struck him as outrageous, illegal, and a violation of his most basic rights. But that's what America was coming to.

This land might yet whip him. Nichols Ranches had already spent thirty thousand in legal fees. He had pushed his line of credit at the Miles City bank to its limit, and he sensed the tension in his bankers now, old friends who wished he'd sell out and pay them off instead of resisting the inevitable. But he did resist, and would resist.

Oddly, he didn't have to. He was executor of his father's estate and could vote the Nichols Ranch shares as he wished. What's more, the probate court had made him trustee of his grandmother's trust, which contained Nichols Ranches shares. Cameron could now vote his grand-mother's interests as well as his father's. He had a large majority of the shares of all the corporations under his personal control. He could call a stockholder meeting and abolish the ranches. But he wouldn't.

Anna Garwood Nichols still believed in the land, in its mysterious beauty and power, in its innate ability to vest its owners with dignity. She believed that land would endure. Stocks, bonds, money, possessions would fall apart, but land would endure, and land would prevail, and land would weather a depression, war, inflation, economic collapse, fam-ine, drought and flood, and all the works of man. Land was eternal, and the ones who bonded themselves to the good earth were the fortunates whose lives were blessed by God. Cameron believed that, too, perhaps less mystically and more practically, but he sensed the power and muscle of the land he stood upon, the fruitfulness of its grasses if he nurtured them. He sensed that some profound love of land had inspired Laslo Horoney, and some lust for land had inspired the various federal land-management bureaus to increase their holdings and drive away rivals. There was only so much land. For generations, few had embraced the faceless plains, where drought was normal and life was sometimes des-perate and never easy. The mountains and river valleys and timbered slopes had been fought over, but not the flat monotonous plains. Until now. Horoney had wanted them for a wilderness, and now every wildlife and land agency in the country had grown concupiscent.

It was time to talk to Anna. He abandoned his early-morning vigil and drove up to Miles City. He had made a point of visiting her frequently, with Dudley gone. Her mind was phenomenal, not what one would expect of a ninety-one-year-old woman. He would tell her this time about the court decision. And he would also tell her about Nichols Ranches' perilous financial condition. The next step would be to start selling the rest of the prized Herefords.

The longhorns might be staving off some wolf kills, but they didn't make much economic sense. John Trouble had reported that the wolves got a heifer after all, one they isolated and jumped. Just as that wolf biologist Kouric had warned, the wolves would occasionally pick off even those well-armed horned cattle. But that was less important than the other realities: less carcass weight, less prime beef, an extra year to grow, less efficient use of fodder. Those were what counted when you added up the columns of figures in the ranch ledgers.

This day the plains glowed with a golden autumnal beauty, rending his heart once again. He smelled smoke in the air. He didn't want to leave here. If he did, he would be a wheelchair case. He was wedded to the land, and it to him, and losing his land would be like losing his limbs.

He found Anna sitting in the lounge, soaking up sunlight and pitying the old people, as she called them. She welcomed Cameron heartily.

"You come more often than Dudley," she said. "My family's so good to me."

"I love to come, and there's often news to share."

"Good news?"

"Well, perhaps."

"Did that professor croak?"

They laughed.

"We've won a skirmish, Anna. The Montana Supreme Court's ordered the new county to provide all services. And it basically invalidated the legislation that gave the Horoney Foundation some tax privileges."

"What does that mean?"

"It may kill Horoney's project in its current form. We'll see what he does."

"You know, it's a good project. He wants to take care of the land."

"Anna—" Her sentiment surprised him.

"Oh, yes, times change. I've been thinking about it, dear. Everything passes except the land. We damaged the land, you know."

"Yes, but for many years we've improved it."

She smiled. "People aren't eating beef as much. Maybe that's passing, too."

"People love beef and always will."

"Cameron, I'm glad you came because I've been wanting to say something to you. You're the trustee now, and can vote my shares, and you're also Dudley's executor and can vote his. I want you to feel free to do what's best."

"Do what's best, Anna?"

"Sell out if that's what is necessary. I'm old and I think in terms of centuries. Our century raised beef. My great-grandchildren may want to raise bluestem grass and flowers and deer and buffalo. That'd be fun, living in a sea of buffalo. Oh, the stories the old-timers told when I was a girl."

"You surprise me."

"When you reach a certain age, Cam, you discover that everything has its time. I sit here and think, how can Anna Garwood Nichols make life sweet for the little ones now? And how can this old Anna make life easier for her dear grandson Cameron? And for her great-grandchildren?" She clasped his hand. Hers felt warm and soft, and her grip was still firm without palsy. "The seasons. It's October outside, but the end of December here." She touched her breast. "There's nothing so lovely as prairie spring, when the grasses burst from the earth, and leaves pop from the cottonwoods. You know what I'd like to leave behind me? Not wealth or cattle or things like that. Prairie enjoying a new spring. Idled prairie."

She caught his eye. "Don't be startled, Cameron. If you should vote the shares to disband Nichols Ranches, I wouldn't see it as a loss or a failure. If you wish to continue with longhorns, I'd be delighted. If our pastures are given or sold to those who wish to nurture them, I'd be pleased and I'd hope I'm strong enough to watch them unload the buffalo when that day comes. What I'm saying, Cam, is that you need your freedom to act wisely. Do what you will with the shares, with my blessing. Really, with Dudley's blessing and with the blessing of all those where I'll be going."

"You're not going anywhere soon."

She settled back in her chair, smiled at him with just a hint of twinkle in those old eyes. Then she added a caveat: "But don't give the land to fools like that Professor Brooke-Carson. I saw him on TV."

"It's a deal, Anna."

"Now tell me about your family, and especially my dear Sandy."

Cam gazed into the sunlight, wondering how to phrase things. "She's a fighter. Billings is good for her. She's lunching with some friends. It's just that—I hardly know her in the evenings."

"Cam, she's doing better. Keep your chin up."

"She's trying, Anna."

"Never give up on her. She's just the finest woman, a lady, a sweet-heart."

"All that and more."

"The world's a beautiful place, Cam. I see troubled people around me. We live with our own flaws, and those of others, and it's still a beautiful world. Sandy's as beautiful as any woman on earth, and you tell her I said so, dear."

He drove home that afternoon feeling elated.

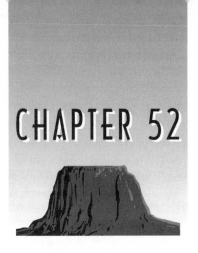

CHAPTER 52

Laslo had become morose and Dolly worried about it, feeling helpless. She regarded all Eastern European males as romantics, and Laslo Horoney the most romantic of all. When things went badly, he saw them in an even worse light. When things went well, he became a poet.

She remembered how he had courted her: roses and orchids, moonlight splashing Caribbean beaches, dancing the rhumba, or bossa nova, or whatever Xavier Cugat was playing, the poetry of Elizabeth Barrett Browning. *How do I love thee? Let me count the ways. I love thee to the depth and breadth and height my soul can reach* . . . His own love poems, yearning and mysterious, filled with the wonder of her and the joy of loving and living. She smiled at the recollection of all that.

She had her own interests, mostly in music, and he had his. But he had the ability to share his visions and interests with her in a such a compelling way that she had been drawn to them. Thus had she started as a disinterested spectator of his great High Plains project, and found herself entranced and absorbed, and loving the rejuvenation of every acre of grassland, and the restoration of its wildlife. So much so that it had become a passion. The restored grassland would be a treasure, something magical—a blossoming of uttermost wilderness in the midst of American civilization. She had no idea how she had arrived at his passions and his vision, except that Laslo struck off sparks of something almost divine in its nature, sparks of vision, a seeing beyond the material world.

Now he brooded within their spacious home, didn't fly anywhere or visit their various cubbyholes, and stared into an empty blue heaven. He had spent a fortune, and for what? The ever-vigilant Hector Truehart, bless him, had at once put his staff to work petitioning the new Montana county to lower its tax assessments on the vast Horoney holdings, and as a result some of the land would be assessed as unimproved range, devoid of even a fence. Wheat croplands, now reseeded with buffalo grass, would be taxed as range. And Truehart's staff had also made sure that the thousands of buildings no longer present on the grassland were not being taxed. The effect was a significant decline in property taxes—which heartened Laslo but did not resolve the problem. No single fortune, however large, could pay taxes on an area as large as a hip-pocket nation.

She couldn't cheer him up. She had never seen him like this, withdrawn and paralyzed. She had already suggested travel, adventure, some moonlit beaches, to no avail. A romantic man in the midst of melancholia could not enjoy such things.

One October morning she ventured into his study, determined to hearten him one way or another, if only with a hug. She loved Laslo as much now as in the brightness and newness of their honeymoon. They had worn comfortably into each other, knew and forgave failings, and had shared their lives.

"There's got to be a way, and we'll just find it," she said, settling in the leather chair opposite him.

He stared at her.

"You've already done more good than you know. This year, hundreds of thousands of acres weren't grazed. The foundation's been buying now for three years. Some of the land hasn't been grazed for two years. Thousands of acres of tilled land have been replanted with bluestem. It's not blowing away anymore."

He nodded.

She touched him. "You're still stuck with me, even if we live on social security in a trailer park."

"Then I am rich," he said, brightening.

"Would it help to think this through together?"

He nodded again.

"Well, all right. You could auction everything off and be done with the project, but we don't want that. So let's just forget it."

"I just don't want to give it to the federal government," he said.

"Why?"

"Those bureaus aren't good neighbors. From the beginning, we've tried to be neighbors with people like the Nicholses."

"All right. That's out. Let's not even think of giving it to the United States government. Not under any terms. That's off the list."

He smiled this time, his cheeks dimpling. "Dolly . . ." He didn't finish, but that one tender word spoke whole books to her. She was helping; he needed her now.

"We still have lots of options," she said. "Things that'll preserve the project, and give us value for all we've put into it."

He looked at her quizzically.

She shrugged. They often communicated with gestures. "Other foundations? The state? Go back to the Montana legislature and cut a new deal?"

"Truehart told me the old deal's dead," he said. "The whole protocol we worked out with the Montana legislature. All gone. It's suddenly ordinary private property again. Ours to do with as we choose. I suppose that's a plus. The foundation can ban hunting. The state can issue all the permits it wants, but we're no longer obligated to let anyone on the property. And we're no longer obliged to let the tribes kill five hundred buffalo each year—that was part of the enabling legislation that was killed by the court. We're in possession again, even if no fortune on earth could pay the taxes."

"Laslo," she said, eagerly, "let's fly up there. I want to walk that land, now, before it's too cold. I want to see what we've wrought. I want to look for mule deer and antelope."

"And wolves?"

"I'd love to see a wolf."

"I got a letter from a wolf biologist—the one, Kouric, who did the studies for Fish and Wildlife. He wants a job. I didn't answer. No reason to anymore."

"Could we get in touch with him? Could he show us the wolves?"

"That pack's on Nichols land, Dolly."

"Could you try? Suddenly I have this craving to see what we've done. To see the brown grasses, ungrazed and tall, to see a wheat farm replanted to buffalo grass. Could we go?"

"You know, Dolly, you're a medicine woman."

That was his yes.

The next morning their white Gulfstream V lifted from Dallas–Fort Worth Airport and hurtled out of late summer and into deep autumn, and settled quietly in Billings on a cloudless day. There they met the wolf biologist, Sanford Kouric, and there they picked up a shiny new four-wheel Explorer and headed for the High Plains.

Dolly eyed Kouric curiously. She had never met a wolf biologist before. Kouric turned out to be thin, serious, not entirely at ease, and maybe even uncomfortable. She understood that. Many people were acutely uncomfortable with the Horoneys, awed by Laslo's wealth and power, and she knew how to put them at ease.

"Dr. Kouric, how did you choose wolves? That's a rare field, isn't it?"

"Well, ah, ma'am, wolves are mythic. Wolves aren't ordinary animals . . . A lot of people hate wolves, and that's reason enough to like them. I like underdogs, if you'll forgive the expression."

"Ah, you're a contrarian!"

"No, not exactly. I just got curious about the myth and the reality. Like whether wolves eat people. I guess probably they have, in the past, though it's hard to document. But there's the folklore, you know."

"And music, Mr. Kouric. One of the loveliest children's pieces ever written is *Peter and the Wolf.* Oh, those horns when the wolf appears. So sinister. Prokofiev was a magician."

"Yes, and Russia is the cradle of wolf myths."

"But surely there was more? You have a doctorate in biology?"

"Yes. I like wolves, so I made them my specialty."

She enjoyed that.

They drove through a chill, clear, golden afternoon, the sun brassy and the shadows long. Laslo took them east on the interstate. His driving always annoyed her. He would accelerate, and then lift his foot off the accelerator, and then press the gas pedal again, fast and slow, a man who couldn't contain himself or his impulse to be somewhere else.

"Laslo, you're doing it again. Set the cruise control."

He smiled and did. She was so glad to see him smile.

West of Rosebud he turned south on a country road, passed a cattle guard and a foundation sign, and traversed a lonely, quiet stretch of hilly prairie. There was no sign of a fence anywhere.

"This is foundation land now," he said. "This had been idle for two years. How does it look to you?"

"I couldn't say," Kouric said. "All I know about grasses is that they're eaten by herbivores, and wolves eat herbivores. If good grass makes more prey, I'm all for good grass."

"Grass feeds the world," Horoney said. "Wheat, corn, oats, barley are all grasses. The meat we eat was grass. Grasses are the real gold."

"Laslo," she said, "could we walk? This is your grass. It's been rested. Let's feel it under our feet."

He drew to a stop without replying, and they stepped into a cutting breeze that had the iron smell of winter in it. She shivered and zipped up her down coat. Her Southern blood wasn't used to this.

They hiked east, with the wind, onto naked prairie that had once been a ranch. The brown grasses bobbed in the wind. She stared at the range, somehow feeling subdued. What had seemed lush pasture from the windows of their vehicle seemed thin and forlorn now. How many years would it require to return the pasture to its virgin condition? If ever?

Horoney stared at it, thin-lipped, seeing what she saw; a vegetative cover so spare that it wasn't even holding down the topsoil on this windy day. Tiny streams of dust eddied along the tan earth. Ancient gray cow flops lay about, sometimes caught in naked sagebrush. What was the value of all this? Wasn't it just desolate wasteland, and hadn't it always been wasteland? The Great American Desert? Even if they poured a fortune into it, wouldn't this perverse land just shrug off the effort, or maybe seduce them with some greenery for a year or two and then laugh at them with the first arid season?

"I thought maybe we'd done some good, but now I wonder if any mortal, with unlimited resources, can do much good," he said.

"Mr. Horoney, much of this country was like this before white men ever set foot on it," Kouric said. "I've seen you on TV talking about the Eden myth. This was never Eden, and the grass here was never thick and knee-high. Not even in wet cycles."

"Yes, thank you, Dr. Kouric. I've bought the myth myself and imagined a wealthy man could restore Paradise."

"Sir, it is a sort of paradise for the species who've adapted to it and know how to use it. Many of these areas are grazed seasonally—only in the spring."

"These are wastes."

"Maybe for ten months out of twelve. Come back and look at this in May or June. Maybe its real value is what it gives the world in a few fleeting weeks each year. Sweet, succulent grass that comes and goes in the blink of an eye."

She took his arm. "We're protecting a fragile land," she said.

CHAPTER 53

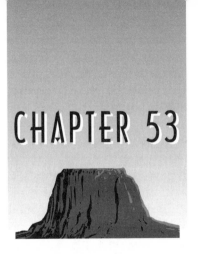

They drove into Nichols's North Ranch and Kouric checked with Mavis Trouble, and then took over the driving. He steered westward, down two-rut ranch lanes that crossed forlorn brown hills and empty valleys. It was the sort of desolate country that inspired mortals to huddle together just for the comfort of being with their own kind, the sort of country that bonded the three sojourners in the Explorer.

"I don't know whether we'll see wolves," he said to the Horoneys. "I don't have any radio gear now. That belonged to Fish and Wildlife. We'll drive to where they denned last spring, and see."

He wondered whether this would lead to a job. Ever since the state supreme court decision came down, he wondered whether the Horoney Foundation would even continue. Maybe that's what this incredibly rich couple beside him were really deciding just now. He suspected that they were. He liked them, especially Dolly.

"This range is in pretty good shape compared to some around here," he said. "The Nicholses were working at it. Not that any of it's even halfway back to the sod system that existed in the old days. We're five hundred feet higher here than when we looked at foundation pasture. More rainfall, better grass."

"You have to know a lot about nature to be a biologist." Dolly said.

"We study systems, yes. In academic terms, there's no such thing as a wolf biologist. My degree's in biology, and my specialty is mammal reproduction. The propagation of a species involves a broad spectrum of knowledge, ranging from entire ecosystems, to animal behavior, to medical or veterinary knowledge. The act of putting a radio collar on a wolf requires some pretty diverse knowledge."

"How *do* you collar a wolf?"

"The original Yellowstone wolves were trapped in Canada with a noose device that clamped around their necks tightly enough to pin them but not tightly enough to choke them. They were sedated with a hypodermic on a pole, for our own safety as well as theirs. Then we could handle the sedated animals. We used a combination of two drugs that work well, but aren't the best available. Trapped animals sometimes die, you know. The whole process is hard on them. The drug we'd like to use, D99, isn't available in the United States, although biologists and vets use it elsewhere. It's an opiate somewhat similar to heroin, and the Drug Enforcement Agency won't let it into the country, even for veterinary use. That drug is safest on a wide variety of mammals. It knocks them out easily, without struggle, and when they recover there are few aftereffects. The ones we use now require an injection of a recovery drug that blocks the sedatives. But that often doesn't work well, and the animal relapses into a sort of drunken conduct that can be dangerous to itself, and others." He smiled. "We do what we have to. When the animal's down we can do all sorts of things. We can take blood, determine its diseases, study wounds, examine the condition of teeth—very important—even see what's in its stomach. Vets do that sort of thing."

Kouric approached the lonely coulee where the alpha had denned months before, and stopped. "All right. We'll walk now. We'll keep quiet. The wind's out of the west and we're southeast of the area we'll be looking at, so we won't be advertising ourselves. But wolves are cunning and brilliant and shy. Bundle up. You're from Texas and you'll feel the wind after a bit. Bring your binocs."

They followed him silently through a bitter breeze. At the lip of the gulch they crawled to an observation point shielded by thick juniper. Kouric glassed the denning area, seeing nothing. All his instincts told him this pack had long since abandoned the area and had moved to happier hunting grounds. After an endless twenty minutes he abandoned the site.

"Sorry. We'll have to try elsewhere," he said.

Silently they returned to the four-wheel and Kouric drove west, down toward the Rosebud. He stopped at a wire gate, but before he could get out, Horoney was dropping the gate to let the Explorer through. In his rearview mirror he watched the billionaire carefully pull the gate taut and drop the wire loop over the post. The man had been around.

"That was the Nichols property line," he said to Horoney after they were en route again. "This is your foundation land here."

They negotiated a long slope into the creek bottoms, where naked cottonwoods dotted the flats.

"Dr. Kouric, when you find a pleasant place along the river, we'll stop. We've some lunch that our flight people put together for us, plenty for all of us," Horoney said. "Dolly and I've come up here to reacquaint ourselves with this country, and feel it under our feet. Would you care to walk with us after a bit? Or do you need to get back?"

"I'd enjoy walking, sir."

He stopped at a spot where the bottoms tried halfheartedly to be pretty and the gray bluffs shielded them from the insolent wind. They walked the river for a while, letting nature do all the talking. A few leaves clung to the cottonwoods and the chokecherry brush had turned into a gray web of twigs. Only the red willow brush stained the land with color. The birds had fled, save for the crows and magpies. The Rosebud purled at low ebb, its waters opaque. A terrible melancholy hung over the quiet valley. Kouric spotted deer pellets and coyote scat and evidence of hares, but kept to himself. He was looking for wolf prints, but found nothing.

"The fall is very quiet here," Dolly said.

"Dr. Kouric, what do you see in this land?" Horoney asked.

"See? Here?"

"Yes, sir. What is its value to you?"

"Its only value is itself. It doesn't exist as something for us to value," Kouric said. He ventured a question he probably shouldn't ask. "Are you wondering what to do, now that the court has killed the enabling legislation?"

"You have it. Paying taxes on a piece of land this size is more than the foundation can handle. But Dolly thought to come here, hoping that by walking it, feeling it under our feet, we might come to some answers. This was her idea, and I'm glad we came. I'm glad we contacted you. I have your letter, and I'm quite unable to reply to it now."

Kouric had thought it was something like that.

"Dr. Kouric, set aside for the moment all the practicalities. Whether we can find the means to continue, or what we can do to salvage the National Grassland. Let's go deeper. Why should we? What value is there in it? This is a dreary little streambed in a little trench in the prairie. Yes, it has its quiet beauty. So do the prairies, as featureless as they may seem. I thought I knew the reasons, but now I know I don't."

Sanford Kouric suddenly felt a weight on him heavier than he could handle. It was as if the fate of the grassland rested on him, and that was more than he was up to. He shrugged. "I don't know," he said. "Its value is for itself, not for what it can do for human beings, or for America, or for civilization. It's not a zoo, not a wildlife display, not an educational park. You could do those things on a few acres. Unlike the rain forests, grasslands aren't major producers of atmospheric oxygen. You could turn this all back to ranching and wheat farming without making great environmental waves. Neither are the prairies eternal. A few thousand years ago, during and after the last glacial retreat, these were forest and swamp, maybe tundra in some areas. Neither are the species prevalent today, or a century ago, graven in stone. The dominating species change once a millennium or so, in endless climax and decline, wrought by competition. There's nothing holy or sacrosanct about the plains as they were before white civilization, even though many of my colleagues might think so. It wasn't a true wilderness—it was hunted by the most ruthless predator of all, homo sapiens. Human hunting was more important to some species than the hunting by all other predators combined. Nature isn't a repository of virtue; nature is neither good nor evil, and it's more brutal to itself than mortals are. Nature isn't God, and not something to worship. It's simply a mysterious, magnificent system of ever-changing life."

"Then the National Grassland is Horoney's Folly."

"No, it's an act of vision and beauty and transcending insight, sir."

Horoney stared at him. "Why?"

Kouric swallowed back fear. "I can't answer that, but I know it's true. Maybe I'll be able to say why after I rationalize it somehow. It's an instinct I have that leaps beyond my very limited powers of thought."

Horoney smiled. "When Dolly and I walked out on that pasture the foundation owns, on the way down here, we didn't see the slightest sign of improvement on ranchland we'd bought two years ago. Not a cow grazed that land since then. You're not an agronomist, but maybe you can tell me. Is it ruined land?"

"Yes, it's ruined. But not forever. The timetable's not what you'd like. An agronomist would probably tell you that there was change after all, but under the surface. Those ungrazed stalks, stronger plants, would improve the root systems. Some of those grasses use roots or rhizomes to multiply, as well as seeds. Try again in a few years."

"Well, that's heartening. I've bought a few roots with a few billion dollars."

"I wish I had better answers for you, sir. We're on the edge of metaphysics."

They returned to the Explorer, backs to the harrying wind, and Kouric was ready for some shelter. He hadn't given Horoney the answers the man wanted, and Kouric had the awful feeling that he'd just scrubbed the most hopeful environmental project in the history of the world.

Back in the four-wheel, Dolly passed out a gorgeous lunch, with everything from a salad with honey mustard dressing to medallions of beef, and saffron-spiced vegetable dishes, with any beverage Kouric could imagine, all of it in elegant pewter dishes, with linen napkins.

Horoney ate little, and gazed upon these prosaic surroundings, his mind full of things Kouric couldn't even imagine. Then, at last, he turned to the biologist.

"What would you do in my shoes?" he asked.

Kouric felt the weight of billions of dollars on his fragile shoulders. "Keep going. Find other foundations to share the tax load. Forget about the buffalo for now if Montana's going to tax them as livestock. Let the prairie recover for five, ten years. But if it's left ungrazed for too long, it won't recover. Eventually there needs to be some sharp random grazing, and churning with hooves, to generate the kind of sod that once covered this country. But that's years away. For now, this land needs release from grazing. But, sir, in your shoes, I'd keep going."

"Thank you, Dr. Kouric. Would you present me with a proposal detailing your salary needs, expectations, and what you would like to achieve as a biologist with the foundation?"

"I would be honored, sir."

"And would you work what you've told me into a concrete plan I can show to my board colleagues? I mean, just from your point of view as a wildlife biologist working with whole ecosystems."

"I will, sir. I'll begin tomorrow."

"It's going to be expensive grass, Dr. Kouric."

"You asked me a while back what good it was, this project, and I didn't have anything very bright to say. In fact, your question scared me. But I'll make a stab at it now, if you'd like."

Dolly said, "Please do."

"It has something to do with our hubris, our conceit, our American passion to conquer every problem, exploit every resource even to its ruin. I've always sensed that nature is wiser and more wondrous than even our best wildlife biologists imagine, and that our real task isn't to manage, but to stop intervening, stand aside, and let the miracle of life assert itself.

"Your National Grassland, Mr. Horoney, will be an inspiration and a rebuke. It will inspire reverence for the miracle of life lived within systems of nature; it will rebuke our pride.

"You lamented that your wealth has wrought only a few blades of grass. And yet grass is the greatest of all gifts. All flesh is grass. Our meat and poultry and dairy products are grass. Our wheat and corn and oats and rice are all grass. Preserve our grass and we preserve the world, and all life upon it. The grass we stand upon is more important than our forests or mountains or deserts.

"When you nurture the grassland, you make a home for all creatures. Giving the world grass is a holy enterprise, and your transforming vision soars above the wildest dreams of the Greens and the small mean programs of the government. Restore the grass, Mr. Horoney, and rejoice."

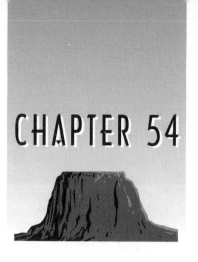

CHAPTER 54

During the next days Horoney and Dolly roamed the High Plains all alone, witnessing what they had wrought. They had flown over this country many times, but now they wandered down gravel roads, stopping at demolished homesteads, pausing at extinct crossroads, and marveling at the vast reaches of empty grassland. They passed tumbleweed thistle and Russian olive trees, and rutted ranch roads with frozen ice in the potholes, and ruined dishes of prairie rimmed with white salts, and a low slope thick with gnarled silver sagebrush.

They rambled without plan, ending up one night in Miles City, another in Gillette, Wyoming, and another at Ashland. Horoney had informed his staff that he would be incommunicado for the time being. He and Dolly intended to turn the great abstraction of a National Grassland into reality, and feel the good earth under their feet.

The voyage proved to be the most exhilarating and desolating he had ever experienced. His spirits lifted whenever he passed what had once been a wheat field, now planted with bluestem or wheat grass. His spirits sank whenever they wandered into an old homestead and absorbed the signs of habitation there. Every building had been burned, knocked down, dismantled, or moved away, but all the marks of life remained. Many of those places had family cemetery plots, some well fenced but others abandoned to the empty future.

Children's swings hung from trees. Forlorn lilac bushes lined driveways. Gulches were still filled with trash, coils of barbed wire, children's tricycles, ancient harness, rusting horseshoes, decaying farm equipment. Many of those vanished families had warred against gophers on their lawns or out in their croplands, but now the gophers were ubiquitous. No one was shooting them with a .22 rifle, or poisoning them, or drowning them with a hose stuck into a hole.

At various homesteads they found the rusting hulks of old cars: a forties-vintage Dodge, an old Hudson, a Studebaker, assorted Fords and Chevies. Several abandoned stock trucks, decaying into rubble. The remains of a motorcycle. A bunch rake, several old tractors, Deere, Ford, Farmall. A plethora of ancient twine-tie balers, rakes, drills, plows, harrows. All these had been the tools of people with dreams, scouring small incomes out of this unyielding land. Where had they all gone, the people who'd settled, raised children, married, divorced, paid taxes, went to church, held dances and parties, suffered through school, dawdled at coffee shops in the nearest hamlet, run up debts they could never repay?

In one place they wandered into a henhouse, and observed the dusty nests made of ancient orange crates, the filth on the concrete floor, an ancient wicker basket once used for collecting eggs. They fled, saddened. Family by family, people had come to the plains, built their homes, cared for themselves, joined the Grange or other prairie organizations, raised small white churches where they were married or buried, baptized and comforted.

Horoney knew that forces much larger than his foundation had driven these people off the land; drought, modern transportation, loneliness had all done their work before the foundation had purchased its first acre. Yet the reminders of settled life remained. Here a shelter belt, row upon row of cottonwoods, spruce, juniper, willow, poplar, chokecherry laid out in military precision as a barrier against the ever-present wind. They would harbor animals now, but their geometric design seemed out of place in a natural world. In one place they found a tree house, cobbled together by children, with ancient steps nailed to the trunk of a cottonwood. What boys had retreated up there? What girls had served Kool-Aid to dolls in it?

The first day out they had narrowly averted serious trouble when their gas gauge showed empty. They had made it to Ashland more or less on fumes. There would be no help now, no one passing by. After that they carried two jerry cans of gasoline, a CB radio and some survival gear, food and water. October wasn't a warm month in these northern climes. Two filling stations remained open on the grassland, one in Ekalaka, and one in Baker, where fifty or so people clung to their former life. Laslo wondered how those people felt about him, even whether it was safe for him to go there. The very thought troubled him. What had he done to other persons? Was it ultimately good?

They passed abandoned electric lines, the wire gone and salvaged, but the old poles poking the overcast sky, waiting to drop in fifty or eighty years. The power of civilization had receded here, pulled away forever. They paused at innumerable crossroads, once thriving places, now piles of ash or rubble. It was necessary to destroy every building, not only for tax purposes but to keep vagrants from denning in them, creating outlaw empires far from the civilized world. He had hardly realized, back in Texas, to what degree this empty part of Montana and Wyoming had nurtured life, often expressed in crossroads places, where there had been a combined store, saloon, and gas pump. Alzada, Hammond, Boyes, Epsie, Olive, Volberg, Belle Creek, Broadus—still alive but hunkered down like trapped animals—Ekalaka, much the same. Plevna, Baker, Carlyle, Saint Phillip, Mildred, Ismay, Willard, Mill Iron, Capitol, Sonnette, Quietus, Otter, Biddle, Ridge. Every one a place where people had lived out their lives, gathered in local cafés or saloons for the day's gossip, dreamed their dreams.

But of all the things that afflicted Horoney the most, the demolished schoolhouses were the worst. Destroying the schools was like demolishing the future. The playgrounds were just as they had been; swings, slides, bars, ancient paint limning a softball diamond on crumbling asphalt, piles of old desks waiting to be burned.

One white clapboard country school, not yet demolished by his crews, yielded a flood of feeling as he and Dolly slipped into its two rooms through an unlocked rear door. Cold air eddied through broken windows.

"Oh, oh, oh," said Dolly as they surveyed the neat rows of ancient desks, much whittled upon by jackknives. The familiar odor of varnished wood leapt to their nostrils. Black coal-burning stoves had once heated the rooms, and beside the stoves were coal buckets, ash buckets, and the shovels and pokers needed to keep a fire going. The blackboards were still chalky; paper still clung to the bulletin boards.

"Think of all the children who learned their ABCs here and went out into the world," Horoney said. "Where are they now? Did we drive them away?"

She took his hand. "No, Laslo." She showed him some notices posted on the board. The last one was dated 1995. This two-teacher rural school had lasted that long. "You see, it's just as we'd been told. This whole country was dying, a day at a time. The few children here must have been bused somewhere."

A green chart adorned the bulletin board, and Laslo studied it. It was some sort of an honors poster: students' names, and gold stars arrayed in rows. Bill Walch, three gold stars; Mary Rose Gump, one green star; Sallie Joseph, two silver stars; Arnold Engstrom, one silver star; Kevin Dettman, two blue stars; Bill Newbauer, one red star; Megan Eckhart, four gold stars . . . Was it for attendance? Grades? Who could say?

Where had they all gone? Had his wealth, his abstract plans, driven them like cattle out of this country?

"Laslo, let's go talk to people. We've been doing this now for three days, all by ourselves. I need to visit with the ones who are staying."

Horoney looked at Dolly, whose voice had a certain urgency, and knew she was right. No matter how disturbing it might be, they needed to visit with the ones who were staying.

They drove quietly across empty plains, once pasture and now nothing but sere brown grasslands, toward Broadus, located right in the heart of the area. Here there was civilization, and even a battered Conoco station. Here, too, was a brick school with cars parked before it, and lights burning within. But flanking the central district were rows of silent dark houses awaiting the jaws of a wrecker. It had been costly for the foundation to depopulate towns, pay each householder a fair-market price for his little home and plot. Millions of dollars that might have purchased rangeland ended up buying small parcels and helping people to relocate. Yet there had been no other fair way. And each of those householders had gotten a much better deal from the foundation than from the government, if the government had employed its power of eminent domain.

Perhaps ninety percent of the town had been turned over to ghosts. But the man in the all-purpose store wasn't a ghost. He was a ruddy old fellow in his seventies, wearing a pair of leather galluses over a dirty flannel shirt. The store carried canned goods, cereals, frozen meats, and a variety of other products, from lightbulbs to screwdrivers.

Horoney didn't introduce himself or Dolly—at least not yet. "Well, sir, how are you doing?" he asked.

"Better'n I expected. We still got a bunch here."

"You still have basic services?"

"Oh, sure, except we got to go to Gillette for most items. But I like it. Old Horoney did us a favor."

"How?"

"Well, I tell you. This town's got a future. Before, it was just fading away, no more'n holding its own. But once them buffalo herds come stomping through, I figure this here's going to be the safari capital of the world. I bought me two motels here. Boarded up now, but just you wait. Where else can anyone see two hundred, three hundred thousand buffalo? Why, we'll have people from Timbuktu coming in to see the buffalo."

"Herds that size'll take thirty or forty years to build, you know."

"Well, I won't likely be around. But this here town'll be the buffalo capital of the world, I figure."

"How do other people feel about it?"

"Aw, who knows. We got fifty-five people left, and we got forty-seven opinions and the rest are too young to have any."

"Was there bad feeling?"

The old man cackled. "Like building nooses for them Horoneys?"

"Well, yes."

"There was that. But I never figured it that way. He helped people git, them that got, and that's more than most would do." He surveyed them shrewdly. "I didn't catch your name."

"I'm Laslo Horoney and this is my wife, Dolly."

"Horoney! I'll be died and gone to heaven."

"We're looking over the plains and thought to stop and talk to folks."

"Horoney are you? You came through here like a ground blizzard; people couldn't see the path until the air cleared. But let me tell you, after it was done, the bitching and moaning stopped. Those that always cussed this land took off like a shot, glad to have the cash to git, mostly cussing you for all the happiness you caused them. They'd cuss any fella that gave them their dream come true. Those that always liked it around here—like me—we're just sitting fat and happy, a million miles from all the troubles of the world."

Laslo permitted himself a smile. "And who are you, sir?"

"Conrad Grossenheider. Me, I got shut of a wife years ago and live alone. I like buffalo, wolves, elk and living alone in that order, and a good steak now and then."

"Well, it's our pleasure, Mr. Grossenheider. Is there anything the foundation should be doing?"

"Oh, there's always those that grouse on the shiniest day of the year, and you can't stop that. There's a few retired folks that thought they'd live out their days here, and they're worried. No doc around, not for a hundred miles, not even a nurse or a physician assistant now. But I hear that Miles City's going to send out a traveling medical bus, come through every two weeks. That'd work pretty good. Even emergencies aren't so bad. Billings helicopter gets here in an hour."

Horoney and Dolly talked a while more to the storekeeper, acquiring a sense that those who wanted to leave the grassland area already had, and those who were staying on did so because they wanted to. That was comforting. But Laslo found himself haunted by what had happened throughout the whole area. A brutal hand—his own hand—had cleared away the warp and woof of civilization as ruthlessly as a plague, or an atomic bomb, or an invading army. Had he really done that? The reality was so different from the nice abstraction. The naked land, mile upon mile without a soul present, without a habitation, without the ensigns of connection to the world—power lines and phone lines—seemed sad and frightening.

But transcending it all came a lyrical line of Walt Whitman's that Sanford Kouric had quoted to them just as they parted in Miles City, days earlier:

I believe a leaf of grass is no less than the journey-work of the stars.

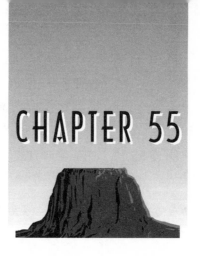

CHAPTER 55

Sandy surprised Cameron one morning, asking whether she might go out to the ranch that day.

"Sure, Sandy," he said. "I'm driving this time, picking up some stock salt."

"I'd like to come. I always enjoy our drives."

That meant she wanted to talk, which was fine with him.

"We'll have to get some groceries," he said. "I don't leave much in the refrigerator these days."

"I'll do some steaks if you like. We can stay over."

"Well, ah, we might need to stock up—"

"There's no booze."

He nodded.

"I will get along without," she said.

He glanced at her skeptically, saying nothing. She would probably ransack Dudley's house, where there was plenty of booze, or go beg from DeeAnn. But that was not something to throw in her face. If she could weather a day or two without her booze, maybe she could build upon that. He smiled.

She smiled back, and for a moment there was the flash of magic between them, the red-haired beauty from Butte and the young rancher from nowhere.

She retreated to her room, and appeared later with an overnight bag and two coats, one light and one intended for tough weather. "I'm ready," she said.

They stopped at one of the eastside ranch-supply outfits—he always enjoyed those places—and loaded up with forty blocks of trace-mineral salt, and signed the chit guiltily. Little did they know how hard he was scraping for cash.

Then they drove east on the interstate. She did not sit on her side, but slid over next to him, the way generations of courting Westerners had sat on the bench seats of pickups.

She wanted to talk about herself; about them. He knew that, but knew he had to let her reach the point where she could. They had done their best talking when they drove, especially in pickup trucks like this one. Something in them responded to the miles of concrete, or the slender lane of asphalt leading to tomorrow, and then they talked and bared hearts. He would wait.

He ached for her. He had never stopped loving her, never stopped hoping, never abandoned the dream of a lifetime together with his slim bride. But it had been hard. Sometimes in Billings he had studied other women, wondering what life would be like with one or another of them, hurting from the emptiness of his marriage, his own bleak sense that he had nothing to look forward to other than a drunk woman sliding deeper into self-immolation.

"Cameron, what's going to happen with the ranches?" she asked after twenty minutes.

"We're still losing money. And we'll probably have to sell one or two units to pay the taxes on Dudley's estate. We did our best to get around that, the corporations, but the government has its hand out, and we're stuck. I'm waiting to hear from Rockwell what we're up against."

"I'm sorry. I suppose if Anna dies, it'll make it worse."

"It could."

"The longhorns aren't working?"

"Not enough to earn us a living. But John Trouble tells me he thinks the wolves are gone. He doesn't hear them. And no longhorns have been killed recently."

"Where did they go?"

"Who knows? What frosts me is the Fish and Wildlife Service still has the provisional wolf-habitat order in place. We can't even seed a hay meadow without permission."

"Even with the wolves gone?"

"When has any bureaucracy admitted to mistakes? Bob Rockwell's working on it, but you know how it goes."

"What does it really mean?"

"We can't change land use. We can't build so much as a stock dam. We can't plow up a pasture and plant alfalfa. We can't put a hayfield back into pasture. We can't build a fence. Not without permission, any-way."

He was starting to boil, as he always did when he contemplated the restrictions the government had imposed on his private land. He had been tempted over and over to defy them, to ranch as he chose, as he needed to survive, and let them bring charges. He'd run it straight up to the Supreme Court. But Bob Rockwell had always cooled him down, reminded him what it would cost.

"I wish things were better," she said. "You work so hard."

"We have a little freedom now. I had a visit with Anna the other day, and you know what? She told me to vote her trustee shares, and Dudley's shares, as I wished. She said a new era was coming, and she got sort of biblical—you know, a season for all things, a time to plant and a time to harvest, a time to be born and a time to die. She said, bless her, Sandy, she said the land needed to be reborn. Imagine it."

"We need to be reborn," she said.

Cam stared at her sharply.

"That's what I'm trying to do," she added.

"That's like saying, I love you," he said.

She caught his free hand and held it.

They sped silently through Rosebud, and turned off into the foundation's land, which lay bleak and empty in the autumnal day, brown and tan against a somber sky.

"It is so lonely," she said. "I'm glad we're in Billings."

He waited for more, but whatever else was on her mind vanished into the silence as he steered the pickup along a desolate road.

"The foundation's in a jam, too," he ventured after a while. "They're required to pay the same taxes as anyone else. I'd guess they'll be forced to turn it over to the government. That's doomsday for us, I figure. Surrounded by the Park Service or whatever outfit gets it."

She pointed at a fence post. "Those are new no-hunting signs."

"Yeah. When the legislation went down the tubes, so did the provisions requiring the foundation to open their lands to hunting. The state can issue permits for this area, but it's mostly private land now and Horoney's people can ban hunting if they feel like it. Horoney's raising deer and antelope, I guess."

"All this land and nothing on it."

"Good for the land—for a while."

They were almost at the ranch gate when she got around to saying what she was trying to say. Or at least that's how Cam figured it.

"Have you noticed anything about me?" she asked.

"I always notice you."

"No you don't. That's because you're gone days."

"Tell me, Sandy."

"I'm doing better. I don't drink in the daytimes. I wait until dinner.

And I'm down to three a day and not cheating, either. Three shots, not three full glasses. That's my rule."

He stared at her. She wasn't smiling. In fact she looked like she was about to blink back tears.

"Tonight I might have one before dinner, but that's all. I want to have a reunion."

"A reunion?"

She smiled. "You know." She had a certain wry grin that dimpled her cheek, and that had meant something private to them ever since college days.

All that was too much for Cam. He surveyed her, bewildered. It was true she looked a little better, or at least he imagined it. It had been what? How many years since they had made love? She'd always been drunk. Or her body reeked of stale alcohol oozing through her pores. Anyone who had ever been around a drunk knew the smell and could never forget it. The woman who once kindled bonfires in him had ended up repelling him.

"I guess you don't want to," she said.

"Sandy! Don't say that!"

"I'm just a drunk."

"Don't say that."

"I will say it. But I'm becoming a controlled drunk. I've made friends in Billings, and I like to go out to lunch and not be out of it and I stopped drinking mornings, and then afternoons until the sun went over the yardarm. I'm not going to quit, but I'm going to control it."

He listened doubtfully. That was the dream of many alcoholics. If she succeeded, she would be one of the lucky few. He elected not to voice his skepticism. She knew all that, and it might only discourage her.

"I don't want to lose you," she said, her face softening into sadness. "From the day we met in Bozeman, I've loved you, Cameron. But I let you down. If you'll just give me the chance to try again—"

He simply couldn't speak.

He reached the old rambling ranch house, and killed the engine. He turned to her and hugged her. He smelled no booze on her breath as he kissed her. The promise of moonlight and roses was in her face.

He carried in her bag and set it on the bed.

"Steaks and candlelight at seven," she said. "Then I get to try on my new outfit."

"Outfit?"

"Just for you," she said. "The children are all gone."

Those dimples were there again.

He nodded, wanting to believe she wouldn't be utterly drunk by then. He couldn't bring himself to believe it, but he hugged her for a minute. Her talk was kindling ancient and long-buried hungers in him. Which he would no doubt have to rebury this evening. But she was making a stab at it, he thought.

"I'll deliver this salt—it goes to the southern units—and be back around five," he said.

She squeezed his hand.

He drove out of the home ranch filled with desire and dread, knowing it was going to be a long day with a disappointing ending. Still . . . This was his own Sandy, and within that woman were strengths and passions that endlessly surprised him.

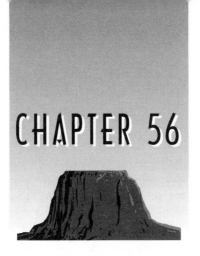

CHAPTER 56

For weeks after his pilgrimage to Bear Butte, John Trouble drew into himself. Sometimes he thought he hadn't given the old ways a chance. He should have stayed four days and let the Old Ones speak to him. That was the way of the elders. He delighted in the old traditions, the belief in spirit helpers, the reverencing of the Medicine Hat and sacred arrows. And yet he didn't for an instant believe that these things had validity as a religion.

There surely was value in the old teachings, such as Sweet Medicine's command to the Cheyenne never to do violence to one another. That was all fine. So was the romance of the old days. He could drum with the best of them, even costume himself in classic Cheyenne clothing, the way Europeans dressed up in their folk costumes, and he could enjoy the old stories and myths and feel that they all have a part in making him what he was.

He was gladly and entirely a Cheyenne. But he was also an American citizen of the twenty-first century. He preferred his pickup truck to any horse; preferred the stability of beef on his table and cereals in his bowl to the uncertainties of the hunt. He preferred money and banking and supermarkets and centrally heated homes to buffalo-skin lodges and no-madism and the uncertainties of life surrounded by hostile tribes. He preferred to plug in a country-western tape rather than listen to a sto-ryteller, or a long ceremonial chant.

But was he happier, spiritually richer, at peace in this white man's world? Horoney's dream of a grassland had suddenly opened that gulf in him—and in a lot of other Indians. The vision of unfenced prairies, massive herds of buffalo blackening the slopes, the chase and kill while riding a fine buffalo pony, life in idyllic villages composed of lodges, the resurgence of the old ways—all that had flared up in his mind, a

seductive dream that mesmerized him day and night as the great grassland project advanced.

Would he be happier with fewer material things, and less comfort?
Would he fulfill his destiny on earth that way? Would his people prosper
in this sea of grass, somewhat insulated from the white men's world?
Would he find more meaning and joy if he were to rise in the morning,
pray for guidance from his spirit-helper, the wolf or coyote or whatever
it might turn out to be, treat his women in the old way, lording over
them as unquestioned master? Would he like the universe better if he
were to abandon the vision of an eternal, omniscient Creator who fashioned creation and set it to evolving, a Creator who cared about all his
creatures?

"You sure are quiet," said Mavis one evening.

He nodded.

"Bear Butte. Off to Bear Butte and then you disappear from my life.
It must be serious."

"I'm feeling like a traitor to the People," he said.

"Ah, so that's it."

"I'm a Cheyenne and always will be. But I'm not. Know what I
mean?"

"I like being a Cheyenne, but not the old ways. If we were living a
hundred fifty years ago, you'd own me and tell me what to do."

"Well, nothing's changed," he said. "Get me a Coke."

She threw a couch pillow at him.

"I guess I can get my own Coke. But it's a good argument for the
old ways," he said.

"If it's the old ways, go get me a buffalo. I want a hide."

He rummaged the refrigerator, keeping his back to her, and found a
Coke.

"Get me one, too," she said, triumphant. "And a cookie."

He did. "Times sure changed," he muttered.

"You can bribe me with a cookie," she said. "I'll do anything for a
cookie."

"I'll bring you four cookies tonight."

They laughed.

They ate and drank quietly, sitting across their dining table. She was
a warm-fleshed woman with big black eyes that glowed with life. He
loved her.

"All Indians got a sweet tooth," he said. "Buffalo Bill once bribed
Sitting Bull with a wagonload of candy. He knew how to bribe an Indian."

"You going to tell me what you're going to do?" she asked.

"Cut off your nose."

They rollicked a moment. That was the old punishment meted out to an adulterous wife.

"John, whatever way you go, I'll go with you. We're on a big journey together."

"You're stuck with me."

"What'll you do if you lose your job?"

"I'll be one bad Indian."

"Do you think you will? Lose your job?"

"Nichols isn't earning anything. He might sell out even if he doesn't want to."

"We'd get unemployment for a while."

"I could go kill some buffalo. Then you could get down on your knees and scrape the hide and soften it and brain tan it into a robe and maybe get a few hundred dollars. You could support me. Like in the old days. Rich warrior, he had four or five wives supporting him."

"I'll tan your own hide, all right, big time hunter."

That evening they joked and worried and didn't know what way to turn, but he had Mavis and she had him, and they were tied together in life, and that was good. He looked at her more that night than he usually did. He liked those smile creases around her mouth and her straight jet hair she wore bobbed. And the goldenness of her smooth flesh. And the sheer cheeriness in her face. That night he pulled her head onto his chest until she nestled into the hollow of his shoulder, and fell asleep.

The next evening he drove to Busby. It was time to report to David Gray Wolf. He had delayed for days, dreading it because he wouldn't make the hat-keeper happy. In Ashland he bought a carton of Camels for the traditional tobacco gift, and headed west, wondering what he was going to say to the traditional Cheyenne who had befriended and instructed him. It would be all right. Indian people followed their own paths.

Gray Wolf invited him in and chased a son out of the kitchen. They didn't go outside because the night was nippy. But Gray Wolf charged his medicine pipe and they smoked it peacefully for a while, establishing the bond they had felt before. Trouble sensed that his host already knew where this would lead.

"Bear Butte sure gives off feelings," Trouble said at last. "South Dakota's done a good job."

"They should return it to the Indian People."

"I guess so. It's just an odd rock to most people."

"You camped there? In that meadow on the south side?"

"Overnight." Trouble figured that would tell the whole story right there.

Gray Wolf nodded slightly. "Go up?"

"Most of the way."

"That's good. We shouldn't go to the top."

"I went up there a way, until I got tired. I could see the whole world from up there. See almost to here. So I sat down and watched the sun set. It was nice."

Gray Wolf nodded.

"David, I got to tell you. The old ways aren't for me."

"I thought so."

"I like the stories. I'm proud to be one of the People."

Gray Wolf slid into silence.

"I'm going to keep the stories alive in my family. And the ways. I'll keep on doing the winter count. That's my office."

"Someone once said the cup was broken. It doesn't hold water anymore."

"Well . . ."

"Stories aren't beliefs."

"No, but they're an inheritance. They're our wealth."

"Beliefs are. Stories are mostly empty. You have another path?"

"I guess so. Maybe a church."

That did surprise Gray Wolf. He tapped the dottle out of the old medicine pipe.

"I got up there and what I saw was Creation. Someone made it," Trouble said.

"I think about that, too."

"We do not have a very good story of Creation. That is where I am stuck."

"We have a religion of personal power," Gray Wolf said. "We receive power when we seek it and it is ready for us. Some find power in spirit helpers. Some find power in medicine herbs. Some people have mysterious powers, and what they say comes true. Some had the power to make war without being hurt. There are many stories, many witnesses. That is what religion's for, having the power to live well."

"That's your way, David, and I've chosen another."

"What'll be your way, John?"

"I'm going to find a church and see."

"Do you think the way they do, that people are guilty or evil unless they worship their God?"

"I'm going to see."

"Then, that is your way. Will you abandon my way?"

"I am Cheyenne."

"Can you live with both?"

"Yes. One is my inheritance. The other might be my future."

"They own the future? Many Indian People think the whites are on their last legs. There is crime and disrespect, and they have thrown aside their own religion and become hollow. I do not think they will last. This grassland is a sign. It says they are giving up. They cannot live upon the grassland anymore and toss Styrofoam hamburger cartons out their car windows. They ravished the earth and now the earth is rejecting them. The rich man buys up the ruined earth, but it is worthless. They have nothing left. He thinks it is his power, his money, doing this, but it is nothing but the whispers in his ear that the end has come for white men."

Trouble shrugged. "We'll see," he said. "Maybe they're at a beginning, not an end. This is a healing act, what this Horoney is doing. My boss, Nichols, he's been healing the land, too, for years. They respect the earth now. Maybe more than we do. Where are Cheyenne healing the earth? Putting pasture to rest? Tell me how many Cheyenne are doing that. None. Maybe we're the ones at the end, eh?"

"It's not the land, it's the spirit that counts. They are hollow, without beliefs. They don't care about anything."

"We see that on TV, but inside people's homes it's better. Just like it's better inside our homes. You read the papers about us, and you think we're all drunken drivers. Well, it's the same with them."

"My friend John Trouble. You are a Cheyenne, and always my brother."

"Yes, David, you are a brother."

They smoked another pipe, and Trouble left the Keeper of the Hat and drove through a mysterious night, his soul more unsettled than ever.

CHAPTER 57

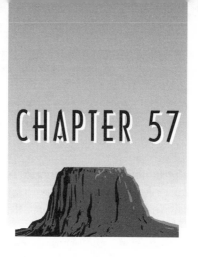

Laslo Horoney found the deputy director of the National Park Service waiting for him on the top floor of the Petroleum Club. What was his name? Ah, yes, Philbert Waite. Number three man. Nicely done, a quiet little inquiry, nothing public or official. Although no agenda for this little luncheon had been mentioned, Horoney had a pretty good idea what it would be about.

"Mr. Waite?"

The man smiled benignly, exuding power and privilege. "Pleasure, Mr. Horoney. Come, let us enjoy a little lunch and a visit."

Waite looked to be the type who jogged five miles along Pennsylvania Avenue or Sixteenth Street or around the mall every morning—a political appointee, trim, lean, shrewd, dark, and assessing. Horoney felt himself being sized up, about the way an undertaker measures for a coffin, which actually wasn't a bad analogy, he thought.

Horoney supposed he would be the host—no one ever expected rich men to be guests—but again, he felt an odd reversal of roles. Waite drifted through the quiet, understated sky-high restaurant as if he owned it.

They made small talk. Waite proved to be not only a raconteur, filled with Yellowstone Park bear stories, but also a man who'd done his home-work, inquiring cheerfully about Dolly's music, Laslo's early-life interest in biology, and similar items straight off a dossier.

All of which was prelude.

Laslo figured correctly that about the time the salad was under their belts, Waite would turn to the matter at hand.

"You know," said Waite, dabbing at his mustache while a waiter slid away the remains of his spinach and bacon salad, "you've done a mag-nificent thing, this national grassland. We've envied you. Single-handedly, you've almost put together the world's largest and most important tract of land ever devoted to preservation." He paused gently. "We'd love to get our hands on it."

That was the joke between them. Laslo smiled.

"Now, of course, we've monitored your progress, and were dismayed when the Montana court set you on your ear with that tax ruling. That was a pity."

"Not from your vantage point," Horoney replied.

Waite smiled, tacitly acknowledging that he had sliced his baloney a little thick. "No, not from ours. Of course, we've waited to see what you'd do—all these little luncheons you've had with the heads of foundations the world over. Am I right in my belief that none of them is willing to ante up funds to pay the annual taxes on what may be the largest land holding in the world?"

"So far," Horoney said. He saw no need to conceal what had become common knowledge. The foundations had shied away from his National Grassland as if it were poison. Horoney's Folly was the word for it now. One by one, the foundations had politely informed him that their objectives lay elsewhere, helping people, doing research, rather than shouldering the tax burden on a sea of grass. He had fared even worse with the Sierra Club and other Greens, which had treated him coldly. Not that any of them had the sort of money that would pay taxes in perpetuity on so much land. Truehart's current figures, now that Montana had pulled out of its deal and the other states were following suit, was that real estate taxes on the foundation land in Montana, Wyoming, and South Dakota would come to 280 million a year. That would decline as lands were reclassified and buildings removed.

Laslo had absorbed that sadly. He might manage one year by going deeper into his dwindling assets than he cared to. And now the vultures, like the gent across the white linen from him, were circling the carcass.

"I should add that we're pursuing other avenues, including new legislative packages," Horoney added. "There are always ways. Especially for someone in my position."

The faintest grimace flitted ineffably across Waite's urbane face. The waiter slipped crab soufflé before each of them, and refilled coffee cups.

The deputy director stabbed his lunch, and then showed his cards. "Well, you know, Mr. Horoney, the National Park Service would love to take your burden off your shoulders."

They laughed.

"It could be arranged, you know. You could define the terms, of course. Give the entire property to the United States government, to be administered by the National Park Service in perpetuity as the Grassland National Park. The whole world would be grateful. The most munificent gift in history."

"Breaking records isn't on my mind, sir."

"Yes, of course. You have a passion to restore the High Plains to its wilderness condition."

"It never really was a wilderness. It was inhabited by tens of thousands of Indians, who were seamlessly part of the ecology and the major predator of several species there. I should add that the Clovis people were probably responsible for the extinction of various species ten to twelve thousand years ago."

"Yes, wilderness is a poor word. Native Americans were and are present."

"Out on the plains, they prefer to be called Indians."

"Yes, yes. One must be sensitive. At any rate, I've been delegated to approach you. A team of our best people has put together a little informal plan for your approval. Nothing final or public, of course. Simply a plan intended to ensure that your dream of a National Grassland, carefully restored and nurtured to its precivilized condition, would be forever enshrined in our administration."

Horoney enjoyed the soufflé, in part because it had too much fat in it to win the approval of food puritans. Waite reached for his tooled-leather portfolio and withdrew a thick and elegantly bound operations plan, handed it to Horoney, and placed a humbler version of it before himself.

"Now, then, here's what we have in mind, Mr. Horoney, always subject to your modification, of course. First a statement of policy: the grassland is to be administered in a way that restores the vegetative cover to its mid-nineteenth-century caliber, and introduces the species long absent from the High Plains, including wolves, buffalo, several types of sheep, elk, and even prairie dogs, so important for the survival of the black-footed ferret. And of course these will be carefully managed so as to preserve the natural balance."

"What's wrong with just letting nature alone, at least for a few decades?"

"Why, things get out of balance and we can't achieve wilderness that way. If there are too many prairie dogs, the grass suffers; too few and the ferret is threatened with extinction. Too many wolves and buffalo and elk and deer herds diminish. On and on. It requires the vigilance of the best biologists in the world."

"What you're acknowledging, then," Horoney said, "is that nature is really an ongoing dynamic, and that what you're really attempting is to freeze-frame a mixture of vegetation and animal life that was perceived to exist just before settlement."

"Why, you could put it that way."

"But without Indians as predators."

"Yes, there'd be no hunting in the national park. As you see, we have a plan for each species, ranging from large ungulates down to rare turtles and insects. You can follow that in the section on species reintroduction and management."

Horoney gazed out the window into a smoggy sky. Dallas had become as polluted as the rest of the cities. "Tell me the rest," he said.

"Well, you know, we'll be able, as a government entity, to achieve what you strived so valiantly to do—consolidate the area into a cohesive unit. We have eminent domain, you know. We can buy and evict. All of these islands of bitter-enders in the area will be bought out just as fast as we get funding from Congress. And you can bet, with a gift like this, that Congress will jump at the chance. I've already had a chat with the Speaker and Majority Leader, and it's in the cards. So, that's a blessing—your dream of a contiguous wilderness realized.

"And that's just the beginning, Mr. Horoney. We're planning a grass-land scenic highway, rather like the figure-eight loop in Yellowstone, with exits on all four sides. Discreet service stations at intervals, of course—can't have people running out of gas out there—and nature exhibits. A whole village, seasonal of course, modeled on a Sioux or Crow encampment. But the real attraction will be hundreds of thousands of buffalo, a sight not seen since the 1870s. We'll install nature walks, showing grasses or small animals like prairie dogs in their natural setting. Educational, of course. The grassland will be the Park Service's premier educational site, if only because no one thinks about grass and prairie."

"You'll need enabling legislation, I imagine."

"Oh, yes. There's administrative costs, and the transfer of Forest Service and BLM land to us, and road-building. We figure it'll cost five billion just to build the highway infrastructure, the park loops and exits." He smiled. "And here's the ace, sir. We've already decided that in your honor, we'll name the administration complex the Laslo Horoney Center."

Horoney wanted to laugh, but confined himself to a quiet objection. "My purposes don't include memorializing myself, Mr. Waite."

"Well, as you wish. We'd be honored to name it that. But your wishes must prevail, of course. We've done some consulting with outside experts on the whole project. Most helpful people, all eager to share the vision with us. Up there in Montana, no one's been more helpful than Professor

Peter Andrew Brooke-Carson. He knows that part of Montana better than we do, and it was his idea to place park headquarters in those beautiful wooded hills now owned by the Nichols family. In fact, we couldn't do better than that very site—good water, accessibility, an existing airstrip—we'll be a park with fly-in capability—ample space."

"I'm familiar with the man."

"Yes, he's been the inspiration, the prod. He's been a whirling dervish in Washington, lining up help for us. He laid the whole park plan in our lap, and of course our expert staff modified it to fit the public need, but I must give Professor Brooke-Carson credit."

"Yes, I give him credit, too. Along with his young research fellows. He has quite a staff, you know. Or seems to. Look at one of his reports some time. My foundation has become very interested in the man's work."

"Yes, Western Research Associates. I've seen the reports. Very impressive."

Horoney turned to a topic that needed airing. "Mr. Waite, what if the Nichols family doesn't wish to vacate land it's held for almost a century?"

"Well, public needs simply transcend private ones. Conflict's regrettable, of course, but they'll be compensated, and won't be hurt."

"I'll look the plans over, Mr. Waite."

"Please do. No rush, of course. You'll find that we've developed plans for every facet of the proposed park. We'll manage wildlife to maintain a careful balance and preserve endangered species. We'll manage the grassland to restore the original mix of herbs and grasses. Did I mention that we've included a bird plan and a separate raptor plan? We want to make the park a showcase of eagles, hawks, falcons, and so on."

"And you'll manage the people, too."

"Yes. We think it'll be more popular than Yellowstone, three to five million visitors a year. Think what that means for surrounding communities—motels and restaurants. And we've plans, you'll see them there, to build the Grassland Lodges, various units in the Grassland Villages located here and there in that vast park. And we've plans to name one for each of you—the Dolly Horoney Inn, the Laslo Horoney Inn."

"I see."

"Not only that, but we'll develop complete communications systems, and buried electrical lines so that not a pole shows in the park. There'll be an employees' village on the Nichols property, like Mammoth in Yellowstone Park, a planned residential community for our people, complete with supermarket, theater, and amenities. It'll be tucked into a fold in those hills and not visible to visitors."

"I see."

"We'll do some discreet fencing. Buffalo are dangerous, you know. We want the public to enjoy the sight, but not be hurt. But all the fencing will be as discreet as that in a modern zoo, concealed, or moated, or gotten up to look like something else. We're going to have to deal with stampedes, you know. Two hundred thousand buffalo on the run can do real damage. Just look at the history books."

"I see."

"Not only that, but we've assembled a whole team to talk with you about our plans. We'll manage this thing in innovative ways because we get to start from the beginning. You've so kindly knocked down everything in sight, so we can come in and design the park the way a park should be designed. We have some fine talent for that, including some great golf-course architects. Not that we'd put a golf course on it— maybe some tennis courts for our employees—but this isn't a playground, it's an educational and theme park."

"I see."

"Well, you read this over, sir, and let us know. We'll fly in our team, well prepared to answer your every question. We think you'll like this option more than any other open to you."

"Thanks for lunch, Mr. Waite."

"Oh! Ah, yes, you're welcome, Mr. Horoney. Glad to consult with you about the most momentous land project in our history."

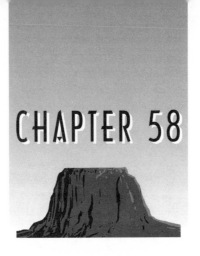

CHAPTER 58

Horoney listened impatiently in his study as Hector Truehart went over the options.

"I've talked to Governor Magruder and the leaders of both houses of the legislature, and the reality is that Montana's not going to alter its tax code to accommodate the foundation. It's going to tax rangeland across the state just as it has, and it's going to impose a personal property tax on livestock, and that's that."

"I was afraid of that."

"Wyoming and South Dakota will follow suit. Montana's the lead state. If its legislature were to find some way to relieve the foundation, the other states probably would. But I have to tell you, the wolves are circling. They're enjoying the rich man's dilemma, and they're thinking maybe they'll take the whole shebang off your hands when you give up."

"Everyone wants it. The Park Service especially. They came to me with elaborate plans to manage it back into wilderness. That's what bureaucracies do—manage."

"Will you accept?"

Horoney shook his head.

"But Laslo, we don't have many options if we can't pay the taxes."

"What, specifically, are they?"

"Turn over the whole thing to the state or federal government. That's one. Another is to sell it back to private holders. And there's an interesting third prospect—simply refuse to pay taxes."

"What does that do?"

"It buys you several years, during which the rangeland recovers. It can take a long time in Montana before rangeland gets auctioned off for tax delinquency. Maybe a decade, if we file motions and delays. That's what you need."

"No. We're good citizens. The foundation's a good citizen. We won't do that."

"I thought so. But it's a rough game, and they're licking their chops up there. Horoney's Folly."

"Two wrongs don't make a right, Hector. I don't have license to abuse them just because they're no longer cooperating."

"That's why I gladly work for you. But you're going to have to come up with something fast. The clock's ticking. The taxes on all that land in three states come to seven hundred fifty thousand dollars a day. A lot of it is not yet classified as range."

"That's a pretty loud tick."

"And they're enjoying it. The whole vision of a National Grassland is less important than seeing what the rich man's gonna do. They are men without vision."

"I don't know what I'm going to do, except that I'm not going to give it to the Park Service. And if I do give it to a public agency, I'll offer it on my own terms. I don't want the land and wildlife managed except for a while to reintroduce and stabilize species. Long term, I want nature to take over and sort itself out. I'm not interested in a park. I'd rather see a game preserve or something like that."

"You could sell it, Laslo. We could divide it into large parcels in a week and hold an auction in six weeks."

"And listen to the howling of those who think we're betraying the cause."

Truehart allowed himself a slight smile. "There'd be howling, all right. And probably injunctions, although I don't know how a court could deny a landholder the right to dispose of his property as he chooses. Shall we consult the foundation board now or later?"

"I need time to think."

"Three quarters of a million a day should invoke a lot of thinking."

"It doesn't. I'm not going to let anyone push me into anything."

"We're not going to get help from other foundations, I'm afraid."

"I'm not counting on it."

"Well, here is a list of properties purchased to date, and annual taxes on them. Maybe you could scale this whole thing down to a zoo."

"Horoney's Folly. An eight-billion zoo."

Truehart stood, walked over and clasped a hand on Horoney's shoulder. "It wasn't a folly. It's the finest vision of a gift the world's ever known."

"Thank you, Hector."

"Maybe if we turned over the land to the three states, it'd all work out."

"I'm thinking along those lines, but it's all so disappointing."

"I'll keep on dickering. You want me to tell them that the foundation might sell the land back to private owners?"

"Not yet. No threats. We're looking for cooperation."

"Montana hunters are hopping mad, you know. No hunting now in a huge area. They're talking lawsuits. The tribes are mad, too. No buffalo hunting. They're blaming us, not the court or the legislature. They're talking lawsuits, too."

Laslo shrugged it off.

"You know," Truehart said, "we may have trouble selling privately if that's what you wish to do. It's all still provisional wolf habitat, and new owners couldn't put up so much as a fence without the permission of the Fish and Wildlife Service. Not a building or a barn, not a well or a windmill. Who'd buy it? Not agribusinesses, that's for sure."

"I guess they have me where they want me, Hector."

"I'll rattle their cage. They can't keep the provisional habitat designation going for long. We have a petition for relief pending in their regulatory mill, but they know how to stall if they want."

"Anything else?"

"Yes, just a little tidbit. We keep finding out more and more about Brooke-Carson. Those big research projects he does for the government are largely the work of doctoral candidates he advises. He does credit them in his reports, but we've found out he doesn't pay them, and his research company pockets a lot of federal money. Even more interesting, he persuades his students to research material he needs as part of their doctoral work—and doesn't tell them much about what it's all for. Very interesting, I would say.

"Oh, and something else. He's an acquaintance of that nut from Jackson who smuggled in the wolves from Canada, and I wouldn't be surprised if they conspired. God knows what else he's been up to, but we're having a close look."

Horoney beamed. "That's very interesting. Perhaps we should fly up there for a talk. Up in the morning, back by evening."

"I'd like to. What do you hope to accomplish?"

"Oh, just a little palaver."

"You want to surprise him?"

"Exactly. Drop in. Catch him unawares. I have a hunch he'll be boastful. I'll set it up for tomorrow, have an aide get his office hours and schedule, and find out whether he'll be absent. We'll fly out early—how about six?"

"I'll be there. You mind if I do the talking? I think I may be able to lead him into some admissions."

"You're good at that, Hector."

"All right. Six at the hangar."

By eleven on a bleak December morning they were in Bozeman. A half hour later they were in Brooke-Carson's office. Horoney found himself staring into a handsome, glacial face, the features chiseled out of a block of arrogance, the hair cut long, the intelligence—and disdain—writ large. The professor wore an Italian-cut brown sport coat, tasseled casual shoes polished to a high gloss, a black turtleneck under an open blue shirt.

"I'm Laslo Horoney, and this is the foundation's counselor and vice president, Hector Truehart, Professor. We thought, if you're free, to take you to lunch. We want to tell you a little about our situation."

"Well, well, so you're the man," Brooke-Carson said, obviously surprised. "Pleased, I'm sure. Well, all right. I'll cancel a little meeting. Let me make a call."

"We have a lunch waiting on my plane if you wish. Or you can select a place."

"No, I'd like to see your plane."

Moments later, they drove back to the Bozeman airport, and climbed the stairs into the Gulfstream V, where Horoney's attendants swiftly spread out an elegant Mexican lunch and served beverages.

"Some bird," Brooke-Carson said, examining with a prosecutor's eye the interior, the pewter and crystal and china service before him, and the blue-jacketed married couple who attended all of Horoney's flights.

About halfway through the enchiladas, Truehart blandly turned the conversation to the National Grassland. Horoney knew he'd enjoy this. No one on earth was better able than Hector Truehart to disarm others and find out things.

"Well, Professor, you're a man of great distinction in your field. We thought we'd seek your counsel. The National Grassland, you know. Of course, you've opposed it—we realize that—but all that aside, you're the one we'd like to consult about the future. Your qualifications are admirable."

Brooke-Carson didn't swallow the bait. "What do you want to know?" he asked abruptly.

"What animals you'd introduce, and in what numbers, for one. Not just ungulates. How would one go about encouraging eagles, or hawks, or black-footed ferrets, or any of the species that once inhabited the area?"

"You've got competent biologists. Why come to me?"

"To find out what we can. Here's your chance to tell us what you'd like to see."

"I'd like to see you turn it over to the federal government so it can be professionally managed and the remaining private holdings won't continue to ruin the project."

"Yes, we understand that. But let's backtrack. You supported the permanent wolf-habitat plan. Why did you do that?"

"Wolves belong there. The plains were once the habitat of gray wolves."

"Ah, yes, and they did return. But they seem to be leaving. One pack's gone entirely."

"The value of the habitat designation is that it freezes the land use. Keeps things from getting worse and destroys the economic viability of an area. The land becomes almost worthless."

"That's what you testified in Miles City, yes. That surely is true. No private entity, including the foundation, can do anything without permission. It's crimping our progress, you know. We have to get permits from Fish and Wildlife to restore cropland to rangeland or burn weeds or pull down an old house—that sort of thing."

"That's what it's intended to do. Drive out all private interest and collapse property values."

"Yes, yes, habitat designation does that. That fellow who put the wolves on there knew what he was up to," Truehart said.

"Delacorte, yes. The man's a hero of our times. He'll be out shortly, good behavior. He never should've been convicted, having done absolutely nothing criminal."

"Yes, it was all for a good cause. You've led that cause for years, which is why we're here seeking your counsel. What would be the best thing for the foundation to do now?"

"The National Park Service is the only entity that can restore the grassland to wilderness. I'm committed to them, and on their advisory boards. Now if you're angling to employ me, I must tell you that I'm not available. I realize you've been leading to that, sounding me out, but I prefer to advise the Park Service, and continue my life of scholarship. I'm an academic, you know, not even tempted by two or three hundred thousand dollar salaries."

"Yes, of course," Truehart said.

"I'm philosophically opposed to the National Grassland in private hands, even if those hands are a philanthropy with all the best intentions. Nature is too important to leave to private groups."

"Yes, we understand your viewpoint."

"But I'm flattered you flew up to ask, gentlemen."

"Well, yes, now that the air's cleared, Professor, tell us what your larger plan is for the West."

Brooke-Carson finally smiled. "Snatch it from developers and drive out agriculture. You've made a good start. By using the endangered species habitat designation, we can reclaim hundreds of thousands of square miles, and turn it into a giant refugia—that's a biological term for an isolated animal or plant refuge—that should occupy about a fifth of the lower forty-eight. I wish we could include more, but there'd be political opposition. We have to be realists, you know. But once your foundation turns over its holdings, we'll have the base we can expand from."

"Turns over?"

"Yes, to the Park Service. I gather you're engaged in serious discussions."

Horoney quashed his instinct to say otherwise, now that Hector had the man talking.

"Well, that's what we're here to discuss," Truehart said. "What would be your second choice?"

"I have no second choice."

"What about turning it back to the states for a giant park?"

"Utterly impossible. You'd run into legal opposition."

"Why?"

"Because states are too vulnerable to voters, interest groups, the public will, lobbying, sleazy exploiters, hunters, all wanting to weaken the parks. You really have no right to do that to land reserved for ecological restoration."

"It's private land, Professor."

"No, it's not. It's owned by a foundation, privileged only if it acts in the public interest."

"Ah, indeed, that's an unusual legal theory."

"It doesn't matter what the law is. It's all technicalities. Your foundation has no moral right to that land."

"And who does?"

"The experts who can make it whole. Thanks for lunch, gents. Teaching's important to me and I must get back."

"Ah, Professor, stay a bit. Teaching, you say. The foundation's been examining your various research projects and reports. Western Research Associates—that's your corporation, isn't it? Your reports impact our foundation, so of course we study them. We're impressed by all those research fellows listed in your reports. They seem to be people without advanced degrees or experience. No contributions to the literature. Do you suppose the Park Service would care? Or Congress?"

Brooke-Carson seemed to fossilize.

"Ah, Professor," Truehart continued apologetically, "we made a call or two. These people seem to be your university advisees, your grad students. At least that's what the registrar's office told us. Do you pay them?"

"It is no business of yours how the research was done. It satisfies the federal government."

"Yes, I'm sure it does. The Park Service and EPA got exactly the findings and recommendations they hoped to receive for all that money. Now, ah, Professor, does Montana State University have any academic code about how students pursuing an advanced degree may be engaged by their advisors—"

"You obviously know nothing about academic protocol."

"Well, then, tell us. We're eager to learn."

"I won't stand for this. Do you have the faintest idea what a laughingstock you'll make of yourselves?"

"Ah, so sorry, Professor."

"Cut the crap."

"You know, sir, we've been comparing the material in the unpublished dissertations of your doctoral candidates—in the university library, of course—with the material that appears in your Western Research Associates reports to the federal government. Very interesting."

Brooke-Carson glared at them.

"Well, Professor," Horoney said, "it's been a pleasure. Would you like a ride back to your office?"

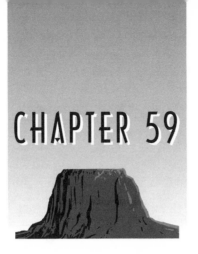

CHAPTER 59

Wearily Cam Nichols listened to his attorney, Bob Rockwell, deliver the bad news. United States Fish and Wildlife had turned the whole grassland into permanent wolf habitat, declaring the wolf a threatened species in Montana, the Dakotas, and Wyoming.

"They exempted some businesses and coal mines and oil and gas fields," Rockwell said over the phone, "and drew a circle around a few dying towns and residences. But it covers pasture and cropland, federal land, state land, and anything else."

"That's the end, then. I can't fix a fence without permission."

"It's not that bad. What you can't do is alter things, such as changing land use. Or build anything, even a road."

"How am I going to sell this now?"

"You probably can't. Not for what it's worth."

"But I'm being taxed at its former market value."

"Well, its market value just dropped to nothing—maybe a buck an acre. That's something we can do—go to your county tax assessor and ask for tax relief based on a new assessment. They'll say an assessment's based on historic value, so you may have to put a few parcels out there and let the market dictate a new price."

"Lot of good it'd do."

"Know what you mean. But we can make a case. Look, Cam, I've talked to Horoney's attorney, Truehart, about this. What they're doing is suing the Fish and Wildlife Service, and he proposes a joint suit or maybe a class action. He says, and I agree, that the habitat designation's a crock. Congress never empowered the service to impose endangered species habitat rules on private property, and anyway, they can't do that without violating the taking clause. Truehart's inviting you to join them—for a nominal fee, no big bucks—and I suggest you do. They'll take the lead."

"I can't afford a lawsuit, especially one that'll take years and end up at the Supreme Court."

"How about a hundred bucks?"

"That's it?"

"That's it."

"All right."

"Truehart doesn't think it'll last long. The feds know they haven't a leg to stand on. It's a case of standing up to the bully until he backs off."

"What about the taxes? Can you help?"

"Sure. I'll draw up a petition and we'll go lay it on your new county tax board. If your land's got little market value, they'd better tax it for a cent an acre, something like that."

"It won't rescue us, Bob. Ever since Horoney started this grassland, I've watched the Nichols ranches slide toward a string of zeros. I was nuts to oppose selling out for twenty-five million."

"You had no choice, Cam. Not with Dudley and Anna calling the shots."

"I don't know. I'm tired of this."

"I called Fish and Wildlife to get a take on this. Their counsel told me they've located the wolves. One pack's still on your land. The other's over near the South Dakota border, in foothills where there's game. After they unloaded Kouric, they put two new biologists on, and they disagreed with Kouric's famous line about the area being habitat only if domestic stock were included as prey. Sounds like a pair of bought-and-paid-for scientists."

"Is this going to help me any?"

"They've got a shaky case, and they ran a lot of history into it—someone ransacked frontier literature for wolf material. Truehart says the foundation doesn't want wolves on foundation lands, not until the buffalo herds are built up to optimum levels. So you're on the same side of the fence. If they want you to sign up for joint suits, I think you should."

"That cuts you out."

"They'll employ me—I know the turf here. There's good in this. If the courts say it's taking—the feds might be forced to buy you out at recent market value, or back off."

"We'll be street people by then. But okay, Bob. Line me up with the foundation. I'll join their suit. I'm good for a fight, and we've nothing to lose anyway."

"That's what I like to hear, Cameron. You're not licked and never will be."

"Neither was my father, but the whole thing killed him."

"Cut that out, Cameron."

"Nichols Ranches was worth twenty-five million in land, and several million more in cattle, depending on markets, and was almost debt-free. Now what're we worth?"

"You'll spring back. We've got to eject some bureaucrats who think your land's their turf."

Cam felt himself sink into sheer exhaustion. "I need to digest this. We'll talk tomorrow. I'll talk to DeeAnn, and call you from the ranch. We're in this pretty deep. But if the ship sinks, it'll go under with our flags flying and the band playing 'Nearer My God to Thee.' "

"Got it. You have any more wolf kills on your place? I'll need to know stuff like that."

"One calf. John Trouble's optimistic. He's telling me the longhorns can deal with wolves. Maybe even drive them away. Actually, we could endure the wolves if those longhorns weren't so poor at putting on meat."

"One more thing. That nut down in Jackson who smuggled the wolves is getting out soon—Delacorte—he's been a good boy and they're springing him. We've got that suit pending. A million in damages. Actually, all things considered, he did more damage. His wolves triggered a permanent endangered species habitat designation. They're going to hear about it in court. I'm pretty sure we'll do fine. We've got him right under the crosshairs, and unlike some, he's got deep pockets— or maybe I should say deep rubbers."

"When's that coming up?"

"Early next year. They've filed postponements, usual stuff, but they've run out of time. You want a fancy log house outside of Jackson?"

"Cash."

"I like your taste. Jackson's being Aspenized. The tooty-fruity rich. I'll be in touch."

Nichols hung up and sagged into the easy chair.

"What was it, Cam?" asked Sandy.

"Wolf habitat. Fish and Wildlife went and did it. From now on, we'll have to get permission to go to the bathroom."

"You're tired."

"I'm just feeling trapped. All I ever wanted to do was ranch."

"I've learned something. If we don't have trouble in our lives, we don't grow."

Cam grunted, but privately he acknowledged the insight. He eyed her, liking what was happening. She was licking her booze problem her own way, by controlling her intake instead of quitting cold. In recent weeks he had acquired a friend during the evenings. He peered up at her wryly, reached out for her, and she settled in his lap.

He pulled Sandy closer, until her head nestled into his shoulder, and they sat like that, the silence more sweet and strong than anything they had to say to each other after most of a lifetime.

"Laslo Horoney's going to do our fighting for us," he said at last. "The foundation doesn't want the permanent wolf habitat."

"I like him."

"I would, too, if he hadn't destroyed Nichols Ranches."

"Is it over? Are we broke?"

"Almost."

"Now what?"

"Sell out, I guess. Pay debts and divide up the crumbs."

He felt her fingers tracing his ear and neck and then his face. He liked having her there in his lap. It was as if a long-lost love had returned from the dead. They had, tentatively, anxiously, made love now and then. It wasn't like when they were young and burning. Maybe it was sweeter. So many years, and so many boozy nights had gone by that this reunion seemed like a new marriage, after a glacial age had separated him from the first one.

"We haven't heard from Martin," she said.

"I've been wondering about it. Part of me wants to yank the support. Another part of me says that the kid grew up wounded and we hardly noticed, and maybe we should let him work things out as long as we can. But we might not be able to soon."

"He's very angry at us."

"I think that'll pass. I thought I saw something in him when Dudley died. Something less hostile, I guess you'd say."

"Do you think we failed him?"

"It's not worth worrying about. We did our best. He'll come home one of these days, and we'll find an adult son. We go through that— leave the nest and reject everything our parents believed in, try out life a while, and then discover our parents aren't so bad after all."

They sat quietly in the chair, and Cam thought he had lost a ranch and won a wife.

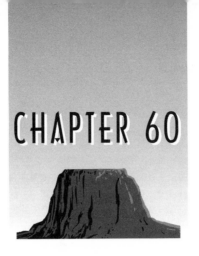

CHAPTER 60

Professor Brooke-Carson negotiated the twisting curves of Teton Pass, pleased that the plows had kept the January snows under control. He descended the slope, entered Jackson, and turned north, his destination the lavish aerie of J. Carter Delacorte, paroled felon.

It would never do to be seen with the man. The professor had insisted that they meet alone and had prepared a cover story: he would spend that Sunday skiing at Jackson's Snow King resort. He didn't really want to visit Delacorte, but in fact he badly needed the nut because his life was about to change. The stupid faculty ethics committee was picking nits about his employment of his advisees in business, and he sensed they were going to inflict maximum pain. That's what those envious campus politicians really wanted: to inflict pain on anyone who rose above mediocrity.

He tooled smoothly north out of Jackson, under the brow of the Tetons, past the elk preserve—wolves had greatly reduced the federal herd, but that was all right—and turned off on a certain rural road that plunged eastward into foothills, and finally into Delacorte's fabulous complex. He heard no barking this time. Gone were the sled dogs as part of the parole arrangement.

He parked, wondering what Delacorte would be like after months in the federal pen in Arizona.

"Peace and love," said his host at the door.

The latex baron led him into the bar and offered a libation, and the professor opted for some Schweppes. He rarely touched insidious alcohol, or meat, or fat, or salt.

"You're looking well," the professor said.

"If I am, it's because I practiced spiritual discipline all those weeks."

"Spiritual discipline?"

"Love and peace. Mantras. Knowing where others were coming from.

I grew to love my guards, care about their families. I forgave everyone, and listened to seascape tapes."

Delacorte led the professor into a study decorated in white ersatz leather—Delacorte was a member of People for the Ethical Treatment of Animals—and stainless steel, and turned on the overhead fluorescents. "This is where I'm at home," he said. "This is my hearth and haven. Have a seat."

Brooke-Carson felt uncomfortable in the room and thought it looked like a surgical chamber.

"I have to know—was it worth it? You're the only man on earth who can tell me," Delacorte said.

"That why you invited me?"

"Yes. The anguish. The mortification. The savaging of my soul. The bars, the locks, the awful food. The helplessness. The discomfort—always cold, even in Arizona. And at bottom, the humiliation. They kept asking me if I was sorry, if I felt remorse. I had to get out, had to, so I said I was, that I'd seen the light, that I understood my conduct violated law and I'd never do it again. That was the worst, the whoring, when my soul cried out, howled in indignation. I committed no crime, you know, smuggling wolves in, not out, enhancing a species, not destroying it, bringing peace to the world, not war. All that piddly stuff about Customs, that was just excuses. They can jail anyone they want, you know; all mortals are vulnerable. It was unbearable. So here I am, living free, but with the parole officers watching my every step. I'm not free to own a dog, won't be for years. They can take everything away and put me back anytime they choose. My God, those people, they know nothing about peace and love and the environment."

Delacorte paused, dramatically, and lifted his hands in supplication. "Tell me, tell me, was it worth it?"

Brooke-Carson wished he had never succumbed. "Yes, of course, Carter. Without you, we'd not be on the brink of victory. The wolves helped."

"Oh, thank you for saying that. From you, that makes it all worthwhile."

"Well, you succeeded. I hear that Nichols Ranches are done for. Horoney wants to give the land to the states, but I've arranged to prevent it. Little talks in the right places. Montana won't accept the land. Yes, you played a key role. We've won."

"I'm in tears, Pete. I had to hear it. Victory. Every hour of every day down there . . . oh, I can't even bear to remember it."

"You'll be doing more condominiums soon?"

"Well, I can't this year. Terms of parole. As far as I'm concerned, that violates my freedom of speech, but they just laughed and told me that, ah, felons didn't have . . ."

"I see. You know, Carter, there's more to do. We need to guide the Park Service. It needs guiding now and then, veers off toward tourists and parking lots. But some sound environmental talk usually puts backbone in them. Same goes for the Forest Service and Bureau of Land Management. They keep straying away from sound environmental policy."

"Ah, I can't help, not for a while."

"The Nichols suit?"

"Oh, that's minor. My dear attorney, Nina Tall Chief, tells me that all Nichols gets out of it is payment for a few cows. Of course they're arguing that my wolves did a lot more damage, land values, all that. So I have to wait."

"Well, we have some urgent projects."

"Peter, I can't. I have to tell you, sales are down. The company's product isn't moving the way it used to. Now that AIDS is almost cured, no one takes precautions anymore. We're seeing gross sales decline ten percent a year, and that's pinching."

"Well, that will pass."

"We're trying new products. Chocolate-coated, fluorescent, all that. But it isn't reversing the trend."

"Too bad."

"Yes, we need another AIDS plague."

"It'd reduce populations. I'd like to cut back world population by three billion."

The professor sipped his tonic, stared out upon the snowy spikes of the Tetons, and decided the moment had come. Delacorte seemed subdued, almost desperate.

"My dear friend," the professor began, "we're at the beginning of a revolution. The next phase will be to recover the northeastern corner of Montana, until the grassland runs from the Canadian border deep into Wyoming. And the next will be to extend it across Wyoming and Colorado, into New Mexico, until we've rescued the High Plains. Of course, it'll all be put in the hands of the federal government. Its environmental bureaus are capable of resisting all the political pressures that'll swirl around them. They'll be like the king's wardens in old England, keeping an eye out for poachers. What a dream, Carter. Species flourishing, pristine grassland, recovering from the damage it suffered.

"This takes money and influence. And moral courage. And sacrifice.

You've seen what your own sacrifice achieved, a lasting memorial in the form of a great national park shaping up swiftly. You suffered down there in that lockup, but you've emerged as a finer man. A man who's walked through fire and blossomed as a saint. You've given an incalculable gift to us all."

J. Carter Delacorte's eyes leaked tears.

"I think you're the man of destiny," Brooke-Carson continued. "The man of the hour. I'm going to ask you to consider something so bold, so daring, that you may just usher me to the door, and I'd understand perfectly. What I'm about to offer you is sacrifice; sacrifice for the great cause we're involved in, no less than rescuing the world. I've dreamed of a new, well-funded foundation, The Great West Foundation. It needs a showy headquarters if it's to be taken seriously. A natural conference center, and a steady income from your company.

"Just like this place. Would you consider turning it over to the new foundation? And financing it through the profits from your company? Sacrifice! Yes, you've just run that gauntlet and come out a whole man, towering of intellect. I sit here and think, what a place this would be to transform the world. Invite heads of state, United Nations officials, the world's leading scientists, politicians. This is the place, Carter. I'm hoping you're willing to climb to the stars."

"I, ah, what's to become of me?"

"You'd be revered."

"I'd need just a little for myself."

"Of course. No one expects you to become a pauper."

"Do you really think this would suffice? It's really a modest little place."

"Yes, perfectly. We don't want grandiosity. Just a pleasant wilderness place that speaks to those who come here of the future of the world. At the Delacorte Center."

"I might, I might!" said J. Carter Delacorte. "Would you be the president?"

"Well, I've been thinking along those lines. The university life bores me, frankly. Too many petty rules, too much politics. I'd like to operate an activist organization, and I'd do it for a modest wage, too. Let's say two hundred thousand. I'm worth all of that."

"Let me think about it. I couldn't afford that, but maybe seventy-five, ah, let's say a hundred thousand. Would you consider running it for that?"

"Oh, I might. Take all the time you want, Carter. I know where your soul will lead you."

CHAPTER 61

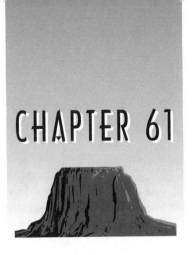

Martin Dudley Nichols wandered through the aisles at Penney's. He wanted a tweedy sport coat, tan cotton pants, and some button-down shirts. He had plunged into the new year with the itch to change everything in his life. His old clothing seemed loathsome to him, Salvation Army stuff he'd worn just because it the most repellent he could find.

He'd blown a whole semester, and by Christmas had nothing to show for the fall term. Then, on New Year's Day, he'd started cleaning his quarters, the need almost a frenzy in him. He ended up piling filthy clothes into plastic bags and hauling them to the trash cans outside. And then he scoured the place, scraping gum off the counters of his kitchenette, filth out of the bathroom sink and tub and toilet. He mopped and waxed the floor, washed windows, vacuumed, and washed all his bedclothes. And when he was done, the only dirty thing left in the place was himself. So he started his shower and scrubbed until he was abrading his flesh. Shampooed his mangy hair. Scraped away days of beard. And then he endured a desperate need for fresh clothing, which he could not buy until the stores opened after the holiday.

There would be time to enroll in the spring semester. Time to line up some courses, begin work on his long-dormant thesis. He'd blown almost a year, and couldn't believe it. He couldn't even say where the time had gone. Sucking beer at a cowboy bar. Sulking around a used-book store on Main Street. Eating cheap. The checks had come regularly, and he'd hated each one even as he deposited them and existed upon them.

The only good thing that entire fall was his occasional visits with Professor Kazin. Sometimes they had lunch. Sometimes Martin just dropped in on the old department chairman. Kazin always made him welcome and never tried to push Martin one way or another. He had been Martin's only friend the whole time, and Martin wondered why the professor had bothered with some stinking bummed-out student too angry to cope with life. But the professor had. Old Kazin might be decades out of fashion, but he was a real person, and not some cold, vain fish like Brooke-Carson.

Martin had come to despise the fraud, with all his maneuvering and grandstanding, all his agitation and power plays and glory-seeking. The death of Dudley Nichols had done it—shown Martin the ruthlessness of the professor he'd once worshiped. What's more, the man was shallow. He knew nothing about paleobiology, and it had been Kazin who gave him a sense of the evolution of nature from the last ice age to the present. Nature wasn't something that had been frozen into its final form just before the arrival of settlers.

Martin made his purchases, knowing he would have to stint on everything else to pay for them. But somehow the new clothing seemed urgent, and fulfilled a need in him. He hastened back to his quarters, faintly shocked to see them shining, and dressed himself in the new tan slacks, blue oxford cloth shirt, and gray woolen coat. Now he would look like any of the academics at Montana State University, but it didn't matter. He examined himself, finding a young adult in the mirror, and felt good. He bagged the last of his stinking old clothing and hauled it to the trash cans.

There he was, all dressed up and nowhere to go.

Something drew him out into the chinook winds again, and he drove to the south edge of the campus and the imposing Museum of the Northern Rockies. He had been there many times, and had lingered long in the world-famous dinosaur rooms. But this time he itched to visit the least popular corner of the museum—unpopular at least among University people—an exhibition of the life and household items of early settlers. When had he ever cared about cracked porcelain dolls and ice skates and battered tin lizzies and ancient Kodaks and venerable gas pumps and old Coke signs and amateur cowboy art and woodstoves?

He had always sensed that the junk had been collected more as a public-relations ploy to keep old Montana families happy than as anything the museum's curators cared about. But this was the very stuff of the first Nichols Ranch, the life of his great-grandparents, and his grandfather Dudley, too, and maybe even the early life of his dad. He found himself almost alone that day, wandering that meandering exhibition of early-twentieth-century life in an isolated and backward state, this time seeing the spirit that lay behind the object; seeing love in doll's clothing and handmade Christmas toys whittled by fathers too poor to buy a child anything from a store. He studied the compact interior of a sheepherder's wagon, marveling that the mobile home sufficed to shelter the tender of a flock month after month.

Life was a struggle in Montana, even more in those days than now. But his forbears had endured, and made a living amid brutal winters when the temperature skidded to forty below, drouthy summers and blistering heat; grasshoppers, floods, and that meanest of all Montana torments, the wind, the wind that whirled up the dust and blew it into the Dakotas. A comfortable day was so rare in Montana that its citizens celebrated with picnics and parties.

He forgave his ancestors.

They had not tried to ruin the land. It had happened, inadvertently, by degrees, the result of desperate measures, times when there wasn't a blade of grass for the livestock, times when floods cut gullies into a defenseless land, times when banks threatened to foreclose. There never was, and never had been, some monster called agribusiness, the devil of his imagination. Who was to blame? From the twenties onward, the people he scorned had taught themselves to protect the land, plant shelter belts, give pastures a rest, rotate stock. The courthouses of Montana had their extension agents, helping ranchers nurture the land. The Soil Conservation Service had been on hand, showing how to halt erosion, plant cover, add nutrients, calculate what burden the land would bear. Was any of this rapine? And was the damage deliberate?

He sat on a bench in the exhibition hall, surrounded by glass milk bottles, a parlor organ, butter churns, porcelain eggs used to seduce hens into laying, tin toys, and mannequins dressed in the lovely gowns of the times. His ancestors, his civilization. Why did no one in the university come here, or speak highly of it? Why did they disdain it as a throwaway exhibit for the public? What *was* it about the people who'd come to Montana, Norwegians and Swedes and Dutch and Irish and Scots and Bohemians, and Basques and Germans and Italians in the last great wave of settlement of the continent—what was it about them these professors scorned? All these people, including the first Nicholses, had dreams and hopes, and many of them worked themselves into an early grave to build something enduring in a brutal land. They had struggled, prayed in their crossroads churches, lived and died, and triumphed—temporarily—over a land that could never be hospitable.

Martin knew why he had come. This was the place where he could forgive his parents. If they had failed in some way, ignoring his loneliness and isolation, it wasn't because they set out to do it. They'd loved him as best they could, made mistakes as all parents did. He knew he would make the same mistakes with his own children, if he should be so lucky to have them. He knew also that no child becomes an adult without forgiving a parent. It wasn't as though Sandy Nichols wanted to drink too much, or Cameron had intended to neglect Martin. His father had ranched in a dry, mean land with more bad years than good, but he had persevered.

Martin realized that in the act of forgiveness he had reached manhood, and that so long as he blamed his parents for anything, as long as he blamed his ancestors, as long as he blamed the family companies, as long as he blamed their civilization, the churches, the newspapers, the lawyers and politicians—so long as he blamed any of those things for his own misery, he would be only a boy. And as long as he remained cynical about his own American civilization, finding nothing good in it or its public figures, he would remain a boy. And so long as he embraced alien ideals, obscure religions, occult wisdom, despising his own American and Christian roots—he would remain a boy. But here in a museum full of settlers' treasures, he had found the real Martin Nichols.

He rose again, traced a finger over a sled runner, touched an ancient buffalo coat, stared at a girl's diary in faded ink, studied a shelf full of Zane Grey and Max Brand Westerns, all the while feeling a tug of something sweet. There in the place they all scorned he came home.

He drove back to his room in twilight, and set about at once to write the letter that begged to be written.

Dear Dad and Mom,
    I'm going to be busy with my studies this semester. I love you and thank you. Come visit me. Billings isn't far away.

Love,
Martin

He discovered he did not have their new Billings address, and was about to call DeeAnn for it when he found it on an envelope from his father. Had it come to that? No address for his parents?

The next morning he visited his faculty advisor.

Leonard Kazin looked him over, registering the sport coat, the shirt and slacks, a face scrubbed and shaved, hair shorn and shiny, but he said nothing about that, simply waving Martin to a chair.

"I want to start a new thesis," Martin said.

That did surprise the old man. "Well, maybe you have something there. What's the trouble with the one you've been wrestling with?"

Martin shrugged, embarrassed. "Too much blaming."

"A good paper should be objective and see all sides."

"I don't know what to do with it."

Kazin sat back, stared at the sky, and steepled his hands. "It's a good thesis—the settling of the plains and the destruction of the biosystems that resulted. Why abandon it? It needs telling."

"It's—judgmental."

Kazin nodded. "Then don't judge. You know what sort of academic writing I enjoy the most? That which is filled with balance and acceptance. Every time I've seen a dissertation brimming with those qualities, I'm reminded that the best scholarship of all rises out of love."

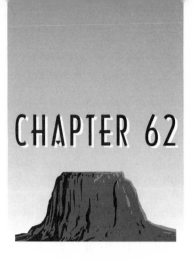

CHAPTER 62

Truehart had set up the meeting in Helena. Laslo Horoney wished he could duck it, but this one would tell the story. He and Truehart had flown up the night before, deplaning into a bitter January night, the arctic air so cold it stabbed their faces. The pilot told them it was thirty below.

Now, this brutal winter morning, he and Truehart waited for the show to begin. A large overheated conference room in the capitol had been set aside for the occasion. Apparently everyone in Montana would be attending.

Strangers filtered in, examined the rich eccentric curiously, and settled into plush brown leather chairs. Some settled at the long conference table, arranged by design of the governor, while others parked themselves in the chairs lining the walls of the room. They weren't all strangers. Among those seated along the walls was Brooke-Carson. Yes, and looking amused, too, as he nodded to reporters and camerawomen and hirsute people holding remote microphones. This had been set up by the pols as a media event, which meant nothing would get done, which probably meant that none of the foundation's proposals would be seriously entertained by anyone in power, and there would be little more than grandstanding on the day's long agenda.

Governor Magruder strode in, along with the lieutenant governor and attorney general, trailing aides in designer glasses. A lot of other yuppie-type people settled in the chairs around the polished table.

The hard-charging Magruder, whose style was to get on with events, plunged immediately into introductions. "Ladies and gents," he said, "I'm pleased to introduce Mr. Laslo Horoney and his executive officer, Mr. Hector Truehart. As we all know, Mr. Horoney's magnificent vision of a Big Lonesome, a High Plains wilderness embracing three states, a National Grassland restored to its original estate, has inspired the entire nation, and especially the people of Montana, with gratitude. Not a day passes that I don't receive letters from schoolchildren filled with joy because the buffalo are coming back.

"Our profoundest thanks and esteem reach out to Mr. Horoney here, and to his able administrator, without whose genius the National Grassland would never have come about." He turned to face the television cameras. "Now let me tell you, I count these visionary men my dear friends, and I want the world to know how much I esteem their project, and the deep sacrifices Mr. Horoney has made to bring us an incalculable gift. Let me put that on record. We are in the presence of greatness. Now, gentlemen, I'd like you to meet our state people, all of whom I've invited here to work wholeheartedly with you to put the grassland on the map."

He introduced Attorney General Zelig, the Buffalo County commissioners, various directors and deputies who administered state lands, state wildlife officers, state taxation experts, legislative leaders from both parties, and the Buffalo County assessor. Then he turned to those who were observing and asked them to introduce themselves. They included federal land-management and fish and wildlife people, observers from the governors' offices of Wyoming and South Dakota, and dozens of credentialed people from the media.

"All right, Mr. Truehart, it's all yours," the governor said.

Truehart rose, looking rumpled and diffident as usual. He surveyed the assemblage carefully, actually sizing them up and selecting those he thought he could talk to. Horoney had seen all this before, and knew that Truehart was the best man on earth for the difficult task entrusted to him. His genius was diffidence, his method was to disarm.

"Governor, distinguished guests, we're here to iron out some difficulties that have resulted from your state supreme court ruling that invalidated portions of the Horoney Foundation's charter," he began. "We really seek your wisdom, and hope to follow your counsel. We realize we're the outsiders here. The foundation's purchased about an eighth of your entire state, and that is just the first phase. So, we are your guests, and we want your preferences to prevail as far as possible.

"You're all familiar with our goal, a magnificent grassland restored to its diversity, resilience, and beauty, a place where nature sings its song unmarred by human hand. You know also that we have fostered a policy in which those wishing to remain upon their land are welcome to do so. We respect the rights of all citizens, and nurture our friends who have made the choice to live within the confines of the grassland. Mr. Horoney's vision, from the start, was not to dispossess anyone, but to protect each hearth, each pasture, so that all may have their, shall we say, home on the range."

He paused, letting the cameras run a moment, his timing magnificent. "Now, as you know from correspondence, we are seeking a means of lowering the taxation to levels that the foundation can handle to create the largest wildlife and wilderness preserve in history. The proposed National Grassland is now about seventy-five percent owned by the Horoney Foundation, twenty percent by the federal government, and the rest consists of state school township sections and private parcels. Of the land privately held, the foundation now owns ninety percent, while the remainder is scattered among people who choose to stay on, plus the holdings of utilities, oil, gas and coal interests.

"We're seeking tax relief. The foundation's paying about seven hundred fifty thousand dollars a day in taxes to three states, and cannot continue at that rate. Our charter, now invalidated by your court, specified a rate that would have amounted to a million dollars a *year* in Montana, which the foundation was quite capable of paying, along with similar taxes in the adjacent states. Part of our problem now is that we've been unable to get land reclassified as unimproved open range, your lowest tax category. There's a backlog before the new Buffalo County's board of assessments that will take years to clear at the present rate. Where we've purchased a wheat farm, we're still being taxed for cropland, and where we've purchased a farmstead, we're still being taxed in many cases for buildings that no longer exist, improvements we've removed.

"We would like to find a way to reduce our taxes. The land within the proposed National Grassland has lost virtually all its market value, and is presently worth a dollar an acre or a figure similar to that. We would like to have it assessed at that value. That would automatically reduce the taxes to a figure we could live with.

"Before we proceed to other proposals the foundation has in mind, I'd like now to hear what you good people have to say about all this."

Horoney knew the way the wind was blowing, just from the faces of those in power. Little smiles, whispering in ears, doodling on pads, pursed lips. He had expected that. This was going to be a media show, not serious business. The Buffalo County assessor and county tax board led off, saying that the assessments, by law, had to be based on recent market value and could not be lowered on the basis of an abstraction. The county commissioners opposed any tax relief, asserting that the court required them to provide full services and invalidated that portion of the charter that would have allowed them to maintain skeleton services; they needed all the money they could get to plow and scrape roads and police their huge domain.

Laslo watched, annoyed. The county needed two hundred fifty million a year for a tax base the way a fat man needed cholesterol. What a bunch of pious little pissants, smiling lugubriously at the cameras, enjoying their turn in the limelight.

The legislative leaders turned out to be flatly opposed to tax relief and were hostile to a new charter, especially the one before them, drafted by the foundation's staff.

On it went. It turned out that nearly everyone in the room was opposed to a privately held National Grassland. The state and federal wildlife and land-management people were all negative. The delegates from Wyoming and South Dakota were negative, too.

What had happened? Laslo sorted through all this, wondering why a project that had won such enthusiastic backing no longer had anyone's support. Turf and greed. The real agenda here, this day, was to corner the foundation and force it to surrender—turn over the entire holding to the federal government and go back to Dallas, where Texans like Horoney belonged.

He sighed, knowing what beetled through the brains of all these worthies. Well, if they wanted to play hardball, he would give them hardball.

That was how it played out. They all saw a goose ripe for the plucking. Millions of dollars of tax money rolling in, and nothing of consequence to spend it on. They'd skin the foundation until Horoney quit and turned it all over to them.

He marveled. What had happened to the vision, the dream of a great grassland, a shining sea of unspoiled nature, the hills black with buffalo, the bottoms filled with game that hadn't been seen on the High Plains in generations? Wolves, human wolves. They were like a wolf pack closing in on prey. Among ordinary citizens, the National Grassland was more popular than ever. Horoney's interviews in the national media had pushed the acceptance of the National Grassland to new levels, something like ninety percent in the polls the foundation commissioned. But public approval was no match for envy and greed, and he knew exactly where this sorry meeting would lead.

Horoney listened icily as Governor Tom Magruder summed it all up. "The consensus here, gentlemen, is that there's little we can do to relieve you. We welcome you, of course, but like all private entities, you must pay your fair share. We'd suggest that you give the land to the federal government. The states—I think I can speak for Wyoming and South Dakota as well as our great state of Montana—would actually find it a burden to maintain on their own. So much land, so little revenue from it. I'm sure we'd take it if you cared to give it to us with no strings attached, but I don't see how the state of Montana can absorb such a gift unless we are free to dispose of it as we choose. The new county, consisting of seven old ones, must not be a burden to the state purse, or to other Montana taxpayers. We must be fair, here. The hard-pressed, overburdened taxpayers of Montana cannot, should not, must not, support a wealthy foundation, no matter how worthy its objectives."

Horoney and Truehart had intended to ask for tax forgiveness if they did turn the land over to the state, but now Laslo shook his head, and Truehart never raised the topic. The meeting had been a disaster, and those who once applauded the great project now sat like a row of vultures waiting for the carrion. Not least was the slippery governor.

Horoney saw how it was, and rose. He surveyed the wolves around the polished table, noting the smugness and amusement in their faces.

"Well, you don't want the grassland, then," he said. "You will tax us as a ranch. You are calling our property ranchland. You are calling buffalo taxable livestock. Very well, if you want a ranch, we'll give you a ranch. If that's what you want, we'll turn the entire grassland into a ranch. We will turn the entire holding to agricultural use and raise meat if that's what it takes to pay your taxes. I came here with a dream and a vision. Since no one here shares that vision, it looks like the Horoney Foundation will be engaged in ranching, not for profit but for educational purposes. We seem to have acquired the largest ranch in the world."

He sat down.

That started them buzzing. It wasn't what they expected.

"Ah, Mr. Horoney," said the governor, sounding rattled, "I'm sure you'll find that the federal government would be pleased to have the land," said Magruder.

"Meat," said Horoney. "Meat raised for the market. If you can't lift your vision above commerce, then we'll give you commerce." He nodded to Truehart. "We're due back in Dallas, gentlemen. Thanks for your time," he said.

Reporters scribbled. Most of the rest sat, stunned. The room exuded sweat and bad breath. TV cameras hummed, gaudy anchorwomen with sprayed-down hair shouted questions, lights flared and lenses panned the crowd. But Horoney just shook his head, and pushed grimly through the mob and into the shocking winter air.

With relief, he slid into the rental van in the capitol's visitor lot and drove himself and Truehart out of there.

"Jesus, it's cold in this machine." Laslo felt the seat bite his behind. He turned up the blower, but it didn't help, and started for the airport.

"My God, Laslo, you could have warned me," Hector said. "Beef!"

Laslo laughed. "I never said beef. I just said it'd be a ranch. How about a buffalo ranch? You think that would pay those damned taxes?"

"Yes, certainly, buffalo meat being such a hot commodity just now. But it's the end of your dream, Laslo."

"No, we'll just keep on. We'll have our National Grassland one of these days."

"But how?"

"That idea of yours. Just not pay a nickel of taxes to anyone and let the land heal itself."

"What changed your mind?"

"They've made up my mind for me. We've tried good citizenship. They tried sleaze. We tried compromise. They tried greed. Now we'll try other means. How long can you postpone delinquent taxes?"

"For years. For decades. We can protest every assessment, file delays."

"And they don't get a cent."

Truehart laughed. "Laslo, you're such a good-hearted soul I never knew the devil was in you."

"It's in me, Hector. Burn the damned tax notices. They'll cry uncle. What's a poor little old county to do when the state and federal government owns a quarter of it, and the remaining owner of any consequence doesn't pay taxes for twenty years? The state ships money to the destitute county, and the transfusion becomes a major item on the state budget, and everybody's mad at us."

"Are you sure you want to do this? In all three states?"

"Wyoming and South Dakota were playing the same game."

"What'll you do?"

"Run buffalo—and run up the tax bills, watch a wilderness bloom."

"And how'll it end?"

"They'll suddenly discover the beauty of a National Grassland run by a nonprofit foundation. It'll beat selling off the land to private holders at tax-deficiency auctions."

"And what'll you do?"

"Watch the greatest wilderness preservation area in the world gradually recover, until the native grasses run deep, the springs flow, the eagles circle, the elk and deer and bear roam, and they all have a home on the range. We have time.

"Meanwhile, I want to thaw my hands in that jet. How the hell can anyone live in Montana? They should give the whole state back to the buffalo."

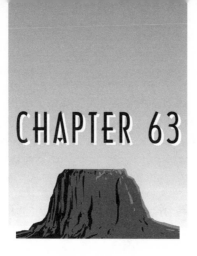

CHAPTER 63

Horoney returned to Dallas in a pensive mood. He had always been an optimist, and wasn't going to permit the perversity of human nature to get him down. They were all rejoicing up there in Montana. They had stuck it to the rich Texan, and somehow the dream of a Buffalo Commons had been utterly lost.

The county tax board got into the act, doing little about the backlog of relief petitions filed by the foundation. They met monthly, considered a handful, rejected most, and once in a while made a token gesture of relief for the foundation, all in the name of fairness, of course, and to protect their rear ends. Horoney supposed they were good enough people, who worked hard, supported families, believed in all the best things. But they had gotten caught up in the sport, and the order of the day was sticking it to the rich Texan who'd bought fifteen percent of Montana, and they were having their fun. If any of them had the eyes to see three feet beyond their faces, Laslo would have been surprised.

He cut off his interviews, even though he received several requests each week from talk-show hosts, newspaper and magazine journalists, National Public Radio, and those seeking a banquet address. He'd had his say. Most of the nation knew of his goal, and approved. The whole concept of the National Grassland had never been more popular.

Truehart stayed busy. The foundation proposed a new tax plan to all three states, one that would pass muster with the state courts. It would simply create a new property-tax category that would apply uniformly across each state, in which land permanently set aside as wilderness would be assessed at one dollar an acre and taxed accordingly. There could be no turning back. Once the land was placed in the wilderness category, it would be without economic value and could not be restored to productive use. It was a good plan, one that would encourage private landholders throughout the area to set aside land as wilderness and habitat.

Huge portions of Montana—and not just the grassland—would end up protected and preserved forevermore.

Not that Truehart was getting anywhere. The governors and legislators positively relished their rejections. Horoney expected that. They would see things differently when it dawned on them that the foundation wasn't paying a nickel in taxes. Next May, when the last of the Year 2000 taxes were due, would tell the tale.

An odd peace settled on him. He could scarcely wait until spring, when he would at last put buffalo on the land. The herd would be modest at first, five thousand from various sources, including the Turner Ranch and the state of South Dakota. But a small herd was what he wanted, so that the wounded grassland would be scarcely grazed, and only randomly, for several more years. He and Dolly would go watch as the big stock trucks pulled in and discharged their shaggy cargo. That would be the culmination, the moment of reality. Would the world be grateful? He doubted it.

The Buffalo County assessor was busily sending the foundation tax delinquency notices. Truehart and his industrious staff kept tabs, and clogged the channels with protests, requests for hearings, and in some cases, lawsuits. Not a cent changed hands. Several weeks later a letter jointly signed by the county commissioners arrived at the foundation, matter-of-factly pointing out that the county could not function without funds, so please pay up promptly. The delinquent amount at that writing exceeded ten million dollars, plus penalties in excess of one million.

Truehart filed that one, too. The snows melted during a chinook, and a promise of warmth eddied through the northern air. In Texas, the weather had turned hot. Soon the hardy prairie grasses would pierce the cold earth, and the High Plains would awaken from their slumber. Horoney yearned to see the grass, walk the wet earth, feel the sharp April wind on his cheeks. Maybe take his new biologist, Kouric, with him so he could learn about the ways of the wild. Kouric was proving himself useful, working up there with everyone, mending the foundation's fences, keeping tabs on winter kill, deer and antelope counts, and the remaining wolf pack.

Horoney turned to his commercial real estate empire, knowing how badly he had neglected it for two years. But no sooner had he begun reviewing the problem areas when he received, by express, an invitation to the White House from President Shiloh Webb, and First Lady Sara McCleary Webb, Republicans who had whirled out of nowhere like the Carters, and won.

Would Mr. and Mrs. Horoney join the secretaries of the Interior, Agriculture, Energy, as well as the directors of the National Park Service,

Forest Service, Bureau of Land Management, Fish and Wildlife, the Majority and Minority Leaders of the Senate, the Speaker and Majority Leader and Minority Leader of the House, and their spouses?

Command performance. Horoney consulted Dolly and accepted. They would twist his arm. They wanted that land. The foundation was the largest private landholder in the United States. They would offer to relieve him of his burdens, maybe even enact legislation appropriating money for Montana taxes. Free and clear, with no loss other than the donated land, sign on the dotted line. He knew what he would say, and regretted having to say it.

They would be quartered at Blair House, courtesy of Uncle Sam. But when they got his reply, they might not be so courteous. This even had a certain arranged quality about it. The federal and state agencies had been exchanging intelligence. The president would know to the penny how much in delinquent taxes the foundation owed the new Montana county. There would be thick files labeled Horoney, and these would include the best psychological assessments the government could come up with, and any little weaknesses that might give the government leverage. Those who read these files would feel power, the ability to manipulate a wealthy eccentric.

The Horoney Gulfstream V landed at National Airport one April afternoon, and a black limousine whisked them to the elegant government hostel across from the White House.

"They'll be looking us over," Laslo said to Dolly.

"With microscopes," Dolly replied. "USDA certified beef."

"There won't be any arm-twisting tonight. Just toasts, flattery, and camaraderie. I'd guess the meeting with *el presidente* in the morning'll be the business end of this little foray."

Promptly at seven that evening, the limo whisked them across the avenue to the White House, and ushers steered them to the black-tie reception. Laslo endured these things rather than enjoyed them, but Dolly clearly was having fun. Laslo's choice for both business and society was always an intimate conversation conducted from comfortable chairs. In the end, he knew the person he was talking to, and that person knew him. But this White House ritual didn't please him. He worked down the reception line, and met the saturnine president, who turned out to operate Lyndon Johnson–style, a big soft paw thrust into Laslo's while the other presidential arm clasped shoulder, elbow, and patted here and there, the presidential touch apparently intended to heal anything ailing Laslo's carcass, including King's Evil. Faith healing. The power of the maximum leader. Friend of Shiloh now and evermore. Laslo liked the first lady better. She stood about five feet tall, peered up at Laslo with her baby blues, and said, "I'm glad you grow it rather than smoke it."

Swiftly, Horoney was introduced to the cabinet members and directors of the agencies who shared an interest in the foundation's project—and itched to lay their paws on all that grass, all for free, without even going to Congress to ask for it. Laslo figured that several of the worthies he was meeting at that time knew to the penny how much in back taxes the foundation owed. Knowledge was power, and these were the world's most knowledgeable men. There were drinks, plied by gents and ladies in black, and then they were ritually herded to the grand dining room, where they were seated by rank, but with the Horoneys next to the president and first lady.

Ritual. Glitter, silver, pewter, finger bowls, thick linen napkins, exotic bouquets flown from the Carolinas, crusty women gauded up in demure evening gowns and hair spray, gents bulging from custom-cut black dinner jackets with silk lapels. Laslo sighed. He wasn't a man who enjoyed power or pomp. He had envisioned a vast grassland wilderness where a man could feel the good earth under his boots, not eating from china with the presidential seal upon it.

Shiloh Webb was Oklahoman and part Comanche, and told Laslo he approved the National Grassland on purely ancestral grounds. But then the seating was completed, the vintage wine poured, and Webb rose, and act that evoked an instant hush.

Webb certainly could be a charmer. He slid into a politico joke or two, some self-deprecating humor, and then proposed a toast to the man who'd put the great grassland together. Pretty flowery stuff, Laslo thought. He picked up all those code words that were intended to massage his conceits, as if they needed a good rubdown. "Visionary," "courageous," "one-of-a-kind," "self-sacrificing," "distinguished," "formidable," "the costliest in history," "the largest such project the world's known," "a man of the hour, the year, the times," and a lot more.

They all liked that, sipped, and awaited a word from himself.

"Dolly takes a different view," he began. "She's the vice president, but actually the guru, and keeps me humble. She's one of the world's finest poker players, as well as pianist and painter and harpsichordist and businesswoman. I'm the wanderer, she's the lady who makes the staff march. Were it not for her, there'd be no National Grassland, you know."

Laslo winked at Dolly. In the morning, when they got down to dealing the poker hands, they'd deal her in. That night, in the quiet of the lavish suite at Blair House, he stared out the window at the endless traffic, felt this city suffocate him, and hoped he had the grace to forgive them.

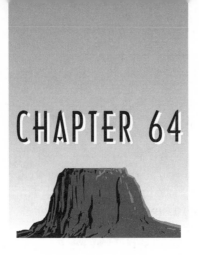

CHAPTER 64

The Horoneys met the president that morning in a White House parlor, far from the Oval Office. Someone had obviously briefed the president right down to a fare-thee-well. No desk stood between Shiloh Webb, Laslo, and Dolly. She figured they knew everything there was to know about Laslo, including the size of his shorts. And one thing they knew for certain was that Laslo's business style was quiet, disarming, and intimate.

So there was Webb, pulled up close, perched on his chair within patting, touching, shoulder-gripping distance from them both, making a little triangle, and there she was, sitting knee to knee with the president of the United States, deciding the fate of millions of acres of land possessed by the Horoney Foundation.

The ubiquitous aides brought tea and tarts, and then the no-nonsense facet of Webb's character emerged at once.

"Laslo, they're howling in Montana that the foundation's not paying its taxes."

Laslo nodded, but Dolly replied. "We don't intend to."

"You what?" The president's piercing gaze settled on her.

"Let them stew," she said.

Webb examined her with a newly appraising glance. "They'll take it away from you. That what you want?"

"That's a dozen years away," she said. "Meanwhile it's the foundation's to do with as it chooses. We'll let the grass grow and the buffalo run, and those who want to stay there won't be molested."

"Are you serious about this?"

She smiled sweetly.

Webb switched his approach. "We take it you don't like the Park Service. What we'd like is for you to donate it to the Fish and Wildlife Service as a national wildlife refuge. You already have a great one there in Montana, the Charles M. Russell refuge along the Missouri River. We've talked it over and we think that's the agency that'd come closest to achieving the objectives of your foundation."

"In one sense, yes," she said. "They'd do a good job with the wildlife."

"And in any other sense?"

"Federal environmental agencies are abusive of the rights of citizens. Fish and Wildlife's among the worst."

The president pondered that. "What's the problem?"

"Wolf habitat. They have no charter to impose it on private lands. The Supreme Court's generally called it taking, because it violates the constitutional protection of private property. If you deprive people of their property rights, you've got to pay them for what they've lost."

She sensed that Webb knew all about this.

"Why should it matter to you—to the foundation?"

"From the beginning, Laslo and I've respected the people of Montana who've roots and homes in the grassland area. We've tried to be good neighbors. The government's shown no sign of that respect."

He glanced at her again. "Well, so Fish and Wildlife's out. Forest Service's oriented to the public, multiple-use policy, and so's the Bureau of Land Management, livestock grazing, all that. You want to give the land to the BLM? We'd run a little bill through Congress, no problem, for the amount of taxes due Montana. We wouldn't pay your taxes, of course—not palatable to the public. But we'd buy the land for an amount equal to your tax obligation, and you'd pay the state and everyone'd be happy."

Laslo said, "We'll just hang on, Mr. President."

"And not pay state taxes?"

"We'll see."

"Am I not getting the whole story?" Webb asked.

"I suspect you already have it."

"I suspect I do. Those clowns on your county tax board've settled only twenty-one out of three thousand seven hundred requests to adjust taxes to your new conditions. And favored the foundation three times. They've saved you exactly two hundred forty dollars. You're paying for wheat farms that don't exist, houses that've been torn out. Right?"

Dolly smiled.

"Bleed the rich Texans, right?"

She had to give Webb credit.

"We'll think about your offer, Mr. President," Laslo said. "Now, we really don't want to take your valuable time."

"I scheduled an hour. Would it help if I stopped this crap that's coming at you from Montana? I can call Magruder and stop it. They're onto you. They know they're not going to see one damned dime, and that you'll drag it out for a decade, fifteen years, twenty maybe before the land goes into a tax auction. They know the state's going to ante up tens of millions every year to keep that giant county afloat, and they're so mad they could spit—threatening to throw you in the slammer, tie you up with criminal investigations, all the rest."

Dolly digested that a moment. "Mr. President, all they have to do is enact the tax legislation we proposed, which would establish a uniform rate for wilderness land throughout Montana."

He grunted. "By God, I like you. I get the picture. All right, Dolly, Laslo, have it your way. These cabinet guys have been putting the heat on me. They want the whole bundle on a platter, preferably after dicing you in a Cuisinart and running you through the Disposall. Let me tell you something. They're all lusting for your land, whoring for it, fighting each other for it, pestering me night and day to put the heat on you. And it doesn't stop there, either. They're talking with Montana, the governor, the agencies, the pols, needling the state to put the heat on you, jack up your taxes. It may not be a conspiracy, but it's a first-class government racket. You're not getting the respect that's owed the humblest citizen. You wouldn't believe how these land and environment and wildlife agencies want that chunk of prairie. They'd damn well kill for it. Me, I figure if they want something that bad, maybe I better get to know the victims." He laughed, went into a frenetic bout of patting and touching and elbow lifting, and handshaking.

Dolly liked him, much to her surprise.

"Hey, keep me posted, you two. This tickles my ass—'scuse me, Dolly. I'm going to order those hounds to quit harassing you. That was how it was supposed to be, you know—cooperate with the Horoney Foundation, integrate their operations with yours. Guess I'll just remind them, and if they don't help you out, we'll have a few beheadings. That was Clinton's executive order, and I'll just tighten it up. Sometimes I think the one person in the country who's got no clout is the old chief himself. Now, dammit, I'm going to write down a number, keep it to yourself, don't put it in an address book next to my name. You'll get me privately, no log-ins, no government switchboard. Call me if you're getting too much heat. I'm good at chewing on people."

He scribbled a moment, handed the number to her, and ushered them to the east end of the White House.

"I think I like him," said Laslo as the limo drove them out to National Airport.

"It's because he likes people," she said.

One June day soon after, when the young prairie grasses bobbed sweetly in the zephyrs, she and Laslo watched a long caravan of stock trucks crawl over the muddy road to a spot on the Powder River where some pens remained, including several loading chutes. There, in an empty land, the teamsters backed the trucks, one by one, into the chutes and opened the gates. Great shaggy buffalo bulled their way out, sometimes jamming the ramp. The pen gates were open. Nothing kept the dark monsters from the shimmering grasses that stretched an infinity toward a sky shot with cumulus clouds with black bellies, some of them spitting rain. She and Laslo watched, ignoring the wind. Many of the buffalo were disoriented, afraid, clinging to the comfort of the pen. But the bolder ones stepped out upon knee-high buffalo grass and wheatgrass, nibbled tentatively, established their sovereign claim to this world where they belonged and always had, and drifted outward, driven by the southwest wind.

This process would take three days. There were that many buffalo to transport from the Gallatin Valley, the Black Hills area of South Dakota, and other places including a large buffalo ranch in southern Wyoming.

She saw fresh-born calves nuzzling up to their mothers, yearlings, big snorty bulls, some angry, some placid, some shocked after hours of hard travel. Most drifted down to the river, sniffed the purling water, and drank. The Powder was famous for its quicksand, but this place was free of it. She swore she saw a mirage: each buffalo was reflected in the sky, a mirror image, a heavenly herd reclaiming its universe, including the muddy earth under their hooves, and the soaring heavens above. She nudged Laslo, who stood rapt and silent, both of them safely in a catch-pen where angry buffalo couldn't hurt them.

They weren't alone. Sanford Kouric watched. Half the foundation staff had wangled a flight in. Some Montana officials watched in enigmatic silence. Some presidential jawboning had worked its way through the federal departments and clear down through state of Montana agencies, and suddenly the pressures on the Horoney Foundation had largely vanished. Best of all, the state legislature had enacted the Uniform Wilderness Taxation Act, which permitted private citizens to convert their property to permanent wilderness status, and be taxed at a minimal rate. That spring, a large chunk of Montana—not including the foundation's land—had been dedicated to wildlife habitat and restoration of wilderness. And no government agency was even involved, except in an advisory capacity.

She didn't know exactly what had happened to change things. No one was saying. But the pols and bureaucrats had caved in. Maybe it was because that nettle and rabble-rouser Brooke-Carson had suddenly resigned his professorship and gone to work for a foundation, where he was being uncommonly silent. Maybe it was because the whole story was appearing in the media. Maybe it was the Horoney Foundation's last-ditch tax rebellion. Maybe Shiloh Webb had gotten busy and knocked a few heads together, all the while smiling and patting his way through the presidency. But suddenly Buffalo County's assessor and tax board began to cooperate. The next thing she knew, the legislature was holding hearings. A month later a bill sailed through and Magruder signed it. The foundation promptly paid the previous year's taxes—at the revised rate—and the new county was adequately funded. Now the buffalo grazed their way down to the river, blackening the tender land with their beauty and power. And no one was saying nay.

"How do you feel, Laslo?" she asked.

"In a bit I'm going to find a sunny slope and lie down upon it and feel the warmth of the earth come through my clothing, and feel the footsteps of the buffalo and watch a hawk circling above me.

"Look at these magnificent animals. Look at them. No wonder the sight of them stirred the pioneers and lifted the hearts of Indians. Look at them! And they're just the beginning. Soon we'll see prairie dogs, and soon the black-footed ferret will flourish. Soon we'll offer a home for elk, deer, antelope, eagles, hawks. Homes, Dolly, we're rescuing the homeless."

"That was always my goal," she said.

CHAPTER 65

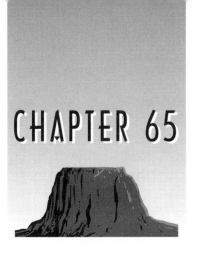

Bob Rockwell was on the line. "Cam, Delacorte wants to settle."

"How much?"

"Twenty-five grand."

"Forget it."

Rockwell laughed. "Tall Chief—his lawyer—said that's how they figure it. The wolves killed a few cattle."

"They're still killing my cattle. And we can't get rid of them. And if he hadn't done that, Fish and Wildlife wouldn't have moved in with the habitat designation, which wiped out our property values, and—"

"Yeah, I know, Cam. I'll tell her to stick it in her ear?"

"But hold the door open."

"What's the damned land worth now?"

"I don't know. Tell her twenty-five's a joke. Forget the land values. Just to keep cattle on country full of wolves, we've had to switch to longhorns. I enjoy the cusses, but they don't make much beef. We've lost a hundred thousand on that whole deal so far. Tell her that. And that's for starters. We're losing more every day. Nichols Ranches weren't damaged much by the foundation; they were demolished by Delacorte. Everything that's happened since then—"

"Yeah, Cam, I'll call her, and get back to you. Trial date's in three weeks. Maybe we can avoid it."

Cam Nichols hung up, fuming. Twenty-five grand. A ranching business falling apart. If there was one man on earth Cam wanted to throttle, it was Delacorte.

He had gotten two resignations in recent days, Billy Marks and Claude Thorn, down on the southern ranches. They were getting too lonely out there, surrounded by foundation land, no one in sight for days, their wives and kids going nuts. His world was caving in on him. He expected more resignations soon.

He felt awash in helplessness. His brain wasn't designed to handle something like this. He knew dryland ranching, not cataclysmic change. Put him in charge of a faltering outfit and he'd rescue it, turn a loser into a profit-earner. Nicholses had always done that, turned those hard-scrabble ranches into paying operations. He knew the weather, the weeds, the soil, the grass. He knew how to survive in tough country. His father and grandfather had learned it and taught him; he'd taught it to DeeAnn, and tried to teach it to Martin—his newfound son.

Cam was stricken by his own helplessness. What do you do when you've done all you can? What do you do when armies march in the night, and you wake up homeless and penniless? Armies were marching across the West. Even a man like Laslo Horoney, well intentioned, sensitive to his neighbors, without a coercive bone in him, wrought such seismic changes that they were off the Richter scale. And he was a good one. What of all the yuppies who swarmed the West, their heads stuffed with romantic notions about buffalo and antelope and Indians, their minds brimming with indignation at those who raised beef—cholesterol—for a living. They believed that ranchers raped the land, and they never looked closely enough at stockgrowing to realize that no rancher in his right mind would destroy his economic base by destroying his pasture. Each rancher lived with his mistakes. That was more than Cam could say about the privileged yuppies, who seemed immune to life's harsh turns of fortune.

But even the yuppies, the me-too environmentalists, were nothing compared to the real armies, the federal bureaucrats allied with their propaganda groups, who wanted to snatch the West from American citizens. Those were the armies of the night, the silent marchers, the ones who paralyzed ranchers with regulations, who poked and probed and fined and chiseled every rancher Cam knew. Those were the night battalions, and before they were done they would murder ranching in a tier of Western states, and turn people like the Nichols family into pariahs and even criminals for unwittingly violating one or another of their myriad regulations.

He didn't have the faintest idea what to do anymore, except try to hang on, raise beef, avoid the razors of the regulators, and pray for rain and grass and hay and mild weather. That's how the spring had gone: hollow, warm, pleasant, but filled with foreboding. He had not tried to replace the departing managers. Instead, he moved beef off those places, sold some Herefords to cover losses, and watched the net worth of Nichols Ranches ratchet downward. He let the vacated ranches go to seed. They needed the rest.

Then one day DeeAnn called. "Mark and I want to come to Billings to talk to you and Mom," she said.

"That sounds pretty ominous, DeeAnn."

"No, don't think that. But we do have some serious things we want to discuss."

"Sure, kid, come on."

"We're going to stop in Miles and see Anna. Put some steaks on for us."

"Now I'm certain this is big medicine."

"Big medicine," she said.

They arrived in time to see Sandy perform her sun's-over-the-yardarm ritual. DeeAnn watched her mother pour exactly two shots of gin into a glass, add tonic and a squeeze of lime, and then cap the gin bottle and return it to the liquor shelf.

"That's it," Sandy said.

DeeAnn looked doubtful.

"That's how I do it. I like my gin. I control it."

Sandy lifted her glass, smiled, and drank.

They watched her, fascinated, distrustful. Cam knew that by the end of this sojourn in Billings, they would see a facet of Sandy they'd not seen before. Her resolve.

DeeAnn led off. "Dad, it's not the same out there anymore. It's spooky. Lots of nothing. No one around for days on end. Mark and I always wanted to stick it out. We're ranchers. We know the business. But the kids—" She shrugged. "Not just the kids. Us. We used to see people at Hart's Corners, but now no one's there. We used to—there were always people. No more."

"You want to get out."

"Well, sort of. We stopped to see Anna and we tried this out on her, and she liked it. She blessed it."

"Try what out?"

She smiled. "Ranching somewhere else."

So that was it. He waited for more.

"We love that land, Dad, but times are changing. It was always a tough place to ranch. I know we have roots there. Mine go deep, like yours. But it's not the only place in Montana. You know what got us down? The wolf habitat. We couldn't do a thing but exist. How can anyone live like that? We want to go somewhere where Fish and Wildlife isn't going to say no to everything we want to do. We want to *own* the land."

"Where?"

"There's an outfit for sale east of Lewistown, right in the center of the state. It's beautiful. Thirty thousand acres, forty-seven sections in two pieces, one of them north and east of the Snowy Mountains, lots of timber on it, well watered, good hay meadow and grass. The other's east of the Judith Mountains, good foothills and grass, live creeks. The ranch is being sold in an estate sale. It's been mostly profitable. It carries three thousand head in bad times, more in good. That's because they make a lot of hay on subirrigated ground. That means we could ship at least eight hundred a year, maybe a thousand. Also, it's beautiful, both pieces. They're about twelve miles apart at their closest points. It's real ranch country, Dad, just meant for stock grazing. Cold winters—the Snowy Mountains are famous for cold—but there's more shelter. Cattle can hole up."

"You've neglected something."

"Six million asked, but it hasn't sold for that and it's been on the market for a while."

"And what do you figure Nichols Ranches are worth, surrounded by the Horoney Foundation's wilderness?"

"Well, that's what Mark and I want to talk to you about. We think you could trade out with Horoney. He gets our two hundred twenty thousand acres for his National Grassland; he buys us this ranch. We sell down our herd to three thousand and keep the cash as a reserve. No mortgage."

"What'll it support?"

"We think it'll support Anna, you and Mom, Mark and me, and provide a little—not much—for my sibs. It'll require one manager on the southern place. Maybe John Trouble, if he's willing to move so far from his people. You could live here. It's closer to Billings than our ranch now. And there's an airstrip on the northern section, and a good airport at Lewistown."

"How do you think those people lying in our family cemetery would take this?"

"I can't speak for them. We need to make changes. I love the land, love ranching, love Montana. But I'm not tied to our place. Not now, with the government saying we can't do anything."

"How do you feel, Mark?"

"I'd like to move if we could, but I'm not a shareholder, so it's up to you."

"Why do you think Horoney would go for it?"

"We're the last hole of any size in his dream."

Cam smiled. "Well said."

"We'd like to show it to you tomorrow. The kids are with Mark's parents. How do you feel about it?"

"I don't know. A place has to talk to me."

"How do you feel about it, Mom?"

"When dreams don't work out, we back off and try to find another, and sometimes the second choice is the miracle we've been waiting for."

"I got to see this place," Nichols said. "It must be Wiley Stark's outfit."

"It is."

He knew most of the major ranches in Montana, and not a few of the smaller ones, too. He'd met Stark, an old bachelor, at many a stock-grower's meeting. Stark had been an old man forever, it seemed.

"I don't think there'll be much of a home on either place," he said.

"That's an opportunity. And we won't have to get permission from Fish and Wildlife to build or remodel."

He laughed, liking her pluck.

"We'll have lunch in Grassrange, and go look. I set this up for after lunch. They'll have the books to show us. And then we'll take a three- or four-hour drive down a lot of two-rut roads."

"Stark raised black Angus."

"Black cows do better than Hereford up there. So maybe we'll have to start over. Dad, when you see this land, and walk these pastures, and see the timber and the clear creeks, and the hills, and the coulees full of brush for the deer, and the wild turkeys, and the way the whole thing lies, and the way these fields look, and the improvements, you'll see what I'm talking about. We should've done this decades ago."

"We're a stubborn family, DeeAnn. The land made us like that."

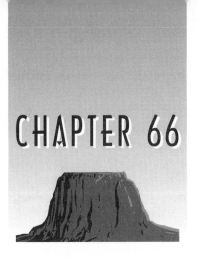

CHAPTER 66

Cameron tried not to think about the beauty. He was a sucker for beauty, and could be seduced into buying poverty gulch if it lifted the soul and delighted the eye.

He wondered whether the manager, a young ag school grad hired by Stark's relatives, had an eye for beauty. He doubted it. The fellow had an eye for quarter horses, but never saw the grace of an aspen or suspected he was living in Eden.

Cam focused instead on Stark's books, which lay before him in the intimate den of a log home set on a bench overlooking a paradise. If you wanted to know the sort of muscle a ranch had, you studied the bad years. 1988, for instance, the year Montana burned, along with Yellowstone Park. It hadn't snowed that winter, and it didn't rain in the spring. The flames had touched this place, at least the southern unit nestled into the northeastern foothills of the Snowy Mountains.

But this morning Cam had driven through vaulting green pastures, lush with knee-high grasses, a place where an occasional black stalk or charred stump was all that remained of a dense woods that died twelve years ago.

The fire year, and the year following, would tell the tale. Stark's books showed a customary profit, no unusual expense for hay or feed, which Stark had in abundance, and no fire expense other than rebuilding fence. The average weight of the shipper cattle had dropped that year, though, and Stark had culled his herd sharply to prepare for a winter without pasture.

Stark had kept good records, and Cam studied them. The ranch had suffered occasional abortion losses, perhaps because so much of it lay next to or within pine timber. That gave him pause. This was cold and snowy country, where animals could easily be trapped by sudden storms. The Snowy Mountains had been well named.

Stark had ranched well, running his nursery stock on the north section, as close to the home place and as far from forest as possible, while running his steers and heifers and mature stock on the higher southern unit through the summers and falls. Nichols doubted that he could do better, and might not do as well anywhere else. A man needed to get the feel of a place like this, just as a man had to understand the land where the Nichols family had put down roots.

He reviewed years of records while his family meandered the ranch. He had seen only a little of the place. One could not examine forty-seven sections in an afternoon. But tomorrow he would fly up here, armed with a plat map, and eyeball the ranch from the air. But all that was business. Something else was going on that made him uneasy. His soul was howling with joy. The southern unit was shot with small icy creeks, Surenough, McDonald, Tyler, many of them dammed by beaver that helped maintain constant flow, a high water table, and lush riparian areas that brimmed with wildlife. From the grassed ridges and valleys below, the land swept upward into black ponderosa pine, the valleys choked with red willow brush and silvery cottonwoods, higher and higher into true forest filled with spruce, pine, fir, aspen, in parks and then denser near the ranch's southern boundary with Forest Service land. From any ridge one could gaze upward to the shoulders of the Snowies, still snow-choked and blue in mid-June, a source of almost perpetual water.

An intelligently laid-out web of ranch roads provided access. Gates were few, and cross-fencing minimal. The animals needed to be able to descend the mountains when snow drove them lower. The ranch had a small Forest Service grazing permit, but mostly relied on its own pasture and hay meadows. The northern unit was laid at the base of the Judith Mountains, and encompassed some of the horse pasture of old Fort Maginnis, a long-gone relic of the frontier. Here was a sea of grass, the land flatter, the views longer, the water scarcer but still adequate, with windmills and springs and some live creeks, like Ford's and Little Box Elder.

Some missile silos dotted the ranch, empty now, a relic of the cold war, somber concrete slabs still guarded by chain-link fence. He wished he could get rid of them. They had once contained multiple-warhead ballistic missiles targeted on the Soviet Union, controlled from Malmstrom Air Force Base near Great Falls.

Cameron knew he would buy Stark's ranch if he could—and if the others wanted him to. And if he could talk Horoney into buying Nichols Ranches at a decent price. This was prime ranch country. A man would struggle with different elements here, more cold, more snow, more swamp and mud and bog, less drought, less cactus, less sagebrush. There were neighbors. This country supported small ranches, family ranches, and that meant people. There were friendly crossroads like Forestgrove. Lewistown was only thirty minutes from either unit. Eight thousand people, amenities, friends. No two-hour school bus rides for DeeAnn's kids. The airstrip, a grassy runway running east and west, would give him thirty-minute access to Billings. This country wasn't going to be a part of the proposed National Grassland, and Laslo Horoney didn't have his eye on it. It had a future. So far, there were no platoons of bureaucrats forbidding an owner to ranch the country. He could build a home without violating some animal's habitat.

DeeAnn and Mark could live in this peeled log one, surprisingly pleasant, rustic, vaulting ceilings, with picture windows opening, variously, upon a sea of grass to the east, the Snowies to the southwest, and the pine-clad Judiths immediately west, and Black Butte to the north. God, what a view. How could anyone live here and not be lifted by the very sight of it, the lush greens that would soon cure into tan, the green-black slopes where ponderosa grew, the streaks of snow high in the blue-and-purple crags?

Some wouldn't see beauty because they hadn't been given eyes to see. Or else their sight was upon the long thick carcasses of fine cattle, or the powerful stifle of a good quarter horse, or maybe even the fat grasses of the hay meadows, dollars and cents by the bale.

He knew how desperately DeeAnn and Mark wanted the place. He could see it in their shining eyes, feel it in their remarks, their efforts to make him see it as they saw it. But there was a question. Two questions. He would talk privately with Anna, just to make sure. And now he would find Sandy and ask her.

He discovered her on the veranda of the log home, prim in a wicker chair, the whole world at her feet, her arm idly scratching a blue heeler. He sat down beside her, saying nothing. All morning they had bounced along two-rut roads, opened and closed wire gates, paused to watch mule and white-tailed deer bound away, stopped to examine black Angus lying on the ground chewing their cud. They had looked at beaver dams cemented together with mud, swampy backwaters, stumps of aspens the little animals had chewed down, game trails up the tumbling valleys, great fenced pastures dotted with islands of forest, some of them several square miles, good and bad fence, some ancient, some taut and straight on metal posts.

She patted his sun-stained hand. "Could we build here and still keep the little place in Billings?"

"Would you like it?" He felt dumb, asking her that.

"Oh, God," she said. He discovered tears in her eyes, and wondered what was wrong.

"If we had only had this all these years, I wouldn't have thrown away so much of my life," she said.

"Maybe we can build. If Horoney agrees, and if we get a good settlement out of Delacorte."

"Could we look at Lewistown?"

"Tomorrow would be better. We can go there and talk to that ranch salesman. Want to fly it tomorrow?"

"Oh, yes."

"Where are DeeAnn and Mark?"

"They're taping everything in sight with their camcorder. I guess they'll show up when they're hungry or the light fades."

"That'll be ten o'clock."

They were heading into the dinner hour—Montanans called it supper time and called lunch dinner—and Cam didn't want to impose on the manager's family any longer, so he hiked restlessly out to the sheds and stock pens, hoping to corral his wayward family. He found them by the creek, DeeAnn relentlessly taping her children's first encounter with icy water while Mark was muttering cautionary advice.

They saw Cam, and fell into an odd silence, one he understood well. There was too much feeling floating around there.

"Guess we'll go talk to that broker in the morning," he said. "I'll call Laslo Horoney. It may not be easy."

DeeAnn wept and kept shaking her head.

"Think you'd like it here?"

She nodded.

"Sandy thinks so, too."

"Is that what did it?"

"No, but it helped. It's a ranch that runs itself. If we stay out of debt, we'll feed our families and then some. You'll ranch here. We'd like to build nearby, sort of like the old place. Put a manager on the southern unit. Like you say, John Trouble if he wants it. The funny thing is, this is a lot less land but we'll be making enough. There was a good story in those ledgers. We'll have one employee, not six or seven."

"Does Mother really want to live here? I mean live here day after day?"

"She's keeping the Billings option open."

"Does she really like it?"

"Yes, she loves it. This place stirs her. The dry plains didn't. Maybe this is a bit more like Butte. Mountains, and water, and cooler summers. But that's not what did it. We've got twenty neighbors within a few minutes. Did you see the mailboxes back there? A regular row of neighbors. Some people I know, stockgrowers meetings. And a beautiful little city of eight thousand just a hop away. Have you ever seen Lewistown? DeeAnn, she's thrilled right down to the bottom of her soul."

"Will she get into trouble?"

"DeeAnn, that's up to her. She drank to escape the prison of Nichols Ranches, and I'm not going to be her jailer. She's got a life in Billings if she wants it. I can fly. That's a usable airstrip up there, with a hangar. If she comes, it'll be because she wants to."

"We want this more than we've ever wanted anything."

"So do I. I'll call Horoney in the morning. Maybe this is all just a fantasy. He's probably thinking he'll pick up Nichols Ranches someday for a lot less."

Later, driving through the summer twilight across the Big Empty, he began worrying that someone would ace him out of the ranch, or bid on just one of the two units, or maybe Stark's relatives had just taken it off the market that very day. He'd call in the morning and learn some wise guy had just signed a buy-and-sell. He was plenty familiar with those somewhat paranoid notions, and understood their source:

The Nichols family had found a new home.

CHAPTER 67

Horoney listened as Cameron Nichols outlined his proposal to sell Nichols Ranches to the foundation. The offer surprised him. He had reconciled himself to living with a large hole in the National Grassland, consisting not only of Nichols's 347 square miles, but another eighty or ninety of state and federal land effectively locked into the middle of Nichols's holdings. Now, suddenly, he could acquire the last and in some ways the most important parcel.

Six million was a lot of money—but less than the twenty-five million the foundation had offered Nichols not long before.

"Cameron, how do you feel about this? Selling at a fraction of what your land was worth?"

"We'll be glad to get out. All of us. Ever since Fish and Wildlife declared the area endangered species habitat, we haven't been in control of our own land. What once was a home and a business turned to ashes."

"But that's quite a loss . . ."

"It was never in my hands. My father controlled the majority before he died. He wouldn't budge, so that was that. Now he's gone and things have changed. I've inherited his stock, and I'm my grandmother's trustee."

"May I ask how she feels about this?"

Nichols laughed. "She's young at heart, and as eager as a half-trained racehorse. I showed her some videotapes of the new place—it's beautiful, you know, mountain foothills stretching into plains, well populated, old ranching community, near a good-sized town, cold creeks, well watered—I showed her all that, and she patted my knee and said she wanted to see it and she'd get taken over there even if it required a nurse or two."

"Does she feel loss?"

"In a way. But she's philosophic. I asked her what her plans would be—that's how I approached a delicate subject—and she said she wanted to be buried in the family plot. That's where generations of Nicholses lie, that's where her husband lies. I asked her whether she'd like the entire plot moved—everyone disinterred and brought to the new place— and she wouldn't think of it. Know what she said? 'I like the idea of buffalo grazing over my grave. They'll knock the fence down, you know. That's good. Our spirits will be there. Oh, to see ten thousand buffalo grazing good grass.' "

"Your grandmother's a great lady, Cameron."

"Yes, she is."

"You feel the new place'll support you adequately—forty-seven square miles instead of three hundred forty-odd?"

"All I can say is, I've studied the books. If we can own it without a mortgage, we'll be all right. Enough for Anna, my wife and me, DeeAnn and Mark, and some for my other children and the others who have minor shares."

"Your family—they all agree?"

"Even Sandy. She's the one I worried about. Sandy loves the place. It's close to all sorts of people. It has trees, and mountain views, and water. She wants to keep the Billings house, and I think that's a good idea. She needs a city around her, and she dreads isolation. But she'll never be isolated again, not if I can help it."

"This new place—it's that beautiful?"

"Well, if you could dream up a fantasy ranch, and set it in foothills, with valleys and meadows and uplands reaching toward snowy peaks, and plains stretching the other direction, you'd have this place."

"Could you love it as much as your home place?"

"I could. My father couldn't. His roots ran deep there, maybe because it was always a desperate struggle to ranch on that dryland. You know, you root down into a place not so much because of things like beauty, but because you've mastered a devil that's wounded and bled you. Your roots are grown out of pain and suffering, drought and cold and wind and all the accumulated skills it takes to survive in a deal like that. I've been thinking about roots—and the truth of it is, pain and struggle make the deepest, toughest roots of all. My father's struggle with the land anchored him to it; mine almost did, too. But when I saw this new place, I knew—*knew*—I had to let go. I'd been too rigid, and I'd hurt Sandy . . ."

Nichols's voice trailed off. Horoney understood in a flash that he and Cam Nichols had somehow drifted beyond business. These were the confidences of friends.

"Cam," he said, "I need to check with the board, but I'm sure we'll do it. Go put down some earnest, and count on us. Make your best deal, up to six million. The foundation maintains large lines of credit with several banks, and this gives me the freedom to sell off properties at will, not at fire-sale prices, and we'll tap that credit line for you."

"You'll do it?"

"Sure. You're fulfilling our dream. Except for some minor commercial properties and a few small holdings, this gives us our Big Empty. It's not just your land we're getting, it's the federal and state land locked up within it. Look, I'll have a confirming fax to you within an hour."

"Laslo . . ."

Nichols couldn't finish.

"Cameron, would you mind if Dolly and I flew up and had a look at your new place?"

"Mind? I'd love to show it to you."

"It'll be a couple of days because I'm tied up with sales here. Time enough for you to put together a buy-and-sell."

"I didn't know you were interested in ranches."

"Well, they're not my line, but Dolly and I've been looking for a little nest in Montana, maybe forty acres where we could pretend to be cowboys."

Nichols laughed. "You're hoping I'll saw off a forty for you?"

"If it's something we'd like."

"Laslo, you'll need a hundred-sixty or three-twenty to play cowboy. A little horse pasture. I just might have some."

"If you don't want neighbors, we'd maybe find a spot in that area, if it's as good as you say."

"Don't want neighbors? Maybe not rich Texans. Sell to a Texan and they buy up the whole state. But we can make you an honorary Montanan."

Three days later the Gulfstream V settled on the runway at Lewistown's airport, and Laslo and Dolly Horoney stepped into a hot June day. There to greet them was the Nichols tribe in a couple of four-wheel vehicles. The area delighted Horoney. To the south loomed the massive ridge of the Snowy Mountains; to the northeast, the black-clad Judiths. The town had a winsome warmth.

Nichols drove them eastward, into timbered country patched with grassy meadows, beneath the big sky of Montana.

"Cam and I are dying of curiosity about one thing," Sandy said. "Why do you want a hideaway here? Why aren't you building a place on the grassland you love so much?"

"That's easy," Laslo replied from the backseat. "We never thought the High Plains, the grassland, made much of a home for people. It's a proper home for buffalo, for animals. Sure, many people have loved their lives there, but for most people, those empty plains have been a struggle, a war fought against weather, drouth, loneliness, dreary vistas, and wind. Wasn't it true that pioneer women trapped there died young, or went mad, or committed suicide? No, we love the great seas of grass for what they are—the best home on earth for buffalo, and the place where grasses flourish. But that doesn't mean we'd like to live there."

"Well," Nichols said, "we'll show you some real ranching country, places where ranching people have made a life. One of those, next to us, is the old N-Bar, a pioneer outfit going back to the eighteen eighties and filled with history."

The country was so heavily timbered that Horoney wondered where the pasture was, but then Nichols turned onto a dirt road that took them across winding pastures nestled into foothills.

"We'll look at the southern unit first," Nichols said. "It's wetter, more wooded, more up and down. Then we'll look at the northern one, which is more open."

They followed a rushing creek that suddenly broadened into a pond surrounded by pine and aspen.

"Beaver pond," Nichols said.

"Oh, could I see?" Dolly asked.

Nichols pulled over, and Horoney found himself chasing Dolly as she raced to the stick-and-mud dam, miraculously cemented together by the industrious beaver. A nearby conical jumble of sticks was no doubt a beaver house.

"Will we see any?" she asked.

"No, they're shy animals," Nichols replied. "But they're here."

"I've never seen one."

"They were trapped out long ago, and stayed trapped out until very recently. Ranchers didn't like them; they could be destructive. They can chew up whole forests of aspen. Build dams that wreck irrigation. But then, not long ago, we all began taking another look. After the beavers were trapped and their dams destroyed, nothing held back the creeks when they ran in the spring, and they cut deep canyons, seriously eroding the creek bottoms. Worse, the water tables dropped because nothing was holding back water.

"A lot of ranchers still kill them. But nowadays, a rancher can call for help and some wildlife people will come out and trap the little devils and move them up into the Rockies, transplant them to good beaver habitat.

There are thousands of new beaver ponds and dams all over the northern Rockies, and they owe their existence to a concerted effort to put the beaver to work. You can guess the result—better control of meltoffs, new lush growth, less soil erosion, better water quality, restored water tables . . . I'm glad to see beaver here. Nichols Ranches"—he smiled, self-deprecatingly—"we'll work with the beaver. Among other things, beaver help to maintain constant stream flow. They'll turn an intermittent stream back into a year-round one."

"Cameron, this is paradise."

"Would you like a corner of it?"

"Of course we would."

"Well, I've an agreement to purchase these two units for five point seven million. You've forty-seven square miles to look at. I'd suggest we drive around both units today, fly them tomorrow, and you can start narrowing down a site. But I hope you'll be close to us. We like neighbors."

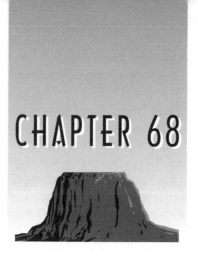

CHAPTER 68

Martin Nichols drove home. The word caught in his throat. For years he had supposed he was one of the homeless. The place in the former Powder River County had never been a home to him. And the place he was driving to was not yet a home. He had never been there. DeeAnn and Mark Cassady were living in the house, and he would be their guest. His parents were building a new home a quarter of a mile away, but living in Billings for the time being.

This summer odyssey would be more than a homecoming. He knew somehow that it was the most important spiritual foray of his life. This trip from Bozeman northeast toward Lewistown would take him through broad valleys and isolated mountain ranges east of the great cordillera of the Rockies. It was all country made for ranching, and if the glowing reports he'd heard were to be believed, the new ranch would be staked out in Paradise.

A homecoming, yes. But more. Some research, too. He would visit isolated communities north of Miles City, areas just barely hanging on, where the web of civilization had pulled thin and fine and fragile; an area slated to become the foundation's next phase of the National Grassland. He wanted to look at those people, clinging to a hard life there, with an appraising eye for his thesis—not to condemn, but to chronicle their resilience and courage. He was done condemning. After that, he would meet the foundation's biologist, Sanford Kouric, and together they would foray out upon an empty sea of grass—empty only to unseeing eyes, because the place teemed with its own life—and look at the wolves, the buffalo, and the silent remains of a desperate life. Kouric would be a good instructor.

His thesis had changed. The material would be much the same, but the viewpoint had altered radically. He had started a thesis filled with rebuke, but blame was no longer the core of his work. The near ruin of the High Plains could not be described in terms of demons, but in terms of tragedy. The whole area could be a seductive Eden when it rained, as it sometimes did for several years. But more often it was barely fit for human habitation, windy, hot, eternally dry, disappointing to wheat farmers three years out of four, to ranchers almost every year. It wasn't settled by ruthless corporations intent on exploiting every last cent from it; the plains had been settled by families like his own, trying to survive in a fickle land and inadvertently hurting the land when they couldn't make ends meet. The plains had been damaged terribly, but the damage had been largely accidental, or else the fruit of ignorance.

Tragedy, then. Those, in the 1800s, who had labeled the High Plains the Great American Desert were righter than they knew. The underlying perception wouldn't please the Greens on the faculty, but he didn't much care. They would have their demons, which were white European civilization and its values, but those were no longer Martin's demons. His dissent meant that he might have trouble getting a degree, and even more trouble if he chose to teach as a career. No branch of science was more trapped in ideology than biology. But that was all right. Academe had become a cauldron of political correctness, and Martin had better things to do than knuckle under to that.

He reached Harlowton in central Montana and drove north past old missile silos, through Judith Gap, and into an exquisite basin filled with prosperous wheat farms and ranches, better watered than those in eastern Montana, better suited for human habitation. He had scarcely seen this area, sere and brown now in the August sun, but the basin and range country appealed to him. This country didn't offend the soul with its flatness. Black mountains cradled the tawny land. Why was this home, when the prairies to the east had never been home? Could land affect his soul so much?

The road took him through the peaceful city of Lewistown, set in a valley girt with mountains, and through a gap in ponderosa-clad slopes. There he turned off, following DeeAnn's instructions, and continued on a dry dirt road, raising a plume of tan dust as he headed for the new ranch. Why was this more than a routine trip? Why was this a passage, taking him from one life to another, from one vision to another? Why did he feel so close to tears? He pulled over, unable to continue for the moment, while the tan dust raised by his tires eddied past him. He needed to cope with something nameless there, at the roadside. Several antelope watched him from a distant knoll. It had grown hot, but the dryness toweled away his perspiration. Why was this place beautiful? He had lived in a forested corner of the Great Plains not so different from this, yet he had not appreciated it. But this he loved, almost before he had walked it or ridden it, and he could not say why.

It all had to do with homes. Laslo Horoney had spoken often about homes during his years of publicizing his great enterprise. Man had the ability to live almost anywhere, but not every place was a good home for mankind. But animals had a much more limited capacity to adapt to homes; they needed the homes for which they were adapted. That was Horoney's whole point, one he often ascribed to his wife, Dolly—that his National Grassland was all about proper homes. In a rush, Martin felt something bordering on love for the man who had expended a fortune returning wild animals and plants and mortals to their proper homes. If Horoney hadn't come along, his family would still be fighting the hard land, bound to it as one is bound to an ancient enemy, wrestling it to the death. And Martin Nichols would be a bitter, aimless youth, rejecting a blessed world.

Martin brushed away tears.

Then he turned the ignition key, and drove up the road that would take him home.

He passed groups of black Angus cattle and knew they belonged now to Nichols Ranches. His father had engineered a trade, purchasing the livestock and turning over the Herefords to Stark's heirs. Just for fun, more than anything else, he had kept the small herd of longhorns, and put them on a sequestered pasture at the north end of the new place. They probably wouldn't earn money, but neither would they lose it on this thick grass. Once, in the open-range days, they had grazed here and elsewhere in Montana. Maybe this would be a home for them again.

His father's excuse was that there might be some wolves floating around someday, but that only made Martin smile. Almost anyone with a sense of the history of the West came to love the big, rangy, monsters and their glorious horns. His father had gotten to boasting about his exotic cattle, measuring horns, devouring history books about the settlement of Montana by those like Nelson Story who drove the Texas cattle north into a virgin land. DeeAnn told him his father's office would soon have a gigantic set of seven-foot horns mounted behind the desk.

The road took him through several cattle guards and into country dotted with ponderosa, and then to a ranch complex nestled on a foothill slope, its back to the sheltering Judith Mountains, it eye gazing upon a grassy empire.

He pulled up before a low, comfortable peeled-log home with great windows that commanded infinite perspectives. This was where his sister and her husband lived while they managed the northern unit. There was a guest cottage and bunkhouse nearby, pens a half mile away, far enough to dull the sound of lovelorn cows and calves during weaning, far enough to diffuse the smell of cattle and manure, the smell of scours and burning hair, and death and new life.

She greeted him at the door, clad as always in her jeans, Western-cut shirt, scuffed boots, and hair worn unstylishly long because Mark loved the way she looked.

"Well, what do you think?" she asked.

His answer surprised him, perhaps because it was nothing he would have admitted a few months earlier. "I stopped on the road and cried," he said.

She gazed at him uncertainly, but he smiled. "Home," he added.

She led him in. "Mark and Dad are out riding the country. They both say they need to ride it and walk it, and you can't just take a truck over it and know it."

"Dad's here?"

"He flies up most days. The airstrip's up the road."

"DeeAnn . . . is everyone happy?"

She beamed. "Wait till we show you the other unit. You won't believe it."

"You're happy."

"I feel I was destined to live here."

"Can you and Dad make money?"

"We think so. This is a well-run, well-maintained ranch. We don't even have plans to change anything."

"How's his house coming?"

"They've picked a site. Decided on the plan. Dream place, vaulted ceilings, fieldstone fireplace, views from every window—not large, just right for them. We've got two hundred fifty thousand to play with, now that that Delacorte nut in Jackson settled."

"What about Mother? She any better?"

DeeAnn glared at him, and then relaxed. "She did it her way. A drink a day. She's fine. This is home for her. The first home she's really had since they were married."

Martin felt bad. For as long as he'd been old enough to grasp that his mother had a weakness, he'd condemned her. Not just for being a drunk, but for ignoring him, abandoning him to a rotten childhood. But none of it was her fault.

"DeeAnn? I'm glad."

She smiled wryly.

He sensed that this had been one of those moments of passage, the moment when he forgave and understood his mortal, fallible, loving parents—and loved them for bringing him into the world and doing their best to give him a good life. He'd been a jerk. He would try never to be one again.

He opted for the guest cottage, and settled in there. Then he wandered the place, liking it, feeling the tan earth under his feet, examining the grasses and browse with a biologist's eye. Damaged, of course; almost all of Montana had been damaged. But nature would heal, given half a chance. And his father would give nature her chance.

He found his old saddle, discovered some saddle horses in a pen, and saddled up. He needed to ride this land just as much as his father did, make it his own from the back of a horse, just as his father did. He hadn't ever before seen this fly-deviled saddler, but it turned out to be a good one, and he turned it out the road past the airstrip, and into the northern pastures, the part he hadn't seen. The hot August breezes sucked the moisture out of him, and he was grateful for the shade of his old hat.

An hour out that road, he discovered his father and Mark Cassady riding home. He pulled up and waited.

"Martin?" his father said.

"Some place, Dad. I like it."

"You do?" His father seemed vaguely disconcerted.

"This is home, Dad. You picked a good one. This is what a ranch should be. There's enough water here."

His father grinned slowly, his gaze assessing Martin. "Your mother'd love to hear that. She loves it, too."

They sat their horses in companionable talk, he and Mark and his father, and then rode slowly back to the ranch house. Martin absorbed all the details, but one astonished him.

"Neighbors? The Horoneys?"

"Yes. Not exactly neighbors. They've decided on a corner of the southern unit, up against the Snowy Mountains. But just a few minutes away. I like them, Martin, and so does Sandy. They're people of vision."

"Why here?"

"They loved it. It's simple enough for Laslo. The High Plains are home for buffalo; these intermountain areas are homes for people. They want to do some amateur ranching, have a country haven to entertain friends. They do that, you know. Nothing grand anywhere, but little hideaways. The beaver did it. Dolly Horoney is nuts about beaver, and she began twisting his arm. Not that it needed much twisting. The Lewistown Airport's just fine for his company jet. They're buying a hundred-sixty we parceled off. That's all. Creek, grass for a couple of quarter horses, aspen, pine, slopes, and some of the best views in the country. I think we'll see a lot of them. The foundation will bring them to Montana often enough."

Martin sensed his father's assessing gaze.

"This is home," he said. "It's home for you and Mom, DeeAnn and Mark. Even if I'm not here much, it'll be home for me, too."

CHAPTER 69

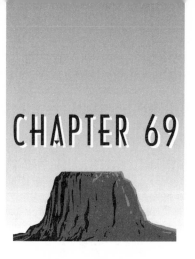

The alpha male lay in tawny grass along a ridge, downwind. Below him, in twilight, a herd of buffalo grazed its way across a sea of grass, its movement in fits and starts, a few animals at a time, though there were many animals.

These buffalo the wolf knew; they were imprinted in his skull, and he had inherited his knowledge of them in his genes. They were food. Flocks of brown birds followed the herd, some riding the shaggy backs of the buffalo. They made their living from the buffalo, the dung, the mites and bugs in the hides, and from the disturbed earth torn by buffalo hooves.

These were dangerous prey, big and mean and able to kick a wolf to death, or toss a wolf to its doom on their short, wicked horns. The alpha male respected those horns and hooves. But hunger drove him and his pack, and when the hunger ran deep enough in his body, he would take the risks a wolf had to take to live. His pack didn't have to kill a buffalo very often. These were big animals, capable of feeding a pack for days. Even the calves were big, blocky animals.

This pack had been feeding on cattle with long horns, as well as an occasional deer and antelope, and smaller animals they could sometimes catch. They had barely subsisted, especially after the long-horned cattle had vanished, driven off by men on horses. Those cattle had taken their toll of the wolves. The alpha male had seen some pups and some females die. He had seen those long fierce horns impale a female right through her gut and toss her twenty feet, where she lay in bloody death.

There were not many wolves, but this was a land they knew. It, too, was imprinted on their souls. The gray wolf was also known as a plains wolf, and these flats and grassy slopes were an ancient home. He belonged here, and lorded over a dominion of his own. He would breed the alpha female and the pack would nurture the pups. That was his existence.

There was nothing else here, no homes, no roads, no poles with wires, no cars or trucks, no people walking or on horseback. He smelled nothing. They had vanished, leaving his home to him. He feared them because of their magical powers, but he had not seen one for a long time, though he sometimes smelled the Stalker, a lone man who came among them and studied them. When that one came, the alpha male led his pack away.

But mostly the wolves were alone, living through the diurnal rhythms, talking to one another at night, or announcing themselves to the moon. Maybe they would talk to one another tonight, because they were spread far and wide.

Below him, the black herd grazed through thick brown grasses that had never been touched this summer or last. Some of the grasses had dropped their seed. Some had been eaten down to the ground by prairie dogs. But no man intervened.

The wolf crawled along the ridge in spurts, not wanting to lose the herd. The thick brown stalks around him protected him from the eye; the westwind protected him from the nose. And he made no sound that the buffalo might hear. Not just now.

A vast silence covered this land. Except when the breezes blew, this was one of the quietest places. The wolf listened sharply for noise, any noise, from the buzz of a rattler to the distant roar of the things that sometimes made white trails in the sky.

The calves were well guarded. There always seemed to be sentinel buffalo keeping watch, and the peacefulness of the herd was deceptive. Buffalo could do anything, even stampede into a pack of wolves. The alpha respected them. But he was hungry.

He watched and waited, and was rewarded with the sight of a limping animal. It was not old. It had injured itself. The twilight thickened and he scrambled closer. Behind him, others of his pack squirmed through the grass, gaining ground. The alpha's behavior told the others he had made his pick. The light faded, and he could not wait longer.

The alpha sprang forward, raced downslope, ears flattened, while behind him half a dozen other wolves followed, somehow knowing which animal they would hunt this dusky moment. A convulsion gripped the herd. Some ran; big bulls headed outward and formed a perimeter. The wolves streaked toward the injured buffalo, which ran at surprising speed, almost as fast as the rest of the herd. But the big bulls formed a wall of horns and hooves around the injured one, driving the circling wolves outward. The lame buffalo never faltered, almost keeping up with the herd as it fled the wolves, heading toward high brushy ground where wolves could not maneuver easily. The earth trembled beneath the weight of so many buffalo, and their hooves churned the tan earth, mauled the grasses underfoot, broke open the soil.

The alpha wolf dived under the horns of a bull buffalo and streaked toward the lame buffalo, but a hoof caught him in the ribs, knocked him over, his breath jolted out of him. He sprang to his feet, feeling pain lance him, but the swift buffalo had gained ground. The alpha limped, his heart not in the hunt this time, and he stopped to sit on his haunches and listen to earth reverberate under the fleet buffalo. He would go hungry tonight, or maybe catch a hare if he was lucky, or trap some small night creature that would give him a bite or two of flesh.

The silence of the High Plains lowered as the wolf lay down in the thick, tawny grass, and rested. A band of blue remained in the northwest, the residue of the dying sun. But the stars winked. The others paused, turning back from the thousand buffalo and gathering around their leader. Not every night was a feast. But they would eat. They always did, enduring starvation, restlessly hunting, until they had meat.

The alpha rose, feeling pain radiate from his ribs. Life was harsh. Few wild wolves lived to be old. He licked his side, his tongue massaging the hurt, his long canines biting at the pain, pulling and kneading flesh.

He was home there. The others waited impatiently. They listened to some coyotes howling in the north, and knew them for interlopers. Tonight the wolves might make a meal of their smaller cousins. This was their home; they would roam and eat and breed, miles from their enemies. Wordlessly the pack turned toward the coyotes, which were baying to one another about meat they had found a mile or two away. A deer, an antelope, a hare, a raccoon, a weasel; who could say? The alpha knew how easily they would drive off the coyotes; and any coyote that resisted would himself become a feast. This was savage nature, far from the moderating hand of man. Little did they know it wasn't wilderness at all, and never would be. It was one man's dream.

AUTHOR'S NOTE

For decades, the High Plains have been losing population. There is not enough precipitation to support dense settlement, and only vast ranches or huge wheat farms are economically viable in many areas. This has inspired dreams and controversy. For years Montana and Wyoming have been afloat with proposals to restore the High Plains to their presettlement condition. These range from the amiable idea that ranchers should pull down their fences and buy into a common herd of buffalo—the Buffalo Commons—to the idea that the federal government should acquire the land and turn it into a massive federal preserve.

These proposals have unleashed unbridled passion and antagonism, much more than they merit, especially from ranchers who fear they will be evicted from their land or forced to change their way of life. These heady ideas are freighted with unexpected implications that reach into the realm of metaphysics and the most basic values and beliefs we mortals possess. What began as a policy debate swiftly exploded into something much larger, fraught with meaning, each side perceiving the other as demonic. The idea stabs people like a sword to the heart.

This novel explores those subterranean passions that lace the whole issue. For some, the buffalo commons is nothing less than an attempt to wreck civilization and progress. For others, it is the salvation of the world, a sacramental act, a restoration of natural order. That, then, is the essence of powerful material for a novel, and I have attempted here to capture the fears and passions of both sides. And thus a story about dreams and anguish was born.

You will discover my prejudices here. I would love to see the High Plains restored to their presettlement splendor, but I love Montana's salt-of-the-earth people, who are tough, unique and honorable. I would like to see a Buffalo Commons in eastern Montana and Wyoming, but I am aware of the pain and dislocation it would cause throughout a vast area.

I am indebted to environmental columnist Alston Chase for his wise counsel and valuable research material. And also to Jim Overstreet for sharing his extraordinary knowledge of Montana ranching with me. My prejudices are mine alone.

Richard S. Wheeler
February 1997